Praise for D. R. Meredith and the Sheriff Matthews mysteries

"Up in the Panhandle, D. R. Meredith has been quietly adding quality volumes to a genre that is possibly one of the most popular categories in fiction today, the murder mystery.... Such complexity of feelings in character is rare in what often is called 'formula fiction.'"
—*The Dallas Morning News*

"It is one of the delights of Meredith's Sheriff novels that she knows the Panhandle country and Panhandle people so well that she can mirror not only what it must be like to be a lawman there but what it *is* like to live here."
—*El Paso Herald-Post*

"Meredith is an artist with words. Her well-rounded characters are vivid, her presentation of idiomatic language makes for realistic dialogue and the almost unknown geographical area seems more than a speck on a large-scale map."
—*Murder Ad Lib*

Also by D. R. Meredith
Published by Ballantine Books:

THE HOMEFRONT MURDERS

D. R. Meredith

BALLANTINE BOOKS • NEW YORK

Copyright © 1994 by D. R. Meredith

All rights reserved under International and Pan-American Copyright Conventions. Published in the United States of America by Ballantine Books, a division of Random House, Inc., New York, and simultaneously in Canada by Random House of Canada Limited, Toronto.

Any resemblance between my characters and any persons actually living in the Texas Panhandle is coincidental and utterly unintentional. The events portrayed are a figment of my imagination and are not meant to mirror actual events, past or present.

Library of Congress Catalog Card Number: 94-94655

ISBN 0-345-38050-9

Manufactured in the United States of America

First Edition: January 1995

10 9 8 7 6 5 4 3 2 1

ACKNOWLEDGMENTS

I wish to thank Tom Ellzey, physical anthropologist, for his advice on old bones—and Charles Moser, my brother, who so patiently advised me on World War II.

PROLOGUE

C.J. TOLLIVER THOUGHT THE SUBBASEMENT OF the Crawford County Courthouse was both the coldest and the spookiest place he had ever had the misfortune to enter. Of course, it was New Year's Eve, and in the Texas Panhandle that more than likely meant it was colder than a well digger's butt in the Klondike. Some years December was downright balmy, but this wasn't one of those years.

C.J. supposed he ought to be grateful that he had a contracting job that kept him inside, out of the blustery wind that sent the chill factor below zero—and never mind that the thermometer actually registered twenty-five degrees. The actual temperature never meant much in the Panhandle in the winter when the wind was blowing—and the wind mostly always blew. A thirty-mile-an-hour wind straight out of the north nearly always meant that it was a hell of a lot colder than what the thermometer registered.

C.J. rubbed his nose and cheeks and decided that tomorrow he would wear his ski mask. Not that he ever skied—no money and no time to spend on what he considered a rich man's sport—but a good ski mask would keep his nose and cheeks from getting frostbit. He had not worn suitable protection this morning because he figured he'd be working inside. He should have known better. The temperature a good twenty-five feet below the surface, which he figured the subbasement was, had to be close to freezing. At any rate, he was so cold his teeth were damn near chattering—even though he was shoveling dirt as fast as he could. He was working up a sweat all right—and he figured

1

his sweat was freezing as fast as it dribbled out of his pores.

But as much as the cold bothered him, the spookiness of this hole in the ground bothered him more. For sixty years, since the courthouse's construction in the Thirties, the sub-basement with its concrete walls and dirt floor had remained mostly undisturbed and generally forgotten. C.J. couldn't shake off the feeling that it ought to remain that way. Maybe the shivers that ran up his spine weren't entirely due to the cold. Maybe it was an instinct left over from the days when men wore skins and lived in caves and slept with one eye open, a subliminal warning that unknown, unfriendly spirits lurked just beyond the firelight. Maybe whatever it was that dried his mouth and sent chills up and down his back and danced just outside his range of vision ought to be left alone to sleep another sixty years. Let the Crawford County commissioners buy an empty building downtown if they wanted more office and storage space—anything but awake what slept in the dark.

And maybe he was crazy as hell, too.

"C.J., tell me again how come we're working on New Year's Eve instead of home fixing to watch a ball game. Tell me again how come it ain't our employees freezing their asses off shoveling dirt instead of us?"

C.J. barely managed not to yell and wet his pants when he heard his partner's voice reverberate around the basement. That was another problem: a man couldn't figure out exactly where a sound was coming from in this hole.

Panting, C.J. leaned on the handle of his shovel and glared at José Herrera. The Tollivers and the Herreras had shared good times and bad ever since José's grandfather had immigrated to Crawford County around 1910 to avoid being caught on the wrong side of Pancho Villa's revolution, and settled on a section of land next to C.J.'s granddaddy. When C.J. decided to go into business as an independent building contractor and wanted a partner, his first choice was his old buddy, José.

That didn't mean that José didn't irritate the hell out of

him sometimes. José never stood in the way when C.J. decided to bid on a job, but he sure as hell managed to get his point across afterward.

"We're working overtime because Crawford County's illustrious commissioners are too damn tight to spend a nickel more than they have to finishing out this hole in the ground, and most of the larger contracting firms refused to offer bids on the job once they found out that the only way in or out of the subbasement is one average-size elevator," explained C.J., irritated that he had to defend his decision for the umpteenth time. Sometimes José was worse than a nagging woman. "That means there's no way to bring in heavy equipment, and the floor has to be leveled by hand. Then concrete has to be brought in a wheelbarrow one at a time. That adds up to a larger payroll than most of the big boys want to meet for a profit that's smaller than they want to mess with. I based our winning bid on the two of us working twelve hours a day, seven days a week, while our employees work eight hours a day, five days a week. We didn't get to be successful by being lazy, José, or hiring done what we can do ourselves, and we sure as hell don't turn a profit by paying overtime when we don't have to."

José mopped the sweat off his forehead with a large red bandanna. "We're gonna be lucky if we break even on this job."

C.J. felt another flash of irritation. "I don't know how you figure that."

José leaned his shovel against one of the concrete walls and lit a cigarette. "Because we're fifty years old and can't shovel dirt very fast anymore—especially not this dirt. It's packed down like concrete in most places. You'd think that as dry as the Panhandle is, this dirt would be loose as sand on a beach."

"What the hell do you know about sand on a beach, José? You ain't never been out of the Panhandle in your life—and there's no sandy beaches around here. Besides, I'd a lot rather have the dirt sort of packed down instead of so dry that it floats in the air. That would be worse than the black dusters we used to have during a bad drought. I hate having to work in goggles and them paper surgical masks."

"We're going to have to sometimes," said José in a gloomy voice. "There are some places down here that are dry as a bone. I can't figure out why half this floor's packed and half isn't."

"Maybe the damn water lines leaked on some of the upper floors, and water dribbled down here," said C.J. "Maybe rain percolated down through the ground and oozed under the foundation in spots. Who the hell knows? It doesn't make any difference anyway. We got the bid, and we're just gonna have to get the job done no matter what we got to work with."

José had a stubborn look that C.J. recognized. It meant he wasn't through arguing. "Another thing, C.J. Both of us have to ride herd on the men every damn minute they work down here. They all spend more time looking over their shoulders than they do looking at what they're doing. Walk up behind one of them, and he's liable to jump right out of his skin. We're not getting much work out of any of them, and we're falling behind schedule. We've bit off more than we can chew this time."

"Why didn't you say something before I bid on the job? Damn it all, José, you're always doing that—letting me take on something, then bitching about it afterward."

José blew out a cloud of smoke and looked around the subbasement. C.J. could see his partner hunching his shoulders up around his neck as if he expected something to sneak up behind him and lop off his head. "I didn't know how it was going to be, C.J. When we looked over this hole before we made the bid, I figured we were in for a lot of hard work but nothing we couldn't handle. But the longer we work down here, the jumpier I get. Maybe if we installed all the wiring first so we could light up this whole cellar, I'd settle down some, but with just a bulb strung up here and there, it seems like the dark places—and it's mostly dark places down here—just get darker and . . ." José's voice trailed off, and C.J. saw him shiver.

"Just get darker and what?" asked C.J., feeling a shiver of his own crawl up his spine. "Blacker? Hell, that's normal. Light always makes the dark look blacker. It's the contrast."

José turned to look at him. "No, not blacker. Thicker. The dark looks thicker where there's no light—like it's trying to take shape."

C.J. felt his belly clench up and the sweat bead up on his forehead. He tried to laugh, but only succeeded in making grunting sounds that echoed around the dark places. He took a deep breath, or as deep a breath as he could, given how tight his chest felt. "Damn it, José! Would you shut up. If you're talking like that around the men, it's no wonder they're all scared as hell."

José shook his head. "The men all feel it without me saying anything."

"Feel what, for God's sake?" yelled C.J., then wished he hadn't. He didn't want to know, or rather he didn't want José putting a name to whatever it was. You call a thing by its name, and it just might answer.

"That we aren't the only ones down here, C.J. Something—or someone—else is here, too, and it's trying to get our attention. And it's losing patience."

"Good God Almighty, José!" yelled C.J., as he grabbed his shovel and stalked off into the dark, scared spitless and ashamed that he was scared and determined that no talk of ghosts or monsters or spirits would get the best of him. Not tough as nails C.J. Tolliver. "There's nothing here! Nothing! Nothing! Nothing!"

He stepped in a slight depression several feet away and furiously dug up shovelfuls of loose, sandy dirt until the dust swirled up to envelope him and set him to wheezing and coughing. Damn it all, he would have to hit a dry spot where the dirt flew up and choked a man. Holding his breath to keep from inhaling any more of the dust-filled air and feeling panic just below his anger, he stumbled back toward José and the naked light bulb suspended above his partner's head. He stepped inside the pool of light and dumped a spade full of dirt at José's feet.

"See! I walked into the dark and nothing got me!" C.J. panted, hoarse from coughing. "Because there's nothing waiting for us. Like old FDR said: We got nothing to fear but fear itself."

José crossed himself and backed away, his mouth falling open and his eyes fixed in his head as he stared down at the ground.

"What the hell," began C.J., then his throat closed up as he, too, saw the thing he had carried out of the dark on the blade of his shovel.

CHAPTER

1

Crawford County Sheriff Roped and Branded

CARROLL, TEXAS—Although it has never been the policy of the *Crawford County Examiner* to mention an elected official's change of marital status other than on the society page, we make an exception in the case of Sheriff Charles Timothy Matthews's recent marriage to Angela Brentwood Lassiter. A surprise victor in the last general election, Sheriff Matthews has been the target of occasional criticism by Crawford County residents. A few disgruntled citizens feel that the sheriff often treads on toes during criminal investigations out of ignorance of our local customs. Some ask how a man born and raised in Dallas could understand our ways. Some folks call Matthews a maverick, an orphaned calf that wears no brand and belongs to no man's herd.

No more is that true.

Charles Matthews now wears the brand of Angela Lassiter, daughter of rancher J.T. Brentwood, and the fourth generation to live in Crawford County. We trust that the new Mrs. Matthews will provide our maverick sheriff with a different perspective on the rest of the herd. Congratulations to the young couple, and we encourage our readers to welcome Sheriff Matthews into the fold. He has always been a fair man whom we have respected, but now he is one of us by marriage.

Crawford County Examiner
December 31

Charles Matthews crossed his ankles and wiggled his toes. Angie had never said a word one way or the other about the habit of putting his feet on the coffee table, but he had seen her looking at the claw marks and dents and scratches on its surface and knew it was only a matter of time. According to conventional wisdom, as voiced by Sheriff Kit Lindman before he was shot helping Charles arrest a murderer, wives didn't approve of husbands putting their boots on the furniture. Charles was willing to admit that Lindman probably knew more about what wives approved or didn't approve of since the sheriff from New Mexico had been married nearly twenty years, and Charles had only been married three weeks. Of course, this was his second marriage so he knew a little more about marital compromise than Lindman gave him credit for. For example, now Charles took off his boots before putting his feet on the coffee table.

He thought it was a good compromise.

Besides, Angie could hardly forbid his using the coffee table as a footstool unless she also forbade Hieronymus Bosch from climbing on it, and Charles knew that Angie would never forbid Hieronymus doing anything his little beagle heart desired whether it be climbing on the furniture or sleeping on their bed or begging at the dinner table. According to his American Kennel Club papers, Hieronymus Bosch might technically belong to Sheriff Charles Timothy Matthews of Crawford County, Texas, but it was Angie whom the beagle worshiped. In the three weeks since Angie and her two daughters had moved into Charles's house on the edge of the Canadian River breaks just outside Carroll, Hieronymus had hardly let Angie out of his sight, following her from room to room like a four-legged shadow. She repaid his devotion with soft words and gentle pats. Charles might have been jealous of his own beagle if Angie had not treated him exactly the same way.

He rested his head against the back of the couch, closed his eyes, and clasped his hands across his belly. Love was a damn wonderful thing.

He heard muffled giggles and felt two little bodies climb on the couch and settle on either side of him. He opened one eye and saw hazel eyes in a pixie face staring back at him. Charles himself got soft inside. At five years old, Jennifer was a carbon copy of Angie right down to her solemn expression and curly auburn hair. He could never see the little girl without feeling helpless against the surge of protective love that rolled over him.

He felt tiny fingers tug on his sleeve and turned his head to smile at Laura, Angie's two-year-old daughter. Although Laura also had hazel eyes, she didn't resemble her mother as much as she did Angie's father, J.T. Brentwood. Laura had the same square jaw and her baby face could take on the same stubborn expression when she wanted her own way.

He cuddled the two girls and closed his eyes again. At least neither girl looked like her father. Angie's first husband, L.D. Lassiter, had been his best friend. He had also been a murderer, a fact that Charles had concealed, as he had concealed that L.D. died at the hands of the brother of one of his victims.

Miss Poole, the dispatcher for the sheriff's department and one of L.D.'s intended victims, called L.D.'s death poetic justice.

Charles supposed Miss Poole's description was valid in a sense, but justice had been the last thing on his mind at the time. His only thought had been to protect Angie from the gossip he knew would erupt if he had revealed that L.D. Lassiter had murdered two people and attempted to murder two more. Charles had broken his oath as sheriff of Crawford County. He had broken the law he had sworn to uphold.

He would do it again under the same circumstances.

He had finally learned to live with his guilt.

For the first time since he left Dallas, after his first wife's murder, he felt his life was under control. He had a wife he loved, two beautiful little girls he wanted to adopt, a comfortable home, a dog, and peace of mind. For the first time in years he was happy, and he didn't intend to let anything disturb that happiness. Finally he belonged.

Still, he was very glad that he didn't have to see L.D. Lassiter's face replicated in his daughters' features. Charles wasn't sure his nascent peace of mind would survive had that been the case.

"Papa Charles, read us a story," said Jennifer, holding out her favorite book by Mercer Meyer. "Please," she added, grinning up at him.

Charles capitulated. Even though he had read the story of Liza Lou's adventures among the ghosts and monsters of the Yeller Belly Swamp at least ten times in the past week, he couldn't resist Jennifer's smile. He knew both little girls worshiped him with the same unquestioning devotion that Hieronymus displayed toward Angie, and he realized he had better enjoy such hero worship while he could. Age would temper their approval. Age always did. Children and dogs were not the same. Children grew up and dogs never did. In the meantime, Charles planned to wallow in the girls' approval until his ego grew to immense proportions. Damn, but love was wonderful.

"Charles."

He looked up at Angie and grinned. He supposed that eventually he would get used to the idea that she was his wife, that she would not disappear when he wasn't looking, that she loved him, but until he did, Charles guessed he would look and act as sappy as Hieronymus every time Angie spoke to him. If he had a tail, he would wag it.

"Charles," she repeated, giving him a quizzical look that indicated his expression was even sappier than he supposed. "Meenie's on the phone. He needs to talk to you."

Charles sat up, a faint irritation marring the perfection of his day. "I can't imagine why. The jail's empty. Crime in Crawford County is taking a holiday. Miss Poole and Meenie haven't had an argument in weeks. Even Slim hasn't destroyed any county property since pheasant season," he said, thinking of his impulsive young deputy.

"Which is unusual considering that Slim can walk through a room and every object in it jumps out of place."

"Meenie sounded worried," said Angie.

Charles patted Jennifer and Laura on their respective heads and rose, a faint—very faint—twinge of concern joining his equally faint irritation to further disturb his placid contentment. "I suppose I'd better talk to him then. Nothing short of catastrophe worries Meenie."

Charles padded into his private study to take the call out of the hearing of the two little girls. As sheriff he might have to discuss anything from murder to armed robbery to rape, and he would just as soon the girls not listen to his end of the conversation. He couldn't change the world for them, but he would censor what they heard about it for as long as he could.

"You better be reporting a mass murder or an invasion by space aliens, Meenie," said Charles, sitting down in a high-backed padded chair and glancing around the paneled room, which held a huge desk, a black leather couch, and chess sets on every surface. "On second thought, if it's space aliens, don't bother me. Call *National Enquirer*."

"If you'd seen C.J. Tolliver and José Herrera when they busted into the office, you might have figured it was the Martians landing from the looks on their faces. I ain't seen any two people so scared since that batch of junior high school boys let loose a cage full of white rats in the girls' gym. I guess that was before your time though."

"Get to the point, Meenie," said Charles.

"Well, C.J. and José been working in the subbasement trying to level out the floor so they can pour concrete, and it appears they dug up more than they bargained for. I didn't hardly believe them when they come running in here, so I went down to take a look, and sure enough, they dug up what they said they did."

Charles took a deep breath, feeling less relaxed by the minute. Ordinarily he enjoyed the way all of his Crawford County deputies had to turn all their reports into a miniseries, but not at this particular moment. "Meenie, tell me in words of one syllable what they found."

"A head."

At first Charles stared at the carved ivory chess set on his desk and considered denying that he had heard the deputy correctly, but decided he would only be putting off the inevitable. Meenie might have a distinct Panhandle drawl, but he was perfectly capable of making himself understood when circumstances demanded. And, Charles admitted to himself, these circumstances definitely demanded it. A murder! Damn it to hell, but he didn't want to deal with a murder on New Year's Eve *and* what amounted to the tail end of his honeymoon.

"Damn it, Meenie, why didn't you say so to start with instead of talking around the subject. Block off the crime scene, and I'll be there in five minutes."

"There ain't no hurry, Sheriff. I figure that head's been there a while. Ain't nothing left but bone and a few strips of dried-up hide."

CHAPTER

2

From the private journal of Megan Elizabeth Poole:

December 31

I have never been a coward and I was not one today, but courage proved a poor defense against the horror that waited in the basement.

The subbasement with its sixty-year-old concrete walls and dirt floor smelled musty, like the inside of a sealed tomb—which Charles supposed was a good analogy because it had certainly been someone's tomb. He knelt down in the circle of light cast by the naked light bulb and stared at the skull. Yellowed bone, grinning teeth, strips of leathery skin, a few hanks of long brown hair hanging onto what remained of its scalp, it was less a skull than the head of a poorly embalmed mummy.

"I don't suppose C.J. and José could have dug into an old Indian burial ground?" asked Charles without any real hope.

A very dirty Meenie Higgins hitched his grimy pants up higher on his nonexistent hips and shook his head. "Twenty-five feet underground? It ain't likely, Sheriff. Besides, Raul and me dug up the rest of him before we called you. Over there." Meenie nodded toward another circle of light several feet away where Raul Trujillo knelt on top of a mound of dirt beside an open grave. "And unless some

13

Comanche warrior found himself a time machine and enlisted in the U.S. Army during WWII, then we got ourselves a white GI."

"A GI?" asked Charles sharply.

Meenie scratched his head and nodded. "I could be wrong, of course. He could be an Indian, but he ain't no *old* Indian. And besides that, there ain't no descendants of the Comanches or any other tribe living in Crawford County, so how come an Indian would end up buried in the courthouse basement?"

Charles rose and raked his fingers through his hair. "Why would anyone be buried in the basement, Meenie?"

The wizened deputy stared at him for a few seconds, then shifted his wad of chewing tobacco from one dust-streaked cheek to the other. "Ain't but one reason that comes to mind, and I figure you already thought of it, so I reckon I don't need to waste my breath answering."

"Was it because he was murdered, Sheriff?" asked a wide-eyed and very clean Slim Fletcher. Evidently Meenie had not trusted the young deputy to help uncover the body, which wasn't surprising considering Meenie thought Slim barely competent to zip his pants without getting his shirt caught.

"It ain't likely he walked down here, died of natural causes, and then buried himself, Slim," interrupted Meenie.

Charles was surprised at the degree of exasperation revealed in his chief deputy's voice, until he remembered that Meenie and Slim had been the only deputies on the eight-to-four shift the last week since they were the only men in the sheriff's department without wives and children. Seven days of Slim's company was likely to make even stoical Meenie a little cranky. Charles supposed Slim would eventually mature into a dependable law enforcement officer—if some other officer didn't strangle him first.

However, sometimes Slim's questions inspired unexpected answers, which was one of the reasons Charles put up with him. "I suspect he was murdered, Slim, but that isn't the principal reason he was buried in the basement," said Charles, dusting off his hands and ignoring Meenie's frown. "He was buried here because someone didn't want him found—ever—and what better place than a subbasement that I doubt anyone fifty years ago anticipated being used as anything but a place to store old desks and filing cabinets the county didn't need, but didn't want to throw away."

Meenie pushed his hat to the back of his head and scratched his balding scalp. Meenie's age was somewhere between fifty and retirement; his faded blue eyes were bright with a cynical intelligence that owed nothing to higher education; his short, skinny frame contained the strength of rawhide; and his leathery, wrinkled face seldom revealed any noticeable expression. It did now. Even through the dirt caked on his features Meenie looked exasperated *and* out of patience.

Charles put his hand on Slim's shoulder and gave him a gentle shove toward the elevator. "Go back upstairs, Slim. Meenie, Raul, and I can handle the crime scene, and I need you in the sheriff's department. You never know when there might be an emergency, and I need a man I can trust to handle it."

The freckle-faced deputy squared his shoulders and saluted. "Don't you worry, Sheriff. I'll take care of anything that comes up." He glanced reluctantly at the skull. "If you're sure you can't use my help? I've been reading some books on how to process evidence. I gave Meenie and Raul some pointers on the latest methods while they were digging up the body."

Charles noticed that Meenie had added outrage to his litany of facial expressions and quickly shoved Slim a littler harder toward the elevator. "Maybe we can discuss some of your ideas later, Slim."

The towheaded deputy dutifully nodded. "I'll just make a few notes while I'm waiting, Sheriff." Charles's last glimpse of Slim before the elevator doors closed was of his pulling a small spiral notebook and a ballpoint pen out of his pocket.

"You just can't keep from borrowing trouble, can you, Sheriff?" asked Meenie, tugging his Stetson back to its accustomed position square on his head. "Slim will wart you on this case until you're ready to strangle him. He's been reading detective stories lately and making mountains out of molehills every time he takes a call. Yesterday old man McCormick reported that some kids broke into his machine shed and took a joy ride on his John Deere tractor. I sent Slim out to his place 'cause I figured he might be able to get the facts without messing up too bad. By the time he finished talking to McCormick, he had the old man about half convinced a bunch of terrorists stole his tractor so they could plow up his wheat field and plant land mines in it."

Meenie spat a stream of tobacco juice toward a dark corner. "I tell you, Sheriff, that kid is going to drive me to drink—and I ain't a drinking man. He's even getting on Miss Poole's nerves. She like to have bit off his head when she came down here a little bit ago. Not that anybody would notice. Slim don't use his head for anything but a place to hang his hat."

Charles clapped his deputy's shoulder. "Now you're exaggerating, Meenie. Miss Poole spent forty years teaching sixth grade before she started working for the sheriff's department as dispatcher. She doesn't have nerves, or if she does, she won't admit it."

Meenie went on as if Charles hadn't interrupted. " 'Course you ought to know about complicating something simple—like telling Slim that the main reason the body was buried down here was because the murderer didn't want it found."

Puzzled, Charles stared at the scrawny deputy. "I think I was straightforward, Meenie. Most murderers leave the bodies where they fall. The ones who don't—well, they have strong reasons for not wanting it known that a murder has been committed."

If anything Meenie looked to be more impatient than before. "It ain't what you said, Sheriff. It's how you said it, and it's gonna confuse Slim, and he don't need you confusing him anymore than he already is."

"Damn it, Meenie, what did I say that's got you so upset?" demanded Charles, raising his voice, then flinching as his words bounced around the basement.

"You let that kid think that *why* the body was buried down here was more important than why he was killed in the first place. Seems to me you got the cart before the horse, and lord knows, Slim ain't too sure to start with whether the horse or the cart comes first."

"I think why he was buried here—in the subbasement—is *more* important, Meenie," explained Charles, feeling a little exasperation of his own. He wasn't in the mood to discuss semantics. He wanted to examine the grave, give instructions on what to do about the skeleton, and go home. "Most murderers who bury their victims do it because they don't want to face what they did. They aren't hiding their victim as much as they're hiding from themselves. That's why most impromptu graves are only two feet deep—just enough to cover the body, to get it out of sight. I don't think that's the case here."

"I don't know how you figure that 'cause this grave ain't much deeper," said Meenie.

"It's at least twenty-five feet if you measure from ground level, Meenie."

"I might have known you'd see it that way. You just can't help making a federal case out of something that's as plain as the nose on your face," said Meenie, turning abruptly and walking toward a brightly lit corner of the basement where Raul knelt beside the opened grave.

Charles reluctantly followed, the scene ahead reminding him more and more of an archaeological dig. Tripod light poles borrowed from Freddie's Fine Photography illuminated the tomb. Like any competent archaeologist excavating a site, Raul crouched beside it, carefully locating on graph paper each artifact and noting its relationship in feet and inches to any other artifact. The sketch would serve as a map of the site and augment the photographic record.

Even the tools scattered about the grave might be found on a dig: two shovels, several trowels, paint brushes of different sizes, a folding tape measure, and a discarded paper surgical mask, evidently Meenie's since Raul still wore his. The price tags dangling from the various tools did weaken the analogy since Charles doubted that most archaeologists patronized Benny's Hardware across the street from the courthouse.

"You look like Indiana Jones, Raul," said Charles.

Raul looked up. His face above the surgical mask was gray from dust and his eyes were red trimmed. "I don't like digging up skeletons."

Charles felt mild shock jar what little was left of his placid mood. Not only did Raul sound snappish, but the customary lilt that revealed his ethnic background without quite being an accent was absent from his voice. Charles couldn't remember Raul ever sounding like that before.

"I know it wasn't a pleasant job, Raul, and I appreciate the way you and Meenie took the initiative instead of waiting for me," Charles began.

"You don't know the half of it, Sheriff," interrupted Meenie. "The dust was so thick you could taste it right through the masks Raul bought. We coughed as much as we dug—except for Slim, and he didn't stop talking long enough to cough. 'Course we didn't let him any closer to the grave than the elevator, and the air's a little better over there." He wiped his face with the red bandanna he always carried, glanced at Raul, and spat into the surrounding darkness. "Slim can ruffle your feathers with all his talking if you let him, and we did, because getting mad at him took our minds off what we were doing and where we were. Seems like the longer we worked, the worse it got."

"Slim's chatter or the dust?" asked Charles, not certain which would bother him more.

Raul pulled his surgical mask off, exposing an oval of skin around his mouth and nose only slightly less dirty than the rest of his face. "Neither one, Sheriff. It's this basement. I don't believe in ghosts, but the longer I'm down here, the more I feel like I'm not alone."

Meenie nodded. "I don't believe in ghosts anymore than Raul does, but there's places that just don't feel empty when they should, and I reckon this is one of them. It makes a man real uneasy—like there's somebody standing behind him when there's nobody there."

Charles stared at his two deputies in disbelief, started to speak, then decided against it. Neither one of them looked in the mood to put up with skeptical remarks. He stepped to the edge of the grave instead. He caught his breath, then slowly let it out. "Dear God," he whispered.

The corpse lay huddled up on its right side, one bony hand with mummified tendons clinging to the joints resting where its head should be, the fingers curled slightly toward the palm as though relaxed in sleep. The left arm was bent sharply at the elbow, its hand caught in the blackened lapel of what, judging from the insignia on the sleeve, had once been a military jacket. The collar of a dirt-stained shirt gaped open where the blade of C.J.'s shovel had sheared off a button and the top of a knotted tie. The corpse's neck protruded from the open collar like the thick brown stalk of a dead plant whose blossom had been sheared off.

Reluctantly Charles examined the rest of the mummy, swallowing hard when he saw one shoe still embedded in the dirt just beyond the skeletal left foot that protruded from the body's rotting trouser leg. The exposed bones and the few remaining tendons were both stained a greenish color that Charles knew was caused by the dye in the corpse's socks. When the decaying uniform was stripped off, every bone and strip of dried tissue would be likewise stained. Bones were only white when bleached by the sun or in some forensic lab; otherwise they took on the color of their surroundings.

Charles cleared his throat, the sound breaking the dusty silence, and fought for objectivity. This was just another murder scene. The skeleton had nothing to do with him personally.

Nothing.

He looked at his two deputies, both dirty, sweaty, and wearing identical scowls. "I apologize," he said, gesturing at the grave. "Exhuming this was more than merely unpleasant, and I can understand why your imagination might kick into overtime. I might start to believe the basement was haunted, too, if I'd been the one to uncover a mummy."

Meenie and Raul glanced at each other, then looked at Charles. "We didn't say it was haunted—just that it made us uneasy," said Meenie, shrugging his shoulders. "Maybe it's because most folks don't like messing around with dead bodies, and Raul and me ain't any different. We don't like it either."

"How much did you disturb the body uncovering it?" asked Charles.

"Not much," answered Meenie. "We dug down a couple of feet with the shovels, then climbed in and used the trowels until we had most of the dirt out of the way. What was left we brushed off with the paint brushes. I think he's pretty much like he was buried—except for his head. The grave's about four feet long and not quite three wide. Whoever killed him had to bend his legs to get him in."

Charles visually measured the depth of the grave. "And about three feet deep."

"I think it was deeper, Sheriff," said Raul. "The ground was sunk in a few inches when we started digging."

Charles looked at Meenie. "Deep enough to validate what I said. It wasn't enough to kill this man. The murderer wanted him to vanish as if he had never existed."

"I still think you're making something hard out of what's easy," insisted Meenie. "We got a killer who wanted to hide what he'd done—"

"But not from himself, Meenie," interrupted Charles. "Otherwise the grave wouldn't be as deep, and he wouldn't have dug it here. Think about it for a minute. If you're right, and the victim is a WWII veteran—"

"He is," interjected Meenie. "I moved his arm a little

and saw what's left of campaign ribbons from the war. And what's left of that uniform looks like what I remember soldiers wearing about that time. It could be that maybe he was killed later and just happened to be wearing that uniform, but I don't think that's likely. Of course, you might figure it that way considering how you like to complicate matters, but I'm gonna stand by what I think. He came marching home from war and didn't get any closer than the courthouse."

"I'll take your word for it—at least until the pathologist, and whatever forensic anthropologist he consults, tells us otherwise," said Charles. "But to continue. Think about how you and Raul felt being down here, and you at least had each other and Slim for company. But what if you had been alone? Now, think about this subbasement fifty years ago. There wasn't even a light bulb down here until last year. Whoever buried this body had to dig the grave by flashlight or lantern, and he had to do it at night when the courthouse was empty. Think about the silence broken only by the sound of your digging and your panting breath and your heart pounding in your ears. Think about the blackness surrounding you and your feeble light. Think about the body lying a few feet away."

Charles drew a shallow breath and shivered. "I don't know about you, but it would take an overpowering reason for me to spend any time alone in this basement burying a corpse—a stronger reason than I had for murdering him. Alive or dead, our soldier was a threat to his murderer. He had to disappear—and he did, until now."

Meenie looked at the pools of light surrounded by blackness that dotted the basement, then glanced at the grave again. "I reckon I see what you mean, but nothing says that the killer didn't have help. Might be two people about to have their New Year start off on a sour note when the word gets out about this."

Charles shook his head. "Fifty years is a long time for two people to keep murder a secret, Meenie. Not that it matters one way or the other. If this soldier's been dead since WWII, then his murderer is either already a tenant in the Carroll cemetery or else is an old man. Either way, I don't think our killer is a continuing threat to the community and neither is the mummy."

"And I think getting married has softened you up some. And that's good," Meenie added quickly. "You were on the verge of being in a real bad mood most of the time, always seeing the worst in everybody. But you don't want to go too far in the other direction either—like with our sergeant here. He's bound to stir folks up some, but you're not looking for that. You think you can run an investigation and try to identify him without causing an uproar. Well, Sheriff, I'm here to tell you that folks who lost kin in the war are gonna think maybe the army made a mistake and their brother or cousin or husband or sweetheart made it home after all and died in the courthouse basement. Grief that's been healed over years is gonna break out fresh. Then those folks are gonna start wondering who murdered their brother or cousin or husband or sweetheart, and the fat will be in the fire for sure."

"You can't be serious, Meenie!" said Charles. "You don't really believe that men and women in their seventies and eighties are going to accuse one another of murder when we don't even know who the victim is?"

"I ain't saying folks are gonna accuse each other out loud, but some of them are going to think it, and that's might near as bad. That mummy is as big a threat as he ever was and he's gonna bring out the worst in everybody, and you ain't looking for the worst anymore." Meenie shook his head, a solemn expression on his face. "You're going to wish C.J. and José had never dug up that body, Sheriff, because they didn't just dig up the dead. They dug up the past, and anytime you do that, it's the same as digging up trouble."

CHAPTER

3

From the private journal of Megan Elizabeth Poole:

December 31 [continued]

I have lived nearly fifty years with a lie.

"Sheriff?"

Charles whirled around, his heart pounding, then felt foolish. Meenie's and Raul's talk of ghosts and his own reaction to seeing the remains of whoever lay in the grave had him jumping at every shadow and sound. Not that Viola Jenkins, Crawford County's only female justice of the peace, constituted a shadow. At barely five feet tall and not much less in girth, solid was a better word.

"Mrs. Jenkins, you startled me."

Viola Jenkins stepped off the elevator and paused, her eyes focusing first on the three men, then glancing beyond them at the grave. "I don't wonder. This place is enough to give anybody a case of the shakes without throwing in a corpse." She closed her eyes momentarily, then opened them to look directly at Charles. "I better go about my business of looking over the body and ordering an autopsy. Although I suppose I don't need to actually look at it. Anybody buried down here is automatically a suspicious death unless the Parker brothers have annexed this basement as part of the cemetery."

Meenie spat toward one of the dark corners. "They

would if they could figure out how to cheat the county out of it."

Charles didn't know the source of Meenie's dislike of Crawford County's only firm of undertakers, and didn't want to ask. He had long ago decided he was better off not knowing.

Viola Jenkins stepped past him and froze at the sight of the skull. "God Almighty!"

"Rest of it is in the grave," said Meenie.

"Miss Poole never said anything about it being in pieces!"

"I don't know why she didn't. She came down here to look same as Slim did, but I reckon it wouldn't make no difference if she had told you," said Meenie. "You still got to look at it."

"I know what I have to do, Meenie," snapped Viola. "I don't need a scrawny ex-cowboy reminding me. I just wish Miss Poole had warned me. I wouldn't have eaten dinner before I drove in from the farm."

Charles saw her close her eyes for a moment before stepping toward the opened grave. Other than a deep breath that lifted her chest she showed no other reaction. Like many of Crawford County's residents, Viola Jenkins was stoic. In a rural county in the Texas Panhandle where one's livelihood depended on agriculture and oil and gas—and the former industry was at the mercy of fierce weather and the Department of Agriculture and the latter to the machinations of OPEC and the United States Congress—a certain degree of stoicism was required. Not that Crawford County was indifferent to pleasure or pain, but its citizens had learned to enjoy one while enduring the other. It was a tough breed that inhabited this southernmost end of the high plains, and Viola Jenkins exemplified that breed as well as anyone Charles knew.

Charles doubted sometimes that his own character measured up to that of the voters who elected him.

"Have you taken photographs?" Viola asked Raul.

The deputy nodded. "All I could without moving him."

The justice of the peace stepped into the open grave and knelt on her plump knees. Charles saw her chest under its orange ski jacket rise with another deep breath. "Let's look him over then," she said in a flat voice.

Charles stepped into the grave and knelt next to her. "I'll search him, Mrs. Jenkins."

She slung her arm across his chest, pushing him back. "No, Sheriff. Not this time."

Charles caught himself before he tumbled backward and stared into her eyes. "I know that legally you're in charge. I know that you can search the body and confiscate everything you find. I know that until the autopsy is done and you rule on cause of death, that body belongs as much to you as to its family," he said gently. "I'm not trying to usurp your office, but I don't see why I shouldn't do the search under your supervision. This will be a damn unpleasant job, Mrs. Jenkins."

She met his eyes. "You think I can't handle unpleasant?"

"No, but I just don't understand why we should handle this situation any differently than all the others we've had since you won election."

"Because I didn't do what the voters elected me to do the last time, Sheriff. I shirked my duty during pheasant season. If I hadn't, then maybe there would have been only one dead body instead of two, and maybe Sheriff Lindman wouldn't be laid up in the hospital with a bullet wound that he came damn close to not surviving. He won't ever be the same man he was before. Nobody is after they've been shot." She drew a deep breath and coughed from the dusty air. "This time I'm going by the book, so move aside and let me get on with it before I lose my nerve and my dinner."

Charles caught her hands and squeezed them. "Living with guilt doesn't mean you can't delegate authority, Mrs. Jenkins."

She pulled her hands free. "To me, it does. Call it my reckoning if you want. Besides, there's another reason."

"What reason?"

"This man was dead a long time before you came to Crawford County. He didn't know you when he was alive, and it's likely he did know me even though I was a kid during the war. I think maybe he would rather have me poking at him than a stranger."

So much for the editorial in the *Crawford County Examiner*, Charles thought bitterly. His status had only changed from that of an unwelcome suitor to an unwanted in-law.

"Are you certain about that, Mrs. Jenkins? Maybe he'd rather trust me because it damn sure wasn't a stranger who murdered him and buried him down here. It was someone from Crawford County. It was one of his own."

CHAPTER

4

SKELETON UNEARTHED IN
COURTHOUSE BASEMENT

CARROLL, TEXAS—C.J. Tolliver and José Herrera dug up more than they bargained for on New Year's Eve when they uncovered a grave in the subbasement of the Crawford County Courthouse. The two contractors submitted the winning bid for renovating the subbasement to provide additional storage for county records, but Mr. Tolliver and Mr. Herrera say they did not include exhuming bodies in their estimate. "If we had known there was a skeleton down there, we would have included medical expenses in our original bid," said Mr. Tolliver at Carroll Memorial Hospital, where he is undergoing treatment for an episode of high blood pressure. "Lord Almighty, I could have died from the shock when I saw that skull grinning up at me."

Mr. Herrera plans several visits to an Amarillo psychiatrist as a direct result of the unpleasant discovery. "I am extremely nervous of dark places now," says Mr. Herrera. "I have to sleep with a light on."

Sheriff Charles Matthews says the skeleton is that of a young man approximately five feet ten inches tall, wearing an army uniform dating from World War II. "Obviously the individual is either from Crawford County or had business here. We ask anyone who might have information about him to call the sheriff's department."

The sheriff adds that a memorial service will be held

within the next week, but that burial will be delayed until the body is identified.

Crawford County Examiner
January 3

Charles paused outside Sheriff Christopher "Kit" Lindman's hospital room and drew several deep breaths. Intellectually he knew that he wasn't responsible for Lindman being shot while acting as his temporary deputy, but he still felt twinges of guilt for not visiting him since the mummy's discovery. If a sheriff is wounded in the line of duty, it at least ought to happen in his own state. Lindman was sheriff of Union County, New Mexico, and claimed to be not too fond of Texas in any event. To be shot by one of Crawford County's homegrown murderers added insult to injury in Lindman's estimation.

Charles pushed open the door and walked in to find the New Mexico sheriff dressed in worn Levi's and a western shirt that hung on his gaunt frame like rags on a scarecrow, standing by the room's only window and reading the *Crawford County Examiner*.

"Are you supposed to be out of bed, Lindman?"

The other sheriff dropped the newspaper and whirled around with a curse in what Charles assumed was Norwegian. Lindman looked to be Hispanic from the top of his wavy blue-black hair to the bottoms of his bare feet. Only his Nordic name, bright blue eyes, and the slight inflection on the ends of his sentences gave away his father's contribution to Lindman's personal gene pool. Kit Lindman almost, but not quite, had a Norwegian accent whether he was speaking English, Spanish, or his father's native language. He was the only man Charles knew who could curse fluently in three different languages.

"I wish you wouldn't sneak up on me when I've got my back turned, Matthews! When the door opened I thought it might be a nurse with a needle in her hand and fixing to tell me to drop my pants."

"You didn't answer my question. Are you supposed to be out of bed?"

"I'm going home today. The wife's down the hall checking me out."

Charles swallowed a sudden knot in his throat. "Were you going to sneak away without saying goodbye?"

Lindman shuffled over to his bed, sat down, and glared at Charles. "I don't appreciate that question at all, Matthews. What kind of man do you think I am?"

"One who got shot while visiting Texas and didn't like it one damn bit!"

Lindman grinned. "That's true enough. The next time I'm making sure it happens in Union County, New Mexico, so my wife can bring me clean pajamas every day. I don't like them hospital gowns that leave my behind waving in the breeze."

"Let's hope you don't get shot again, period," said Charles.

"'I'm damn sure going to try to avoid it in the future. I may even start wearing one of them bulletproof vests. On second thought, I don't think I will. Union County doesn't have your kind of crime. But to answer your question, I wasn't sneaking out. I was gonna come by your office and jaw a little on my way out of town. Say a proper goodbye, friend to friend, in surroundings that don't smell like alcohol and bedpans. Goodbyes are important, Matthews. A man has to tie up loose ends so he doesn't get tangled up and trip when he least expects it. And speaking of loose ends, I've been reading about your skeleton in the local paper." Lindman paused, his eyes expectant.

Charles pulled one of the visitors' chairs close to Lindman's bed and sat down. "We found one."

"I know you found one, damn it! I learned that much from the paper, but what about it? Have you identified it yet? Come on, Matthews, tell me about it. I've been bored as hell with nothing to do but wait for your visits and my wife's visits and give that doctor of yours a hard time."

"You're not happy with Dr. Wallace?"

"Sure I am. He saved my life, didn't he? I'm just used to giving orders instead of taking them, and besides, arguing with the doc helped pass the time and beat the hell out of watching TV. So are you gonna tell me or not?" Lindman asked abruptly.

Charles supposed there was no reason not to discuss the skeleton with Lindman. The other sheriff certainly seemed more interested in the discovery than anyone else in Crawford County with the possible exceptions of Meenie and Viola Jenkins, and Charles suspected both of them wished the dead sergeant had lain undisturbed for eternity.

"Then Meenie said that we were digging up trouble, and I'll have to be honest and admit that just for a minute I wondered if he might be right," admitted Charles, after recounting the events of the last three days. "But we haven't had a single person claim that our unidentified mummy is his or her nearest and dearest. In fact, except for you, I haven't heard anybody express more than mild curiosity about Sergeant John Doe."

The New Mexico sheriff swung his legs up on the bed and leaned back against the headboard. "If I was in your shoes, Matthews—and there's plenty of times when I'm hurting like hell that I wish I was wearing your boots and—"

"That I was lying in that hospital bed," finished Charles, feeling a fresh twinge of guilt. "Damn it, Lindman, there are times when I wish it, too."

"Then you're a bigger fool than I think you are," said Lindman, frowning at him. "I was intending to say that I'd rather be enjoying myself as a brand-new married man than lying here waiting to heal up. Shit happens, Matthews. It wasn't your fault I got shot."

"If I hadn't coerced you into acting as my deputy when all you really wanted to do was go pheasant hunting . . ." began Charles.

Lindman shook his head. "You're the damnest man I ever saw for wanting to feel guilty. If you can't find something close to hand, you'll go off looking for something.

Hell, you didn't coerce me. When that body showed up in the stubble field on the opening day of pheasant season, I was like an old coon hound. My nose was twitching and my legs were quivering and I was ready to hunt even when it wasn't my field I was hunting in. If you hadn't asked me to help, I'd have volunteered. Damn it all, Matthews, I'm a sheriff, and hunting down criminals is what sheriffs do. The fact that it wasn't my criminal in my county or even in my state doesn't have a damn thing to do with it. It turned out to be a good chase even if I did catch a bullet for my trouble. That don't mean I'm not going to give serious thought to finding another place besides Crawford County, Texas, to shoot pheasant next year. Nothing against your county, but some damn strange things happen here—like your mummy."

"You sound like Dr. Akin, our pathologist for the Panhandle. When I talked to him this morning, he was convinced there might be some kind of chemical in the water in Crawford County that causes its residents to occasionally act oddly."

Lindman snickered. "From the look on your face, I'd say you didn't much like the doc's comment."

Charles grinned reluctantly. "I guess I'm a little sensitive, yes. Until I was elected sheriff there hadn't been a deliberate homicide in this county for eighty years."

"I reckon there was at least one—that you know about anyway," said Lindman. "Or did your Dr. Akin come up with a different date than WWII on your mummy?"

Charles leaned back in his chair and stretched out his legs. "Sort of. I found a 1946 coin in the mummy's pocket when I did a preliminary search of his clothes before Mrs. Jenkins sent him over for the autopsy. Akin called in a physical anthropologist who worked a few years for the Smithsonian before he quit to manage the family ranch, and the anthropologist agreed that 1946 was a good ballpark figure, although it might be '47 or '48 or '49 or maybe even '50. Evidently dating unidentified bones isn't as an exact science as I thought and neither is determining the exact age of the skeleton at the time of death if he's over thirty—which fortunately our soldier isn't. The anthropologist estimated his age at twenty-eight, give or take a year, so I have a murder victim in his late twenties who probably died as early as 1946 or as late as 1950."

"Then your soldier was murdered?" asked Lindman.

Charles nodded his head. "Dr. Akin and the anthropologist did agree on that. The back of the skull was caved in so they ruled it a probable homicide from blunt-force trauma."

Lindman snorted in disgust. "Probable homicide? Do they think the victim cracked his skull falling down your courthouse stairs, and the custodian didn't want a corpse littering up the halls so he buried him?"

"They don't think so, no, but you can bet if this case ever comes to trial the defense attorney will argue accidental death in spite of the circumstances."

"You think it will ever come to trial?"

Charles shook his head. "Nearly fifty years is a long time. The murderer and any witnesses involved are probably dead or close to it. I have Meenie and Raul sifting the dirt from the grave for evidence, but I doubt if we'll find any. Somebody was careful. Every bit of identification was removed from the body including his dog tags. The dental records—if the army finds any—will narrow it down since Sergeant Doe had perfect teeth. Not even a cavity, which is highly unusual considering there was no fluoride in the water at that time. He probably had never been to a civilian dentist in his life. I'll still try to find out who Sergeant Doe is, but I won't lay awake nights worrying about it."

Charles ignored the faint uneasiness he felt at denying any strong interest in the mummy. It wasn't guilt.

Of course, it wasn't.

"You might say that the case is a historical mystery. It's an interesting puzzle, but whether or not I ever solve it won't make any difference in the present," he continued.

Lindman sat up and looked at Charles intently. "Now that's where you're wrong and Meenie's right. That's what

I started to tell you before you interrupted me. If I was in your shoes, I'd be worrying about the fact that nobody in Crawford County is acting curious. That's like the dog that doesn't bark in the night. He ought to bark and your folks ought to be more curious, and if they aren't, then you ought to wonder why not. It ain't natural, Matthews, for a small town not to talk. It means folks are hiding skeletons in their closets, and I'd be afraid they wouldn't appreciate one of them turning up in public. If I was you, I'd work real hard at trying to identify that body. That way you might narrow down the number of people with reason to be uneasy. It's too late to cover up the discovery, which would be my other suggestion."

"For God's sake, Lindman, we're talking about senior citizens, and I can't think of a one in the whole county who doesn't have a reputation for leading a blameless life."

"There ain't a human being anywhere on this planet who is blameless. Everybody has secrets he doesn't want known. Everybody has secrets he's tried to live down. Mind what I say when I tell you that skeleton is a loose end, Matthews. He's somebody who didn't get to say a proper goodbye. He's a story that didn't end, and I suspect it's a story with more than just one character."

"There are at least two. The victim and the killer."

Lindman shook his head. "There's more than that. Otherwise, it doesn't make any sense for the killer to bury your sergeant like he did. He would have just let him lay where he fell."

Charles felt a dull pain in his belly, a reminder that the ulcer he always denied having wasn't as healed as he thought. "I know that, Lindman, but I think you're exaggerating. You and Meenie both."

Lindman leaned over and grasped Charles's arm. "I guess what I'm saying is that if you can't let sleeping dogs lie, Matthews, then you at least ought not to wake up the whole pack. Find out who he was, and for Christ's sake, watch your back. Don't go thinking that just because the folks who knew your sergeant are old that they're not dangerous. An old dog can be just as vicious as a young pup—especially if somebody goes to digging up a bone he's buried."

CHAPTER

5

The original settlers of Crawford County were of Scottish, Irish, and English descent. The isolation of the region, a common culture based upon the demands of agriculture, and intermarriage among its inhabitants produced a cohesive society in which public disapproval of individual members was more highly feared than any penalty imposed by legal authority.

> *Sociological Traits of a Rural Culture in Crawford County, Texas*
> An unpublished dissertation by James Crane

Charles stepped out of the elevator into the dust-filled air of the subbasement and blinked his eyes. "Where did all the lights come from?" he asked, walking toward the grave site where Meenie and Raul crouched, each holding a makeshift sieve made of screen wire tacked to the bottom of a shallow wooden frame.

Meenie looked up, his face tan from the fine grit that rose in a small cloud as the deputy shook the sieve. "I called an electrician to string more lights 'cause I ain't fixing to work down here if I have to spend half my time thinking that something's creeping up on me out of the dark. Them tightwad county commissioners had best pay his bill, too, or they can sift through this dirt themselves and see how they like working in the dark."

Charles refrained from making any remarks concerning ghosts, haunted basements, or overactive imaginations. Judging from the scowls on his deputies' respective faces, neither Meenie nor Raul would appreciate such comments now any more than they would have three days ago. Besides, the basement was an unpleasant place in the best of circumstances, and knowing it was a burial ground added to that unpleasantness. He felt a shiver run up his spine and wished Lindman had never warned him about loose ends, stories without endings, and a man who never got to say a proper goodbye.

"Have you found anything yet?" he asked.

Raul pulled his mask down. "Nothing but a button from his uniform and a few tiny bones that probably came from his feet or hands."

"We've sifted through all the dirt from the grave, Sheriff, plus six feet in every direction," said Meenie. "I don't figure we're gonna find anything else."

"Check the rest of the basement and dig up any place that looks suspicious," said Charles.

Meenie came as close to looking appalled as Charles had ever seen him. "Damnation, Sheriff! Ain't one skeleton enough?"

Charles shrugged. "More than enough, but I'm taking your advice and looking for the worst. Maybe our murderer used this basement as a cemetery more than once."

"This was a lot smaller town fifty years ago, Sheriff," said Meenie. "I don't guess there were more than three thousand people living here. I don't hardly see how even one person disappeared without anybody noticing, but I know for certain that two or three couldn't turn up missing without there being an uproar, and there wasn't one 'cause I've lived here all my life and I'd remember that kind of fuss."

"Then you don't know who our sergeant might be?" asked Charles.

"Damnation, Sheriff, if I'd knowed, I would've said something before now." He set his sieve in the dirt and stood up, giving his pants a hitch as he did. "If you want to look for more bodies, that's up to you, but Raul and me would appreciate it if you'd find somebody else to do the digging. Handling skeletons and mummies kind of puts a man off his feed and spoils his sleep."

"You have a point, Meenie," said Charles.

The deputy looked relieved. "I figured I did."

"I'll send Slim down to help you dig," said Charles, stepping back in the elevator and pushing the button for the third floor. As the doors slid closed he heard Meenie utter a profanity—something Meenie never did—and Charles wondered if perhaps he ought to let sleeping dogs lie as Lindman advised.

He was still wondering when he walked off the elevator on the third floor and turned down the wide hall that served as a reception area for the sheriff's office. Painted an institutional green, whose shade reminded Charles of the stained bones now resting in the morgue in Amarillo, the hall held a cracked vinyl couch, a coffeemaker on a metal table, and two molded plastic chairs guaranteed to give anyone who sat in them a backache. At the end of the hall was a door that couldn't be closed because the carpenters who built the courthouse in the Thirties had hung it crooked. Charles had heard the carpenters had been suffering a gigantic hangover at the time—a result of celebrating the end of Prohibition. He didn't know if it was true or not, but it was as good an explanation as any and made a good story.

In the wall beside the door was a rectangular-shaped opening behind which the dispatcher sat. Except Miss Poole wasn't sitting there now, and Charles frowned as he stepped through the open door.

"Miss Poole, have you taken up poker as a vocation?"

Although Megan Elizabeth Poole's thoughts had been distant in time and space from her corporeal existence as dispatcher for the Crawford County Sheriff's Department, she nevertheless had a certain facility gained in forty years of teaching sixth grade for maintaining a facade of attentiveness to her surroundings. Heaven knew what mischief sixth graders might have undertaken had they ever suspected that she occasionally allowed her mind to wander, not to mention the gossip such vagueness would cause. Of course, during most of her career, old-maid schoolteachers were expected to be a bit odd, a natural result of being unmarried and, by extension, unwanted, but Miss Poole had always eschewed living up to such stereotypes. She would not be thought of as odd. She was unmarried, yes, but that was her business, and in no way did her unwed state mean she was lacking either the feminine attributes or the mental faculties of other women. She had made her bed years ago and had grown used to lying in it.

She was Megan Elizabeth Poole, spinster, with a reputation for having a sharp mind, a tart tongue, and a disposition unsympathetic to foolishness. She was what time had made of her and what she had made of herself, and she had no intention of losing the respect with which she was held by Charles Matthews by appearing to be a dithery old woman who wasn't too certain where she was at a given time.

Nor did Miss Poole intend to lose the respect in which she held herself by succumbing to self-pity.

She carefully squared the corners of a deck of cards she had just shuffled and laid them to one side of an old metal desk that sat in the middle of the squad room and served as a worktable. "I am not playing poker, Sheriff. As you can see, Slim is the only other person here at the moment, and he doesn't present a challenge."

The young deputy's freckled face turned a bright pink. "I can't help it if I'm unlucky at cards. Some people are, Miss Poole."

"Nonsense, Slim," said Miss Poole, in the same brisk tone of voice she had always used with students who failed to turn in their homework. "A successful poker player is merely familiar with mathematical probability. As I recall, I warned you when you were in my sixth-grade class that one day you would find mathematics a necessary tool. I also recall that you didn't listen. Perhaps you should be studying mathematics instead of spending your time reading those lurid mysteries."

"You read mysteries, too, Miss Poole," protested Slim. "I've seen you."

The dispatcher smoothed the knot of iron gray hair at the back of her head, and leveled a hard look at the young deputy. "I read Miss Christie and Miss Sayers as well as a selection of more modern intellectual mysteries. I do *not* waste my time on paperbacks that feature body parts on the cover and fornication as a major element in the plot. Good heavens! I don't know how the detective has the time, not to mention the energy, to solve the murder when he's so busy seducing nubile young women."

Slim's complexion turned even more crimson, and Miss Poole tried to remember if his family was prone to hypertension. "How do you know what's in my books if you don't read them?" protested the young deputy.

Had she been troubled by a weak ego, Miss Poole might have felt threatened by her former student's question. Instead she was pleased. Perhaps she had not failed in her duty as Slim's teacher after all. "An excellent question, Slim. It demonstrates independent thought. However, it is not necessary to do more than skim the first few pages of such books to ascertain the presence—or absence—of literary merit. Also, I have noticed that there is some correlation between blood on the cover and gore on the pages."

"Miss Poole!" interrupted the sheriff. "Your taste in literature is not the point. Your behavior is. It doesn't matter to me if you were playing poker or tiddledywinks, just don't do it on the county's time. What if a civilian had walked in? A taxpayer? What would he think of an employee spending her time playing cards instead of working?"

Miss Poole felt disconcerted by his question before regaining her customary self-possession. "I didn't think of that, Sheriff. I apologize. I have found that a game of solitaire is soothing to a troubled mind, and I didn't consider that my actions might be misinterpreted."

The sheriff looked a little disconcerted himself, and Miss Poole wished she had held her tongue. Charles Matthews was far too intelligent not to wonder at her uncharacteristic behavior. "What is the problem, Miss Poole? Family? Finances? Health?"

The dispatcher shook her head slightly and straightened the black wool blazer she wore over a very proper high-necked white blouse. She felt her face grow warm and knew there was a faint tint of pink in her cheeks as though she was embarrassed. She noticed that the sheriff looked alarmed rather than merely disconcerted and no wonder. She doubted Charles Matthews had ever seen her embarrassed. It was not an emotional reaction in which she indulged under normal circumstances. Of course, these were not normal circumstances. On the other hand, she was not turning pink from embarrassment, but from anger with herself. She must be more careful with her words.

"Thank you for your concern, Sheriff, but I am quite healthy and have sufficient means to live a comfortable life. I have merely let the discovery of our skeleton distress me."

"It's not a skeleton," said Slim. "It's more like a mummy. There's skin and stuff on the bones."

Had she been younger and not possessed of such rigid self-control, Miss Poole doubted she could have held back the sob she felt burning in her throat at the image Slim's words evoked. But she was an old woman by most people's standards and a strong one. She had done with crying years ago.

She gave him a hard look. "You should have paid closer attention in health class, Slim. That *stuff* is more than likely dried tendons. I'm not certain, of course, but I doubt that I'm wrong."

"Slim, go help Meenie and Raul," the sheriff ordered.

"Yes, sir!" exclaimed the young deputy as he straightened his shoulders and saluted.

Charles sighed. "I wish you'd stop saluting. I feel like I'm back in the army."

"Yes, sir! I'll remember." He stuck his hands in his back pockets as if he thought one or the other might salute on its own and began backing toward the door. "I guess I better get on down there. I read this book the other night about some serial killer in Connecticut or Ohio or one of those other eastern seaboard states who buried his victims. The book explained how the police went about finding the graves. I expect I need to tell Meenie and Raul." He turned and ran for the elevator.

Miss Poole allowed exasperation to distract her. "I hope his sense of direction is better than his knowledge of United States geography, or he will arrive on the roof instead of the basement. Ohio an eastern seaboard state indeed!"

"Slim can always find his way into trouble—which I suspect is what my sending him to the basement will cause—but I'll worry about that later. Right now, suppose you tell me why you are so distressed, Miss Poole?" asked Charles. "Do you think you might know the identity of our Sergeant Doe?"

She rose and dropped the deck of cards in the top drawer of a dented filing cabinet to give herself a moment to choose her words. She must be very careful in her answer. "This is my town, Sheriff. My grandfather built the first house in Carroll before it was even the county seat of Crawford County. That was 1903, and my family has lived here ever since. I literally know everyone, and in most instances knew their parents and grandparents. It is very unpleasant to admit that someone I have known most of my life murdered a man."

"Miss Poole," said Charles. "Every murder since I've taken office has been committed by someone you knew. Why is this one so much worse?"

She turned around, feeling further disgusted with herself. A lifetime of honesty is not a good training ground for becoming a practiced liar. "Perhaps because I feel betrayed by this murderer, and I didn't feel that way about the others. They were a younger generation, after all, and that does make a difference. I could take a more objective view. But this murderer is someone I know—or perhaps *had* known is the proper tense—since I was a child. He is one of my own in a sense, and I have shared a lifetime of experience with him, yet he is—or was—a stranger. It is as though the earth has suddenly shifted under my feet without warning. It is very unsettling."

The sheriff looked a little unsettled himself. "You're talking like Meenie—and Lindman. They both think we dug up trouble."

"Meenie and Sheriff Lindman are frequently right."

"Lindman believes we should identify the corpse as fast as possible before our senior citizens go on a rampage."

Miss Poole frowned for a second. "I'm not certain I agree with Sheriff Lindman. The person responsible for the murder—if he is still living—knows the identity. Those who were involved with the victim before his death undoubtedly have also guessed his identity. Perhaps it is no one else's business."

The sheriff frowned back at her. "It's my business, Miss Poole."

She arched her eyebrows. "Is it, Sheriff? It's too late for the guilty to make amends."

"I'm not as concerned with the guilty as I am with the innocent."

"It is the innocent of whom I'm speaking," said Miss Poole, gazing over his shoulder into space. "If the guilty is dead, which probability says he is, then it is his family and friends who will be shamed by his deeds. Is that really necessary?"

"Damn it, our Sergeant Doe survived the Second World War, and he wasn't just a clerk at some Stateside army post either. He wore a Purple Heart on his uniform. He was wounded, Miss Poole! In the name of patriotism, or to save a buddy's life, or because he believed he was fighting for a just cause, he walked in harm's way."

She laid her hand on his arm. "And you feel a sense of comradeship with him? Because you fought in Vietnam?"

She realized her mistake the instant she felt his arm stiffen beneath her touch. She should never have mentioned Vietnam. The sheriff's face took on the forbidding expression it always assumed whenever anyone mentioned his wartime service, and she knew that she had awakened a resolve best left alone.

"I'm prying, aren't I, Sheriff?"

"Let's just say that our sergeant deserves to be buried under his own name. He earned that right." He lowered his voice. "Why is Crawford County so damn determined not to care, Miss Poole? He was one of yours. It was your history he shared, not mine, but not a single person in this county seems to give a damn about him but me!"

Miss Poole straightened her shoulders. Perhaps it was not too late to weaken his resolve by reminding him of his status as an outsider in Crawford County despite his recent marriage. It was a sensitive point with him. "You answered your own question, Sheriff. It is our history and we know that we can't relive the past. Whatever lives were altered by Sergeant's Doe's death cannot be set right. It's too late. I'm not fond of fanatics who bolster their arguments with Scripture, but I'll succumb to the temptation on this occasion. Let the dead bury their dead."

"Doesn't he deserve a last goodbye, Miss Poole?" asked the sheriff softly. "Won't Crawford County at least call him by name?"

She turned away and walked across the cracked asphalt tiles to one of the windows. Bracing her hands on its sill, she looked westward toward the farms and ranches with their neat barbed-wire boundaries that began at the edge of town and spread across the flat plains to the New Mexico border. This was her land, its people were hers. She knew their names, their histories. They were an agricultural people with more in common with early man, who first put away his migratory ways as a hunter-gatherer to become a farmer and herdsman, than with Sheriff Charles Matthews, a man of the city who never grew his own food. After all, cities were a very recent development in mankind's social evolution. In ancient days she suspected she might have been a witch woman, the keeper of the tribe's totem and its protectress against these city dwellers. But this was now, and she was merely an elderly dispatcher for a sheriff's department in a not very important county, and she could not stop what must come to pass. And she should not stop it. The sheriff was right. Crawford County must say goodbye.

She turned toward him and saw him waiting, his face that stern mask behind which he frequently hid an empathetic nature. She doubted he was feeling empathetic at the present time.

"What is Crawford County's answer, Miss Poole?"

She gave him a sharp glance. "I'm hardly an oracle, Sheriff, but you are right, of course. Crawford County must claim its own, if Sergeant Doe is indeed ours, not some transient who stopped here on his way to somewhere else."

"You don't believe that, do you, Miss Poole?"

She shook her head. "No, I don't. It would be too convenient a solution, and life is seldom convenient."

"Do you have any idea who he might be, Miss Poole?"

She swallowed back another sob as she recalled the image of the grinning skull she had not wanted to look at, but had felt compelled to view. "He was hardly in a condition to be recognized, Sheriff, and that is as honest an answer as I can give. I don't know who he was."

She wasn't lying, she thought as the sheriff disappeared into his office and slammed the door. She *didn't* know for an absolute fact. But she suspected, and was surprised to discover that her grief was as sharp as it had been nearly fifty years ago—sharper even, because it held so much regret.

CHAPTER

6

From the private journal of Megan Elizabeth Poole:

January 3

I read James Crane's dissertation on Crawford County
again this evening and again found much with which to
disagree. James is a former student of mine, and even as
a sixth grader, he was prone to be judgmental.

Charles dropped his Stetson on the battered filing cabinet
next to a chessboard whose pieces showed a game in progress, one of the many he played by mail. He had taken up
chess during the long, pain-filled weeks in the military hospital recovering from his own near-fatal wounds and watching others die from theirs. The game's stylized ritual
restored symbolic order to the pieces in which he felt his
life had been broken. In the intervening years between then
and now, thinking about intricate chess strategy not only
helped pass the time but kept war memories at bay. Only
occasionally did those memories break through into his ev-
eryday life.

Unfortunately, this was one of those occasions.

He turned away to sit down and prop his boots on the
top of his desk. His heart pounded in his chest and he knew
his muscles would ache tomorrow. Damn it, why did Miss
Poole have to mention Vietnam? He always tensed up
whenever a civilian referred to the war. It was a reaction he

couldn't help, a defense mechanism of that war's veteran to the probing of a nonveteran. It was a reaction he learned as a nineteen-year-old when he stepped off the plane in Dallas after being released from the military hospital. Feeling a thousand years old and with his uniform hanging on his skeletal body, he only wanted to go home to finish healing and put his life back together. With the war over and everyone anxious to forget it, he didn't expect to be spat upon by a well-fed young man wearing a sweatshirt with a peace sign on it. Too weak from his healing wound to fight, and too dazed from the painkillers to speak without slurring his words, Charles had wiped the spittle off his cheek, straightened his shoulders, and walked away on unsteady feet. He never forgot the expression in the young man's eyes. He wondered if Sergeant Doe had seen that same arrogant self-righteousness and ignorance and contempt in the eyes of his murderer, the expression of a man who had never seen the face of war but felt justified in judging those who had.

Charles rubbed his cheek where the spittle had struck him. So long ago. A lifetime ago.

He studied his office with its green asphalt tiles, chipped plaster walls, hissing radiator, and three sturdy wooden chairs grouped in a semicircle in front of his desk until his heartbeat slowed and his tight muscles began to loosen. Finally, reluctantly, he focused on the several small paper bags sitting on the corner of his desk, each labeled and initialed and smelling of the grave. Lowering his feet to the floor, he leaned over and opened one of the bags, spilling its contents on top of his desk. Gently he touched a still-recognizable combat infantryman's badge. The other sacks held a sharpshooter's badge, campaign ribbons for the American and European theatres of operations, a good conduct medal, Purple Heart, lapel insignia, and the decaying remnants of three yellow bars originally sewn on the mummy's uniform sleeve—one bar for each six months spent overseas.

Had the murdered soldier not been buried in dry sandy soil, it was probable that little would have remained of cloth or ribbon or human tissue. Perhaps even the medals would have rusted away. Perhaps no one would have known he was a soldier. But Crawford County's arid climate had preserved Sergeant Doe. Had Miss Poole not mentioned Vietnam, Charles might never have recognized him. Different time, different war after all.

But Miss Poole's words ripped away his willful blindness. However many years and whatever the relative merits that separated their respective wars, the indisputable fact was that both Charles and the mummy in the unblessed grave were shot in their country's service. It was a bond between soldiers, a kinship granted not by birth, but by blood spilled, and Charles could deny it no longer. Be damned if he would bury a brother in arms in an unmarked grave, and if his efforts to identify Sergeant Doe disturbed Crawford County's complacency, then to hell with Crawford County.

Dropping the dead soldier's badge back in its paper sack, Charles reached for the phone and dialed directory assistance. "St. Louis, please."

Twenty minutes later he carefully replaced the receiver, took several deep breaths to relieve his frustration, and buzzed Miss Poole. "Would you bring me a cup of coffee, please? In fact, just fill up that thermos you keep in your desk drawer."

There was a moment's silence before the dispatcher answered. "Are you expecting company, Sheriff?"

"No."

"That much caffeine will irritate your ulcer."

Charles gritted his teeth. "Miss Poole, when I need a medical opinion I'll call Dr. Wallace. Just bring me my damn coffee! Please," he said, clicking off the intercom and leaning back in his chair, trying to ignore the twinges of pain in his belly.

"If you're going to yell, I don't know why you bother using the intercom," said Miss Poole a few minutes later as she set a coffee mug and thermos on his desk.

"Didn't anyone ever tell you not to criticize a frustrated man, Miss Poole?"

The dispatcher raised her eyebrows. "Not that I recall."

"It's one of those things your mother should have told you along with the facts of life."

She uncorked the thermos and poured him coffee. "My mother died when I was quite young, Sheriff."

"I'm sorry, Miss Poole. I didn't know."

"No reason why you should. You're a newcomer, and I'm not one of those little old ladies who dwells on the past. Not my past at any rate," she amended. It was as close as she would come to admitting to occasionally gossiping about everyone else's past.

"Then I'll tell you, Miss Poole. Never criticize a frustrated man."

She sat down in one of the wooden chairs in front of his desk. "A lifetime of observation has taught me the effects of frustration on the male psyche. However, I refuse to excuse bad manners on that account. Suppose you tell me why you're frustrated instead of taking out your ill temper by yelling or throwing things. It will be good practice for your marriage since I doubt that Angie will have any more patience with your masculine habit of keeping things to yourself than I do."

"Miss Poole, you are criticizing again!"

"Nonsense! I'm stating facts. There's a difference."

"I suspect any difference exists in your *female* psyche."

She tilted her head to one side and thought. "That's a possibility—but I doubt it."

"I don't," said Charles. "And another thing, while we're on the subject of my psyche. I don't intend for my personal life and my professional life to overlap if I can help it. My home is my refuge—the one place where my life is very nearly perfect—and I have no intention of disturbing my domestic peace by bringing home problems from work and dumping them on Angie."

Miss Poole tapped her nails on the chair arm. "Her first husband kept things to himself."

"Damn it all, Miss Poole, it's not the same thing at all! L.D. Lassiter was a philanderer and a murderer! You couldn't expect him to discuss his latest seduction or murder at the dinner table!"

Miss Poole leaned forward with an intent look on her face. "Angie is too intelligent a woman to make the same mistake twice. She won't allow herself to be shunted aside again."

Charles glowered at her. "I'm only trying to protect her from the unpleasant side of my job."

"My father often made decisions in the name of protecting me. I frequently resented him—as any intelligent woman would."

Charles wiped his hand over his face and wondered if Miss Poole had been as strong willed a child as she was a woman. If so, he was surprised her late father hadn't strangled her out of the sheer frustration of trying to win an argument. "Miss Poole, I don't know why you and everyone else in the county is so damn interested in my marriage, but I've heard all the advice I can handle. The subject is off limits. When I'm in this office I am not Angie's husband, I'm Sheriff Matthews of Crawford County, Texas."

Miss Poole sat back and folded her arms. "And I am not your wife, and as your employee I believe I'm entitled to know why you're frustrated. Ranting and raving and keeping secrets interfere with the efficient operation of this office."

Charles ran his fingers through his hair. Miss Poole was right, of course, but she generally was. Cooperation was necessary to solving crimes. He sighed. He wished he could go home right now. Between Sheriff Lindman's and Miss Poole's advice, Meenie's complaints, Slim's potential for creating chaos where none existed before, and his own belated sense of kinship with the dead soldier, Charles needed peace and quiet and uncritical acceptance.

He reached for his mug of coffee. "I just called the National Personnel Record Center in St. Louis, Miss Poole."

He noticed the watchful expression in her eyes and the stillness of her body, and wondered if she was as ignorant of the dead soldier's identity as she claimed, then discarded the idea. Another attribute of Miss Poole was her unfailing honesty. She would no more lie than she would arrive for work in mismatched and untidy clothes.

"Yes?" the dispatcher prompted, and Charles started, realizing he had been staring at her without speaking for several seconds.

"The army can't help us identify Sergeant Doe—at least not immediately. It seems the Center had a fire in 1973 that destroyed all army records for the years 1912 through 1959. They have managed to reconstruct most of the missing files through veterans' discharge papers and affidavits and company rolls and various other means, but our soldier was dead before the fire. No one would know that his record was one of those destroyed, so no one would come forward to help reconstruct his file."

Charles saw Miss Poole's shoulders relax, but her watchful expression remained. "What do you mean by not immediately?" she asked.

He gestured toward the small paper sacks on his desk. "The army can compile a list of names of all the men ever awarded our corpse's various badges and medals, then correlate the lists to find a name common to all of them. There will be tens of thousands of such names because during the course of the war tens of thousands of men received the same medals as our soldier did. We'll be lucky if the army can identify him by the turn of the century." He slammed his fist on his desk. "Damn it all, Miss Poole, I don't intend to wait that long!"

Miss Poole blinked, then stared at him in disapproval. "Breaking your hand or the office furniture won't speed up the army, Sheriff."

"I don't intend to wait on the army. As you said, Sergeant Doe is one of our own. It's Crawford County's responsibility to uncover his identity."

"You've already published an appeal in the *Crawford County Examiner*, and no one came forward with any information. I don't know what else you can do."

"There are a number of things I can do. I can examine

draft records. I can order a facial reconstruction done if I have to, but I *will* identify him."

"And from there it is only a step to identifying his murderer, given how small the town was in those days and how impossible it was to keep secrets."

"Possibly."

"I would say probably is the correct word, Sheriff, but will you take that step?"

Charles hesitated as he struggled to find an answer he could live with—that the town could live with—and realized there was no such answer. A man could break his oath once and justify it to himself. More than once, and he was morally dishonest. There was no compromise.

"Damn it all, Miss Poole, why did this have to happen now, just when I'm married and finally feel like I'm part of this community?"

Miss Poole closed her eyes briefly before squaring her shoulders and meeting his eyes. "Then you've made your decision. You will take that step?"

"I have to, Miss Poole."

She sighed. "I thought that might be your answer."

"I'm sorry, but I don't have a choice."

"There are always choices, Sheriff, some more destructive than others. You made the right one, but don't expect Crawford County to be pleased—or cooperative."

Built a mile outside Carroll's city limits, where the flat prairie turned rugged as it descended toward the Canadian River breaks, Charles's house was both larger and more sprawling than most of Crawford County realized, since only its west side could be seen from the highway, and only then from a distance. Charles had built it that way on purpose. He hadn't wanted anyone to ask what a single man with no known romantic attachments—or none he admitted to—needed with such a large house because it was a question he could not answer. Building a house for a woman who at the time was married to someone else might have struck locals as a sick fantasy—which Charles supposed in a sense it had been. He certainly had no way of knowing at the time that Angie would ever be free to marry him. But one man's sick fantasy was another man's hopeless dream, and having enough money to indulge in any number of hopeless dreams, Charles had done so.

He parked in front of the house and rested his head against the steering wheel. "Goddamn it all, it's not fair!"

He raised his head and looked through the windshield at the stone and timbered house with its lawn of native buffalo grass whose arduous cultivation had fueled gossip and head scratching in the county for months. No one understood why Charles planted a lawn of grass most thought of as cattle forage even if it was disease resistant and required little water. He never told anyone why—not even Angie. Buffalo grass was native to the Panhandle, even if it had largely disappeared, and he wasn't. Surrounding his castle with native grass was another attempt to fit in.

Now his castle was under siege, or might soon be, according to Miss Poole. He had won his fair maiden and assumed he would live happily ever after. He forgot that outside the castle walls life waited with all its conflicts and dilemmas and ugliness.

Charles slid out of the car and hurried up to the double wooden doors. Suddenly he wanted to be inside his house—his castle—holding the wife he never thought he'd win, listening to the high-pitched voices of children he never thought he'd have, and enjoying tranquillity for as long as he could. And Miss Poole might be seeing conflicts where none existed. Certainly he'd seen no indication of any except his own deputies' reluctance to do more in the way of investigation than they absolutely had to.

He stepped inside the house. "Angie?"

Only the silence of a dark and empty house answered him, and for a second he wondered if his hopeless dream had not come true after all. When he barked his shin on Jennifer's bicycle, which was parked in the middle of the dark entry hall, he knew it had. Dreams never included such mundane objects as children's toys scattered over the floor like booby traps.

He limped into the den and dropped onto the couch, not noticing the wooden blocks on its cushions until their sharp edges bit into one hip.

"Damn it!" he roared, leaping up and barking his other shin against the coffee table. Grabbing his newly injured leg, he tripped, lost his balance, and sprawled across the top of the coffee table and onto the floor. With the tiny corner of his brain not involved in coping with pain, Charles wondered why he bothered installing a security system before his marriage. Any intelligent burglar would avoid like the plague any house with kids.

"Charles?"

He heard the back door slam and quickly sat up, biting his lip when his bruised hip protested the movement. "In here, Angie."

"What are you doing sitting in the dark?" asked Angie, switching on the light, then staring at him with a puzzled expression in her hazel eyes. "What are you doing sitting on the *floor* in the dark?"

"Papa!" screamed Jennifer, running into the den followed by Laura and a howling beagle and flinging herself on his lap, stepping on one shin in the process. His lap already being claimed, Laura sat on his legs. So much for his lifelong assumption that little girls were soft and cuddly. Judging from the increased pain in both shins, these two girls were all knees, elbows, and hobnail boots.

"Can we? Can we?" cried Laura, bouncing up and down on his legs.

"Oh, God!" said Charles, biting back a more pithy epithet.

"Hush, girls!" shouted Angie, over the bedlam of girlish shrieks and barking canine.

Silence fell except for Angie's voice, and Charles concentrated on his cuddling the two girls. Despite barked shins, scattered toys, noise, and confusion, he wouldn't trade places with anyone he knew. He wondered how in the hell he could do his job without it spilling over into his private life and destroying his dream.

"Charles?"

He lifted his head, noticing when he did that both his stepdaughters were watching him as expectantly as Hieronymus always did whenever Charles opened the refrigerator door. Hieronymus always hoped for a slice of cold chicken or a piece of bologna. He wondered what the girls hoped for.

"What do you think, Charles?" asked Angie.

Charles stared at her, then cleared his throat of the large knot that had suddenly formed there when he realized that while he was thinking of what his job might cost his family, Angie had been talking. Lindman had warned him against tuning out a wife. In the New Mexico sheriff's opinion, not being listened to would send a wife into a conniption fit faster than almost anything else a husband could do short of adultery. Charles wasn't certain exactly what kind of behavior a conniption fit entailed, but he didn't want to find out either. Not now. Time enough later if Miss Poole was right.

He smiled at Angie. "Whatever you decide is fine with me."

The girls bounced up and down on his body and clapped their hands while screaming "Thank you, Papa" in their shrill voices. Hieronymus reared up and licked his face.

Charles grabbed at the two little girls and hoisted them to their feet, then got to his knees, which was a better defensive position. Whatever he had agreed to seemed to make both girls and dog ecstatic. He wondered what it was.

Angie tilted her head and narrowed her eyes. "I'm surprised you didn't argue, Charles."

Charles shrugged his shoulders. "You're a sensible woman, Angie. You wouldn't do anything dangerous or foolish, so why should I argue?"

"Because you don't like horses."

"Horses? What do horses have to do with this conversation?"

Angie sighed. "I didn't think you were listening to me.

You had a glazed look in your eyes. Still worried about whose skeleton was found in the basement?"

"Never mind my skeleton. What about horses?"

"Dad came by this afternoon," Angie began, then hesitated before bursting into speech again. "I'm afraid he wasn't very tactful, Charles. You know how he is. He sometimes talks before he thinks and he was sorry afterward he said anything in front of the girls, but he did."

Charles felt the hair on the back of his neck stiffen much as he imagined the lord of a castle's might if he saw a band of mail-clad knights riding toward his castle with mischief on their minds. In Charles's opinion Angie's father was just as capable of causing disaster as any enemy knight.

"What did he say?"

"Since we live on the edge of town, and you own a section of land back of the house, Dad offered to send a couple of cowboys to build a stable and a small corral behind the back fence. I think that will be far enough from the house so we won't have a problem with flies."

"A stable and small corral?" asked Charles.

"Yes. For the horse. Dad has a horse too old to work cattle anymore that he's willing to give the girls, but he wanted to be sure you'd agree. He seems to think that you're afraid of horses."

"I am *not* afraid of horses! I just don't enjoy riding them," explained Charles, thinking that was the understatement of the year. He would rather walk a mile barefoot over broken glass than ride a horse, and furthermore, J.T. Brentwood, Angie's father, knew it.

His relationship with Angie's father was ambivalent to say the least, and he wouldn't put it past the old reprobate to have offered the girls a horse just to make him look bad. J.T. Brentwood's tolerance for men he called "city boys," who were any men not raised on a ranch in the Texas Panhandle, was close to nonexistent. Not only did Charles grow up in Dallas, but his family's considerable wealth was based on stocks, bonds, banks, and mutual funds. To J.T.

Brentwood any wealth not based on land and cattle was suspect.

Charles glanced at the two little girls, and knew their adoring eyes would fill with tears and disillusionment if he exerted his authority and denied them a horse. Damn J.T. Brentwood.

"Don't you think the girls are too young to be riding horses? Maybe a pony instead? A small pony?"

Judging from the shocked expression on Angie's face, Charles decided he had just said the wrong thing, but he hadn't a clue as to what it was.

"Charles," said Angie quietly. "I can't remember when I didn't ride a horse. And I don't mean a pony!" Her voice rose on the last word, and he flinched.

"I just thought a pony would be safer," he began.

Angie raked her fingers through her hair and sighed. "I'm sorry, Charles. I shouldn't jump on you for an honest mistake. I keep forgetting that you're a stranger to Crawford County. You don't understand about horses and growing up in the country. You grew up in a different world."

Charles felt as though a wide chasm had opened beneath his feet. How many times in the past four years had he been accused of not understanding the folkways of Crawford County? Too many times to count, he decided, including Miss Poole's comments this afternoon, and each time he felt the loneliness of the outsider. But he didn't want to be an outsider in his own marriage. He didn't want Laura and Jennifer to think of him as a stranger who didn't belong in their world—even if he didn't. Besides, Angie wasn't asking him to *ride* the damn horse, just accept his presence. And J.T. Brentwood probably didn't have an ulterior motive behind his offer—although Charles wasn't as sure of that.

He cleared his throat again. "You're right, Angie. I don't understand your and Crawford County's attachment to overrated, romanticized, four-legged beasts. I may never understand. But I'm willing to compromise. Tell J.T. we'll take the horse, but it had better be so decrepit that it can hardly put one hoof in front of another, be nearly toothless, and as tame as Hieronymus. I don't want the girls bucked off, nipped, or kicked by some half-wild horse."

He nodded his head to emphasize his demands, suddenly feeling better. He had bowed to Crawford County's ways and bought himself some goodwill at the same time. Once Angie learned the cost of marrying Sheriff Charles Matthews, he might need whatever goodwill he managed to accrue.

He wondered why doing right often cost so much more than doing wrong.

Angie studied him, her face solemn. "Are you sure, Charles?"

"Absolutely," Charles lied.

CHAPTER

7

In certain isolated cultures a stranger will be adopted and initiated into the tribe, usually as a result of marriage, but sometimes because of his leadership abilities. He will often be called upon to settle disputes, determine guilt and innocence, and assess punishment. He is trusted to be impartial, while at the same time is expected not to interfere with local custom. The appearance of such strangers in Crawford County is rare.

> *Sociological Traits of a Rural Culture*
> *in Crawford County, Texas*
> An unpublished dissertation by James Crane

From the private journal of Megan Elizabeth Poole:

January 4

I know of only one other stranger besides the sheriff.

By the next morning Charles was looking forward to investigating the mummy no matter how many toes he stepped on. At least he would have the upper hand. He wasn't married to the mummy's daughter, and the mummy hadn't shown up at his front door with two cowboys, a pickup load of lumber, and a smug expression the way J.T. Brentwood had. Charles hadn't even finished his first cup of coffee when the old rancher walked in the kitchen and laid a list of scribbled instructions in front of him.

"What's this?" Charles had asked through clenched teeth.

J.T. took off his hat and sat down, tilting his chair back and grinning. "I figured that since you didn't know from nothing about taking care of a horse that I'd better write it all down for you. I'll bring in a load of hay and some grain when I deliver old Blaze. You got plenty of grass in that section back of the house, but a little grain to supplement won't hurt. Give him some in the evenings, and you might want to run a water line out to the corral so you won't have to carry water."

"Carry water?"

"And be sure to shovel out his stall about once a week."

"Shovel out his stall?"

J.T. gave him a pitying look. "Horse manure, son. You don't want the girls stepping in manure every time they want to go pet Blaze. I'd have thought even a city boy could figure that out."

"Wait a minute," began Charles.

"The girls and I can take care of the horse, Dad," said Angie, frowning at her father.

J.T. glared at Charles. "That's mighty dirty work for womenfolk."

"I'll hire a man to do it," interrupted Charles.

"That's a silly expense to go to for just one horse," said J.T. "You too proud to shovel your own manure?"

"Dad!" cried Angie.

Charles slammed his cup down on the table and pushed back his chair. "J.T., you just provide the horse, and I'll take care of the rest of it."

He had fled the house and driven to town, telling himself all the way that marriage was a compromise. He just hadn't expected a horse and J.T. Brentwood to be part of the compromise.

He wondered how one went about hiring a part-time cowboy.

Charles shivered as he slid out of his patrol car into the freezing weather that turned his breath into a tiny white cloud the second it left his mouth. He hurried into the courthouse, actually looking forward to a cup of the thick sludge that Miss Poole passed off as coffee. A little caffeine stimulus and he would call a staff meeting and lay out his campaign to identify Sergeant Doe.

"Coffee, Miss Poole," he ordered as he walked through the squad room, noticing in passing that at least the elderly dispatcher was seated at the radio and not playing solitaire.

Miss Poole started, then gave him a hard look. "Your coffee is waiting in your office, and Meenie, Raul, and Slim are in the basement. And if I were in poor health, your habit of barking in my ear might give me a heart attack."

Charles thought about refuting her, but he'd already come out second best this morning in one verbal confrontation with a Crawford County oldster and he wasn't up to losing another. He escaped to his office instead.

Tossing his Stetson on top of the filing cabinet, just missing the chess set, he dropped into his chair and poured a cup of coffee. Pulling a yellow legal pad out of his desk drawer, he centered it in the middle of his desk and picked up a ballpoint.

He wrote the numeral one on the pad and took a sip of coffee, spitting it out almost immediately. "Miss Poole, what in the hell did you do to this coffee?" he roared.

The dispatcher appeared in the doorway. "I didn't do anything to the coffee."

He held out his cup. "Miss Poole, your coffee is black as tar and strong enough to dissolve the enamel off a man's teeth. I caught the custodian using it instead of floor stripper, for God's sake! This stuff is not up to your usual standards. It's so weak I can see the bottom of the cup."

Miss Poole crossed to his desk and peered into the cup as though she was afraid it might explode, then stared at him. She licked her lips. "Slim has been underfoot so much recently that I must have let him distract me while I was making coffee. He was chattering worse than a magpie this morning."

Charles raised one eyebrow. "Is that a fact?"

Miss Poole picked up the cup. "I'll make another pot.

And I do apologize. No wonder you barked at me when you came in. I've observed that men are often in a bad mood before having their morning coffee. I imagine caffeine has a soothing effect on the male psyche."

Charles watched her as she marched to the door, then remarked softly. "I believe you said Slim was in the basement with Raul and Meenie."

Miss Poole's back stiffened, then she glanced over her shoulder at him. "Well, I meant he was in the office earlier this morning."

"Meenie and Raul let Slim's chatter distract them while they were exhuming Sergeant Doe. Meenie said it kept them from thinking about ghosts."

"I'm not as young as I used to be, Sheriff, but I'm not senile either. I don't imagine I see things that don't exist." Miss Poole slammed the door behind her.

Charles stared at the closed door for several seconds before he took a deep breath and expelled it. He had never known Miss Poole to slam a door. He had never known her to lie either, but she had just done one and he suspected she had also done the other. The Second Coming couldn't distract Miss Poole from whatever appointed task she set for herself, certainly not one she considered as essential to health and happiness as making coffee. She admitted yesterday that the mummy's discovery distressed her, so why bother lying about it this morning? Why not admit it instead of blaming Slim?

He got up to ask her when a slight woman in her late thirties with two parallel lines etched between her eyes by either bad temper or chronic indigestion slammed open his door and stalked toward him. "It's about time you showed up. Do you know it's nearly nine o'clock and I've been waiting nearly an hour? And I want you to speak to Miss Poole. She put me in the district courtroom to wait instead of calling you when I told her to. She said I was hysterical and needed to calm down."

Miss Poole hurried into the room. "I'm sorry, Sheriff. She got past while I was away from my desk."

Charles couldn't imagine anyone getting past Miss Poole. Either this woman was cleverer than she appeared, or Miss Poole was more upset than he thought. "It's all right. I'll speak to her."

Miss Poole nodded and disappeared, and a second later Charles wondered if he shouldn't call her back as the woman leaned across his desk and grabbed his arm. "I'm not hysterical, Sheriff! I'm worried! There's no telling what my father might do, and I want you to talk to him."

Charles jerked his arm free. "Just wait a minute, Mrs. Brett," he said, thankful for the two furrows between her eyes. Otherwise, he might not have recognized her. He was still trying to put names to all the eight thousand faces in Crawford County, and it helped when one particular face possessed a distinct feature.

"Who is your father, and why are you worried about him?"

She gave him a disgusted look. "I can't imagine how you ever got elected when you don't even know who your constituents are. My father is William Treadwell."

Charles ran through his mental list of county residents. "You mean Mad Dog Treadwell?" he asked.

"A few close friends call him that," she admitted with obvious reluctance.

Lying seemed epidemic in Crawford County lately. So far as Charles knew, everyone called her father Mad Dog, friend or no, and had ever since 1945 when Treadwell chewed a bar of soap to simulate rabies in order to avoid taking a high school algebra test. In fact, the old man even registered to vote under that name.

"Why are you worried about your father, Mrs. Brett?"

The lines between her brows deepened into crevices as she frowned, her eyes darting from side to side as though looking for eavesdroppers, an unnecessary precaution in Charles's opinion. Anyone who cared to know whatever Mrs. Brett was about to say didn't have to hide behind the radiator or listen at keyholes to find out. He could visit the doughnut shop where local businessmen and farmers gath-

ered to drink coffee and exchange gossip. Charles often
thought most of the town's citizens were telepathic. It was
the only explanation for the lack of secrets among the inhabitants. Crawford County gave new meaning to the term
open society.

Mrs. Brett lowered her voice. "My father has locked himself in his house and won't come out. I think he's getting
senile, Sheriff. You might have to break down the door."

Charles rang Mad Dog's doorbell, waited, then pounded
on the door. "Mad Dog, it's Sheriff Matthews. Are you in
there?"

"I told you, Sheriff, you'll have to kick in the door. Did
you hear me, Daddy?" shouted Mrs. Brett over the sound of
the wind shrieking around the corner of the house. "The
sheriff will kick in the door."

"I might have knowed you'd raise a fuss, Pauline."

Charles stepped off the porch to see the top half of Mad
Dog Treadwell leaning out a second-story window. Although in his middle to late sixties, Mad Dog had less gray
in his black hair than his daughter had in hers, and his
broad face, although leathery from a life spent outdoors,
had fewer lines. His shoulders and torso still looked thick
and solid beneath the red flannel shirt he wore. Bright blue
eyes unfaded by age shone with health and youth and mis-
chievous good humor.

No glazed look of encroaching senility in those eyes.

"Your daughter was worried about you, Mad Dog," said
Charles.

Mad Dog grinned. "Well, I guess that's her problem,
ain't it, Sheriff."

"Better come down and unlock the door so she can see
that you're all right."

"She can see me just fine from where she's at."

"Daddy, you come down here right now!"

Mad Dog's eyes lost their good humor. "I ain't doing
any such of a thing. I've argued with you all I intend to.

You're just like your mother. She never knew when she'd lost a fight either."

Pauline Brett pointed to the door. "Kick it in, Sheriff."

"This house is my property, ain't it, Sheriff?" called Mad Dog. "That means I don't have to let nobody in if I don't want to, don't it?"

Damn it, but he hated domestic squabbles, Charles thought. "That's right, Mad Dog."

"I don't even have to let in my own daughter if I don't want to?"

Charles sighed. "That's right, too, Mad Dog, but wouldn't it be better if you and Mrs. Brett talked about your disagreement?"

"Not if it means letting her in the house."

"Would you let me in?" asked Charles.

Mad Dog's eyes narrowed in suspicion. "What for?"

"Because it's cold as hell out here and I'm tired of yelling over the wind, and maybe if you'll talk to me, I can help you two settle your differences," explained Charles.

And maybe he could sprout wings and fly, too.

Mad Dog scratched his head. "I ain't got no objections to you trying, Sheriff, but you'll be wasting your breath. I'm gonna do what I want to do with my life. I ain't got that much of it left and be damned if Pauline's gonna tell me how to spend it."

"I just want you to be sensible, Daddy," protested Pauline Brett. "This new hobby of yours is dangerous. You could break your neck."

"What kind of—" began Charles.

"I suppose you want me to take up playing checkers down at the church like the rest of them old codgers," said Mad Dog. "Most of them won't even go fishing anymore 'cause they're too scared to get out of shouting distance of their doctors. Afraid they might die if somebody in a white coat ain't standing ready to stick tubes everywhere a man's got a cavity or hook him up to machines to do for him what he used to do for himself. What kind of life is it if a man can't even take a piss without help?"

"Daddy . . ."

"Mad Dog, Mrs. Brett . . ." said Charles a little louder.

Mad Dog shook his fist in the air. "I'm gonna look danger in the face and spit in its eye like I done all my life. I ain't having nobody say Mad Dog Treadwell lost his guts in his old age. I ain't having nobody call me a coward. Do you understand that, girl? I ain't lived all these years the way I have to end up losing my neighbors' respect. I ain't afraid to die!"

"I won't allow it, Daddy. . . ."

"You ain't got anything to say about it, Pauline."

"Quiet!" shouted Charles, and two startled faces swung toward him. He drew a deep breath. "Mrs. Brett, your father put out oil-well fires for a living. I can't imagine what hobby could be more dangerous than that, but—"

"Hang gliding," interrupted Pauline Brett, her hands on her hips and her chin jutting out.

"Hang gliding," repeated Charles. "Hang gliding? Good God, where can he hang glide on the prairie? The highest point around here is the mesa south of town, and I don't think it's more than thirty feet high."

"The breaks along the Canadian," interjected Mad Dog. "Some of them cliffs above the river ought to be high enough if I get a running start and the winds are just right."

"Your daughter's right, Mad Dog. You'll break your neck."

"I told you so, Daddy," said Pauline.

Mad Dog jutted out his chin at the same stubborn angle as his daughter's. "It's my neck, Sheriff. I reckon I can risk it if I want to."

"Stop him, Sheriff!" ordered Pauline Brett.

Charles shook his head. "I can't."

She glared at him with the outraged disbelief of a woman who has always gotten her way. "Then I'll have him committed."

Charles felt a little outrage of his own. "Your father's not crazy, Mrs. Brett—at least not in a legal sense, and I don't believe you'll find a doctor who will swear he is. If he wants to break his neck, I guess we have to let him."

CHAPTER

8

One of the inexplicable anomalies of Crawford County culture is its tolerance for odd behavior among its individual members.

> *Sociological Traits of a Rural Culture*
> *in Crawford County, Texas*
> An unpublished dissertation by James Crane

From the private journal of Megan Elizabeth Poole:

January 4 [continued]

James always saw us as more rigid and humorless than we really are. Every society must have its fools. Nevertheless, I wonder at Mad Dog Treadwell's behavior.

"I don't know why Mad Dog took so long to tell Pauline to mind her own business," remarked Miss Poole after Charles returned to the courthouse. "She always had a bossy nature even in the sixth grade, and giving in only encouraged her."

Charles thought if anyone ought to know about bossy natures, it was Miss Poole, but didn't think it would improve employee relations to mention it, especially not when he was about to question her.

He cleared his throat and leaned against the dispatcher's desk. "Miss Poole, why did you blame Slim for the coffee?"

Startled, Miss Poole looked up at him, then her face slowly turned red and she glanced down at her hands. "I might have known you wouldn't believe my fib, Sheriff," she finally said. "And I'm ashamed for bringing up Slim's name. Heaven knows, he doesn't need my help to get into trouble."

"Why did you, uh, fib, Miss Poole?"

She met his eyes. "When you get to be my age, you begin to worry about your mind slipping. I didn't want you to think I'm becoming a forgetful old lady who needs to be pitied."

"And the skeleton in the basement had nothing to do with it?"

She raised her eyebrows. "I hadn't considered that, but it's quite possible that thinking about its discovery might have distracted me. In fact, it's probable. I don't know why I didn't think of that at the time. Too worried about getting old, I guess." She smiled at him. "Thank you, Sheriff. You relieved my mind. And now you best see what Howard Worchester wants. He's waiting in your office."

Charles didn't much care what Howard Worchester wanted. To be honest, he didn't like the man and didn't want to waste time talking to him—time better spent thinking about how to identify Sergeant John Doe.

And wondering why Miss Poole had lied two days in a row.

He limped into his office and tossed his Stetson on the filing cabinet. "What's on your mind today, Howard?" he asked, sinking gingerly into his chair and studying the man sitting opposite him on the other side of the desk.

Howard Worchester was the antithesis of the old homily that plump men are jovial, kindhearted, and generous. Charles doubted the man had smiled in the past decade, and the only thing generous about him was his waistline. He even figured his tip at the doughnut shop with a calculator, and at Halloween one year gave each child a penny.

Howard touched the tips of his pudgy fingers together.

"This is very embarrassing for me, Sheriff. I don't like the general public knowing my business. I enjoy my privacy."

Charles didn't believe a desire for privacy had anything to do with it. In a town as small as Carroll, secretiveness was power and Howard enjoyed power. "I don't repeat anything said to me in this office, Howard, unless I'm on the witness stand testifying in a criminal case. If you're about to confess to a crime, then you have something to worry about. Otherwise, you don't."

Howard leaned forward and the wooden chair creaked under his bulk. "I appreciate that, Sheriff, and I'll remember how cooperative you were come your reelection campaign. I don't imagine you'd turn down a contribution."

"I don't accept contributions," said Charles, clenching his teeth. "That way no one owns me. Now, what did you want to tell me?"

Howard cleared his throat and glanced around the office, and Charles wondered why everyone he'd talked to this morning seemed worried about being overheard.

"You see, Sheriff, it's this way. I'm planning to have my father committed, and I wanted you to know first so you could handle taking him to Amarillo without any undue fuss."

Charles braced his elbows on his desk. "You'd better talk to the county attorney before you make arrangements with me to transport your father. An involuntary mental commitment requires two medical opinions and a legal hearing. Do you have two medical opinions, Howard?"

Howard frowned and rubbed his plump hands together. "No, but I don't anticipate a problem once I explain the situation to the doctors."

"Exactly what is the situation?" asked Charles. "I haven't heard of Jeremy doing anything out of the ordinary."

Howard pulled a white handkerchief out of his pocket and wiped his forehead. "I'd call an eighty-five-year-old man marrying a twenty-five-year-old waitress an act of senility, wouldn't you? His mind is failing, or he'd realize that she's just after his money."

He twisted his handkerchief into a knot, and Charles wondered if Howard wasn't pretending it was his father's neck. "Well, I don't intend to let some slut shake her tits in my father's face and persuade him to give her every cent he has in this world. He's incompetent to handle his own affairs, Sheriff, and I have to save him from himself."

He sounded so earnest and sincere that Charles almost believed him. Almost. If the smug expression on Howard Worchester's face had not reminded him of J.T. Brentwood's.

That was reason enough for Charles to visit another of Crawford County's senior citizens.

Jeremy Worchester was tall with skin the color of rawhide shrunken around his bones as if the arid climate and hot summer sun had sucked all fatty tissue from his body, leaving a dried brown husk. Except for the shrewd green eyes behind wire-rim glasses and luxurious silver hair that glittered in the sunlight pouring through the huge picture window behind him, the old man looked very much like a mummy himself.

Jeremy folded his hands over his belly, crossed one handmade cowboy boot over the other, and smiled at Charles. His teeth were stained from a lifetime of smoking unfiltered cigarettes, but their yellowed ivory color suited him more than pure white would have.

"What kind of business do you have with me, Sheriff?" asked Jeremy in a deep baritone voice in which a listener could catch only a faint quiver of age.

"Does this have to be an official call, Mr. Worchester? Can't I drop in to have a cup of coffee?"

The old man chuckled. "You ain't very good at bullshit, Sheriff, and that's what you're trying to hand me. You're a friendly enough sort, but you ain't the kind of man who drops in on the voters without being invited. Even if you were, the next election ain't for another year, so I reckon you got something on your mind besides your hat. Why don't you spit it out so I can get back to work? I've got to go over my portfolio, make sure my stockbroker is staying honest. You know, the trouble with being a rich man is trying to find someplace to invest your money so the government won't steal it to fritter away on some damn fool project, but at the same time keep it handy in case you want to do some frittering of your own."

"I heard you were getting married, Mr. Worchester," said Charles.

The old man's eyes sharpened. "Did you? I wonder where you heard that. I ain't told but one person—besides my bride to be, that is—and Howard is tighter than Dick's hatband with information. Ask that boy what time it is, and he'll figure out a way to avoid answering. So how come he broke the habit of a lifetime and told you his business?" Jeremy broke off and shook his head. "Never mind. I answered my own question. He wouldn't talk about his own business, but he might about mine—if he figures there's something in it for him—something being money."

Jeremy sat up straight and pointed a bony finger at Charles. "Well, let me tell you something, Sheriff. I don't appreciate folks interfering in my personal affairs and that includes you and my son. How about you getting on out of my house and telling my son that if he's got something to say to me, he can say it himself and not send the high sheriff to do it for him."

"Your son didn't send me, Mr. Worchester. In fact, he doesn't know I'm here."

Jeremy shook a cigarette out of a crumbled pack and lit it, peering through the smoke at Charles. "Is that so? Then what are you doing here?"

"Howard is worried about you. . . ." began Charles.

"Howard hasn't worried about anybody but himself since he was born sixty-five years ago," interrupted the old man. "And age hasn't mellowed him."

"He's afraid this young woman will take advantage of you," said Charles.

Jeremy laughed, then leaned over and tapped Charles on his knee. "Son, nobody's ever taken advantage of me. I'm too ornery and too mean, and for damn sure a little bit of a thing like Marcie Gray can't do it."

"Marcie Gray," repeated Charles. "The, uh, shy young girl who works at the Dairy Creem Drive-In?" Actually, he thought mousy would be a better description. She was young, certainly, but she wasn't beautiful, and placid was the word best suited to describe her personality. By no stretch of the imagination could she be called a rich man's sex toy.

"That's the one," said Jeremy, exhaling another cloud of smoke. "She's a fine little girl, but afraid of her own shadow and always worried about doing the right thing. That's a refreshing change from Howard. He never worries about the right thing, unless there's money in it for him. Oh, I'm not saying my son does anything illegal," the old man said quickly, "but sometimes what's right is wrong. At any rate, he's sticking his nose in my business and I won't tolerate it."

Charles studied the irate old man and came to a decision. Jeremy Worchester might be unable to perform certain of his marital duties, but Charles had no doubt about the old-ster's ability to manage his financial affairs. "Your son believes you're senile, Mr. Worchester. He's planning to commit you to stop the marriage."

Jeremy stiffened, then stubbed out his cigarette and looked at Charles. "Was it hard to do the right thing, Sheriff?"

"I beg your pardon?"

The old man chuckled. "I suspect that technically it was the wrong thing for you to come warn me—violation of confidentiality or interference with justice or some such thing. I don't imagine sheriffs are supposed to interfere in legal proceedings between family members or to take sides. But I tell you, son, you did the right thing. You don't think I'm crazy and you don't intend to let Howard sneak up on my blind side to prove I am. Well, you can rest easy. I'm warned. If anybody's crazy in my family, it's Howard for thinking he can beat me. I'll put a call in to that band of lawyers I keep on retainer and tell them to get to work spiking Howard's guns while Marcie and me just slip out of town once it gets dark and get ourselves married soon as we can round up a marriage license and a preacher. Present Howard with a done deed. He ain't getting but half my money no matter what kind of tricks he tries to pull because half is all he's entitled to. To be honest, he ain't entitled to that much, but he is my son and I can't bring myself to cut him off completely. I keep hoping he'll change when I know in my heart he never will. Old men's hopes are pathetic sometimes, but hope is all we got."

He leaned back and closed his eyes, a spasm twisting his features, and Charles leaned forward to grasp the old bony shoulder. "Mr. Worchester, are you all right?"

Jeremy's eyes snapped open, and he brushed away Charles's hand. "I'm fine, Sheriff, just took a minute out for regrets. A man does that when he get to my age and his flesh and blood is a disappointment to him. Useless exercise though. Regret never changed a thing and it sure as hell won't change Howard. Now you get on back to your office and don't worry about me. I may be an old bastard, but I'm a tough old bastard. I reckon Howard forgot that."

CHAPTER

9

From the private journal of Megan Elizabeth Poole:

January 4 [continued]

I am not a skillful liar.

The thunderous faces of his reception committee stopped Charles abruptly in the squad room doorway. Dirty, disheveled, reeking of sweat, and wearing identical expressions of desperate men stretched to the limit of their endurance, Meenie and Raul glowered at him.

"Where you been?" demanded Meenie.

Charles stepped into the room and shrugged off his fleece-lined coat with a casualness he didn't feel. "Preserving the peace of Crawford County. I take it that since you're up here on the third floor instead of in the basement you've finished that stage of the investigation."

Meenie spat toward a spittoon without looking and Charles flinched. The law of averages said that one day the deputy would miss. "I reckon we have, and we didn't find any more bodies just like I thought we wouldn't. 'Course there was a time or two when I thought about planting a fresh one, but Raul allowed as how Slim's mama might miss him if he didn't make it out of that basement alive."

Charles glanced around the office. "Where is Slim?"

"At Dr. Wallace's," answered Raul.

73

"Why?" asked Charles, noticing that the lilt was still absent from Raul's voice.

"He tripped on the blade of the shovel and fell in the open grave. I think he sprained his ankle—the left one," said Raul.

"Both his ankles are left ones," added Meenie. "That's 'cause he's got two left feet."

"For God's sake!" exclaimed Charles. "Is he all right?"

Raul shrugged again. "I don't know. Miss Poole took him."

"Then who's been answering the phone and acting as dispatcher?" asked Charles.

"Raul and me," answered Meenie.

"Why didn't you call me? When one of my men is hurt I want to know about it."

"We didn't know where you was," said Meenie. "Miss Poole said you whipped out of here with a face like a thundercloud and didn't say where you were going. She figured that maybe something had happened at home, and you'd already told her that you didn't want nobody asking questions about what was going on at your house, so she didn't ask. We tried to raise you on the radio, but you didn't answer."

Charles felt his face turn red. "I, uh, turned off my radio. I needed a quiet place to think, and it seems like the only quiet place these days is my patrol car."

"You might try the basement," said Meenie. "It's quiet as the grave down there."

Charles closed his eyes and counted to ten before looking at his deputies. "I don't need any bad jokes. I've had a hard two days, and nothing I've done has a damn thing to do with identifying Sergeant Doe. Now I have to go check on Slim, but when I get back, I want the two of you in my office. I have a few ideas about this investigation."

"Before you see about Slim, you better stop by the Baptist church," said Meenie. "Reverend Lundy has called twice wanting to talk to you."

"About what?" asked Charles.

Meenie shrugged. "He wouldn't tell me. Said he had a

problem with a church member that he wanted to talk to you about. Nothing criminal according to him, but he thought maybe you might help."

"Why would he think that?" demanded Charles. "I deal with criminals, not theology. Besides, why doesn't he call the chief of police. The Baptist church is in the city's jurisdiction, not the county's."

"Because the chief of police ain't as important as the sheriff. Reverend Lundy's an old man, been preaching at the Baptist church fifty years or more, and I guess his thinking is a little out of date. He thinks you're a Texas high sheriff like we used to have in the Thirties and Forties. Used to be the county sheriff was the first person you called when there was a problem, like your husband was drinking too much or your wife was a little too friendly with the neighbor's husband or your kids were running wild. The sheriff would talk to the husband or the wife or the kids and kinda settle things down before they got out of hand. I guess if we still lived in caves and ate our meat raw, the sheriff would be the chief or the medicine man. He'd be the man we looked to first. I guess Reverend Lundy still thinks that way," said Meenie.

Any man interested in finding his way to the hereafter from Crawford County had a variety of paths from which to choose. Within the city limits of Carroll were four Baptist churches, two Methodist churches, one each belonging to the Disciples of Christ, the Lutherans, the Presbyterians, the Episcopalians, the Mormons, the Assembly of God, the Church of God, the Church of Christ, the Catholics, and several claimed by no particular denomination and best described as vaguely Protestant and definitely evangelical.

First Baptist was the first church established in Crawford County, but neither its position as a pioneer nor its longevity accounted for the fact that it was also the biggest religious organization, with nearly fifteen hundred members out of a county population of only eight thousand. In

Charles's opinion the responsibility for the church's success rested squarely on the frail shoulders of its minister.

Reverend Lawrence Lundy, addressed as Brother Lundy by almost everyone, whether members of his congregation or not, was a tall, thin man in his late seventies with sparse white hair, soft gray eyes, and a kindly disposition that did more to keep his parishioners on the straight and narrow than any number of hellfire and brimstone sermons. No one wanted to disappoint Brother Lundy.

Including Charles.

The minister ushered him into his book-lined office. "I appreciate your coming, Sheriff."

Charles removed his hat and coat and sat down. "If this isn't a criminal matter, I don't know what help I can give you, Reverend Lundy."

"I don't know either, but as sheriff you have some experience with human nature. . . ." His voice trailed off and he looked hopefully at Charles.

"Mostly with the worst side of human nature, Reverend. In fact, I probably know more about it than you do since I'm faced with the results every day. For a sheriff, sin is less philosophy than reality."

"That's true of my profession also, Sheriff," said Reverend Lundy.

The elderly minister sat down behind a desk so strewn with papers and books its top was hardly visible. He brushed clear a spot just large enough to rest his clasped hands on and peered at Charles from behind the thick lenses of his horn-rimmed glasses. "In the years since I was ordained, I've listened to tales of every imaginable depravity that man is capable of committing. Every minister does. When I was a younger man, I often questioned why God demanded we love one another when so many of us are not loveable at all. It is one thing to believe that man is born in sin. It is quite another to see and to hear day after day how much he relishes the circumstances of his birth."

He gave a self-deprecating chuckle. "In other words,

Sheriff, I labored in God's vineyard and every so often I wondered if all the grapes had a blight."

"I see," said Charles, then realized he was lying. "No, I'm afraid I don't see."

Reverend Lundy shook his head. "I'm sorry, Sheriff. Sometimes preachers are too wordy for the good of their congregations. I've always thought that Sunday afternoon football has done more to improve sermons than all the courses in seminary. We've had to learn to get to the point, and my point is that after nearly fifty years in the ministry, I can recognize a sinner. I can even recognize the signs of a man contemplating sinning. I recall a young man many years ago who cast his net among the ladies of the choir. I stepped in before he caught one, but I still remember how surprised he was that I saw through him. Of course, in his case it wasn't difficult. The man was tone deaf and flinched from the time the organist played the opening chord until the last note died away. I'm afraid he was more interested in the sins of the flesh than the sound of music—which he couldn't hear in any case."

The minister leaned forward with an earnest expression on his face. "Bobby Burns was right, Sheriff. If we could see ourselves as others see us—see how transparent most of us are—much heartache and pain and, yes, crime could be avoided."

"And you think one of your parishioners is planning to commit a crime, and you want me to talk to him before he does?" asked Charles.

"Gracious, no! Nothing like that. In fact, Sheriff, even sin isn't the problem. It's lack of sin."

Perplexed, Charles stared at the minister. "I beg your pardon?"

"It's difficult to encourage a sinner to repent if he sees a church member he's always assumed was already on a first-name basis with the Almighty uncertain of her standing. It makes personal salvation look like parole that God can revoke."

The minister pounded his fist on the top of his desk,

scattering papers on the floor. "That's not what Baptists believe, Sheriff! Once a man is saved, he's saved for all eternity. If his conversion is sincere, of course. If it isn't, then that's another matter, but sincerity isn't the issue here. Mrs. Dodd's behavior is."

"Mrs. Dodd?" asked Charles, thinking of the kindly, white-haired old lady who was such a champion of good works that she had even succeeded in shaming Howard Worchester into donating five dollars to Meals On Wheels.

"Yes, Judge Dodd's widow, but of course you wouldn't have known Judge Dodd. He died twenty years ago on a cold day much like this one, a heart attack while shoveling snow. He was found frozen stiff with the shovel still in his hands as I remember. The funeral was delayed somewhat as he was a portly gentleman and took some time to thaw."

Reverend Lundy cleared his throat as if recalling where he was. "At any rate, Mrs. Dodd was devastated, but still refused to indulge in unseemly displays of grief, as I unfortunately have witnessed other widows do. I've always distrusted the sackcloth and ashes approach to mourning, Sheriff. Too often it's appearance over substance. That's why I don't understand why Mrs. Dodd is suddenly behaving this way after twenty years of widowhood."

Charles leaned forward. "How *is* Mrs. Dodd behaving?"

Reverend Lundy rubbed a liver-spotted hand over his face. "Oh, dear, I'm not telling this well. I'm usually much more organized. I hope my dithering around the subject is a sign of my concern rather than one of old age. At any rate, Mrs. Dodd has taken to wearing widow's weeds, including elbow-length gloves and a long black veil that hangs from the brim of her hat. When I look out from the pulpit I can't decide if she's suffering from the onset of some disfiguring disease or if she's taken up beekeeping."

Charles coughed to cover up a smile. "Reverend, Mrs. Dodd's behavior may be a little eccentric, but I don't think either one of us can tell her what to wear."

"It's not her costume that disturbs me as much as her habit of rededicating her faith at the drop of a hat—and in a Baptist church the hat drops often. That woman's life is so squeaky clean that I sometimes think she must wash her soul in detergent every day, and her coming forward after every sermon is discouraging the real sinners."

The minister leaned forward, an earnest expression on his face, and lowered his voice. "If Mrs. Dodd with her record feels she must plead her case before God several times each week, then those who regularly break, or at least bend, the Ten Commandments must believe their cases are hopeless and that there's no point in even going to court."

Charles expelled a breath and sat back. Mrs. Dodd's behavior might be coincidence or it might not be. "Reverend Lundy, when did Mrs. Dodd began acting strangely? Was it this past weekend?"

The minister started to answer, then hesitated, his gray eyes suddenly focusing on Charles with all the intensity of lasers. "Of course, the skeleton in the basement. My heavens, you do look for the worst, don't you, Sheriff? However, I'm afraid the onset of Mrs. Dodd's behavior predates your discovery by at least two months."

The Dodd house always reminded Charles of an economy-sized Southern mansion with ivy-covered brick and a two-story porch supported by thick white pillars. He felt as if Scarlett O'Hara in hoop skirts and a flirtatious smile might saunter around the corner of the house at any minute.

But the woman who opened the door didn't resemble Margaret Mitchell's fictional character, although her ankle-length black dress did look like it belonged in a Civil War museum. It had long sleeves, a high neck, jet beads sewn on the bodice, and a faint smell of mothballs.

"Who is it?"

"It's Sheriff Matthews," said Charles, wondering why she didn't know him. She always recognized him when collecting money for one of her charities. Perhaps her age was making her forgetful.

"What do you want?"

"Reverend Lundy and I are concerned about you."

"Why?"

"Reverend Lundy seems to think you're distressed about something," said Charles.

"Why would he think that?"

Charles asked himself for the tenth time since he left the church why he let the minister talk him into visiting Mrs. Dodd. A person's religious peculiarities were not the business of the Crawford County sheriff. Even Reverend Lundy ought to have understood that instead of looking so earnest and hopeful and helpless as he pleaded. "Please talk to her, Sheriff. She won't say a word to me, but she respects the authority of an elected official. Her husband was a district judge, you know."

Charles had agreed and wished he hadn't. But nobody liked to disappoint Reverend Lundy.

"I guess he finds your wearing mourning a little out of character. I didn't even know women wore hats with veils anymore," said Charles finally.

The elderly woman was silent a moment, then pulled a pair of glasses from a pocket of her dress. She put them on and looked up at Charles. "Ugly, aren't they. The lenses are so thick that I look bug-eyed wearing them. I never did like glasses even when I was young. I used to walk around in a blur in public rather than wear them. I couldn't even see well enough to recognize you when I answered the door. I got the first pair of contact lenses sold in Crawford County, Sheriff. I imagine you didn't know that. Well, don't feel badly. Not many people did. But I can't wear contacts anymore. My vision is too bad and I need trifocals."

Mrs. Dodd's brown eyes did look protuberant behind her thick lenses. "You wear a veil because you don't want anyone to see your glasses?" asked Charles.

"I'm vain," admitted Mrs. Dodd. "And I'd look silly wearing a veil without the rest of the outfit."

Charles thought she looked sillier wearing mourning than wearing glasses, but what did he know? "What about your rededicating your faith every Sunday, Mrs. Dodd?"

"And Wednesdays and Fridays—Bible study and prayer meeting, Sheriff. I come forward on those days, too."

"Can you tell me why, Mrs. Dodd?"

"Vanity is one of the seven deadly sins, you know," said the old woman, wringing her hands and blinking.

"I believe you're thinking of pride," said Charles.

"Am I? Well, pride leads to vanity."

"And you're feeling guilty, so you try to expiate your guilt by coming forward?" asked Charles, feeling out of his depth discussing theology and deciding Reverend Lundy owed him one.

Mrs. Dodd nodded. "Yes, I'm feeling guilty—but don't tell Reverend Lundy. He's a good man, but he's still just a man. I don't think he'd understand, and he'd try to talk me out of coming forward, and I won't be talked out of it. I absolutely won't!"

She closed the door in his face, and Charles walked back to his patrol car, resolving to stick to criminal matters in the future. Crawford County eccentrics would have to manage without his help.

So help him God.

CHAPTER

10

From the private journal of Megan Elizabeth Poole:

January 4 [continued]

Jeremy Worchester is as big a fool as Mad Dog Tread-well. Imagine a man of his age marrying a child as young as Marcie Gray. Still, I am surprised. Jeremy has always impressed me as a man of common sense. How-ever, men do foolish things to deny declining virility. Be-sides, little Marcie isn't a femme fatale. She's more of a house wren.

Miss Poole looked up when the sheriff walked into the squad room. Or perhaps stomped would be a better descrip-tion, she thought. Something must have upset him. He never set his feet down so hard otherwise, as if he was stepping on whatever irritated him.

"Where's Slim?"

"I took him home," she replied. "I presume you heard what happened."

He took off his hat and ran his fingers through his hair. Another sign he was upset, Miss Poole thought. He never messed with his hair like a nervous woman unless he was angry or frustrated.

"Meenie and Raul told me. I went by Doc Wallace's af-ter I left Mrs. Dodd's, but you had already left. The doctor said Slim just sprained his ankle so I assumed he would come back to work."

Miss Poole folded her hands. "Dr. Wallace taped Slim's ankle and suggested he use crutches for a few days. I was the one who persuaded him to spend the rest of the day at home. I wanted time to put away every breakable object in the office. Slim waving crutches around is tantamount to a demolition crew."

The sheriff nodded. "Very wise of you, Miss Poole. Now, where's Raul and Meenie? I told them both I wanted them in my office as soon as I got back. And you, too."

She heard the note of irritation in his voice and frowned. "They went home to shower and put on clean uniforms, then have a late lunch—or early dinner, since it's nearly three o'clock. You can't expect them to work in dirty clothes and go without food."

He frowned back. "I never said I did, Miss Poole. I just lost track of time. In fact, I don't think I even ate lunch myself. All these interruptions . . ."

His voice faded away as she watched him remove his hat, shrug off his coat, deposit both on a filing cabinet, and drop into a chair behind Meenie's desk. He wanted to talk, or else he would have gone into his office. That was good. She wanted him to talk. She wanted to know where he'd rushed out to after talking to Howard Worchester. Most of all she wanted to know why he talked to Mrs. Dodd. She didn't like Mrs. Dodd, hadn't liked her for over forty years. Ever since Albert . . .

Miss Poole abruptly got up and walked to the coffeemaker. "Would you like a cup of coffee?" she asked the sheriff.

He cocked one eyebrow. "Did you make a new pot?"

She felt herself flush. She might have known he wouldn't forget. "Yes, and this one is nice and strong."

She turned away and poured two cups of coffee, checking to see that it was indeed up to her usual standards. She must remember to check over her work, whether it was making coffee or filing papers, until this distressing business was behind her. More important, she must keep past and present from overlapping in her thoughts.

She handed the sheriff his coffee and sat down again at the dispatcher's desk, taking a tiny sip of her own coffee to wet her suddenly dry throat before asking questions. She had always prided herself on being a forthright woman, and soliciting information in such an underhanded fashion was having a detrimental effect on her salivary glands *and* her conscience. So far she had found nothing to recommend the lifestyle of a sneak.

"What business did you have with Mrs. Dodd?"

"I didn't have any *business* with her!" he snapped. "I was doing a favor for Reverend Lundy, and that's the last time anyone in this county will con me into interfering with other people's personal affairs. I can't stop Mad Dog Treadwell breaking his neck hang gliding or Jeremy Worchester making a fool of himself or Mrs. Dodd wearing a black veil to her ankles and confessing her faith every Sunday. I don't have jurisdiction, Miss Poole!"

He slapped the top of Meenie's desk and glared at her for want of anyone else to glare at, she supposed. "I had noticed Mrs. Dodd's sudden passion for mourning," she remarked, taking another sip of coffee.

"It's not sudden according to Reverend Lundy. It seems she's been dressing like Queen Victoria mourning Prince Albert for the past two months."

Miss Poole's hands trembled, and she barely held on to her coffee cup. For the space of a heartbeat she was young again and felt sick to her stomach. Mrs. Dodd's given name *was* Victoria, but that was as far as the analogy went. Albert had not been anything like the British consort. . . .

She shook her head to clear it of grief and memories best left for later. Meanwhile, she needed her wits about her. "Mrs. Dodd always enjoyed playing charades," she said, intent on observing the sheriff closely. "Did she tell you why?"

He looked at her curiously, and Miss Poole wondered if she had revealed her thoughts during her brief lapse of self-control. "She did, but her reasons are personal and have nothing to do with this office," the sheriff finally said.

Miss Poole doubted that, but wasn't about to say so. "I'm hardly likely to gossip about department business, Sheriff."

The curiosity vanished and Charles Matthews's face took on an expression of square-jawed stubbornness. "Didn't you hear me? It's *not* our business, Miss Poole, and I don't intend to mention the subject again."

Miss Poole released a pent-up breath. The male psyche was frequently so predictable. Push a man in one direction and he immediately wanted to go in another. In this instance it was just as well. She didn't *want* him discussing Mrs. Dodd again with anyone.

The sheriff saw the determined expression on Miss Poole's face. Damn, but the woman was stubborn. Tell her something was none of her business, and she would stick her nose in it, come hell or high water. Well, not this time, he decided, leaning forward over Meenie's desk. "Miss Poole, leave Mrs. Dodd alone. I won't have her embarrassed by your meddling. I know you don't like the woman, but—"

"How do you know?" interrupted Miss Poole.

Charles sat back and shook his head. "Miss Poole, I may be from Dallas and have limited experience with small towns, but I do understand group dynamics. You and Mrs. Dodd are contemporaries, yet I've never seen you speak to her or serve on any of her committees. . . ."

"We're not contemporaries! She's at least ten years older than I."

Charles raised an eyebrow at his dispatcher's outrage. He wouldn't have thought Miss Poole cared about such matters as age. Apparently, he was wrong.

"I didn't know that," he said. "Mrs. Dodd certainly doesn't look to be that much older. . . ."

"Are you saying I look older than I am?" demanded

Miss Poole. "Are you saying that I'm a dried-up old maid?"

Charles ran his fingers through his hair again. He wasn't in the mood for this. "I didn't mean that at all, Miss Poole. I should have picked my words more carefully."

"You certainly should have!"

Exasperated, he glared at her. "I apologize if I unintentionally hurt your feelings, Miss Poole, but my order stands. Leave Mrs. Dodd alone!"

"Sheriff!"

Meenie stood in the doorway with Raul behind him. Both looked spit polished with pressed uniforms and scrubbed faces. At least, Raul did. Meenie merely looked clean. The starch hadn't been invented yet that would hold a crease in Meenie's pants.

"Sheriff, I got to talk to you. Lord Almighty, but you got to do something!" exclaimed Meenie.

Charles didn't like the worried expression on his deputy's face; he didn't like Meenie's mention of God, which for the wizened ex-cowboy almost amounted to profanity; and he most definitely didn't like the sound of urgency in Meenie's voice. The three together indicated a crisis of biblical proportions.

"For God's sake, what's wrong?"

"Do you know what the police department's doing?" demanded Meenie, shifting his tobacco to the other side of his mouth.

"I hope nothing more serious than handing out parking tickets. The last time Chief Brian and his stalwart boys in blue tried anything that resembled real law enforcement, they endangered life and property—like those two patrolmen firing on that fleeing armed robber and hitting a parked car and a streetlight instead."

"This ain't funny, Sheriff," said Meenie, leaning over the spittoon to expectorate.

Charles stared at his deputy in alarm. Meenie Higgins could hit a spittoon from ten paces with his eyes closed; he didn't need to lean over it. In fact, if the Carroll police could shoot as accurately as Meenie could spit, a recent editorial in the paper wouldn't have suggested the town was safer if the police patrolled with unloaded guns.

"Then why don't you tell me what in the hell is wrong instead of playing twenty questions!" he demanded.

"Gimme hats," said Meenie.

"What?"

"The police are wearing gimme hats. You know, Sheriff, them hats that look like baseball hats, except these got 'Carroll Police Department' stitched across the front instead of a team's name."

"I know what they are, Meenie," said Charles through gritted teeth. "What I don't know is why the devil you should care if the police wear gimme hats or sombreros or sew lace around the hems of their pants."

"The city commissioners said the police had to wear gimme hats 'cause they were cheap. Well, me and Raul was down at the Dairy Creem having a sandwich and we heard a couple of the county commissioners saying how they thought the city had a good idea. I always knew them commissioners were about half-worthless and cheap to boot, but I never thought they'd be traitors to their state. A Texas deputy sheriff might as well trade in his britches for bloomers as to give up his hat."

Charles rose and leaned over the desk, placing both hands palm down on its top. Otherwise, he might be tempted to strangle his chief deputy. "I am the sheriff of Crawford County. I am responsible for investigating serious crime, and I have a serious crime to investigate in case you've forgotten. I have a damn mummy in the basement! But what have I been doing in the last five days? I've been listening to aging children whine about their parents or playing backup for Reverend Lundy or arguing with Miss Poole or with you or watching my devil of a father-in-law build a corral in my backyard!"

"What do you want with a corral, Sheriff?" asked Meenie, shifting his tobacco. "You don't like horses."

"Never mind!" yelled Charles. "The point is I've had to

put up with every damn distraction imaginable from every eccentric in town, and I don't intend to have my own deputies frittering away time and energy on some minor matter instead of concentrating on the *mummy*!"

Meenie Higgins drew himself up to his full height of five feet seven inches or so in his high-heeled boots. "A Texan's hat ain't no minor matter, Sheriff."

Charles glared at the deputy. Damn it to hell, but he would never understand these people. "Meenie, if I'll guarantee the commissioners that I'll personally pay the difference between the cost of gimme hats and the present cowboy hats worn by members of this office, will that satisfy you? Will you be able to devote your mind to the business at hand?"

Meenie wrinkled his forehead in thought. "I reckon that your guarantee will do for the time being, but it ain't no permanent answer. What if you get beat in the next election? What's gonna happen then?"

Charles walked slowly to the filing cabinet, jammed on his own hat, and reached for his coat, all the while counting to one hundred under his breath. Had Meenie and Miss Poole always been such cantankerous curmudgeons, and he had just never noticed? Or was there a virus suddenly infecting Crawford County natives over fifty? A variation of Legionnaires' disease?

"I'll worry about the next election when the time comes, Meenie. In the meanwhile, you and Raul write up your reports and play dispatcher. Miss Poole, find any open file on missing persons dating from the Second World War."

"Any such files will be stored in the basement under the county clerk's office, Sheriff," replied his efficient dispatcher. "I mean the regular basement, not the subbasement where the"—she hesitated, then drew a deep breath—"mummy was found."

"I know the difference between the courthouse's two subterranean dens, Miss Poole," interrupted Charles. "Just get on with it."

"No one has looked through those records since the nineteen thirties, Sheriff. I believe the clerk just stacks the boxes of files one on top another. It's a terribly inefficient and confusing system."

Charles wiped his hand over his face. "Miss Poole, with the exception of Angie and myself, I haven't talked to anybody in this whole county in the last five days who isn't confused or confusing, so why should the storage system be any different? And I don't care if no one has looked through those files since Roosevelt's administration—Teddy's, not Franklin's—I want them searched!"

Miss Poole gave him a disapproving look. "You certainly are testy, and according to my reading of the latest in management theory, being testy and judgmental are not good management techniques. Patience and an open mind are recommended."

Charles's jaw ached from clenching his teeth, and he consciously relaxed it. "Miss Poole, I'm going home for an early dinner and an evening of peace and quiet. Tomorrow morning I'm going to institute some management techniques of my own. I'm going to give orders, and all of you are going to obey them without any excuses or comments. And another thing, I don't want any more calls or visits from civilians about matters that don't concern crimes. I'm a sheriff, not a psychiatrist and not a family counselor."

Charles nodded his head emphatically and walked out the door. Maybe telling off the help wasn't a good management technique according to Miss Poole's expert, but he doubted the man had ever lived in Crawford County. If he had, he'd be in a mental institution—or else in prison for the mass murder of his employees.

CHAPTER

11

From the private journal of Megan Elizabeth Poole:

January 4 [continued]

Thank God for gimme hats and the peculiar affinity Texas males have for cowboy hats. Otherwise, Meenie Higgins might have asked about Reverend Lundy and Mrs. Dodd and, to use a common expression, the cat would have been out of the bag. The sheriff missed the significance of a certain fact he learned, but I doubt that Meenie would. Despite his atrocious grammar, Meenie is quite intelligent. However, I must be fair to the sheriff. He was in New Mexico clearing Raul of a murder charge two months ago while Meenie had stayed in Crawford County and ran the sheriff's department—with my help, of course. That does not excuse Charles Matthews from keeping himself informed on events that occurred in his absence. A student is always held responsible for make-up work, and I did save all the newspapers he missed reading while he was away.

It is my duty as a member of the sheriff's department to point out pertinent information, but I have no intention of doing so, at least, not at this time. Meenie is right: nothing good comes of digging up the past. It is too late—over forty years too late. Victoria Dodd did not murder Albert, and much as I dislike the woman, I refuse to see her harassed by the sheriff over a crime she didn't commit. I do intend, however, to find out how Mrs.

Dodd knew Albert was buried in the basement, and it *is* Albert. Her behavior no longer leaves me room to doubt—if I ever really did. More to the point, I intend to find out why Victoria Dodd held her peace all these years. It certainly wasn't because she was fond of me—Megan Elizabeth Poole.

Charles parked in front of his house so Angie's father wouldn't see the patrol car. It was barely four o'clock in the afternoon, and his sainted father-in-law would still be on the premises supervising his cowboys' efforts at building a corral. J.T. Brentwood's idea of quitting time was whenever it was too dark to see, and Charles wasn't in the mood to listen to any of the old man's comments about city boys who were too soft to put in a full day's work.

Charles slid out of his car and quietly pushed the door shut instead of slamming it. Not that he thought slamming a car door could be heard over the sounds of hammering interspersed with a few mild profanities emanating from the pasture behind his house, but he didn't want to take a chance. J.T. Brentwood had very acute hearing.

He stepped through his front door and listened. The house was quiet, so Angie, both girls, and the dog must be outside watching the corral being built. Otherwise, Hieronymus Bosch would be dancing around his feet and uttering high-pitched, unmistakable whines of reproach. The beagle believed that Charles's habit of going to work each day constituted dog abuse. Any kind master would stay home and tend to the delicate emotional needs of such a wonderful dog as himself—or so the sorrowful expression in his brown eyes seemed to say. Charles wasn't sure whether the beagle or J.T. Brentwood was more expert at instilling undeserved feelings of guilt, but he had all the guilt he could handle at the moment, courtesy of a dead soldier.

Charles tiptoed toward his office. He needed solitude, or in Angie's words, he needed some quiet time. He felt a twinge of guilt at the thought of Angie. What kind of husband sneaked into his own home without greeting his wife—and children? What kind of husband planned to hide in his office instead of joining the family he had longed for and dreamed about so long? What kind of husband planned to spend the next two hours, or however long before being found out, contemplating his next move in any one of the twenty chess games he played by mail?

A desperate one, he decided, stepping into his office and flipping on the light; a man seeking to restore his powers of rational thought; a man needing to believe that he controlled some facet of his life, even if it was only determining which chess piece to move.

"Hell and damnation!"

He stopped just inside the door, staring helplessly at his chessboards, all twenty of them, which formed a huge square on the floor in the middle of the office. The chess pieces of varying sizes, designs, and materials, lined each side of the square, while in its center huddled two forsaken dolls dressed in beaded ball gowns.

Charles skirted the square of chessboards and dropped on the couch. He leaned forward and rested his forearms on his knees, letting his hands dangle uselessly. Twenty chessboards, twenty games by mail in progress. He would have to write each of his opponents and ask for a review of the moves because he couldn't remember the placement of the pieces in each separate game. At the moment, he wasn't certain he could even remember his own name.

"Hell and damnation!" he repeated.

"I'm sorry, Charles."

Angie stood in the doorway, clasping her hands together, her face paler than usual. Hieronymus Bosch stood by her side, cocking his head and wagging his tail as he looked at Charles, but was mercifully silent.

Angie walked to the couch and knelt in front of him. "I was going to warn you before you saw this"—she waved one hand at the square of chessboards—"but I was asleep when you came in. Hieronymus woke me up."

"What in the"—he caught himself before a certain four-letter word slipped out and amended his question—"what happened?"

"It's really as much my fault as the girls', Charles. I never specifically told them not to play in your office and not to touch your chess sets. Between trying to keep them in the house, so Dad and the cowboys could cuss whenever they hit their fingers instead of nails—cowboys aren't much good at any work that doesn't involve riding horses—and fixing lunch for everyone, I didn't keep a close enough eye on Jennifer and Laura. I was just glad they weren't under-foot." She raked her teeth over her full lower lip. "It's been a confusing day."

"A confusing day," repeated Charles.

"But the girls had a reason for what they did."

"A reason?"

"Yes. The girls thought all those squares of polished wood looked like a parquet floor, so they made a ballroom. Then they danced on the chessboards."

Charles peered at the chessboards, noticing their scuffed surfaces for the first time.

"They pretended a wicked witch turned all the servants into chess pieces—sort of like *Beauty and the Beast*. The movie?"

Charles nodded.

"I sent them to their rooms and told them they had to apologize when you came home."

Charles nodded again.

Angie clasped his hands. "I know I told you to treat the girls just as if you were their real father, and I know you're angry—and you have a right to be—but I hope you won't spank them."

"Spank them?"

"Not only would it break their hearts, but they really didn't realize they were doing anything bad."

"Bad? For God's sake, Angie, murder is bad! Robbery is bad! This is—well, this is wonderful!" He leaned back against the couch and laughed. "A ballroom. A parquet floor. God, that's brilliant and imaginative and—reasonable."

"Charles, you're hysterical!"

He leaned over and lifted Angie onto his lap. She was soft and silky and firm in all the right places. "No, I'm not. I'm relieved. It's the first time since C.J. and José dug up that damn mummy that anybody born and raised in Crawford County had a rational explanation for their behavior."

Miss Poole checked to see that she had properly buttoned her winter coat, a calf-length, wheat-colored wool she particularly liked. After the coffee incident, she distrusted her powers of concentration, a situation she was unfamiliar with since she hadn't allowed outside events to disturb her since—well, since Albert left in 1945 to take part in the last push to Berlin.

Satisfied that all her buttons were securely fastened, she rang Victoria Dodd's doorbell.

After a long wait during which Miss Poole felt the north wind whirl around her legs, leaving them feeling like nylon-clad columns of ice, Victoria Dodd opened her wooden front door a few inches.

"Yes?"

"Good evening, Victoria," said Miss Poole.

"Who is it?"

Miss Poole felt indignation at the unnecessary question. "You know very well who it is, Victoria, since you have a more than adequate porch light. You might have known I'd come see you."

Victoria blinked. "Miss Poole?"

"There's no need to be so formal, Victoria. You never called me Miss Poole in the old days."

Victoria licked her lips. "Well, you're not a skinny teenager anymore, are you? You're an old-maid schoolteacher, and old-maid schoolteachers are always addressed by their last names."

Miss Poole gritted her teeth in irritation. The woman acted as if the married state was a badge of honor awarded to only the most worthy instead of a voluntary act that sometimes left both parties feeling as though they should have enlisted in the army instead.

"Then perhaps I should address you as Madame Bovary," said Miss Poole.

"Who? I don't believe I know her."

Miss Poole sighed. She had always known Victoria Dodd's looks exceeded her education. "Never mind. Let me in."

"You haven't changed a bit. You're still trying to push your way in without being invited."

Miss Poole felt herself flush. "If you're referring to that episode in the church choir room, I wasn't aware that invitations were required. After all, one doesn't expect to interrupt a married woman attempting to seduce another woman's intended."

"You're still jealous after all these years," said Victoria Dodd, an accusation wasted on Miss Poole who wasn't about to admit anything of the kind.

"I was appalled at your behavior, as any young girl would be when she catches an older woman she respects in a compromising position with a man to whom she isn't married. And I felt betrayed that you picked on a man who had proposed to me!"

"You were not engaged to Albert. He was flattered by the way you followed him around panting like a dog in heat—Albert was a little vain—and was too nice to tell you to leave him alone. Anything else was all in your head, *Miss Poole*!"

Miss Poole felt her cheeks grow even hotter with remembered humiliation. Her father had used similar words a few hours after the unfortunate choir room incident. He was waiting for her when she came home. . . .

"Megan Elizabeth, you are late," he said in his deep slow voice. "It is nearly midnight and you have school tomorrow. Where have you been?"

Miss Poole remembered how his large hands were

clenched so tightly that his knuckles were white. Her father had never struck her nor raised his voice when speaking to her despite his reputation for having a hot temper. He had looked so angry that she remembered wondering if he would break that habit of a lifetime and slap her as he so clearly wanted to. She remembered feeling afraid of him for the first time in her life.

"I was with Albert. We were talking."

She noticed a vein throbbing near her father's temple. It always throbbed when he was angry. "Did he explain his disgraceful behavior this evening?"

She was speechless for a moment, wondering how he knew, but then her father learned everything sooner or later. He had his ways.

She raised her chin. "Yes."

Her father's features always reminded her of a predatory bird's. His pale blue eyes were hooded, and his nose jutted like a beak over a wide, thin-lipped mouth. He watched her like an eagle watched a rabbit. "What did he say? Never mind answering, Megan Elizabeth. I'm familiar with the kind of lies men like him tell when they are intent on persuading a woman of their innocence. No doubt he told you it was not his fault."

"It wasn't," she began.

Her father held up his hand. "And you believed him. Of course, you did. You're an innocent young girl, and he turned your head—just as he has turned the head of every woman in town foolish enough to listen to him. It's unseemly the way you follow him about, begging for his attention as though you had no pride. I trust you haven't allowed him to take advantage of you in your anxiety to please. Have you?"

She stood silent, feeling the hot color wash over her face. Let him think what he wanted. He would anyway. He had always been a man who believed the worst of life, and her brother's death from lockjaw following so quickly after her mother passed away only confirmed his opinion.

Her father sighed. "Well, I intend to put a stop to it,

Megan Elizabeth. I have been in touch with the army and Sergeant Albert Finnigan will be ordered back to the front. If his wound is healed enough to paw young women in the choir room, then he is healed enough to fight for his country. You will neither see nor talk to him again."

She remembered blinking back tears. "I'll wait for him, Papa, and we'll marry when the war's over."

Her father closed his eyes briefly, then looked at her. "Then you'll wait in vain, Megan Elizabeth."

And she had, for she didn't lay eyes on Sergeant Albert Finnigan again until C.J. Tolliver uncovered his grave on New Year's Eve. . . .

"You told my father that Albert took liberties with you," said Miss Poole as she refocused her attention on the present and Victoria Dodd. "That's how he knew, isn't it?"

Mrs. Dodd looked away as if she, too, were remembering a painful scene. "Yes," she whispered, turning back to look at Miss Poole. "I told him. You have to understand. I was married. I couldn't have my husband hearing about—about what happened. I was embarrassed and frightened and ashamed all at once, Miss Poole. It was nearly fifty years ago, and people didn't think much of a married woman who kissed a man who wasn't her husband. We didn't have magazines and talk shows that discussed a woman's needs. We only talked about a woman's duty. People weren't very liberal then."

"I'm not very liberal now," interrupted Miss Poole, feeling disgusted. She never accepted self-serving excuses from students, and she didn't intend to accept any from Victoria Dodd. It was one thing to repent a sin; it was another to justify it. "But I'm not here to talk about your behavior in the past. I'm here to talk about your present behavior. If memory serves me, and it usually does, the *Crawford County Examiner* published an article two months ago concerning the renovation of the courthouse—about the time you took up professional mourning, Victoria. How did you know Albert was buried in the basement?"

Mrs. Dodd gasped. "Oh, my God!"

"If God hasn't paid any attention to your prayers every Wednesday and Friday and twice on Sunday, I don't think He plans to listen now, Victoria. Answer me! How did you know Albert was buried in the basement, and why did you hold your peace all these years?"

"What else could I do?" Mrs. Dodd burst out. "What other choice did I have? Should I have told what I saw in the courthouse that night and destroyed another life? Should a whole lifetime of good works go to waste because some-one lost their temper during an argument? Albert was al-ready dead! Sending someone to jail wouldn't bring him back. Don't you see, Miss Poole? It was an accident! No one *intended* to murder Albert."

Miss Poole wished she could believe Victoria Dodd, but she wasn't a woman for wishful thinking. She *knew* Albert Finnigan was murdered, deliberately and with malice afore-thought.

"Go away, Miss Poole," said Victoria Dodd, her voice sounding as old and weary as her withered face looked. "Let me mourn my dead and atone for my sins in private."

Albert wasn't Victoria's to mourn, thought Miss Poole, but she supposed it didn't matter now. "The sheriff is deter-mined to identify Albert, so there will soon be no privacy for either one of us."

Miss Poole turned and walked down the sidewalk toward her car. She could feel Victoria Dodd's eyes watching her.

CHAPTER 12

From the private journal of Megan Elizabeth Poole:

January 5

I didn't sleep well last night after talking to Victoria Dodd, and I dreamed of my father and Albert when I did doze off. I find little comfort in knowing that Albert did not reject me, that he came back to Crawford County just as he promised me he would, when outside of my dreams I cannot even remember what he looked like. The discovery of his body only meant that I traded one hurt for another. My father promised I would never see Albert again, and my father always kept his promises. I know he believed he was doing what was best for me when he murdered Albert, but when I think of all the years that he watched me grow old and disillusioned, I find that I can't forgive him. He made my choice for me, and no intelligent woman will forgive that.

I don't forgive Victoria Dodd her lies either. I wonder what she was doing in the courthouse that night. I forgot to ask her. I fear the sheriff would say I was remiss in my interrogation.

"Sheriff?"

Charles looked up to see Meenie sticking his head around the door. "Either come in or get out, but don't stick your head in like you're afraid I'll bite it off."

99

D. R. Meredith

Meenie stepped inside Charles's office and hitched up his pants. He shifted his wad of chewing tobacco to his other cheek and glowered at the sheriff. "Lately I ain't too sure but what you won't and today's worse than most. You come roaring in here spitting out orders right and left without a howdy do to anybody. Anyhow, I been picked to ask what kind of burr you got under your saddle this morning."

Charles swung his feet off his desk and rose to glower back at his deputy. "You could have gone all day without mentioning saddles to me—or anything else that has to do with horses!"

Meenie's mouth twitched once. "I hear your daddy-in-law ain't too happy about the way you're carrying on about his giving Miss Angie and the girls a horse."

"Where did you hear that?"

"From the horse's mouth," replied Meenie, his mouth twitching again, and Charles wondered if his deputy was developing a sense of humor in his old age. "J.T. was having coffee at the doughnut shop this morning same time as me, and he was talking about it."

"Then you must have been there awfully early because the old reprobate was at my house before the sun came up."

"Well, you know how country folks like to get an early start."

"In a pig's eye, Meenie! The only early start J.T. Brentwood is interested in is seeing how early he can start in on me. My esteemed father-in-law was still sitting in *my* kitchen working on his second pot of coffee when I left *and* lecturing me on the parasites commonly found in a horse's digestive tract. Parasites for God's sake! I don't care about parasites and I damn sure don't intend to have anything to do with a horse's digestive tract. And I'm not carrying on—whatever that means!"

Charles drew a breath, wiped his hand over his face, and consciously tried to tell his belly it didn't hurt. He gave up and reached for his antacid pills in his desk drawer. He popped two in his mouth and chewed. "Where's Miss Poole?" he asked to change the subject.

Meenie lifted his hat and scratched his balding head. "I figure she's in the same place she was when you came to work this morning and asked that same question. She's downstairs looking for them missing person reports you asked for. Waste of time if you ask me. I can't call to mind the last time anybody in Crawford County went missing more than a day or so, and that was generally done on purpose and you generally found them in one of two places. Either fishing down on the river—and that don't happen but a week or so in the spring 'cause the Canadian ain't got enough water to keep a fish alive 'cept during the spring runoff—or else in Butch Beauchamp's back room at the Electric Horseman, swilling down rotgut and playing cards."

Meenie sat down in one of the wooden chairs in front of Charles's desk and tilted it back before continuing. "When Butch figures a man's lost as much as he can afford, or drunk as much as he can hold without getting mean, then Butch calls the man's wife to come get him. Butch is real responsible that way."

"Gambling is illegal in Crawford County and so are open bars that sell more than beer and wine," said Charles.

"Butch's back room is a private club," said Meenie, "and I swear to God you're worse than Miss Poole's daddy when it comes to a man taking a nip or two on a cold night or playing a hand or two of cards, and he was worse than a Holy Roller preacher. That man was death on sin, and he considered pert near everything a sin."

Charles debated asking Meenie to define the term Holy Roller preacher, but decided against it. No one in Crawford County ever talked about Miss Poole, and he didn't want to distract Meenie while he was breaking what amounted to a taboo. "I guess that explains why Miss Poole is straitlaced and a spinster," said Charles. "She probably didn't have a chance to be anything else."

Meenie wrinkled his forehead in thought and Charles resigned himself. The more wrinkles in Meenie's forehead, the more convoluted his story, and his wrinkles, by

Charles's count, just missed double digits. "Well, Sheriff, it's funny about Miss Poole. She's a mite older than me, but she was old Daniel Poole's daughter, so folks paid attention to what she done, even kids like me, and I seem to remember that Miss Poole was all set to jump the traces and marry some feller her daddy didn't like."

"Who was it?" asked Charles, sitting back down and propping his feet on the desk again. Listening to one of Meenie's stories beat the hell out of hearing about parasites.

"I don't rightly know. Like I said, I was just a kid and all I know is what I heard my mama say. It was just rumors mostly, something about Miss Poole looking for a white dress. My mama went on and on about that white dress 'cause it was during the war and there weren't no white dresses to be found in Crawford County and, what with gas rationing, nobody could drive to Amarillo just to go dress shopping, not even old man Poole's daughter. Anyhow, she never got married, and her and her daddy acted like they didn't hear you if you was to ask. Something happened, though, 'cause when Miss Poole came back to Crawford County after getting her teacher training, she never spent another night under her daddy's roof. She rented a little two-room shack down by the railroad tracks and lived there until her daddy died back in 1960, I believe it was. That's when she moved back into that great big white house she lives in now."

Charles was interested in spite of himself. "So she never spoke to her father again?"

Meenie shook his head. "It wasn't nothing like that. They spoke. They just didn't live in the same house. It was like Miss Poole didn't want to take anything from her daddy—money and the like. Folks around here talked about it a lot because in them days an unmarried lady lived with her folks."

"When did all this happen, Meenie?"

Meenie rubbed his chin and squinted up one eye as he thought. "I reckon all the marriage talk was going around about 1945, so you can see why her daddy was pitching a fit—if he was and nobody knows for sure—because Miss Poole was only sixteen that year and still in high school. Besides, every able-bodied man had gone to war, so whoever she wanted to marry had to be either lame, blind, dumb, or so damn no good that even the army didn't want him."

Meenie opened his pocket knife and began to trim his fingernails as he talked. "My mama always thought Miss Poole was sweet on Mad Dog Treadwell 'cause you always saw them together at bond rallies and scrap-metal drives and the like that folks on the homefront had to support the war effort. Now me, I figure Miss Poole was smart enough to know her and Mad Dog wouldn't get along for five minutes after the preacher pronounced them man and wife. Anyhow, nobody never found out who Miss Poole was sweet on. I guess it's the only secret in Crawford County that somebody didn't find out."

The radiator along the wall opposite Charles's desk hissed and clanked; the wind rattled the ill-fitting windows; and a phone rang out in the squad room. The air smelled of dust and age and the cheap wax the county bought for the ancient tile floors. Somehow it was a fitting background for the story Meenie told. The courthouse was an institution in Crawford County and so was Miss Poole.

"Sheriff?"

Raul stepped inside the office, a hesitant expression on his face.

"Come in, Raul. I've sworn off chewing on my deputies." Charles noticed Raul didn't look convinced.

"The library called. They want you to come over," said Raul.

"Tell the librarian to call the police. The library is within the city limits of Carroll and out of my jurisdiction."

"I told the librarian that, but she said that since the county provided her budget, the library was county property and that means you're responsible. Besides, she said she wouldn't call the Carroll police if Jack the Ripper walked into the reading area and started butchering the patrons."

Raul shrugged his shoulders. "That wasn't exactly what she said, but it's close enough."

Charles reluctantly got to his feet. "What does the librarian want? Did she say?"

Raul nodded. "She wants you to talk to Miss Smith."

Charles froze in the middle of putting on his coat. "Miss Smith? The old lady with the fluffy white hair and a vague look in her eyes? The one who used to be head librarian until she retired?"

Raul nodded.

"She was the only librarian Crawford County had for over forty years," remarked Meenie, folding up his pocket knife. "The old lady must be in her eighties by now."

"What's the problem with Miss Smith?" asked Charles. "Has she taken up hang gliding or is she planning to marry the captain of the high school football team? Or maybe she's dressing up like Alice in Wonderland?"

"No, Sheriff," said Raul, taking a step back toward the door.

"It doesn't matter what she's doing, Raul. I told you yesterday that I'm not talking to any more eccentrics. I'm not intervening in family arguments or doing social work. I'm not taking any calls that don't concern a crime. Now, you go back and tell the librarian."

"This is a crime," said Raul. "Miss Smith is cutting all the pictures out of the county history books."

Miss Rachel Smith looked like everyone's idea of the perfect grandmother: thin white hair that swirled around her head like spun sugar on a cone; faded blue eyes behind gold, wire-rim glasses; skin the color and texture of old parchment; a periwinkle blue wool suit, thick support hose, and what Charles's mother always called sensible shoes.

Charles and Meenie questioned Miss Smith in the library's workroom, a misleading description of a space barely big enough to hold a small round table and four chairs, a narrow cabinet with a sink, shelves along one wall that held books in various stages of cataloging or repair, and a tall filing cabinet whose lock was missing. The room smelled of freshly brewed coffee, new books, library paste, and lilac water—but Charles decided that odor emanated from Miss Smith.

Charles watched the retired librarian add four heaping spoonfuls of sugar to her coffee, and concluded the elderly woman's veins must run with syrup instead of blood.

Miss Smith sipped her coffee, then blushed when she noticed Charles staring at her. "It's because of the Depression and the war. No one could afford white sugar during one, and it was rationed during the other." She touched the corners of her lips with a tiny white handkerchief and smiled at him.

Charles cleared his throat. "Yes, well, I can see your reasoning. It's, uh, reasonable. I guess."

She smiled again, a dimple that Charles had never noticed before appearing in her right cheek.

Feeling at a loss, Charles glanced sideways at Meenie for help in questioning Miss Smith, noticed the chief deputy's scowl, and quickly decided that he had better handle the interrogation himself. Meenie wasn't feeling very charitable toward librarians in general since the present head librarian insisted that he spit out his chewing tobacco. She didn't allow tobacco products of any kind in the library whether they were chewed or smoked or inhaled.

Charles returned the elderly lady's smile and began. "Miss Smith, do you know why Chief Deputy Higgins and I are here?"

Miss Smith patted her spun-sugar hair. "I'm a little absentminded, Sheriff, but I'm not senile. Of course, I know why you're here."

"Could you tell me why, Miss Smith?"

She blinked, looking confused. "Don't you know, Sheriff? I would have thought you were too young to be so forgetful."

Charles tried a more direct approach. "Miss Smith, why did you cut the pictures out of the county history books?"

The retired librarian ducked her head and stared at her coffee cup.

"Miss Smith, did you understand the question?" asked Charles gently.

"Certainly," she replied in a faint voice, still staring at her cup.

"Well?"

The elderly woman was silent, her lips pressed tightly together.

"Miss Smith, will you answer my question, please?"

Still not looking at him, she shook her head.

Meenie's chair creaked as he scooted closer to the retired librarian. "Miss Smith, that battle-ax at the front desk made me spit out my chew, so I'm in kind of a hurry to get out of here, and I bet you are, too. If I remember right, the county commissioners tried to fire you about 1950 because some old biddy, a lot like the one out front, caught you smoking during working hours and said you set a poor example for youngsters. I don't recollect how you wiggled your way out of that mess—"

"I threatened to file misdemeanor charges against three of the commissioners who owed large library fines. It's against the law not to pay library fines although most people don't know that," interrupted Miss Smith in a soft voice.

Charles revised his opinion of the retired librarian. He respected anybody who made politicians back down for whatever reason, and for an unmarried woman to do it in 1950 said something about Miss Smith's character. She wasn't as harmless and vague as she appeared.

Meenie grinned and continued. "Anyhow, I figure you got some kind of sympathy for a man who has to go without his chew, so how about you tell the sheriff here why you won't answer his question."

Miss Smith looked up and smiled at Meenie. "Because my reasons are private and I don't choose to tell him."

"Miss Smith, you defaced public property and that's against the law!" exclaimed Charles. "Not only that, but the public property you defaced were books. As a former librarian, don't you even feel bad about destroying books?"

Miss Smith sniffed and dabbed at the corners of her eyes. "Of course," she said in a muffled voice, "but I did what I had to do and I'm ready to take the consequences."

"Damn it all, Miss Smith, I can't throw an elderly lady in jail!" said Charles in exasperation.

Miss Smith's blue eyes widened in surprise and what Charles suspected might be amusement. "I don't see what other choice you have, Sheriff. It's your duty."

Charles descended the narrow staircase into the storage area beneath the county clerk's office and halted on the bottom step, appalled at what he saw. Naked light bulbs dangled from the ceiling and the air smelled of old moldy paper. Shelves choked with oversized ledgers in crimson-and-gray binders lined the walls and marched up and down the length of the room. Stacks of cardboard boxes tied with yellowing twine leaning drunkenly against one another took up most of the rest of the floor space.

"God Almighty!" said Charles, sinking down on the bottom step of the staircase.

Miss Poole and the county clerk, a tall bony woman named Zelma Dunkerson, peered around the end of one shelving unit. "If you were addressing your Creator, I doubt that He is down here," said Miss Poole with disapproval in her voice.

Charles grasped the wrought-iron banister and pulled himself to his feet. "I'm not in the mood for your idea of levity, Miss Poole."

"Then I doubt if you're in the mood to hear what else I have to say, Sheriff."

"You're going to tell me that you can't find any missing persons reports for the relevant period, aren't you, Miss Poole? Well, I'm not surprised. God Himself couldn't find anything in this mess."

Miss Poole dusted her hands off. "As a matter of fact it's not as bad as it appears. There was much less paperwork before 1960 than after—less government bureaucracy I believe—and I was able to sort through the records fairly quickly. You're right, of course. There are no missing persons reports for 1940 to 1950."

Charles sighed. "A dead end in other words. Well, wash your hands and come back upstairs. I just arrested an old lady and I want you to interview her because I'm not doing too well at it."

"There are, however, missing records."

"What records?" asked Charles.

"Marriages, births, and deaths for 1940 through 1950, Sheriff," said Miss Poole. She glanced toward the county clerk. "Zelma discovered the disappearance this morning."

"Do you have any idea how long these records have been missing, Mrs. Dunkerson? I mean, when was the last time you saw them?"

"I never saw them, Sheriff, but then I wasn't looking either. To tell the truth, I still wouldn't know they were gone if I hadn't been keeping Miss Poole company this morning and decided to tidy up a little by dusting all these old ledgers on the shelves. That's when I noticed the ones for that ten-year period are gone. And they haven't just been misplaced either, because somebody pushed all the ledgers together so there's no gap on the shelf to catch the eye."

"Who's been down here besides you and Miss Poole in the last week?"

"No one! But they weren't stolen last week anyway. Miss Poole pointed out that the dust wasn't disturbed. In other words, the records were taken long enough ago for more dust to settle."

"Then who has access to this area, Mrs. Dunkerson?"

"Anyone who works in the courthouse and needs to look up old records. Everything is down here, Sheriff: trial transcripts, property deeds, criminal records, minutes of the commissioners' court—everything!"

Zelma Dunkerson wrung her hands, the first time in his life that Charles actually saw a woman perform that particular gesture. "I don't know what I'm going to do, Sheriff.

It's going to be a nightmare to duplicate those records. In fact, I don't know if I can. So many folks who were adults during that time and registering marriages and births and deaths are dead themselves. My God, a whole decade in Crawford County's life is gone."

Charles abruptly sat down on the stairs again. "My God," he whispered. "My God, but I've been a fool."

CHAPTER

13

From the private journal of Megan Elizabeth Poole:

January 5 [continued]

The sheriff is a highly intelligent man. He frequently can't see the forest for the trees, but that is because he has an obsessive mind and tends to disregard events he doesn't believe have any relevance to his investigation. That is why he paid little attention at first to Victoria Dodd and Mad Dog Treadwell. I, of course, was in a position to know that Victoria's behavior was a direct reaction to Albert's discovery. I must admit I dismissed Mad Dog, but that is hardly a reflection on my own intelligence since Mad Dog has always made such an effort to live up to his name that one tends not to distinguish between his escapades. Once Rachel Smith was caught busily mutilating county history books, however, I knew the sheriff would reexamine recent activities of Crawford County senior citizens. Although he is convinced residents of this county are the most eccentric in the Panhandle, even he realized that he could no longer excuse their behavior on that basis. In spite of what happened to me personally, I was very proud of his reasoning. I have read that one sign of genius is the individual's ability to make connections between seemingly unrelated events. The danger for a genius with an obsessive mind is that he sometimes makes connections that seem logical and correct, but which are actually neither.

The three suspects sat in sturdy oak chairs in front of Charles's desk, while Raul and Miss Poole leaned against the opposite wall between the two windows. Meenie, as usual, stood within comfortable spitting range of the spittoon at one end of the desk, his hat pulled low over his forehead, but not low enough to hide the scowl of disapproval. Charles ignored him. Meenie had voiced his opinion earlier, and Charles didn't need reminding by nonverbal means. He knew he was violating every rule, both written and unwritten, for a successful interrogation by questioning Rachel Smith, Mrs. Dodd, and Mad Dog Treadwell at the same time. Conventional wisdom held that all suspects should be questioned separately so their stories, lies, and alibis could be compared for discrepancies. However, experience over the past three years taught him that conventional wisdom didn't always work in Crawford County, so he might as well go with his instincts, and his instincts told him that he might learn more by watching the reactions of the suspects to one another than he could learn from watching them one at a time.

On the other hand he wouldn't bet on it.

In Crawford County, only a fool believed in a sure thing.

"What the devil do you want, Sheriff?" demanded Mad Dog Treadwell. "And I don't believe that horse manure Meenie give about you needing my help, so don't bother repeating it. Unless you got an oil-well fire that needs putting out, I don't know of nothing I can help you with."

Charles rested his folded hands on the top of his desk and studied the ruddy-faced man sitting between Rachel Smith and Mrs. Dodd. "Then why did you come, Mad Dog?"

Mad Dog rubbed one hand across his chin several times as though checking for whiskers. "Well, Sheriff, I was curious and didn't have nothing better to do. Thought I'd come down to see what you had on your mind. I like to drop in every now and again to keep up with what's going on here in the courthouse."

Charles didn't consider Mad Dog a genius, but he conceded the oldster's IQ was at least as high as the temperature on a hot day. Mad Dog was too smart to believe Meenie's reason for bringing him to the sheriff's office, but he wasn't quite smart enough not to come, and he definitely was too dumb to keep his mouth shut once he got there. In the nearly three years Charles had been sheriff, Mad Dog Treadwell had never set foot in the Crawford County courthouse.

Charles shifted his gaze to the sedate old lady sitting on Mad Dog's right. Rachel Smith was intelligent, maybe the most intelligent of the three. She had smiled at everyone, called Miss Poole by her given name, thanked Raul for holding the door open for her and complimented him on his manners, brazenly lit a cigarette in defiance of the NO SMOKING sign, and said not one word of any substance.

Charles next considered Mrs. Dodd, sitting on Mad Dog's left. He agreed with Reverend Lundy. She did not look like a beekeeper in that damn hat and veil. "Mrs. Dodd, will you please remove your veil? I like to be able to see the people I'm talking to."

"I can't, Sheriff. I told you why the other night." The veil fluttered with each word like a curtain blowing in a gentle breeze.

"Oh, for goodness' sake, Victoria, you'll do anything for attention," said Rachel Smith as she reached across Mad Dog and whipped the veil and hat off Mrs. Dodd.

Several things happened almost simultaneously. Mrs. Dodd screeched and Mad Dog scooted his chair back to get out of range of the widow's long polished nails as she lunged across his lap after Rachel Smith. The chair legs caught on a warped tile and tipped over backward. Mad Dog landed with a loud thud and a breathless "Goddamn women!"

"Stop it, ladies!" ordered Charles, rearing up out of his

own chair, but if the ladies in question heard him, they didn't bother answering, being occupied in a tug of war over Mrs. Dodd's veil.

Meenie stood with an open mouth and a horrified look. Meenie was never at his best dealing with females he considered ladies, even those engaged in unladylike activities.

Raul danced around the two women uttering useless admonitions and waving his hands.

Miss Poole, as usual, suffered no doubts as to the proper course of action. She darted in, nimbly avoiding Mad Dog's flailing arms and legs in the overturned chair, seized a fistful of each lady's hair and jerked both women out of their chairs and up on their toes. Off-balance and indignant, they dropped the hat and veil in favor of trying to break out of Miss Poole's grip. Mad Dog Treadwell, who had managed to right himself aided by grunts and expletives, recovered the fumbled garments, made a quarterback sneak between the two struggling women, and stuffed both hat and veil in the spittoon by Charles's desk.

He then swung around to face the two women. "You two old biddies stop your clawing and shut the hell up!" he shouted in a loud enough voice to reverberate off the plaster walls.

Everyone froze in a tableau of raised arms, open mouths, and ringing ears.

Charles recovered first. "Thank you, Mad Dog," he began when Slim slammed the office door open and hopped through on his right foot and crutch, an impossible feat when Charles thought about it later.

"Everybody just hold it right where you are!" bawled Slim, pointing his remaining crutch at the room's occupants and swinging it from right to left as though unsure from which direction an attack might come. "Don't you worry, Sheriff. I'll take care of things!"

"Don't swing that crutch, Slim!" ordered Charles, feeling an ominous sense of pending disaster.

Given the fact that Slim was wearing a brand-new, slick-soled cowboy boot on his only foot touching the floor, and given the fact that balance is more certain if both crutches rather than only one are used for their intended purpose, and given the further fact that swinging a heavy wooden object builds up centrifugal force that is directed away from its axis, the axis in this case being Slim, what happened next didn't surprise either Charles or his other deputies. Slim Fletcher was a perpetual accident waiting to happen; only the form of that accident was in doubt. Muttering an "Oh, God," but lacking any hope of divine intervention, Charles witnessed the inevitable with as much stoic acceptance as he could muster.

Slim's boot skidded in one direction on the heavily waxed floor while the rubber-tipped crutch, tucked under his right arm and supporting what weight was not resting on his booted foot, skidded in another. His body turned on its own axis instantaneously, and he appeared to levitate parallel to the floor for a fraction of a second before succumbing to the force of gravity and dropping like a stone to land spread-eagled on his back. The instant he felt himself slip, Slim let go of the second crutch, which had by that time gained considerable centrifugal force as a result of his swinging it back and forth at an immoderate rate of speed. Propelled by this centrifugal force, the crutch sailed through the air on a trajectory perpendicular to its radius, skimmed across the top of Charles's filing cabinet, scattering the pieces of his only remaining chess-by-mail game not already vandalized by his stepdaughters, missed Meenie's head by inches, ricocheted off the wall, and crashed through a window on the opposite side of the room.

Mad Dog Treadwell rushed to the window and looked out. "I'll be damned, Sheriff, that crutch must have picked up some speed falling three stories and got a real good bounce off the sidewalk because it put the damnest dent in the hood of one of your patrol cars."

"It's your patrol car, Sheriff," said Meenie, peering over Mad Dog's shoulder.

Charles sank down in his chair and popped two antacid pills. "Somehow I'm not surprised."

Mad Dog turned around and looked at Charles. "Is it always this exciting around your office?"

"Pretty much," said Charles, chasing the antacid pills with two aspirins.

"I'll fix your car, Sheriff," said Slim, still supine on the floor. "I've been reading this book on how to do your own bodywork—"

"Slim!"

The young deputy flinched. "Yes, Sheriff?"

Charles took a deep breath and then another before speaking. "Slim, I appreciate your offer, but I want you to crawl out of my office, call your mother to come pick you up, and go on sick leave until your ankle heals, and whatever you do, don't come near this courthouse again with those crutches!"

"Yes, sir!" said Slim as he rolled over, got to his hands and knees, and crawled out of the office.

Charles got up and closed the door.

"You don't let Slim carry a loaded gun, do you, Sheriff?" asked Mad Dog.

"He's not as inept as he appears," said Charles.

"Nope, he's worse," said Meenie, shifting his tobacco from one cheek to the other and gazing in consternation at Mrs. Dodd's veil trailing over the edge of the spittoon. Finally he spit in his empty coffee cup.

Charles touched his badge to remind himself that in theory he was the authority figure in this room. It was time to take charge while he still retained a modicum of sanity—if, in fact, he still did.

"Slim's behavior is not the issue," he said, staring at each of the three oldsters in turn.

Rachel Smith and Mrs. Dodd busied themselves straightening their hair, in disarray from Miss Poole's usage, while Mad Dog brushed the knees of his pants. None seemed interested in meeting Charles's eyes.

"The issue is the discovery of a mummy in the courthouse basement," he said, observing the three.

Their hair suddenly forgotten, Rachel Smith swallowed

and ducked her head while Mrs. Dodd bit her lip and clutched an old-fashioned brooch pinned at her throat. Mad Dog Treadwell stared at the toes of his boots.

"Even though the mummy was a homicide victim, he'd been dead for nearly fifty years. Surely he didn't represent a threat to the living after so long, and *I* certainly didn't," Charles continued. "I wasn't interested in arresting anyone for a fifty-year-old murder. I only wanted to know what name to put on Sergeant Doe's tombstone. I expected Crawford County to be as concerned as I. I expected my office switchboard to be flooded with callers guessing the mummy's identity. I expected letters and cards. I expected people to stop me on the street. But none of that happened. A few residents even told me that Sergeant Doe's identity was none of my business. In short, no one seemed to care except me."

He rose and walked around his desk to stand in front of his three unwilling guests, but it was Miss Poole at whom he looked. Charles wanted to shake her, just to see an expression on the dispatcher's impassive face.

He leaned back against his desk and folded his arms. "But you see, Sergeant Doe has no one else to say his name, not even the army. His records, along with thousands of others, were burned. There is no proof that Sergeant Doe ever enlisted, that he ever fought and was wounded, that he was ever discharged. Officially he doesn't exist. He never *happened*!"

He saw Mrs. Dodd flinch at his words, while Mad Dog grimaced and Rachel Smith closed her eyes. Miss Poole's face seemed a little paler, but Charles still detected no expression.

"The loss of army records is a coincidence, but in my opinion the theft of Crawford County records of births, marriages, and deaths for the decade from 1940 to 1950 is not. Someone destroyed the official history of life, love, and death in Crawford County during the decade of the victim's murder. Officially, from a philosophical perspective, life didn't exist in Crawford County. It never *happened*!"

Charles paused and watched his three guests glancing at one another. He would swear they seemed surprised. Not that surprise was synonymous with innocence since he would also swear they possessed guilty knowledge—just not knowledge of this particular crime. That was reserved for another.

"None of us were born in that decade. Mrs. Dodd married the judge before the war, I got married in 1951, Miss Smith never married at all, and sure as hell none of us are dead even though Mrs. Dodd dresses like she's anticipating the event, so what do those records have to do with us?" demanded Mad Dog, frowning at Charles.

"Did you ever read the Sherlock Holmes stories, Mad Dog?"

"I seen the movies."

"Maybe I better explain then. My friend, Sheriff Lindman, who is a wiser man than I am, reminded me of Holmes's quote about the dog that didn't bark in the night. Lindman said the dogs of Crawford County ought to be barking. And they were! I just didn't hear them until those records turned up missing. The specter of Sergeant Doe frightened someone enough to steal those records, someone living in Crawford County during the war, someone who is now elderly."

"Crawford County's full of old coots, Sheriff," said Mad Dog. "Why the hell are you picking on us?"

"Because the old coots as you call them aren't barking, Mad Dog. And if they were male and able bodied, they were probably off fighting the war. For the most part only women and children and those too old or too infirm to fight remained on the homefront, and who are the only dogs barking? Who are the only elderly residents of Crawford County who are acting out of the ordinary? Miss Rachel Smith, a woman who loves and reveres books, snips all the pictures out of the library copies of the county history book five days after the remains of Sergeant Doe are found; Mrs. Dodd, who was a grown woman during the war, suddenly starts wearing mourning—"

"I told you why, Sheriff," interrupted Mrs. Dodd.

"Yes, your glasses were ugly I believe you said."

"That's right."

"You're not wearing your glasses today, Mrs. Dodd"—Charles leaned down and cupped the widow's face between his hands—"and I believe I can detect contact lenses. So do you have another explanation for your costume?"

Blinking, Mrs. Dodd stared at him and licked her lips. "I started wearing mourning long before—before whoever that was turned up."

Charles released her and sat back. "Two months before if my information is correct, and if Miss Smith hadn't ripped off your veil and I saw you without your glasses, it's possible that I might have sent you home. I say possible because I don't believe in coincidence Mrs. Dodd. Now that I know you lied to me, I believe in it even less."

"If she started dressing like that two months ago, then it ain't no coincidence," interrupted Meenie. "There was a story in the newspaper around about that time. I remember 'cause me and Miss Poole was talking about it. You were in New Mexico, or I reckon you'd have read it, Sheriff."

Charles almost wished Meenie hadn't spoken. He didn't want his suspicion of Miss Poole bolstered. It was strong enough as it was. "You didn't mention that when we were discussing Mrs. Dodd's behavior, Miss Poole."

The dispatcher looked paler than before, but she remained silent. Charles wasn't surprised. Miss Poole was intelligent enough and had worked in the sheriff's department long enough to learn a smart defendant's basic creed: if you don't plan to confess, don't say anything at all.

He turned his attention back to Mrs. Dodd. "You started your period of mourning when you learned the subbasement would be renovated. Do you have an explanation for your behavior?"

Mrs. Dodd followed Miss Poole's example and remained silent.

"Did you know the sergeant was buried in the basement,

Mrs. Dodd?" asked Charles. "Is that why you suddenly started wearing black?"

Mad Dog Treadwell stood up, his hands clenched. "Just a damn minute here, Sheriff. Are you accusing Mrs. Dodd? Well, you're just plain crazy. Mrs. Dodd wouldn't murder—"

"Of course, she wouldn't, Sheriff," said Rachel Smith quickly—too quickly, in Charles's opinion.

"—nobody," finished Mad Dog.

That wasn't the word Charles had seen the old man's lips start to form before Rachel Smith interrupted.

"I'm not accusing Mrs. Dodd of murder," said Charles. "I'm not accusing any of you of murder. I only want to know who was buried in the basement. I only want a name and I think the three of you know what that name is."

"Three! You keep saying three but you never have said why I'm included in this little party, Sheriff," said Mad Dog Treadwell. "Hell, I was a kid during the war."

"Actually you were a teenager, older than Miss Poole, but not by much."

Charles paused abruptly and met Miss Poole's expressionless eyes. He heard Meenie clear his throat and Raul shuffle his feet. He didn't need to look at his two deputies to know that they were staring at him, wondering why he had paused and why he was staring at Miss Poole.

Charles deliberately picked up his cup of coffee and sipped the tepid liquid. "Excellent coffee, Miss Poole, strong as usual."

"Thank you, Sheriff."

Despite what he suspected, Charles admired his spinster dispatcher. Miss Poole would never hide behind a veil; she would look her accuser in the face and spit in his eye. But then why the devil did she lie to him? What was the dead sergeant to Miss Poole? He could only think of one explanation that seemed to fit the facts.

"If you ain't got no better reason than that, Sheriff, I'm going home," said Mad Dog.

"There is the matter of your new hobby, Mad Dog," said

the sheriff. "I find it a little out of the ordinary that you would suddenly take up hang gliding. That's a little unusual even for an eccentric like you."

"I been thinking about it for a long time. Just didn't decide until lately."

"Four days after C.J. Tolliver dug up a mummy?"

"Damn it, Sheriff, not everything everybody does in Crawford County is because of that feller in the basement! It's a coincidence."

"And I've already said I don't believe in coincidence. Give me a name, Mad Dog. Whose grave was in the basement?"

"Hang gliding?" said Rachel Smith. "At your age? You're a fool, Mad Dog."

Mad Dog straightened his shoulders and pushed out his chest. "No, I ain't. I just got a lot of guts."

"And not a lot of sense," said Rachel Smith. "What are you trying to prove?"

"And what are you trying to hide, Miss Prim and Proper Smith, cutting pictures out of county history books? Is there a picture of you being naughty in there?"

Rachel Smith flushed, but she didn't lose her composure. "I don't think this is the time to toss accusations at one another. The sheriff is doing a good enough job of that."

The hint was broad enough that Mad Dog couldn't miss it. "You're right about that, and I'm getting a little tired of it. Put up or shut up, Sheriff. Throw us in jail or let us go."

Charles's regard for Rachel Smith's intelligence went up another notch. Once again she distracted Mad Dog before he gave anything away.

"Short of a confession, Mad Dog, I can't throw anyone in jail, and even a confession isn't enough. I would have to prove that confession with other evidence, and after fifty years, there's no evidence left."

If the oldsters felt reassured by his words, he didn't see any indication of it in their expression. He tried again. "All I want is a name. What harm can it do to tell me his name?"

There was no sound but the wind whistling through the broken window. "Damn it, I've already told you I'm not a threat! You don't have to be afraid of me!"

One face finally revealed an expression. Mad Dog Treadwell looked surprised.

Rachel Smith stood up. "If you don't intend to charge me with defacing public property, Sheriff, I believe I'll go home now. Victoria, Mad Dog, if you're ready to leave, perhaps we can impose on Deputy Trujillo to drive us home. He has such nice manners, and young people so often don't these days."

Raul looked at Charles. "Sheriff?"

Charles felt his stomach burning despite the antacid pills. Anger and frustration always made his stomach hurt. He waved his arm. "Take them home, Raul."

"Thank you, Sheriff," said Rachel Smith, glancing back at him just as Raul opened the door.

Charles thought later that if Rachel Smith hadn't smiled in such a lighthearted and relieved way, he might never have said what he did. Or maybe he would have.

"Short of Mrs. Dodd having an attack of conscience tonight and telling me how she knew someone was buried in the basement two months before anyone else did, I suppose I'll have to find my own answers. I will, you know. I won't bury that soldier without a name, and your efforts to hide the history of Crawford County won't stop me. There are other original sources besides official records and informal county histories if a person is sufficiently curious about the past of a town and its people. I'm sure I'll find the wartime issues of the *Crawford County Examiner* very interesting—and informative."

He certainly found the looks of dismay on three faces informative. The fourth face was as impassive as ever, but then Miss Poole possessed extraordinary self-control.

CHAPTER

14

From the private journal of Megan Elizabeth Poole:

January 5 [continued]

What is Rachel Smith hiding? Although Albert always was polite to her, I do not recall his ever mentioning her except in passing. She was always such a romantic though that I suppose she made more than she should have of the time he spent in the library. She should have realized that it was not for love of reading, or of her, but because he always met me there after school. The meeting place was my idea since in those days the library was housed in a room next to my father's office on the second floor of the courthouse, and I always hoped my father would be impressed by Albert's spending his leisure time there. It was a futile wish. My father never approved of Albert; in fact, he despised him although I would not admit it at the time. I could not imagine anyone not liking Albert. Apparently Rachel Smith certainly did.

I wonder why she's so sure that it was Albert in the basement.

"I've heard of making bricks without straw, Sheriff, but I ain't never seen them made out of hot air until now," said Meenie as soon as the door closed behind Raul and the three oldsters.

Charles sank down in his chair and rubbed his temples. The aspirin hadn't stopped his headache. "If you're referring to what I just told my suspects ..."

"Jumping the gun calling them suspects, aren't you? Maybe Mrs. Dodd dressing up looks suspicious, and Miss Smith cutting up the county history books don't look too good either, but that's all it is, just looks. Just because things look a certain way doesn't mean that's how they are. And you're sure stretching a point with Mad Dog." Meenie shifted his tobacco and spat in his coffee cup again. "You didn't have a lick of proof to back up anything you said to start with, and you didn't learn anything you didn't already know except that Miss Smith don't like Mrs. Dodd one bit, and Mrs. Dodd told you a fib about her glasses."

Charles glared at his deputy. "Damn it, why does everybody say fib instead of lie? Is a fib a lesser offense?"

Meenie shook his head, reluctantly in Charles's opinion. "I reckon not, Sheriff. It's just I don't like to think Judge Dodd's widow would be telling a windy."

Charles rolled his eyes dramatically toward the ceiling. "A windy! A fib! Next you'll be calling a lie a slight exaggeration. Good God, Meenie, just because somebody has gray hair, is female, and the widow of a long dead county judge—"

"District judge," interrupted Meenie. "He was a district judge."

"I don't care if he was the chief justice of the Supreme Court, that doesn't mean his widow can't lie! She lied and Mad Dog lied. The only one of the three who didn't lie was Rachel Smith, but then she was too busy interrupting the other two to make sure they didn't say too much."

Meenie nodded. "Yeah, I reckon she took charge of what was said." His expression insinuated that she was more in charge than the sheriff. Charles couldn't disagree.

"Did you also notice that not a single one of those three denied knowing the mummy? Don't you think that would be the first thing they'd do? Wouldn't you expect them to say they had no idea who that might be in the basement?

But in fact, only Mrs. Dodd and Mad Dog even obliquely mentioned Sergeant Doe—once—and Rachel Smith didn't mention him at all."

Charles rose and began to pace his office, clutching his hands behind his back. "I'm convinced that all of them know our soldier's name, and furthermore I'm convinced that Mrs. Dodd knew he was buried down there, which means she either killed him or knows who did."

Meenie lifted his hat to scratch his head, something Charles had noticed him doing whenever he needed time to think. Meenie Higgins wasn't an impulsive talker. He weighed each word as though it was gold, particularly if he was about to argue with Charles.

"I can't see Mrs. Dodd dragging a dead body down to the basement and burying it," he finally said, replacing his hat. "She ain't very big for one thing, and a dead body always seems to weigh more than a live one. I can't see her doing it anyway. I reckon it takes a stronger stomach and nerves than what she's got to dig a grave with nobody but the dead for company. That basement jangled my nerves and I figure I'm a lot tougher than Mrs. Dodd."

Charles raked his fingers through his own hair as he picked his own words carefully. "As it happens, I agree with you. I don't think Mrs. Dodd has the character to commit murder, but I still believe she knows who did and is protecting him—or her. But why is she wearing mourning? Why call attention to herself now?"

"Maybe she's feeling guilty about what she's hid all these years?" suggested Meenie.

"Why? If we're right, and I think we are, she protected his killer for more than fifty years. Why feel guilty about it now?" Charles shook his head. "No, I don't buy the guilty conscience, Meenie. It's a good devise for fiction when an author can't think of a better motive for a character's peculiar actions, but in real life—no, I don't believe it. If Mrs. Dodd's conscience is hurting her, it's more likely from fear than remorse. The body's been found. The whole story is liable to come out."

Meenie scratched his head again. "Well, it don't seem to be coming out very fast, does it? Seems to me the smart thing would have been to sit tight."

"But Mrs. Dodd couldn't count on that, Meenie. She reacted in anticipation of the body being identified and so did Rachel Smith and Mad Dog. They're all afraid, but not of me. Mad Dog even looked surprised at the suggestion that they might be. They're not afraid I'll think they committed murder. They're afraid of Sergeant Doe himself. He's nothing but bone and hair and hide, but he's still a threat. But why, Meenie? What did a judge's wife, a spinster librarian, and a teenager have in common with Sergeant Doe? What did they have in common with each other? For that matter, what do they have in common now? Nothing that I can see except Sergeant Doe. Rachel Smith evidently doesn't even like Mrs. Dodd and didn't hesitate to embarrass her earlier."

"Maybe she wanted to see Mrs. Dodd's face just like you did," said Meenie. "Sort of keep an eye on her."

"That's a possibility I hadn't thought of, Meenie. What's your opinion, Miss Poole? Does Miss Smith habitually embarrass people, or did she want to watch Mrs. Dodd's reactions just as I did?"

The spinster dispatcher hesitated before speaking, and Charles knew she was weighing her words. "I've never known Rachel Smith to be unkind. Perhaps she didn't want Mrs. Dodd to have the opportunity to hide when she couldn't."

"She made an effort to hide though, didn't she?" asked Charles. "Why else would she cut the pictures out of the county history? And speaking of that volume, Meenie, round up a copy. I want to see what Rachel Smith was so afraid of that she went against the habits of a lifetime and defaced library books."

Meenie lifted his hat and scratched his head. "I reckon I got one at home somewhere if I can find it."

"If your personal quarters are no neater than your handwriting, perhaps I'd better get mine," said Miss Poole, starting for the door. "My books are arranged by subject."

Charles caught the dispatcher's arm. "No, Miss Poole, you stay. I need to talk to you and I'm afraid it won't wait." He inclined his head toward the door. "Go on, Meenie. Find me a copy of that history."

He waited until the deputy departed before releasing the dispatcher. "Sit down, Miss Poole."

The dispatcher sat in the chair vacated by Mad Dog and smoothed her skirt over her knees. "What is it, Sheriff?"

Charles sat down beside her. "Miss Poole, you know who he is, don't you?"

She didn't bother asking to whom he was referring. "I can't imagine why you think that."

Charles sighed. "You were the first dog I heard barking, Miss Poole, but I fell into the same trap as Meenie. I didn't want to believe you would lie, so I let myself be distracted by my other barking dogs—until this morning."

Miss Poole sat like a prim and proper lady at some bygone tea. Her back was straight and didn't touch the chair, her folded hands rested on her lap, her skirt covered her knees, and her feet rested flat on the floor. No crossed legs for Miss Poole. She was a proud, uncompromising, straightforward lady of Crawford county, and it made Charles's heart ache to look at her.

Finally, she turned her head to meet his eyes. "I suppose Meenie's telling you about the newspaper story further aroused your suspicion."

"Are you going to tell me it slipped your mind?"

"No."

"Do you have an explanation?"

"Victoria Dodd did not commit murder, and I had no intention of allowing you to harass her."

Charles rubbed his chin as he studied her determined face. Her features were as perfect as those on a cameo, and it occurred to him that she must have been a beautiful young girl. "You seem as sure of that as Rachel Smith and Mad Dog. Would you care to tell me why?"

"For all the same reasons that you and Meenie discussed."

Charles waited for her to say more, but like Meenie, Miss Poole was not an impulsive talker. However, she had a better reason. "Miss Poole, I like you as well as I like anybody I know. You and Meenie have been my mentors and kept me from digging a hole for myself because I was ignorant of Crawford County ways. You've protected me and trusted me and in the case of L.D. Lassiter's death, you even lied for me. . . ."

"I didn't lie for you," said Miss Poole in the stern voice of a teacher correcting a student. "I merely kept what I knew to myself since I judged the literal truth would serve no one. Occasionally poetic justice is more satisfactory than legal justice."

Charles wondered if he was the only person in Crawford County who called a lie by its name. "Poetic justice would give back our soldier's identity, Miss Poole. Give me a name, please."

He watched her swallow convulsively and pressed harder. "Don't deny that man's existence by denying him a name, Miss Poole."

He listened to the wind shrieking around the old courthouse until he finally admitted the wind was all he would hear. Miss Poole would not speak. Whatever loyalty and affection she held for him weighed less with her than the secret she kept.

He hesitated. He could stop now, bury the remains of the young soldier, and go on with his own life. Who would he be hurting after all? The soldier was dead. Calling him by name wouldn't restore his life and it might destroy others.

He rose, feeling old and used up, and walked to the broken window. The bitter wind ruffled his hair as he looked down at the bare elm trees that circled the courthouse, then raised his head to look toward the west, toward the farm and ranch land that produced so much of Crawford County's wealth and determined so much of its culture. Take away their tractors and electricity and mechanized irrigation systems, and the people differed little from their agricultural ancestors who first turned over the soil or herded livestock.

They lived in a timeless world of crops and cattle that was alien to him. He was a stranger. What right did he have to wreck the peace of this land? What right did he have to dig up trouble?

He touched his badge. Because he was here and he was sheriff.

He turned away from the broken window and bitter wind and walked back across the room toward Miss Poole. He sat down beside her to finish what he had begun. "Not telling me about the newspaper article isn't the primary reason I'm questioning you, Miss Poole. It was the records."

Her eyes widened. "I beg your pardon?"

"Don't act so surprised, Miss Poole. The only one of my barking dogs with the opportunity to steal those records was you. You were also the only one familiar enough with criminal investigation procedures to push the other ledgers together so there wouldn't be a gap on the shelf and to restore its dusty condition. What did you do? Blow dust on the shelves?"

Her cheeks turned bright pink. "I did nothing of the kind. I might withhold information to protect another person as I did in Mrs. Dodd's case, but I would never steal county records. I have no reason to in any case."

Charles wanted to believe her and a week earlier he would have. But not today. Today he trusted Miss Megan Elizabeth Poole about as much as he trusted the sun to set in the east.

"I understand you planned a wartime wedding."

The pink faded from her cheeks in favor of dead white. "Then you misunderstood. I never married."

"According to my informant, the wedding never took place, but that's not to say that a marriage license wasn't issued. Those licenses were numbered and carbon copies were kept in the county clerk's office, Miss Poole. Is that why you stole the records? Because there was a carbon of a marriage license signed by you and Sergeant Doe, a license never used because your father interfered? Something caused an estrangement between you and your father that lasted until his death. Was it Sergeant Doe?"

Miss Poole stumbled rising from her chair, and Charles caught her around the waist. "Miss Poole, are you all right?"

She leaned against him for a few seconds, then straightened her shoulders and stepped away. "I'm perfectly fine, Sheriff. I've just never been called a thief before and I'm afraid I lost my composure."

"I'm sorry, Miss Poole," said Charles. And he was. He should have remembered that she was an elderly woman and been a little more subtle.

She patted his arm. "Don't apologize. Your reasoning was quite logical. Under the same circumstances I would have drawn the same conclusions. I'm sure you'll reconsider once you've had time to think about it."

"Anything's possible where Sergeant Doe's concerned, but until I know his name and his relationship to you, consider yourself on administrative leave. Goodbye, Miss Poole."

Other than an indrawn breath, Charles saw no other reaction to his words until she nodded her head. "I'll try to use my free time productively, and Sheriff, talk to Meenie before you dig yourself too deep a hole. Hot-air bricks make a poor ladder." She walked toward the door.

Her words set off faint alarm bells. Miss Poole's definition of productivity might not be the same as his, especially since she already had interfered once in the investigation. There was no telling what she might do with free, unsupervised time on her hands.

Breaking out in a sweat, Charles followed her. "Miss Poole, keep out of this case."

She opened the door, then glanced over her shoulder. "There are people waiting to see you." She stepped through the door, leaving it open.

"Miss Poole," Charles began, making it as far as the threshold before he found himself crowded back into his office by the two people he wanted least to see.

"How dare you drag my father down here like he was a criminal! The neighbors have been calling me all afternoon. And then telling him that you wouldn't allow me to take him home! That he had to ride with that deputy! I'm not putting up with it, Sheriff. I'm calling a lawyer." The crease between Pauline Brett's eyes looked as deep as the Grand Canyon.

"I never told your father any such thing, Mrs. Brett," began Charles, trying to edge around her and make a rush to the door.

Howard Worchester's rotund shape blocked the doorway. "My father's run off, and his neighbor told me she saw your car in his driveway. You warned him, didn't you, Sheriff?"

"Call it preventive law enforcement, Howard. Your father's entitled to my protection against false imprisonment—which, in my opinion, your plans to commit him would be."

Howard's face turned red and seemed to swell. "Crawford County doesn't pay you to take sides in a family dispute, Sheriff. I'll be calling my attorney about a lawsuit."

"That could be expensive, Howard, and I don't think your father will allow any attorney he has on retainer to sue me. You'll have to pay a lawyer out of your own pocket." Charles watched the red fade from Howard's face until he looked bloodless, probably from shock at the thought of having to let loose of a nickel to pay a lawyer.

"Then I'll circulate a recall petition and get you thrown out of office."

Charles thought it likely Howard would do exactly that. Recall petitions didn't cost any money. "Get out of my office, Howard, before I charge you with threatening a peace officer."

Howard's jowls shook with indignation. "You can't talk to me like that."

Charles felt his muscles tighten and he knew that if Howard Worchester didn't move in the next few seconds, there would be no need for a recall petition. Sheriffs who assaulted citizens generally ended up serving the remainder of their term of office in their own jails.

"Move, Howard! And you, too, Mrs. Brett."

Something of the rage Charles felt must have shown on his face because Howard backed out of the door, turned, and lumbered across the squad room and out of the sheriff's department like an overweight bear. Pauline Brett hesitated, then scuttled after Howard, bumping into Raul at the outer door.

"Excuse me, ma'am," said Raul, removing his hat. Rachel Smith was right, thought Charles; Raul did have beautiful manners.

Pauline glared at him. "Don't try to butter me up; I'm still suing," she declared as she disappeared through the door.

Raul walked into the squad room. "Suing?"

Charles wiped his hand over his face. "I'll explain later, Raul. I'm not in the mood to talk about it now. Take care of the phones, please, while I'm gone, and call somebody to fix the window in my office."

"Where's Miss Poole?"

Charles hesitated, reluctant to tell him. If he was wrong about Miss Poole, he didn't want the other deputies knowing he'd ever doubted her; if he was right, he didn't want her humiliated. The thought of Megan Elizabeth Poole as an object of curiosity or worse, pity, her relationship with the dead soldier the subject of gossip at the doughnut shop, made him cringe. Damn it, why couldn't life ever be simple—black or white, guilty or innocent? Why did it always have to be so complex, like a tapestry of interwoven lies and motives?

"She's taking a few days off—at my suggestion. All the players in this drama are contemporaries of hers, and I think the whole business is distressing her. She's not a young woman, Raul."

Whatever Raul might have replied was interrupted by Reverend Lundy, "Sheriff, I need to speak to you about Mrs. Dodd."

Charles had noticed the minister waiting in the squad room with Howard and Mrs. Brett, but had forgotten about him. "Why don't you talk to Mrs. Dodd instead, persuade her to tell me who the devil was buried in the basement. Tell her confession is good for the soul." He veered around Lundy and headed toward the reception area.

The minister trotted after Charles. "I don't believe you understand the situation, Sheriff. . . ."

Charles made it through the reception area to the hall and turned toward the elevator. "I understand it perfectly, Reverend. Four of Crawford County's upstanding, God-fearing, respectable citizens are too busy protecting their spotless reputations to care about some GI who got himself shot up defending their right to be upstanding, God-fearing, respectable, and *free*! He's just trash to be buried, and trash doesn't have a name!"

Charles reached the elevator and hit the down button, then leaned against the wall and closed his eyes. His chest was tight and his belly felt as though it was on fire. He was exhausted, frustrated, angry, and disgusted, and he'd left his hat, coat, and antacid pills in his office. He rubbed his forehead and wished he could go home instead of the newspaper office.

"Compassion hurts, doesn't it, Sheriff?" said Reverend Lundy. "Or at least that's always been my experience."

Charles opened his eyes. "Is that why Crawford County wants to avoid it? They don't want to hurt?"

"Guilt and fear hurt, too, Sheriff."

"Don't you think that soldier was afraid, Brother Lundy?"

Charles stepped into the elevator before the minister could answer. His hand hovered over the panel of buttons for a few seconds before he made a decision he doubted he would ever be able to explain and didn't intend to try. How could he when he didn't fully understand himself?

When the elevator doors hissed open again, Charles stepped out. He flipped a switch on the wall next to the elevator and the lights came on. But not all. Meenie and Raul had disconnected the extra lights they had strung, and now only a few bulbs glowed like feeble candles in the waiting darkness.

Charles walked toward the opened grave, growing more chilled with each step, until he stood at its edge. There was nothing to see: no bones wrapped tight in dried flesh, no rotting uniform, no metals too corroded to catch the dim light, nothing. The tomb was empty. All that could be touched or seen of Sergeant Doe lay unclaimed—and unnamed—in the morgue in Amarillo.

But Charles knew that which could be touched or seen was the least important part of a man. The body was a shell left behind like the husk of a cicada, form without the substance. "What kind of a man were you?" whispered Charles, lifting his head to look into the darkness beyond the grave. "And why do the living still fear you?"

The darkness did not answer.

The dead are mute.

CHAPTER
15

AMERICAN BOMBERS RETURN

LONDON (AP)—Formations of American bombers, shepherded by darting swarms of fighters, returned from across the Channel today, apparently from their first mammoth air battle over Germany.

The Allies at the same time resumed their big air offensive against the German's mystery targets on the northern French coast.

Crawford County Examiner
January 14, 1944

D-DAY DAWNS

LONDON (INS)—American and British troops invaded northern France today, landing in overwhelming strength along the coasts in a stupendous operation that Prime Minister Winston Churchill said had been "successfully effected."

Crawford County Examiner
June 6, 1944

DON'T PAY BLACK MARKET PRICES
FOR WHISKEY!

Due to government controls there is a real whiskey shortage in this country and bootleggers are taking advantage of thirsty customers. The shortage is likely to continue unless the government permits some resumption of beverage distilling, and YOUR HELP IS NEEDED. Don't buy from bootleggers and black market operators. Don't pay a penny more than government prices.

Crawford County Examiner
July 22, 1944

DRAFT CALLS INCREASED

WASHINGTON (INS)—National draft is due for sharp increases until Germany is defeated. The War Department boosted its recruitment demands from 60,000 to 80,000 per month for January and February.

Crawford County Examiner
December 19, 1944

GERMANS GAIN
PAY TERRIFIC PRICE AS
SAVAGE FIGHTING RAGES

PARIS (INS)—Fighting deepening on the western front in support of American troops battling to stem the continuing bitter Nazi counterattack.

Crawford County Examiner
December 19, 1944

The Colchesters had owned the *Crawford County Examiner* since 1904 when Benjamin Colchester had driven a wagon loaded with type, paper, and a printing press across the windswept prairie from Amarillo to the fledgling town of Carroll in search of opportunity and no competition. The first issue of the *Examiner*, according to Jack Colchester, managing editor and the latest scion in the publishing dynasty, was printed on water-stained paper as a result of his great-grandfather's miscalculating the depth of the Canadian River when he crossed it. Undaunted, Benjamin Colchester had taken a penny off the price, then began a campaign to make his newspaper the one of record for the northern Panhandle. He succeeded through perseverance, hard work, and a strategy based on cynicism and human psychology: he mentioned, however briefly, the name of every subscriber in each issue of the paper for the first five years of publication. Charles's favorite story of the irascible publisher was when he refused to print the mayor's name because the gentleman in question failed to subscribe to the paper, referring to him instead as Mr. X when he mentioned him at all. Within a month the mayor capitulated and bought a three-year subscription. Within a year Benjamin married the mayor's daughter although gossip said that relations were never too cordial between the newspaperman and his wife's family.

The *Examiner* was still housed in the long, narrow limestone building erected by Benjamin Colchester in 1925 to replace an old frame one. Rumor said he paid for the building with profits from a foolproof distribution system he ran for the local bootleggers. Being fond of strong drink himself, he disapproved of Prohibition, calling it "an experiment in tyranny that fosters neither true sobriety nor moderation, and is based on the arrogant assumption that the moral precepts of a self-righteous few may be forced upon the many."

Jack Colchester lacked his great-grandfather's iconoclastic nature, being more likely to protect local customs and traditions than to destroy them. He was a diplomat, not a crusader.

He stared at Charles. "You want to read all the issues of the *Examiner* published between 1940 and 1950? What in the devil do you expect to find, Sheriff? A headline announcing a special burial in the courthouse basement?"

"If you're going to jump me, you'll have to take a number and wait in line, Jack. I've already got more people on my back than a wide receiver on Sunday afternoon, and damn it, I'm not even carrying the ball. I've been threatened with a lawsuit and a recall petition, nobody is telling the truth, my office routine is disrupted, my domestic life is under siege . . ."

"I heard about J.T. Brentwood and the horse," interrupted

Jack. He grinned and the dimple in his left cheek deepened. "Knowing how you feel about horses, I got a real kick out of the story, but if you want my opinion, old J.T. is doing you a favor. Outside of marrying Angie, I can't think of anything that will make you more like 'just plain folks' than shoveling horse manure."

Charles barely repressed a shudder. "Good God!"

"I'll even come out and take a photograph for the front page to immortalize the occasion."

"You're talking like cleaning up after a horse was an initiation rite."

Colchester rubbed his chin, his pale blue eyes thoughtful. "Maybe it is in a sense. A smell of sweat and horse shit will go a long way toward making you one of us, Sheriff, and I think that's what you want. There was a time when I would have rolled in horse manure and run naked down Main Street if I had thought it would prove I belonged."

Charles started to laugh, then realized that the editor was serious. "What are you talking about, Jack? You were born and raised in Crawford County. You're what—the fourth generation? You never had to prove anything. Just being a Colchester was enough. This town is your birthright while I'm still an interloper."

Colchester looked pensive for a moment. "I guess there's no way you could know. What few people do don't talk about it anymore. You see, Sheriff, I'm adopted. I was about thirteen when my folks told me and I felt like somebody cut the ground out from under me. All of a sudden I wasn't a Colchester but some stray the family had taken in because nobody else wanted him. I felt like I didn't belong anymore, and it took me a lot of years to get over it."

He touched the dimple in his cheek. "I even went to the doctor to ask if he could get rid of this. None of the Colchesters had a dent in the cheek, and to my mind it was like a brand on my face that said I was a maverick in the herd. Well, the doctor had sense enough to call my family. Old Benjamin was still alive then, and he came roaring down to the doctor's office in his old Ford and jerked me out of there like I was a kid instead of nearly twenty years old. He brought me here, to this newspaper office, the citadel of the Colchesters. He sat me down in that very chair you're sitting in, Sheriff, except it's been reupholstered a few times, and told me that it didn't make a damn bit of difference how or where or to whom a man was born, what counted was what a man made of himself. I didn't have to *be* a Colchester to become one."

Charles raked his hand through his hair. "It's not a good analogy, Jack. You were raised as a native son of Crawford County and I wasn't. My shoveling out a stable isn't going to change that."

Colchester leaned back in his chair and propped his feet on the corner of his desk next to a microfilm reader. "Maybe not, but it's good public relations, and you need a little extra goodwill. Damn it, Sheriff, I don't want to see some good old boy beat you in the next election just because you opened up the closet and pulled out all the skeletons."

Charles rose and leaned over Colchester's desk. "Are you warning me off this investigation, too, Jack?"

The editor shook his head. "I guess what I'm telling you is a variation of old Ben's advice to me: you don't have to be a native son to act like one. Treat our skeletons like they were your own, and don't drag them out for everybody to look at unless you know for damn sure they have something to do with this business."

"And how will I know which ones do and which ones don't, Jack? Will the closet doors have signs? I beat my wife but I didn't kill the soldier? I had an illegitimate child but I don't know whose body is buried in the basement?" Charles saw Colchester flinch and knew his last question drew blood like a spear in the heart. "Damn it, Jack, I'm sorry."

The older man lifted his feet off the desk and rose. "Don't apologize. Sometimes my skin wears thin when I least expect it. Must be all this talk about old Ben and not belonging. You'd think that after all these years it wouldn't bother me, but every now and then I feel the ground shaking under my feet again. And if I feel that way, and I'm not even hiding a guilty secret, how do you suppose the folks who are must feel? Damn it, they're all old, Sheriff! If anybody still living killed that soldier, don't you think he's expiated his sin? Can't you leave him in peace?"

Charles felt a chill run up his spine, as though someone with icy hands had touched him. Someone—or something. "Do you believe in ghosts, Jack?"

"Christ, no!"

"I don't either," said Charles slowly. "But I know whoever slept in that grave isn't at peace, and he's going to haunt me until I learn his name."

"Why the hell should he haunt you? Because you're the sheriff?"

"No, because I'm not a native son. I'm the only one he can trust."

Colchester came around the desk and grasped Charles's arm. "Good God, I can't believe we're having this conversation. Come on, Sheriff, I'll show you the morgue. Maybe you can find your soldier there."

The editor led him to the very back of the limestone building, to a room of shelves holding bound copies of the *Crawford County Examiner*, and handed him a pair of white cotton gloves. "Wear these. These old papers are fragile, and I don't want them touched by bare hands." He pointed to a shelf. "1940 to 1950 are those volumes, and you can use this table. We don't have a paper to get out tonight, so the staff will be leaving at five and I will, too. I'm going home and having a stiff drink, maybe more than one. You're welcome to stay later if you'll lock the front door when you leave. And, Sheriff, I hope you find your body."

"Do you really, Jack?" asked Charles, studying the tall, thin man whose face looked older than it had a few minutes ago.

Colchester looked around the newspaper morgue, but Charles was certain he wasn't really seeing it. His eyes had that unfocused look of a man looking inward at his own heart. "Yeah, I do." He grinned. "Put it down to memory. I remembered that I'm not really a native son either. Us interlopers have to stick together. Besides, I'm nameless myself if you want to look at it that way, and sometimes it bothers me—like now."

The editor hesitated in the doorway, then waved a hand and walked out. He was one more victim of a fifty-year-old murder, and Charles wondered how many more there would be. None, if he could help it. He lifted down the volume labeled JANUARY–JUNE 1940 and opened it. The musty smell of old newsprint reminded him of the courthouse basement, which he supposed appropriate since the world recorded in that print was as dead as his unknown soldier.

As Charles skimmed volume after volume he heard the newspaper staff leave one by one until he was alone in the old building, lost in a past only the elderly remembered. He noticed that prime rib roast was twenty-four cents a pound in 1941, a penny less than apples and four cents less than a dozen eggs. He also noted that a politically correct historian would immediately label the homefront newspapermen as racist pigs and burn them in effigy for their use of such derogatory terms as "dagos" and "Nips."

Charles forced his wandering mind back to the present. As interesting as dispatches from the front or grocery ads or the pleas to buy war bonds might be, World War II was a story whose end he knew. The mummy in the basement was the unfinished tale. His was a mystery story that could only be told in flashbacks and solved only if Charles could establish his identity.

The first step was listing the suspects who might be guilty, not of murder, but of being the victim of murder.

Fortunately the *Crawford County Examiner* provided such a list in each issue from 1941 through 1945.

MEN AT WAR

We at the *Crawford County Examiner* announce a new column that will appear each week in this space on the front page. We dedicate it to Crawford County's very own men at war, those noble individuals who answer President Roosevelt's call to arms. We will list each man who joins our armed services and print news of them that comes our way. We invite the families to share letters and cards from their fighting men with the readers. All personal exchanges should be deleted first as we have no desire to eavesdrop on tender moments between husband and wife or mother and son.

Now that the reader knows what we plan to do, let us begin with the names of those brave young men, and some not so young, who volunteered for duty at sea with our navy. Put our name on a torpedo, boys, and deliver it to a Nip U-boat with our compliments. . . .

Benjamin Colchester
Crawford County Examiner
December 15, 1941

Charles grinned as he read the rest of the column and copied the names of men who had joined the army. He wished he'd moved to Carroll in time to have met Ben Colchester before his death. The old man was never afraid to state an opinion or to take sides on an issue. No wonder Jack suffered an identity crisis when he discovered he was adopted. Living up to a legend would be hard enough if you were a blood relative. If you weren't, it might seem impossible.

He lost track of time as he copied names from subsequent columns, then checked each name against the obituaries and the legal notices through 1946 and made a separate list of those men who survived the war. Or at least those men whose families had not given obituaries to the paper or those who had not had their wills filed for probate. Finally Charles marked through the names of those men he knew were still alive.

The names unaccounted for made a distressingly short list, and all were members of prominent Crawford County families.

"Damn it!" exclaimed Charles as he studied the list. "These men couldn't have disappeared without their families raising hell about it, which means they probably came home and died peacefully in their beds sometime during the last forty years or so. I'll have to ask Miss Poole."

He heard his voice echo in the empty building and shook his head in disgust. "Terrific, Matthews," he said aloud. "Not only are you talking to yourself, but you forgot you suspended Miss Poole. The best damn source of information on everybody in Crawford County, and you have to kick her off the investigation."

He flipped a page of the October 1946 issue and stared unseeing at a photograph on the society page. "On the other hand," Charles wondered aloud, "could I trust her to tell the truth if one of the names on my short list is Sergeant Doe? I don't know. God help me, but I just don't know."

He rubbed his eyes and then focused on the photograph. He leaned over to peer more closely at the grainy picture. "Speak of the devil," he murmured and read the caption.

Miss Megan Elizabeth Poole, escorted by her father, Crawford County judge Daniel Poole, was crowned 1946 Homecoming Queen Friday night during halftime activities at Carroll High School's football game with Dumas High.

Charles smiled. He had been right about one hunch today. Miss Poole had been a beautiful young girl. She would have been even more beautiful if she had been smiling in the photograph. Which brought up an interesting point. Why wasn't she smiling? Didn't every young high school girl dream of being Homecoming Queen or was that a politically incorrect assumption? And why did her father escort her? Wasn't that traditionally the privilege of the captain of the football team?

Charles studied the picture again trying to discern the expressions of Miss Poole and her father. Like those of a prisoner and her guard, he decided. He abruptly slammed the bound volume shut and pressed a hand against his belly, which suddenly felt as if he had swallowed a razor blade. He wished he had. It couldn't hurt as badly as the realization that his analogy of prisoner and guard might be an apt one. Motive, means, and opportunity were the three questions any murder investigator must answer, and Charles had failed to even ask them. Now he didn't have to. He knew the answers, all but the means, or weapon. Best two out of three wasn't bad after nearly fifty years.

Miss Poole won hands down, though. She even got the bonus question right. She knew the victim's name and he didn't.

Charles shoved the bound newspaper aside. He wished he hadn't seen that photograph, or if he had, that the caption hadn't been so informative. Miss Poole's father had been county judge and the county judge always had keys to the courthouse. Opportunity. Miss Poole had been jilted by Sergeant Doe. Motive. The means, or weapon, didn't matter. Any blunt object would do.

"Damnation, Miss Poole!" he exclaimed aloud and slumped forward against the edge of the table. It was a fortuitous move. Otherwise, the intruder's bullet would have gone through his heart.

CHAPTER

16

From the private journal of Megan Elizabeth Poole:

January 6

I shall never forgive myself that my day of epiphany came at the sheriff's expense. Whoever shot Charles Matthews murdered Albert; therefore, my father is innocent. It is a simple matter of logic. If I had been honest from the beginning, it's possible I or the sheriff would have arrived at this conclusion at the time of Albert's discovery, more likely the sheriff than I. Charles Matthews for all his emotional angst and unfortunate tendency to complicate a simple problem with extraneous details is a remarkably logical man with a bent for psychological analysis. After investigating, he would have pointed out that my father, despite his reputation for being hot tempered, never in his life committed a violent act. It is unlikely that he would have deliberately committed murder even to prevent my marrying Albert, but if he had, he would have admitted it. My father often failed to explain himself, at least to me, but he never lied. Burying Albert in an unmarked grave was a lie in a sense.

I was too overwrought to view the situation from the proper perspective and jumped to conclusions, the very thing I always warned my pupils not to do. I realize now that I never forgave my father for requesting that the army send Albert back to the front, and allowed my old resentment to interfere with my normal mental processes.

But despite my resentment and my certainty that he murdered Albert, I protected my father's name even to the point of lying and I am uncertain of my motive. But I am very certain that my dishonesty has led to a good man lying on the verge of death.

Although the words and the concepts behind them are out of fashion these days, I will use them anyway. I sinned and I must atone. I must direct the investigation of Albert's death and the attempted murder of Charles Matthews. There is the matter of my suspension from duty, but I believe even the sheriff would agree that under the circumstances I am the most qualified person to be in charge. After all, I know all the suspects and am in awe of none of them. Neither Rachel Smith's age nor Victoria Dodd's social position nor Mad Dog's gender shall prevent my giving them the "third degree" I believe it's called in those lurid books Slim prefers over decent literature. I *will* learn the truth, and God forgive me if it's too late for Charles Matthews. He is most grievously wounded.

Miss Poole laid down her pen and closed her journal. Until the sheriff recovered sufficiently to hear her apology, acknowledging her guilt in her journal would have to do. She didn't subscribe to the breast-beating school of public confession unless tax money was involved. Besides, she knew her people. Protecting one's family was a long-standing tradition, and no one would censure her for keeping silent about her father, certainly not over a fifty-year-old murder. Crawford County would more likely blame the sheriff for sticking his nose in business that didn't concern him. Not that she believed people would ignore the attempt on his life, but at the same time she knew a substantial number would think he brought it on himself. Human nature was frequently less than admirable and sometimes perverse, her own included.

But at least she admitted it, which was more than Victoria Dodd, Rachel Smith, and Mad Dog Treadwell seemed prepared to do. The very idea! Shooting the sheriff! What a despicable and self-serving act—particularly when he said he wasn't planning to arrest anyone. Whatever the rest of Crawford County thought, Miss Megan Elizabeth Poole absolutely refused to excuse such behavior.

Her duty clear in her mind, Miss Poole buttoned her coat, turned off the lights, and drove to the hospital.

She realized the moment she walked into the small waiting room opposite the surgical ward that everyone excepting herself and Dr. Wallace was suffering from psychological shock. Of course, Dr. Wallace's appearance wasn't reassuring. His green scrub suit was stained with both sweat and blood, and no one, certainly not the three people gathered around him, doubted whose blood it was. Angie looked like a ghost, so white and insubstantial did she appear. Her eyes, usually such a lovely hazel color, were muddy brown and sunken from exhaustion. Even Raul and Meenie looked dazed, Meenie in particular. His face was pale with more lines about the eyes and mouth than she had noticed only a few hours ago. It could be the early effects of tobacco deprivation since the hospital forbade tobacco use of any kind, but Miss Poole doubted it. Lacking a family of his own, Meenie had adopted the sheriff whether Charles Matthews knew it or not. The scrawny deputy couldn't suffer more than he was now if the sheriff actually was his son.

Raul, on the other hand, had a wife and five children, so his grief sprang from a different source. The sheriff had risked his own life to prove the deputy innocent of a murder charge in New Mexico, and Miss Poole knew that Raul felt a bond to Charles Matthews that was strengthened by custom and culture. In Crawford County a man never forgot a debt.

Whenever the shock wore off, both Meenie and Raul would be very dangerous men. Miss Poole didn't think they would shoot the guilty party, whoever it might be, at the first opportunity, but she wouldn't swear to it either. She decided that it was a very good thing that she would be in charge. She didn't plan to shoot anyone—unless it was absolutely necessary, of course.

Miss Poole walked up to Angie and put her arm around the younger woman's waist. "Lean on me, dear, while we listen to what the doctor has to say."

If Angie heard her, she gave no indication of it. Her attention was focused on Dr. Wallace. No one else existed for her. "Will he live? Will he be all right?"

Dr. Wallace took her arm and lead her toward a couch. "I want you to sit down, young lady. No standing on your feet. And yes, he'll live and I think he'll even be all right eventually. He was lucky this time. If the path of that bullet had been another inch in nearly any direction, you'd be talking to the Parker brothers instead of me. As it was it nicked the left lung, one of his ribs, and left a messy exit wound. Oh, I plugged up the hole, used tiny stitches to minimize the scar, but every time he takes off his shirt he's going to know how close he came to buying the farm."

Dr. Wallace swallowed and rubbed his face with his surgical mask. "Damn it all, Angie, I'm tired of patching up that boy. My grandmother could make a quilt with fewer stitches than doctors have put in his hide over the years, starting when they put his gut back together in Vietnam. He's running out of safe places to be shot."

Angie moistened her lips. "You said he'd be all right eventually." Her voice broke on the last word, but Miss Poole watched her take a deep breath and straighten her shoulders. Angie Brentwood Lassiter Matthews had grit. "What did you mean by that?"

"Angie, I wish you'd had a good cry and got all the fear out of your system before you started asking questions," said Dr. Wallace. "It unnerves a man to see you hanging on to your composure with your fingernails. I've seen corpses with more color in their faces than you have."

"Answer my question, Dr. Wallace."

The doctor sighed. "The bullet wound isn't the problem. Don't get me wrong, Angie. It's no piece of cake recovering from a bullet, but I'm a damn sight more concerned about the smoke he inhaled before Slim pulled him out of that building. Breathing smoke when you have a slow leak in one lung isn't a good idea. It's not a good idea at any time, but especially not under those circumstances. I'm going to have to watch him like a hawk, make sure complications don't set in."

"Smoke?" asked Miss Poole, startled. "Meenie, you didn't mention a burning building when you called me. And Slim saved him? Our Slim?"

Meenie cleared his throat. "I reckon even Slim's shenanigans are bound to turn out right sometimes. Law of averages I guess. Anyhow, Slim was out riding around in his mama's car and drove by the *Examiner*'s office and saw smoke leaking out the front door. Anybody else would have called the fire department and hung around waiting for them to get there. But not Slim. He didn't even call the fire department, said he didn't think of it—which don't surprise anybody who knows him. He breaks out the glass in the front door with his crutch and runs in the building, or hobbles would be more like it. Gonna save people, he said. Thinking not being Slim's long suit, he didn't stop to think that it was dang near midnight and there wasn't nobody in there to save. Except there was. The sheriff was in that back room where all the old newspapers are. That's where the murdering bastard started the fire, Miss Poole. Used them old newspapers like they was kindling."

"The murderer hoped the fire would destroy the evidence of a bullet wound," said Miss Poole. "A very foolish assumption on the part of someone since the Branch Davidian tragedy proved that even incinerated bodies will reveal bullet wounds."

"Oh, God," cried Angie, bending over and hiding her face in her hands.

"You two hush up!" snapped Dr. Wallace. "Talking about how damn bad it could have been isn't helping Angie deal with how bad it is. I won't have it, do you hear me? You want to talk about how close the sheriff came to being a crispy critter, you go somewhere else." He knelt down in front of Angie and patted her shoulder. "It's all right, little lady, none of those horrible things happened."

Angie pushed his hand away and stood up, clutching a large shoulder bag. "I'm not little and I don't know how much of a lady I am either, Dr. Wallace."

"I was trying to reassure you, Angie, not put you down," said Dr. Wallace. "Charles is still in one piece, thanks to my fine hand with a needle. He's just a little singed around the edges and is liable to have a hell of a cough for a while, but I promise that when you take him home, everything will be in working order."

"I believe you, Doctor," said Angie, "but Miss Poole and Meenie don't need to watch what they say around me. I know Charles could have died and I know I'm responsible that he was in that newspaper office at all. When he didn't come home at five o'clock, I should have called to find out where he was. But I didn't. Because I was afraid. Charles— Charles hasn't found being married as wonderful as he thought. There's my father—who isn't the world's greatest diplomat—and the horse and the girls leaving toys all over the house and playing with his chess sets, and Charles tries to be so nice about it all, but it's obvious he's wondering what he got himself into. So when he wasn't home for dinner and he didn't call, I thought he was working late because he wanted some peace and I didn't want to nag him."

She took a deep breath and paced the length of the small waiting room, then whirled around and faced them. "To hell with being sweet and accommodating and never speaking my mind. He married me and he can take the bad with the good, and that includes my nagging when I think he needs it. He's my husband and I want him alive because I'm pregnant and it's not right for his baby to grow up without a father!"

"Lord Almighty," said Meenie, whipping off his hat and putting it over his heart. Judging by the awed expression on his face, Miss Poole decided that the deputy considered Angie's pregnancy on a par with the Immaculate Conception. "You don't worry about that, Miss Angie," continued Meenie. "Me and Raul are gonna camp out in the sheriff's room to keep him safe until he can look after himself."

"That's right," agreed Raul. "We will guard his door like he was family."

Angie smiled as she reached into her shoulder bag and pulled out a revolver. "I appreciate that, Meenie, but I plan to keep my own vigil. If someone dares threaten my husband again, I'll kill him or her without a second thought."

"Madre de Dios!" exclaimed Raul. "Mother of God, that's a Colt .45!"

"Yes, and I'm a very good shot," said Angie.

"Angie, you put that gun down right now," ordered Dr. Wallace.

If Meenie hadn't spat out his tobacco before entering the hospital, Miss Poole was convinced he would have swallowed it. She didn't think she had ever seen the deputy so shocked.

"Now, Miss Angie, ladies ain't got no business waving guns around." It was obvious to Miss Poole that Meenie was none too comfortable with the idea of women arming themselves.

"I'm not waving it and I'm not a lady," said Angie.

Miss Poole decided it was time to take charge. "Angie is correct in both remarks. She is holding the revolver in what seems to be a competent manner, and she is a woman. Every woman is capable of protecting herself and her family if necessary. It's part of equal rights."

"I thought equal rights has more to do with a lady's paycheck and not listening to dirty jokes than it does with losing their common sense and running around with a gun like a damn fool man."

"Losing one's common sense is also an equal right," said Miss Poole, deciding that Meenie wasn't too comfortable with the feminist movement either. "However, that doesn't mean a woman should do so. Angie, I don't believe you can properly care for the sheriff while he is incapacitated and hold a gun at the same time. You would never forgive yourself if it accidentally discharged."

Angie hesitated a moment, then returned the revolver to her bag. "You're right, Miss Poole. I'm not thinking too clearly tonight."

"That's understandable, dear."

Suddenly tears welled out of Angie's eyes and ran down her cheeks. "He doesn't even know I'm pregnant, Miss Poole." She sank to her knees and wrung her hands.

The three men started toward Angie, but Miss Poole waved them back and helped the young woman up. "If you gentlemen will excuse us, I believe Angie is going to take Dr. Wallace's advice and have a good cry."

CHAPTER
17

SHERIFF SHOT;
CRAWFORD COUNTY SHOCKED!
Local Rancher Up in Arms at Son-in-Law's
Attempted Murder

Sheriff Charles Matthews was shot in the back by an unknown assailant during an investigation into the fifty-year-old murder of an unidentified soldier who had been found buried in the subbasement of the Crawford County Courthouse. While engaged in reading old newspapers at the *Examiner*'s office in search of clues to the soldier's identity, Sheriff Matthews was apparently unaware that he was not alone. The assailant jimmied the back door of the *Examiner* and crept through the dark building to the newspaper morgue to shoot the unsuspecting sheriff. Although the bullet was not fatal, its force propelled the wounded man forward into a stack of bound newspapers. Miss Megan Elizabeth Poole, spokeswoman for the Crawford County Sheriff's Department, stated that investigators believe the sheriff was knocked unconscious when his head struck the corner of the July–December 1946 volume of bound newspapers. "Had it not been for this fortuitous accident, it is probable the assailant would have realized that Sheriff Matthews was still alive and fired another shot," said Miss Poole. "In fact, if the gunman had left then, it is possible his assault would have been successful because the sheriff would have bled to death. But criminals often trip themselves up and that was the case here. After deactivating the *Examiner*'s smoke alarms, the assailant set fire to the newspaper's morgue in an attempt to destroy evidence of his crime. The fire was observed by an alert Crawford County deputy, David 'Slim' Fletcher, who entered the burning building and saved Sheriff Matthews."

Miss Poole added that rumors the attempted murder of Sheriff Matthews would be investigated by the Carroll Police Department are untrue. "The assault on Sheriff Matthews is related to the investigation of the murder of the young soldier, and thus is the responsibility of the Crawford County Sheriff's Department even though it occurred in the city's jurisdiction." Miss Poole further assured the *Examiner* that a report by informed sources of a fistfight between Chief Deputy Meenie Higgins and Carroll police chief Edward Brian over jurisdiction was greatly exaggerated.

Crawford County reacted to the shooting of Sheriff Charles Matthews with shock and indignation. "It's a terrible thing to happen," said one local resident who prefers to remain anonymous. "I didn't vote for Sheriff Matthews because I didn't think he knew folks well enough, but I don't appreciate somebody using a gun to remove him from office."

Crowds of local citizens who gather at the hospital for Dr. Gilbert Wallace's hourly medical bulletins on Sheriff Matthews's condition agree that yesterday's assailant will receive short shrift in Crawford County. "I don't care if the sheriff was wasting his time on something that happened before most of us was born, that don't give anybody the right to shoot him," said one man.

J.T. Brentwood, Sheriff Matthews's father-in-law and owner of the Branding Iron Ranch, roundly condemns both the assailant and Crawford County. "He's been a damn fine sheriff, and Crawford County ought to be ashamed of the way it balks every time he asks for a little cooperation. If folks had come forward with their ideas about that damn mummy instead of figuring it wasn't any of their business or the sheriff's either, my son-in-law wouldn't be laid up in the hospital. I don't want to hear any more remarks from half-wits about how sorry they are the sheriff got shot, but that he didn't have no business investigating an old crime. He was hunting the truth, and Crawford County ought to be, too. What kind of folks are we if we say the truth has got a time limit on it? Pretty damn sorry is what. And as for that no-good son of a b——h that shot my son-in-law, I got a warning for him, too. When the sheriff married my girl, he became family, and I don't allow anybody to criticize him in my hearing, and I for damn sure don't allow nobody to shoot him. Whoever shot my boy had better walk looking over his shoulder 'cause I'm on your trail. You should have known better than to tangle with J.T. Brentwood's kin."

Crawford County Examiner
January 8

From the private journal of Megan Elizabeth Poole:

January 8

I'm not as young as I used to be, and the past two days waiting at the hospital have been exhausting. Other than visiting with the fire chief, meeting with Chief Brian of the police department, and holding a news conference, I haven't accomplished a thing toward arresting one of my three suspects. The fire chief's information about the smoke alarms was helpful, though. Although I suspected the fire was arson, it was necessary to be sure. I'm not certain that arson rules out any of my suspects. As a man who spent his career fighting oil-well fires, Mad Dog Treadwell certainly is no stranger to setting a fire of his own. I am rather surprised that he wasn't more efficient. Wadding up pages of old newspapers seems amateurish to me, more like what Victoria Dodd might do. However, staying in the same room with a suppos-

edly dead man long enough to set a fire requires a colder
nature than I attribute to Victoria. Being self-centered
and silly is not the same thing as being cold natured. Rachel Smith, on the other hand, is a very strong-willed
woman. I can see her planning and carrying out a murder. I'm surprised her cover-up attempt was so sloppy,
though. She is a very meticulous woman—or was. She is
getting along in years, so perhaps she's not as mentally
astute as she once was.

However, this is all speculation. Dr. Wallace assures
me that the sheriff will be conscious and able to respond
to questions this afternoon—at least for a short period. It
is possible that he saw something or heard something before he was shot that may help identify his assailant.
Meenie keeps insisting that this delay gives my three
suspects time to discard clothes that might be evidence.
His concerns are legitimate, but as I pointed out rather
forcefully, we can't obtain a search warrant without probable cause, and we have no real evidence against any of
the three. We need evidence to search for evidence. Perhaps the sheriff can provide some.

Charles dreamed that he was tied to an altar in hell and
the devil had built a fire in the middle of his chest. Three
lost souls danced around the altar, swaying and dipping in
unison and casting strips of yellowed newspaper onto the
fire while the devil watched from the darkness. The flames
soared higher and in their flickering light Charles saw the
demons' faces. Mad Dog, Rachel Smith, and Victoria Dodd
bowed to him in turn as the music reached a discordant cre-
scendo, then fled as the devil snapped his fingers.

Charles writhed against his bonds as he tried to free himself.

"Hold him down, boys, or he'll rupture them stitches!"

"Charles, lie still!"

*"J.T., stop giving Meenie and Raul orders and hold the
sheriff's legs. And for heaven's sake, take off that gun belt*

first. We don't need any accidents with firearms. I'll get Dr. Wallace."

"Damnation, but Miss Poole is the bossiest woman I ever did see. Like I don't know how to handle a gun."

Charles heard the voices from a great distance. Why were Meenie and Raul and J.T. Brentwood helping the devil? And Angie. Why was Angie in hell?

He felt strong hands pressing down on his shoulders and heard voices again.

"Do something, Dr. Wallace!"

"I'm trying, Angie, but there's not much I can do but help hold him down until he wakes up. And I wish he'd hurry. I don't know how a man can get himself shot to hell and still be so damn strong. Talk to him, Angie, maybe he'll wake up for you."

Charles felt soft hands stroking his cheeks and heard a voice coaxing him toward the light he could just see beyond the thinning edges of his dream. He struggled toward wakefulness just as the devil turned and showed his face.

"Miss Poole!" Charles screamed as his dream vanished, and he opened his eyes, blinking until he could focus and forcing his mind to fight off the last vestiges of unconsciousness and disorientation.

Angie's face filled his vision. "Charles, it's Angie. You're in the hospital and you must lie still. Please."

"What was that he just said, Doc?"

"I couldn't make it out, J.T. The man's throat is probably as dry as the Sahara. Give him a drink, Angie, but just a sip. I don't want him getting nauseated. And J.T., you can get off his legs now. And get your gun belt off the window ledge. Damn it, I feel like I'm in Beirut every time I walk in this room. Meenie, you and Raul let up on the sheriff, too. I don't think he'll thrash around now that he's awake."

Dr. Wallace leaned over Charles. "You hear me, Sheriff? Don't be wiggling like a trout on a line, or I'll have to order restraints again. You jerked your IVs out so many times while you were unconscious that the nurses got tired of sticking them back in. I don't know what kind of night-mares you were having, but they must have been hellish."

Charles would have laughed but his mouth was too dry. He sucked water through the straw Angie held to his lips, studying her face as he did so. She looked tired, no, ex-hausted was more like it, and her chin kept quivering. His glance traveled around the room, stopping on each face for a few seconds. Meenie, Raul, J.T. Brentwood, even Miss Poole looked as if they had gone without sleep for longer than was good for them. Everyone in the room looked like the very devil. . . .

Miss Poole!

Charles fixed his eyes on her and tried to remember why the devil wore Miss Poole's face. He closed his eyes and concentrated. The photograph! The photograph of Miss Poole and her father in a back issue of the *Examiner*. Op-portunity, motive, and means. He remembered it all now—except how he ended up in a hospital bed with tubes and needles stuck in his body and his chest feeling like some-body ran a hot poker through it. Shot? Had someone—Dr. Wallace?—said he was shot? Or was that just part of his dream? He had to find out.

But first things first. He couldn't stand to see Angie's chin quiver.

He pushed the water glass away and tugged on a lock of her hair until she leaned down so he could kiss her. If his breath smelled as bad as his mouth tasted, he was surprised she responded so enthusiastically. God, but love was won-derful.

When he finally let her go, Angie's cheeks were pink and he felt stronger, his mind clearer. But God, he hurt! Well, pain wasn't a stranger and neither was waking up in a hospital. The important thing was not to give in to the pain until someone filled in his missing hours.

He held on to Angie's hand and turned his head to look at Meenie. There was something odd about the deputy, and it took several seconds for Charles to realize what it was. Neither of Meenie's cheeks was swelled out with a wad of tobacco. His mouth made up for his sunken cheeks though. Both lips were split and swollen double their size. If Charles didn't know better, he'd think Meenie had been in a fight.

Charles swallowed, then cleared his throat. "What happened?" His voice sounded rusty to his own ears, but at least it was audible and his words weren't garbled.

Everyone broke into explanations at once until Charles held up his hand. "Stop! Meenie, give me a report—and start with your mouth."

The deputy's face turned red and he hitched up his pants. "I got in a little disagreement, nothing for you to worry about."

A disagreement? Meenie disagreed with nearly everyone on a daily basis, but he never fought. "Who?" asked Charles.

Meenie hesitated and looked toward Miss Poole, who sighed. "You had better tell him, Meenie. He won't rest until you do, and you don't want him hearing an exaggerated, inaccurate account from someone else."

"Chief Brian," mumbled Meenie, looking down at the floor.

Charles licked his dry cracked lips. Chief Brian was at least twenty years younger and fifty pounds heavier than Meenie, and a member of another law enforcement agency besides. "If this was over those damn gimme hats," began Charles.

Meenie looked up, a guilty expression on his face. "Maybe I said something about his hat—just in passing you might say—but that ain't what we were fighting about. The chief wanted to take over the investigation 'cause the *Examiner* office is in the city limits, and I told him his boys couldn't catch a killer if he'd left his driver's license and a city map at the scene, and they for sure couldn't find out who shot you."

Miss Poole cleared her throat, and Charles looked at her. "I settled the matter of jurisdiction after tempers cooled—a fire extinguisher is a very effective tool for separating quarreling men, but it does leave a mess—and Chief Brian is perfectly willing for the sheriff's department to head the investigation."

Charles started to laugh, but coughed instead, finally spitting out black-and-red-streaked phlegm into a tissue. "Did I swallow gunpowder?"

"Smoke inhalation," said Dr. Wallace.

"Somebody tried to roast me, too? I'm a hard bastard to kill, aren't I?"

"It's not funny, Charles," snapped Angie. "Everyone's been scared to death for two days. The babysitter says the girls have cried themselves to sleep since it happened, and Hieronymus sits by the front door with one of your old shirts in his mouth and whines. If he were human, he'd cry, too. So don't you dare try to make something humorous out of some *bastard* shooting you in the back!"

Meenie in a fight with Chief Brian, Miss Poole spraying them with a fire extinguisher, the girls crying, Hieronymus chewing on his shirt, someone shooting him in the back. Life as usual in Crawford County. In a sense it was reassuring that nothing had changed since he'd been unconscious.

"In the back? I was shot in the back?" He raised his head from the pillow to look at his deputies, then at Dr. Wallace. "Is that right?"

Raul nodded. "We think he stood in the doorway about four feet from where you were sitting."

"You were damn lucky, Sheriff," said Dr. Wallace.

Charles let his head fall back on the pillow and stared at the ceiling. It didn't fit. Being shot in the back didn't fit at all.

Thank God.

"That's wonderful!" He raised his head from the pillow again and smiled at the incredulous expression every face. "If everybody would leave, please. I need to talk to Miss Poole in private."

Angie's expression changed from incredulous to mutinous. "I'm not leaving you."

"I'll live, honey. Don't worry about me. Go home and go

to bed. Tell the girls I love them, and take my shirt away from Hieronymus before he chews the buttons off and swallows them. Buttons always give him a bellyache. J.T., take her home."

He watched J.T. sling a gun belt over his shoulder and lead a protesting Angie out of the room, followed by Meenie and Raul. A very reluctant Dr. Wallace lingered by the door. "Five minutes, Sheriff. That's all. Then I'm busting through that door and knocking you out again. I figure the only way you'll rest is if you're unconscious."

Charles lifted one hand to wave the doctor away. "We'll talk about it. For now, tell Meenie to take that gun away from J.T."

Dr. Wallace rubbed his chin and grinned. "That gun was a compromise, Sheriff. J.T. threw a ring of armed cowboys around the hospital, and Meenie threatened to arrest the whole bunch, but Angie persuaded J.T. to send his men back to the Branding Iron Ranch, if Meenie would deputize her father so he could keep his gun. Your wife could talk Meenie Higgins into damn near anything."

"J.T. Brentwood a deputy!" exclaimed Charles.

Dr. Wallace grinned again. "Scary thought, isn't it? But at least he's a better shot than the police department. I didn't let Chief Brian and his Keystone Kops in the hospital." He held up his hand, fingers spread wide. "Remember, five minutes."

The door closed behind Dr. Wallace, and Charles took ten seconds out of his five minutes to let his heartbeat slow. Crawford County was going to hell in a handbasket, and he had to stay calm if he planned to slow its descent.

He beckoned to Miss Poole. "Sit down and tell me everything you know so far about my attempted murder."

"Certainly, Sheriff. I have formulated a theory about the event, based on what evidence we have," said the elderly dispatcher as she sat in a chair by the bed, folded her hands in her lap, and crossed her ankles.

Her account of the events and her suppositions didn't include a word about her interfering in the investigation while she was technically suspended from duty. Charles smiled. Miss Poole looked startled—as well she might, he thought, since she probably expected him to chew her out.

"Miss Poole, I saw a photograph of your being crowned Homecoming Queen. You never mentioned your father was county judge."

"I don't believe the subject ever came up."

"It's just as well. I would have suspected you of murder much sooner than I did."

Miss Poole's mouth gaped open with astonishment, the first time Charles had ever seen that happen. Very little astounded the ex-schoolteacher. "I beg your pardon?"

"You had the opportunity and the motive. You could have stolen your father's keys to the courthouse, met Sergeant Doe there late one night, and killed him for caving in to your father's opposition to the marriage. Of all the suspects, I believe you have the strongest nerves. Even as a teenager, I can see you burying Sergeant Doe without having hysterics."

"I have never murdered anyone!"

Charles touched his bandaged chest where pain was kicking into high gear. "If I hadn't been shot in the back, you would still be my number one suspect. As it is, I know you're innocent. You would never shoot anyone in the back. That's the coward's way, and no one can accuse you of being a coward."

"Thank you for that assessment of my character—I think," said Miss Poole.

"You're welcome. Now suppose we start over from the beginning. Who are you protecting, and who is buried in the basement?"

"My father and I believe it is Albert Finnigan in the basement."

Charles blinked. "Your father?"

"He had the opportunity and the motive, Sheriff, and my father always kept his word. He told me I would never see Albert again when he had him transferred back to the front, and I didn't until C.J. dug him up." Her chin quivered for a few seconds before she controlled it. "But my father's been dead for over thirty years, so he couldn't have shot you, which makes it highly unlikely that he killed Albert."

"Miss Poole, I made a list from the *Examiner*'s Men at War column of all the Crawford County men who volunteered or were drafted into the military during WWII. Albert Finnigan's name wasn't on that list. Who was he?"

"He was a sergeant in the army who had been wounded in combat and sent home to recover. He had no family, so when he was released from the military hospital Crawford County offered him a home until he was well enough to return to active duty. He roomed with Judge Dodd and Victoria because they had a large home and no children. Our home was larger, of course, but my father thought it would be unseemly to quarter a single young man in a house where an impressionable young girl lived without a mother to serve as chaperon."

"He was afraid people would talk about you," said Charles.

Miss Poole tilted her head thoughtfully. "There was that—a young lady's reputation was a fragile thing and more carefully guarded in those days—but I don't believe that was my father's primary reason. He was a very strong-willed and forbidding man. I'm not certain anyone would have dared cross him by talking about me. No, I think my father had a very low opinion of human nature and feared the worst, as we used to say. He was afraid Albert would seduce me."

"So he didn't trust the sergeant."

"He didn't trust any young man who ever came calling, but he mistrusted Albert the most. Perhaps it was because Albert was handsome and such a romantic figure. The wounded hero. And my father was very Victorian. He believed young women were easily led astray and would give away their virginity to the first good-looking man who gave them a corsage."

"He didn't think much of a man's character, did he?"

"Nor a woman's intellect, I'm afraid."

"No wonder he looked like a guard and you his prisoner in that photograph!" said Charles, feeling pity for the young girl Miss Poole once was.

She nodded. "A good analogy, but the prisoner escaped."

Charles doubted that she had. Judge Poole had wanted to keep his daughter chaste and he had succeeded. "But you still lied to protect him."

She glanced down at her folded hands. Charles noticed her knuckles were white. "My father was a good man in all respects except in his determination to keep me dependent. He was respected, and to see his name in a banner headline in the *Examiner* for a rash action I was certain he regretted seemed so useless. He was dead, Albert was dead, and I am a spinster. Nothing would change except that I would become an object of curiosity and pity, and my father would become grist for pop psychologists in supermarket tabloids. Yet, I had a responsibility to Albert." She looked up at Charles, and for a moment her expression was the same as in the photograph, that of a prisoner. "I haven't slept well since the grave was discovered."

Charles reached for her hand and squeezed it. Like Jack Colchester, Miss Poole was also a victim.

CHAPTER

18

From the private journal of Megan Elizabeth Poole:

January 8 [continued]

It never occurred to me that *I* might be suspected of murder. The sheriff's exoneration of me is flattering, but it defies logic. If I were desperate enough to commit murder to conceal my relationship to Albert, I would do so in a manner most calculated to succeed. Given the differences in age, physical agility, and strength between myself and the sheriff, facing him face-to-face would have been a foolish tactic on my part. Apparently he has a higher opinion of my character at present than I do. My actions throughout his whole investigation have shaken my faith in my own morality. The road to hell is not paved with good intentions, but with self-justification. Thank God Charles Matthews is more charitable toward me than I am toward myself. If he were a more logical man, I would be in jail.

"Sheriff, I'm sorry."

"I accept your apology. And I apologize for accusing you of stealing county records, so we're even."

"I was the logical suspect."

The sheriff closed his eyes for a moment, and Miss Poole observed a spasm tighten his features. The poor man was in pain, and she had best summon Dr. Wallace. Further apologies could wait until later. She tried to free her hand from the sheriff's grip, but he held on with surprising strength and opened his eyes.

"You're not responsible for my being shot," continued the sheriff. "The law takes into account the individual's intent, Miss Poole. You didn't intend any harm to me by protecting your father's reputation, and it wouldn't have made any difference if you had told the truth."

"I'm not a child, Sheriff. You don't need to pat me on the head and tell me it's all right. If I had identified Albert, then there would have been no reason to shoot you."

He smiled, a rather pitiful effort she thought, but a smile nevertheless. "I wouldn't presume to pat you, Miss Poole, but most particularly not on the head. And I would have been shot anyway. Albert Finnigan is still a threat to someone, but not as big a threat as I am. Someone was afraid that I wouldn't be satisfied with merely knowing Albert's identity. Our X was afraid I'd keep asking questions. But if I were dead and my body too badly burned to determine cause of death, then the questions would never be asked because Crawford County wants to forget Albert Finnigan. There might be a few jokes down at the doughnut shop about the mummy's curse, but that would be it."

She decided that pain must be robbing him of his mental faculties. "That's foolishness, Sheriff. When you're thinking more clearly I'm sure you'll see the intent was to keep Albert's identity a secret."

"Then why didn't X shoot you, Miss Poole? Or don't our three suspects know you're aware of Albert's identity?"

"Victoria Dodd knows," said Miss Poole slowly. "And it's safe to assume that Mad Dog and Rachel Smith know, too, or at least suspect."

"Do you think they trusted you not to eventually spill the beans? After all, you work for me."

"In their position, I wouldn't."

"Then why weren't you the victim?"

It was an excellent question—and she didn't have an answer.

The sheriff twisted the sheet in his fists and his expression was fearsome. Of course, he looked terrible anyway. His lips were cracked, and one half of his face was blistered red from the fire while the other half, which had rested on the table after he lost consciousness, was a tattletale gray. His brown eyes, which could look as soft as melting chocolate or as hard as stone depending on his mood, were a dark mahogany, as though rage was adding a red tint to their color.

"It's not the skeleton in the grave they're afraid of, Miss Poole, it's the skeletons in their closets! Only one of them murdered Albert Finnigan, but they're all guilty of something. They don't want me asking questions about their activities on the homefront."

"That means Albert's murderer isn't necessarily the same person who tried to kill you," said Miss Poole, her hands turning cold as she carried the logic of her statement to its extreme. "If that's the case, then my father could have killed Albert, after all."

The sheriff's eyes lost their mahogany tint as sympathy softened them to chocolate brown. "I don't know, Miss Poole. I never knew your father, but he did have motive and opportunity."

Miss Poole leaned back and closed her eyes, casting her mind back nearly fifty years. "They all had opportunity, Sheriff. They all had access to keys." She felt him grip her hand again and opened her eyes. "Victoria Dodd's husband was district judge, and the library was on the second floor of the courthouse until 1950, and Mad Dog Treadwell's father was sheriff for two terms, from 1944 to 1952. Mad Dog lived in the courthouse with his family in an apartment in the attic above the sheriff's department until he went off to college in the fall of 1945."

"What?" demanded the sheriff, rising up on one elbow to stare at her, then groaning and falling back on his pillow.

"The apartment hasn't been used in decades, and the staircase was finally boarded up and plastered over years ago. I guess no one ever thought to mention it to you."

He clutched his chest and rolled onto his side facing her. "No one in Crawford County ever thinks to mention a damn thing to me, Miss Poole. 'Turn left where Dinky Holman's Billiard Parlor used to be' or 'it's that road that runs by old man Cheney's place' were the kind of directions you people gave me when I was trying to learn my way around. I nearly went crazy looking for the billiard parlor until Meenie told me it went out of business during the Truman Administration. And the Jones family bought the Cheney place fifty years ago, but Crawford County still calls it the Cheney place. And nobody tells me about the one historic location I might be interested in, the apartment above my own damn office!" He broke off in a spasm of coughing.

Miss Poole seized tissues and handed them to him. "I'm sure Dr. Wallace would agree that you need to avoid these emotional outbursts, Sheriff."

He glared at her as he spat into the tissue and motioned for water. She held the glass while he sucked on the straw. Finally, he pushed the glass away. "Don't lecture me, Miss Poole."

His voice sounded weaker and very hoarse, and she considered breaking off the conversation, but she hadn't asked him the one important question. "Did you see or hear anything or anyone just before you were shot?"

"Don't you think I would have said something before now?"

She pursed her lips. "I suppose so."

He rolled over on his back and looked up at the ceiling. "Tell Meenie to interview our suspects and find out if they have alibis. If they do, try to break them. Find out which ones own a gun of whatever kind I was shot with—"

"We didn't find the bullet, but Dr. Wallace thinks it was a forty-five," interrupted Miss Poole.

"Figures. This is the Wild West, after all. Anyway, tell Meenie to check out the guns, and for God's sake, try to find out what they're scared of. Opportunity, means, motive, he knows the drill."

Miss Poole rose and smoothed her skirt. "I'm certain he does." No need to mention that she planned to do the interviewing herself. It might provoke another emotional outburst. "Do you want me to send the doctor in when I leave? You look as though you're experiencing some pain."

He grunted. "You have a way with understatement, Miss Poole. Send him in. I think I've reached the limit of my stoicism for the day. I'm not as good at it as the rest of Crawford County."

"Then I shall report in tomorrow with preliminary results of the interviews, Sheriff." Just as she reached the door, his voice stopped her.

"Miss Poole?"

"Yes, Sheriff?"

"What did Meenie say to Chief Brian about the gimme hats?"

Miss Poole sniffed. "To the best of my recollection he said, and I quote: 'I ain't turning over no investigation to somebody that wears a sissy hat and still has the gall to call himself a Texas peace officer.' "

Miss Poole checked her hat in the rearview mirror before sliding out of her car. In her youth no lady went calling without a hat, and she saw no reason to change her habits just because this visit was business rather than pleasure. In her opinion hats made a statement, and hers, a broad-brimmed red felt with a high crown and three tail feathers from a pheasant tucked in the hatband, stated that Megan Elizabeth Poole was a person to be reckoned with. She had bagged the pheasant herself during last month's hunt.

She locked her car and dropped her key into her red leather bag, which matched both her gloves and shoes. Her job as dispatcher didn't require her to wear an official uniform, and she saw no reason to adopt the pale pastels or black that so many women her age wore.

She checked to see that her deputy's badge was securely pinned to her coat above her left breast where she privately thought every plainclothes detective should wear hers. Satisfied with her appearance, Miss Poole rang Mad Dog Treadwell's doorbell and waited, then rang it again. She knew he was home because his muddy Ford Explorer with TREADWELL'S OIL WELL FIRE DEPARTMENT painted on each side was parked in the driveway. Mad Dog never stirred off his property if he could help it unless he drove that Explorer.

Miss Poole hesitated, then turned the doorknob and eased open the door. Mad Dog was older than she and perhaps he'd slipped and fallen or suffered a heart attack or a stroke. Widowers often failed to look after their health properly. She supposed it had something to do with the male ego being infected with a Real Men Don't Get Sick Syndrome. Look at the sheriff's refusal to admit he had an ulcer.

"Mad Dog," Miss Poole called, slipping inside the house and pausing in a large entry hall. Through an archway on her right was the living room done all in shades of white; to her left was the dining room done all in shades of green. From the dusty, neglected appearance of both, Miss Poole judged neither room had been used since Mad Dog's wife died last spring. Certainly there was no sign of Mad Dog. Not that she blamed him; she wouldn't want to be caught dead *or* alive in either room.

"Mad Dog," she called again, continuing down the hall past the staircase to the back of the house. She would search the first floor, then the second floor and attic. Miss Poole hoped Mad Dog hadn't fallen in the bathroom or if he had, that he was dressed. Not that she couldn't handle a potentially embarrassing situation with her usual aplomb, but she doubted that Mad Dog could. Men didn't like to be caught with their pants down either in metaphor or reality.

She glanced in the kitchen, noticing with surprise that there were no dirty dishes stacked in the sink.

"What the hell are you doing here?"

Miss Poole gasped and whirled around. Mad Dog Treadwell stood in a doorway across the hall from the kitchen, his face streaked with dirt, a cobweb caught in his hair, and sweating profusely. "My heavens, you startled me. Where were you, Mad Dog? I rang the bell twice."

"It doesn't matter a hill of beans where I was, and I don't have to answer the door if I don't want to, either. Question is, what are you doing standing in my hall all dressed up like Donna Reed on her way to church when I didn't invite you in?"

The reference to Donna Reed stung. Donna Reed would never bag her own pheasant. Miss Poole lifted her chin. "I thought you might be ill and unable to answer the door. As a peace officer I'm very sensitive to my duty to the elderly and possibly infirm. I thought you might need assistance and I'm proficient in CPR."

"So you're Florence Nightingale, huh?" Mad Dog stalked toward her until he was practically nose to nose, and Miss Poole flinched at the odor of his sour, yeasty breath. "Elderly and infirm, am I? I'm not but two years older than you, Megan Elizabeth Poole, and I bet you wouldn't like people calling you an old woman. And I bet you wouldn't want an old biddy snooping around your house without an invitation either."

Miss Poole suffered a moment's self-doubt. Was it possible that subconsciously she had hoped Mad Dog was absent so she could look for evidence without benefit of a search warrant? She shook her head. No. Absolutely not.

"I was not snooping!"

"Had to think about it a while, though, didn't you?" He stepped back, staggered until he caught himself, and pointed down the hall at the door. "Now that you know I'm alive and kicking, how about you walk back out that door and close it behind you."

"I think not, Mad Dog. I've come to interview you concerning your—"

"Interview me?" interrupted Mad Dog. "You ain't a real deputy, Megan Elizabeth, in spite of that badge you're sporting. You're a dispatcher, and since when do dispatchers interview folks?"

"Since the sheriff was shot," she snapped back. "And I

am a real deputy and I will interview you—either here or at the sheriff's office. Take your pick."

"You ain't going to drag me down to the courthouse again," said Mad Dog, folding his arms and leaning against the door frame.

Over his shoulder she glimpsed an informal den complete with worn leather furniture and a stuffed antelope head above the fireplace. "Perhaps you'll be more comfortable talking to me in here," she said, marching past him into the room. "Judging by the empty beer bottles and overflowing ashtray, it's where you spend most of your time. You shouldn't be drinking alone—the habit often leads to alcohol abuse—but if you do, I'd recommend that you not burn a fire in your fireplace and certainly not one big enough to roast a side of beef. No wonder you're sweating. It's as hot as July in here."

"You get out of there!"

Mad Dog's shout was followed by a heavy thud, and Miss Poole glanced over her shoulder to see him levering himself off the floor. "Solitary drinking often leads to accidents, Mad Dog."

He stood up and squared his shoulders. "I ain't had but two beers today, Megan Elizabeth, and I don't need a lecture from you just because my feet got tangled up. Now, if you want to talk to me, let's go in the living room. No beer bottles in there and maybe the temperature is more to your liking." He took her arm and tugged her toward the door.

Miss Poole jerked out of his grip. "I'll thank you not to manhandle me. And I have no intention of conducting an interview in that living room. For heaven's sake, Mad Dog, all the furniture in there is white and your clothes are filthy and you've got a cobweb in your hair. What have you been doing, crawling around in your attic?"

For a split second Mad Dog's face went slack, and Miss Poole distinctly saw fear in his eyes. "It's none of your business what I've been doing!" He blustered, reaching for her arm again.

Miss Poole twisted away and darted around the couch,

her mind working faster than her legs. Why would Mad Dog be afraid of her knowing he was in the attic? Was he hiding something up there? A gun? The gun he used to shoot the sheriff? She felt chilled in spite of the roaring fire. She was alone with a man she suspected of attempted murder, and thanks to her own manipulations, Meenie and Raul didn't know where she was.

Mad Dog rounded the end of the couch, his eyes red with fury or the effects of excess drink—Miss Poole wasn't sure which, but men in either condition were unpredictable and needed firm handling. Sometimes even a show of force. With a quick side step she reached the hearth and seized a poker from the metal stand of fireplace tools.

"Stand back!" she commanded, brandishing the poker like a rapier. "Or I'll skewer you."

Mad Dog froze. "Are you crazy?"

"No, I'm defending myself against your repeated assaults."

"Damn it, I haven't assaulted you! I'm just trying to get you out of my den!"

He snapped his mouth shut but it was too late. "Of course you are," said Miss Poole slowly. "You're not hiding something in the attic—you were, but you're not now. You brought whatever it was downstairs—to this room. That's why you don't want me in here. That's why you built such a huge fire. You're going to burn it—so it isn't a gun."

"A gun!"

"That you used when you shot the sheriff!"

Mad Dog stared at her, his mouth gaping open. "Is that what this is all about?" he burst out. "For Christ's sake, I didn't shoot the sheriff! Are you calling me a coward, shoot a man in the back?" He sounded outraged—and relieved, which only increased Miss Poole's uneasiness.

"Where were you between midnight and one o'clock on January 6?" asked Miss Poole, trying to watch his face while at the same time taking quick peeks around the room for whatever it was Mad Dog Treadwell didn't want her to see.

"I was right here—in that chair—watching a movie on television, and you can't prove different," he said, pointing over her left shoulder for a second before suddenly swinging his arm in a half circle. "No, I wasn't, I was stretched out on the couch. Yeah, that's right, I was on the couch, same as I was when I heard you pussyfooting in the hall. I'd just finished a beer and was fixing to take a nap. Mighty comfortable piece of furniture, that couch. I spend a lot of time there just resting and thinking."

Miss Poole doubted Mad Dog spent much time at the latter activity or he would know when to shut up. Charles Matthews always said that the longer you let a suspect talk without interrupting, the more likely he would give himself away, and Mad Dog certainly had. She backed up several steps until she could see the chair he was so anxious she disregard.

There was nothing to see: just a worn leather chair, a copy of the *Crawford County Examiner* spread across its lumpy seat, with a rusty old tin trunk covered in dust beside it. Dust? Miss Poole studied the trunk more closely and saw a piece of torn spiderweb hanging from a cracked leather handle on one end—which no doubt matched the web caught in Mad Dog's hair.

Miss Poole raised her eyes and pierced Mad Dog with the same kind of look she had used with sixth-grade boys caught bringing slingshots to her class. "Is this what you didn't want me to see?" she asked, tapping the trunk with her poker. "What's in it, Mad Dog? Albert Finnigan's duffel bag?"

Even Mad Dog's lips turned white. "Albert Finnigan?"

"His duffel bag wasn't found with his body. Did you hide it in this trunk after you killed him?"

His face turned from white to red. "I didn't kill anybody, damn it! And it you don't believe me, just open that up and look. You won't find anything but pictures and keepsakes from my family. My wife was always after me to put the pictures in an album after my folks died, but I never got around to it."

Miss Poole studied his face. He looked sincere, but he was talking too much again. Therefore, despite his protestations to the contrary, the trunk held a secret. She leaned over and lifted the lid.

"See, what did I tell you? Nothing but family pictures, my old report cards, my daddy's campaign buttons and signs from when he ran for sheriff, genealogy papers my mama collected, junk like that. But no duffel bag or anything else of Albert Finnigan's. My God, I didn't even remember his name until you mentioned it, Megan Elizabeth. I haven't thought of him in years."

"You really should avoid lying, Mad Dog. You're no better at it now than you were in high school."

"So now I'm a murderer *and* a liar."

Miss Poole shrugged. "If the shoe fits." She laid the poker on the floor, grasped the trunk's leather handle, and tugged it in front of the chair.

"I don't have to listen—hey, what are you doing?"

"I have no intention of kneeling or sitting on the floor at my age. Besides, this carpet is filthy. I'm going to sit in this chair and look through—"

"No!" he shouted, rushing over and grabbing the handle on the other end of the trunk. "This is my family's private papers and such. I'll put it over to the couch, and we'll go through it together if you're so damn nosy."

Miss Poole let go of the trunk. "You're certainly fond of that couch, Mad Dog."

"I told you, it's comfortable," he said, pulling the trunk toward the piece of furniture in question. "Come on, Megan Elizabeth, take a seat."

Miss Poole stayed where she was, looking down at the chair he was so frantic she not sit on. Yet Mad Dog had obviously been sitting there while he looked through the trunk. And he hadn't been sitting on the copy of the *Examiner* because the paper bore no imprint of his buttocks. So why did he get up and carefully spread the newspaper over the seat before he investigated who had entered his home without an invitation?

Miss Poole snatched the newspaper off the chair.

The seat of the chair was covered with old Kodak photographs.

And a hat! An oblong, olive green cloth hat.

Dazed, Miss Pool sank to her knees on the dirty carpet. All she could think of was that hats made statements—and this one certainly did. It had sergeant's strips on the side.

"Albert!"

CHAPTER
19

From the private journal of Megan Elizabeth Poole:

January 8 [continued]

Memories are unstable. Just when one thinks a memory is fixed upon the mind like a photograph in an album, it transmutes into another form. Or perhaps not. Perhaps as a memory fades we fill in the blurred outlines, altering it to suit ourselves until finally very little is left of the original. We cannot objectively recall what happened an hour ago. How can we expect to recall people and events that occurred nearly fifty years ago without confusing fact with fiction? The truth is we remember what we want to remember and suppress what we don't. Will we ever know exactly what happened in the courthouse so many years ago? How far can I trust Mad Dog's memories?

[Miss Poole laid down her pen and massaged her fingers. Every so often when it snowed or rained, both infrequent occurrences in the Panhandle, thank heavens, her joints ached a little. She flexed her hand as she read her entry. More philosophical than her usual style, but sorting through the past often called for philosophy. She picked up her pen and wrote a final line.]

For that matter, how far can I trust my own memories?

* * *

Miss Poole reached out and traced the sergeant's stripes, then picked up the hat and rubbed her cheek against its rough wool. For a moment she imagined she smelled a faint trace of Albert's hair oil, but that was wishful thinking. What she really smelled was the musty odor of wool too long hidden in an old trunk. She laid down the hat and picked up one of the photographs.

"Megan Elizabeth?"

She heard Mad Dog calling her over the sound of her heart pounding in her ears, but he was in the present and she was confronting the past. The images of herself and Albert Finnigan were blurred as if she were looking at the picture through water, then realized she was, if tears might be considered water. She blinked and wiped her eyes on her sleeves, a breach of behavior but one she forgave herself. These were extraordinary circumstances. For the first time in nearly fifty years she was seeing Albert's face. His features were clear and unmistakable, as though the photograph had been taken yesterday instead of April 1945. Odd that she remembered the date so clearly when her memory of his face had dimmed. She closed her eyes and superimposed the photograph over her memory, until the two became one and took on color and substance. . . .

Megan Elizabeth Poole sat on the trunk of the fallen cottonwood tree next to Albert. His eyes were nearly as gray-green as the budding leaves of the sagebrush on the prairie above the grove of trees on the bank of the Canadian River where they sat. His hair was a more ordinary medium brown, and a little longer than the regulation military haircut, but then it had grown out since he arrived in Crawford County six weeks ago. His face was more thin than not, his lips full and always smiling. Her father distrusted that characteristic, saying that Albert smiled too easily and without thought, and depended too much on charm rather than character. But then her father wouldn't like Albert under any circumstances because he was the man she had chosen to marry.

Megan Elizabeth leaned her head against Albert's shoulder. "Isn't it beautiful along the Canadian? I want to build a house on the bank above us so we can look out and see the whole valley."

Albert folded his arms. "Got your life all planned, don't you, Meggie?"

No one but Albert ever called her Meggie. "But it's your life, too," she protested, raising her head to look at him.

Squeezing her hand, he stood up and moved a few steps away. "Not until the war's over, Meggie. Right now I belong to Uncle Sam, and I don't plan for the future because I don't know if I have one."

"Don't say that!" she said, jumping up and grasping his arm.

"I'm a soldier, Meggie. Soldiers sometimes don't come home again."

"Then let's get married now, Albert. I'm sixteen. I'm old enough."

He tucked a strand of hair behind her ears. He wasn't smiling now, and his somber face scared her. "You're too young to be thinking of getting married. You don't want to be a sixteen-year-old widow, Meggie. Besides, you don't know what kind of a man will come home. I might be maimed or crippled or just different, I don't know."

Megan Elizabeth swallowed, blinking back tears. "It doesn't matter. I'll wait for you and I'll love you until I die."

"And if I don't make it back to Crawford County, I'll remember you, Meggie, and wish you well. Not many men have a young girl as beautiful as you who loves them. I'm lucky, but I guess I've always been lucky in that way and most of the time I don't deserve it. But I can't turn down what's offered me. Too selfish, I suppose—or too scared that I might not have another chance."

"Hey, you two, look at the birdie!"

Megan Elizabeth turned and a flashbulb exploded in her face. "Mad Dog Treadwell, go away. . . ."

Miss Poole looked over her shoulder. "I forgot you took pictures that day at the river."

Mad Dog sat on the couch, his elbows resting on his thighs and his hands dangling between his knees. He looked up. "I wanted to be a photographer. I think that's why I didn't get those pictures out and burn them like I should have when old C.J. dug up the body. I just kept putting it off until today when I read in the paper about the sheriff getting shot. I knew Meenie and Raul would come after me, and I didn't want anything in the house to connect me to Albert."

He wiped his face on his sleeve before continuing. "It was like killing my kids to have to burn those pictures, and I finally went out and bought a six-pack. I thought I could do it a little easier if I was drunk. But I couldn't even get drunk 'cause I don't much like beer. Strong drink and oil-well fires don't mix, so I never developed a taste for it. When you rang the doorbell I didn't even hear it. I was sitting there just looking at those photographs, sort of lost in the past, when I heard you call. If it hadn't been your voice, if it had been Meenie's instead, I doubt I would have heard him at all, and I'd have been caught dead to rights."

Mad Dog dragged himself off the couch and shuffled over to Miss Poole like a man twice his age. He hunkered down beside her. "But I was thinking about you and me and Albert, so your voice jarred me out of my daze. I didn't have time to hide the pictures, so I dumped them in the chair and covered them up with the newspaper. I thought I could keep you out of here, but I forgot that every damn time we're within shouting distance of each other, we find something to fight about. You remember that summer before you went off to college—'47, I think it was—when I asked you to marry me? You remember what you said?"

Miss Poole remembered. "I was shocked, Mad Dog. I had no idea you had matrimony in mind when you stopped by after supper every night."

"Well, it sure as hell wasn't to visit with your daddy. He may have been a good man, but he lowered the temperature of every room he ever walked in. Anyhow, when I finally got you alone on your front porch without your daddy rid-

ing shotgun and popped the question, do you remember
what you said?"

"Of course I do. There's nothing wrong with my memory. I told you I was waiting for Albert, and how dare you
think I would throw him over for you."

Mad Dog pondered for a moment. "It doesn't sound so
bad now, not like I remembered it. I guess it wasn't so
much what you said as how you said it, like I was something you scraped off your shoe after walking through a
cattle chute."

"I could have been more tactful, but I wasn't expecting
a proposal. Besides, Albert was your friend, Mad Dog.
How could you betray him by going after his girl?"

"Albert Finnigan was no friend of mine. I hung around
him 'cause I needed some advice I figured he could give me,
and to make sure he kept his hands to himself around you.
But you were a damn fool to still be waiting for him two
years after the war ended. He wasn't coming back for you,
and I told you so. And so did he that day at the river—I
heard him—but he was damn mealymouthed about it."

"He didn't tell me any such of a thing!" exclaimed Miss
Poole.

" 'If I don't make it back to Crawford County, I'll remember you, and wish you well,' " mimicked Mad Dog.
"That's what he said, Megan Elizabeth, and that doesn't
sound to me like a man dead set on getting back home to
the woman he loves. Sounds more like a man trying to let
a girl down easy."

"That's not true! He meant that if he were killed in battle, he'd remember me as he died."

"Maybe you believed that when you were a kid, but
you're not a kid anymore, so how come you don't look at
him like a full-grown woman? Why don't you see him like
he was? A damn bee collecting as much pollen as he could.
He was leading you on like he was leading every woman
in town. Just look at the rest of those pictures if you don't
believe me."

Mad Dog rifled through the photographs, holding them

up one by one. "Look at this one with Victoria Dodd. He's holding her plastered to his side until you can't see daylight between them. And look at this picture, see how he's standing with his arm hanging over Rachel Smith's shoulder like he's getting ready to grab one of her assets? Don't you remember standing off to the side when I took these pictures? Don't you remember, Megan Elizabeth?"

Miss Poole took the two pictures and studied them. "These weren't taken that day, Mad Dog. See how Victoria and Rachel were huddled in their coats. It was a beautiful day at the river. The sun was shining and the wildflowers were in bud on the prairie."

Mad Dog grabbed her shoulders. "It was cold as hell, Megan Elizabeth. The wind was whipping across the prairie straight out of the north, and the Canadian had ice on it. Nobody wanted to go on a picnic but you, and you bullied Brother Lundy into sponsoring it because it was the only way you figured you could latch on to Albert without your daddy jerking you home. Wildflowers and sunshine, my hind end. The only wildflowers and sunshine that day were inside your head."

"You're mistaken, Mad Dog," said Miss Poole with as much dignity as she could muster. She wished her heart would stop pounding and the hollow feeling in her stomach would go away. Such physical symptoms distracted her from logical thinking.

He released her and sighed. "Look at that picture of you and Albert, Megan Elizabeth. You've got a coat on, and that patch of white stuff on the ground behind you is snow leftover from a blizzard the week before." She hesitated and he picked up the photograph and stuck it in her face. "Look at it, damn it!"

If she had not been a strong woman, Miss Poole thought she might have fainted when she reluctantly looked at the picture again. It was true, all of it. She *was* wearing a coat, and there *was* a patch of snow on the ground. She closed her eyes and cast her mind back nearly fifty years. She remembered it now—all of it—the bone-chilling cold, her nausea inspired by jealousy when she saw Albert hugging Victoria and Rachel while Mad Dog took pictures. How could she have failed to remember?

"Look at this group shot I took. Look at Albert standing there between Victoria and Rachel with his arms around both of them. And where are you?" Mad Dog pointed his finger at her unsmiling face. "Standing here at the end next to Edna Manning. Don't you think that Albert would have demanded you stand next to him if he really thought anything of you? You're damn lucky you didn't end up like Edna Manning, your belly swelled up and no husband because your GI boyfriend ran off. That girl was ruined. It's no wonder she took a dive out of a second-story window."

Miss Poole blinked back more tears as she gazed at the picture. It showed everything Mad Dog claimed it did. But that was only one picture. Mad Dog wasn't there with a camera the night before Albert left Crawford County.

"But he came back for me, didn't he?" demanded Miss Poole.

"He came back for somebody, I guess. I don't know if it was for you. I think he came back to pick up where he left off, but the war was over and nobody was the same—except you. Everybody but you wanted to get on with their lives and didn't want any reminders of what they'd done on the homefront. There wasn't any homefront anymore—just home, period, and Crawford County wasn't home to Albert Finnigan."

"Is that why you killed him, Mad Dog, because you didn't want him picking up with me where he left off?"

"If I'd killed him, I'd have made damn sure his body was found the next day so you would know he was dead. Wouldn't make any sense to kill him otherwise."

Miss Poole scooted backward, picked up the poker she had laid down, and got to her feet. Mad Dog's answer was logical—if he was telling the truth. But until he explained the evidence, she was safer with her feet on the floor and the poker in her hand. "What about the hat, Mad Dog? If you didn't murder Albert, where did you get his hat?"

Mad Dog looked exasperated. "Would you put that god-damn poker down. If I didn't strangle you years ago when you were acting so pigheaded and nasty about turning down my proposal, I ain't going to do it now."

Miss Poole took a firmer grip on the poker. "I didn't catch you with evidence of a murder years ago either, Mad Dog. I'll keep the poker handy until you answer my question. And don't curse."

Mad Dog's face turned red, and she could hear him grinding his teeth. "I found the g——damn hat!"

"Where? On Albert's head after you bludgeoned him?"

Mad Dog took a step toward her before he caught himself and stood clenching his fists. In Miss Poole's experience, men always did that when they were angry. "Would you stop jumping me before I finish what I'm saying? You've got a terrible habit of doing that, Megan Elizabeth, and one of these days you're going to do it to a man who's not as good-natured as I am, and he'll belt you in the mouth. Now, will you let me finish?"

Miss Poole swallowed. It was possible that she finished men's sentences for them, but men ought to learn to speak up. "Please continue."

Mad Dog wiped his face on his sleeve again. The room was hot as Hades, and Miss Poole felt perspiration on her own forehead. "It was in 1946, early June—I don't remember the exact date—and I came home from a river bottom party down on the Canadian. We lived in the dinky apartment above the sheriff's office then if you remember—"

"I remember," said Miss Poole. "There's nothing wrong with my memory."

Mad Dog cocked his eyebrow. "Yeah—unless you want there to be, like when you're remembering Albert. Anyhow, I came home along about one o'clock in the morning and let myself into the courthouse. I remember I took the stairs because the elevator shaft ran right next to my folks' bedroom and I didn't want my dad waking up and catching me coming in so late. We weren't on real good terms because I told him I wasn't going back to Texas A&M in the fall, and he was mad as hell about it. He couldn't understand why I wanted to go to work fighting oil-well fires instead of being a newspaper photographer like I'd planned."

"Why did you change your mind, Mad Dog?" asked Miss Poole. She'd been curious about his abrupt career change for years and thought that as long as she had him on the defensive, she might as well ask.

Mad Dog shrugged and looked down at the photographs on the chair. "Seemed like the thing to do at the time. Photography was a sissy kind of a job—or I thought it was—and I didn't want Crawford County calling me a coward. But that doesn't have anything to do with the hat. It's just explanation as to why I took the stairs. I found the hat on the second-floor landing and picked it up. It had Albert Finnigan's name stenciled inside, and I thought the bastard had come back. I don't mind telling you that scared the hell out of me, and the next morning I asked my dad if anybody had come looking for me the night before. He said no. I dropped in at the billiard parlor—that was before it closed down—and asked if anybody had been in looking for me, but nobody had. I couldn't figure where Albert had gone, so I went over to your house that night. Do you remember? I asked you if you'd heard from Albert yet?"

Miss Poole licked her lips. "Yes, I think I do remember. You were white as a sheet and stumbling over your words."

"You never did answer me 'cause your daddy did it for you. He said, 'No, and she won't either.' I figured he must have caught Albert before he got to you and chased him off." Mad Dog stopped abruptly and stared at her, his mouth hanging open. "He killed Albert, didn't he, Megan Elizabeth? That's why you're over here trying every which way to trap me. You don't want it to be your daddy, so you're looking to hang it on somebody else. All these years that I've had a soft spot for you, and all the time you think so damn little of me that you'd rather see me in jail than admit your father had a screw loose where his little girl was concerned. Well, you've finally done it. You've finally killed off any feeling I had for you, so you can get out of my house."

He stalked toward her, and she brandished the poker. "Stay away from me, Mad Dog!"

He grabbed the end of the poker and jerked it out of her hands. "Don't shake that thing in my face, *Miss* Poole. I said get out and I meant it." He seized her around the waist and heaved her over his shoulder and started toward the door.

She held on to her hat with one hand and pounded on his back with her other. "Let me go, Mad Dog! You're assaulting a peace officer!"

He tramped down the hall, and she heard him open the front door. She felt herself lifted and the next thing she knew she was standing on Mad Dog's front porch. Her hat was covering one eye, her blouse was coming untucked from her skirt, and the front of her beige coat was covered with grime from Mad Dog's dirty shirt. She was rumpled, filthy, and humiliated.

Mad Dog towered over her, his hands on his hips. "I didn't let you bully me when we were young, and I ain't about to start now."

Miss Poole felt her eyes sting and blinked. She'd cried more this afternoon than she had since she was twenty years old, and enough was enough. She had to keep her mind on her business.

"I would never send an innocent man to jail just to protect my father, and I don't appreciate your thinking I would."

"My God, we just can't keep from fighting, can we?"

"Oh, hush up while I'm talking, Mad Dog! My father didn't shoot the sheriff—somebody else did—and it's his attempted murder I'm investigating! Do you have an alibi or not?"

"Hell, I told you I didn't!" exclaimed Mad Dog. "But I wouldn't shoot a man in the back! I'm not that big a coward."

Miss Poole wondered why a man who risked his life fighting oil-well fires could think anyone in their right mind would assume he was a coward. Mad Dog's courage—or foolhardiness, depending on your point of view—was the best reason to believe he wasn't guilty. But that wasn't evidence.

"What about your guns, Mad Dog? I'll have to take your handguns to have a ballistics check done on each one."

"Handguns? I don't have any handguns. All I've got are rifles and a shotgun. Anything I shoot, I'm going to eat, and a handgun ain't real good for hunting."

"Then let me search your property," began Miss Poole.

"Oh, no, *Miss* Poole. I've had all of you I can take. I'll ride with you to the sheriff's department right now without going back in the house, so you'll know I'm not hiding anything, and Meenie and Raul can come out and search."

"But what about the hat and the photographs, Mad Dog? Meenie will arrest you when he finds them," said Miss Poole.

"You weren't worried about my hide a few minutes ago, so why are you worried now?"

Miss Poole felt a nervous quiver in her stomach as she thought about her answer. Why was she worried? After all, Mad Dog could be lying. "I don't believe you're guilty because I think you would be a more efficient arsonist."

"Now I'm an arsonist! Anything else you want to accuse me of? How about rape and child molestation?"

"Certainly not!"

Mad Dog raked his fingers through his hair, and Miss Poole noticed it was as thick as it had been in his youth. She thought he still had his own teeth, too. He was altogether a fine looking man for his age, which wasn't unexpected since he had been a handsome young man. Not refined or scintillating or charming or romantic as Albert, of course, but nobody was.

"I guess I'll have to be satisfied that you admit I'm not a dirty old man," said Mad Dog, taking her arm. "I'm ready to go if you are, but you better straighten your hat or let me drive. You can't see out of but one eye. By the way, it's a nice-looking hat. Did you bag the pheasant?"

CHAPTER
20

THE MUMMY IN THE BASEMENT
IS IDENTIFIED

Deputy Megan Elizabeth Poole, spokesperson for the Crawford County Sheriff's Department, announced that the mummy unearthed in the courthouse basement has been identified as Sergeant Albert Finnigan, formerly of Dallas. Wounded in the Battle of the Bulge, Sergeant Finnigan spent his convalescence in Crawford County from February to April 1945. While living here the sergeant spoke to civic groups, appeared at war bond rallies, and led several scrap-metal drives, according to Deputy Poole. Below is a photograph of Sergeant Finnigan speaking to a group of seniors at Carroll High School. Anyone who remembers the sergeant is asked to contact the sheriff's department. Deputy Poole did not elaborate on how identification was made. "We have an informed source whose word has been verified by other persons. We will not be releasing any names at present."

Asked if the informed source was a suspect, Deputy Poole would only affirm that the officers were pursuing several leads and would be questioning a number of residents who had known Sergeant Finnigan. At this point in the press conference a heated argument conducted in whispers broke out between Deputy Poole and Chief Deputy Meenie Higgins, but your correspondent is unable to report the cause as Deputy Poole turned off the microphone loaned by our local radio station KCCT. The

Crawford County Examiner wishes to protest the abrupt end to the press conference and to remind the sheriff's department of the public's concern about this investigation.

Crawford County Examiner
January 9

From the private journal of Megan Elizabeth Poole:

January 9

Meenie did not arrest Mad Dog, but it was a near thing. Although the search of his house and other property, which lasted until the early hours of this morning, turned up nothing in the way of evidence except the photographs and hat, Meenie remains convinced that Mad Dog knows more than he is telling. Even my logical arguments in Mad Dog's favor failed to persuade the chief deputy. I finally had to call upon the sheriff to mediate.

"If Mohammed can't go to the mountain, then Miss Poole will bring the mountain to Mohammed," remarked Charles, relaxing in the recliner in his hospital room and facing Mad Dog Treadwell who shrugged and grinned.

"I don't know about that Mohammed fellow, but if he's shot up as bad as you, he don't need to be bothering about no mountain either," interrupted Meenie. "I told Miss Poole you ought to be left alone to heal up instead of messing around with business." He glared at the dispatcher who sat in a hard plastic chair beside Mad Dog.

Charles was a little tired of everybody from his chief deputy to his wife telling him he was an invalid. He still hurt—God only knew when he would stop hurting—but his mind was clear, his throat better, his voice stronger, and his patience thinner.

"I feel fine! I had a good night's sleep, Dr. Wallace removed all the needles and tubes from my various veins and orifices, and best yet, I confiscated J.T.'s forty-five the minute he walked into my room this morning. I feel wonderful, terrific, great. I certainly feel up to taking command of the investigation into my own attempted murder—at least by proxy."

And not a moment too soon in Charles's opinion—particularly after he read of this morning's aborted news conference. Meenie and Raul were good ground troops—none better in his opinion—but ground troops needed a general. As for Miss Poole, she was either a guerilla fighter against the opposing force, or a loose cannon within her own ranks—probably both.

Charles rifled through the photographs taken from Mad Dog's house, then touched Albert Finnigan's hat, noticing it smelled like moldy wool. Finally he glanced through Mad Dog's two statements: one written by Miss Poole that included her conversation with the old man, and one taken by Meenie after the search.

Charles looked up at Mad Dog Treadwell. "You've read both these statements and agree they are an accurate record of what you told Miss Poole and Meenie?"

Slouching down in the molded plastic chair the hospital provided for visitors, Mad Dog stretched out his legs and crossed his ankles. "Wouldn't have signed my John Henry on them if they weren't—although I don't know why Megan Elizabeth had to write down all that personal stuff. It's water under the bridge and ain't any of your business anyhow."

"That personal stuff, as you call it, tells me that you probably didn't kill Albert Finnigan."

Mad Dog looked triumphant. "Said all along I didn't."

"If you were serious about supplanting Albert Finnigan in Miss Poole's affections—"

"Damn right I was serious," interrupted Mad Dog.

"—then you were truthful when you said you would have wanted the body found."

"Damn right I was truthful," said Mad Dog, nodding his head.

Charles shifted forward in the recliner, wincing as the movement sent pain spiraling through his chest. "However, your statement also tells me that you could have shot me."

Mad Dog jerked upright in his chair. "Where the hell did you get that idea?"

"You were going to burn the photographs and the hat because, and I quote: 'I didn't want anything in the house to connect me to Albert.' Also, further on in your conversation with Miss Poole, you said that when you found the hat it scared the hell out of you. You immediately started asking around town if anyone had been looking for you. Miss Poole states that you were white and trembling when you arrived at her home to inquire about Finnigan."

There was a wariness in Mad Dog's eyes that didn't match the grin on his face. "Yeah, well, I suppose I was. I didn't want that bastard showing up and throwing a monkey wrench in my courtship."

Charles inclined his head. "You were afraid 'he would pick up where he left off' I believe is the way you put it."

Mad Dog rubbed his palms on his jeans, and Charles noticed his hands left moist streaks on the denim. "Yeah, that's right, and I didn't want him marrying Megan Elizabeth."

"But you didn't really believe he would, did you, Mad Dog? Didn't you tell Miss Poole that Finnigan was interested in Crawford County women, period, not a particular woman? Didn't you tell her that you believed Finnigan was trying to let her down easy?"

Mad Dog swallowed. "Yeah, but he might have changed his mind."

"I'll give you the benefit of a doubt, Mad Dog. Your romantic rivalry with Finnigan might have been in the back of your mind, but it wasn't the real reason you were scared of him in 1946. Otherwise, you wouldn't still be scared nearly fifty years later, so scared that you lied about his identity, so scared that you were planning to burn photographs that are really innocuous as far as you're concerned. You're not even in those pictures! But Finnigan is, and you don't want anyone reminded that you knew him. Why not, Mad Dog? What kind of a hold did Albert Finnigan have on you? What did he know about you that you're afraid I'll find out?"

More than Mad Dog's hands were sweating. His forehead was wet, and Charles could smell the other man's acrid perspiration and see the wet circles forming on the underarms of his flannel shirt. "Finnigan didn't have any *hold* over me, Sheriff," Mad Dog blustered. "I just didn't want to have to talk about the son of a bitch. I didn't like him when he was alive and I don't like him any better dead."

Charles nodded. "You told Miss Poole he wasn't a friend of yours."

"That's right! I didn't trust him as far as I could throw him."

Charles leaned forward in his chair. "Then why were you interested in his advice, Mad Dog?"

The other man turned white. "What?"

"You told Miss Poole that you needed some advice you thought Albert Finnigan could give you. What did Albert Finnigan advise you to do, and why do you think Crawford County will still care after nearly fifty years that you took that advice? What are you ashamed of, Mad Dog?"

Mad Dog Treadwell couldn't have been more still if he had turned to stone. Charles almost wished he had. Stone didn't hurt the way he knew Mad Dog was hurting. The pain was there in the other man's face, in his eyes.

But Mad Dog Treadwell could fight pain as well as Charles. He straightened his shoulders and drew a deep breath. "I ain't got anything more to say except that I didn't shoot you in the back. You want to arrest me, go ahead, but you want to ask any more questions, you talk to my lawyer."

Charles folded the statements and placed them, the photos, and Finnigan's hat in a folder and dropped it beside his chair. "Go home, Mad Dog." He heard Meenie's cry of protest and motioned to the deputy to keep quiet. "I can't arrest you because I can't prove means and opportunity. Meenie and Raul didn't find the gun on your property and no one saw you at the newspaper office. I can't even prove motive. I know you've got one, but I don't know what it is. I'll find out, though—now. I was telling you the truth before when I said I wasn't going to arrest anyone for Finnigan's murder. All I wanted was a name. But that has all changed."

He put his hand over the bandage on his chest. "I don't like being shot, Mad Dog. It makes me angry. I want to know who did it, and I'll dig up dirt from here to China on you and Rachel Smith and Victoria Dodd until I know everything there is to know about Albert Finnigan and the three of you. All of you should have told me the truth in the beginning. The last thing you should have done is wake this sleeping dog with a damn bullet!"

Mad Dog stood up, his eyes unfocused—like a man looking back over his past and picking out all the things he wished he could change.

"Talk to me, Mad Dog," urged Charles. "Tell me about you and Albert Finnigan. Give me a reason to eliminate you as a possible suspect."

Mad Dog blinked and his mouth tightened as he caught Charles's look. "I reckon I'll have to play the hand I dealt myself, Sheriff, and I ain't showing my cards until you call. Could be I'll win, then I won't have to show my hand at all."

"Don't gamble on it, Mad Dog."

"My life's been a gamble since I found Albert Finnigan's hat," he said as he turned and walked to the door. He opened it, then hesitated and glanced back. "Megan Elizabeth, you were right to turn me down—but you did it for the wrong reason."

Charles watched the door swing shut behind Mad Dog, then saw Miss Poole get up. "Don't follow him. He won't tell you any more than he already has."

Her eyes held something of the same unfocused expression as Charles had seen in Mad Dog's eyes, as though she, too, was looking back. Finally she blinked and cleared her throat. "I don't know how you can be sure of that. I was successful the last time I talked to Mad Dog, although I'll admit that I failed to correctly interpret what he said. Your analysis was brilliant, Sheriff."

"You caught him by surprise and so did I, but that won't happen again. Mad Dog isn't a stupid man and he won't allow himself to be bluffed, and that's what you'd be doing if you questioned him again." He looked at her sharply. "Unless you know what he's hiding, Miss Poole."

Miss Poole shook her head. "I have no idea. Mad Dog has always been eccentric, of course, beginning with his chewing soap to avoid an algebra test his senior year."

"If eccentricity were illegal or immoral, half of Crawford County would be in jail. Either no one knows what Mad Dog did, which I find hard to believe given the efficiency of the doughnut shop as a conveyor of gossip, or everyone knows but misinterprets whatever it was. I'm betting on the latter. As long as nobody took a second look at his eccentric behavior on the homefront, Mad Dog was safe. In fact, I'll bet he exaggerates his eccentricity and has done so since the soap-eating episode, so that any oddity or contradiction is overshadowed by his outrageous behavior. It's a case of Poe's purloined letter."

Charles eased forward out of his chair until he finally stood up on legs that felt like limp spaghetti. He supposed he was a fool for making the gesture, but a commanding general, even one with a hole in his chest, needed to project an image of strength, particularly when his army had soldiers like Miss Poole in its ranks. He just hoped he had enough stamina left to hand out marching orders to his troops before he collapsed.

"There's a record somewhere of whatever Mad Dog did that he's ashamed of, or he wouldn't be afraid of my questions. He's betting I won't find it, and I'm betting that I will. But I can't call with the hand I have now and he knows it. I need an ace, and Meenie, I want you and Raul to shuffle the deck until you deal me one."

"We already shuffled the only deck we got when we searched Mad Dog's property, Sheriff," said Meenie, his face still bearing fading bruises from his fight with the police chief. "Me and Raul did everything but tear up the floors looking for evidence. We didn't find nothing but that hat and them pictures. No gun, no traces of ashes he might have tracked in from setting the newspapers on fire, and sure as the dickens nothing you could call an ace."

Raul spoke for the first time. "Meenie and I questioned the neighbors that live around the newspaper office, Sheriff—at Miss Poole's suggestion. No one saw or heard anything."

Slanting a look toward the dispatcher, Charles tightened his lips to prevent a smile. He had wondered why Meenie allowed Miss Poole to interview Mad Dog by herself. The answer was he didn't. Miss Poole conned Meenie and Raul into knocking on doors in a futile search for possible witnesses while she questioned a probable suspect without interference. The retired schoolteacher certainly didn't suffer from a lack of confidence.

She did, however, suffer a lack of common sense.

Charles felt his legs begin to quiver and surreptitiously shuffled the few steps to the window, scooted the vases of flowers and the potted plants that lined its wide sill out of the way, and sat down. "Miss Poole, do not, I repeat, do not question another of our suspects without letting Meenie know where you are. If I was the target before, you're the target now. Since you identified Albert Finnigan, you're a bigger threat to the killer than I would be in a hundred years. You know too damn much about every person in this county."

"She ain't gonna be questioning any more suspects," said Meenie, hitching up his pants and glaring at Miss Poole. "She's the dispatcher and she ought to be dispatching. She ain't got no experience at interrogation. She was just lucky with Mad Dog."

Miss Poole drew herself up and glared back. "Luck had

nothing to do with it, Deputy Higgins! In my forty years of teaching sixth graders I have interrogated—"

"That's enough!" shouted Charles, or at least he tried to shout, but all he succeeded in producing was a hoarse croak followed by a coughing spasm.

"Shut up!" shouted Raul as he held a glass of water against Charles's lips. "This is no place to fight, Meenie."

Meenie and Miss Poole looked horrified—better yet, they looked guilty. A little guilt was a terrific behavior modifier, or at least Charles hoped so. He nodded his thanks at Raul, a little amazed that the reserved deputy would actually shout. He didn't ever recall hearing Raul raising his voice before.

"Meenie, you and Raul look through the newspapers for 1945 and 1946. Copy every article about Mad Dog Treadwell, I don't care if it's on the sports page or the society page. Whatever he did that he's so ashamed of happened in one of those two years. Then check the public records—real estate transactions, arrest records, draft records, whatever. And Meenie, make photocopies of the birth and marriage announcements in the newspaper along with the obituary sections. He—or one of our other suspects— had a reason to steal those records from the courthouse. I want to know what it was."

"Sheriff, the fire burned up the old newspapers," said Meenie, looking worried. "We told you that, don't you remember?"

Charles frowned. "I wasn't shot in the head, Meenie. There's nothing wrong with my memory. The library and the county museum have the paper on microfilm. Divide up the issues between you and get with it. I expect those photocopies by tonight." He shifted his eyes to his dispatcher. "Miss Poole, interview Rachel Smith and Mrs. Dodd—"

"Just hold your horses, Sheriff," interrupted Meenie. "You already said it wasn't safe for her to be running around asking questions, and I sure don't think it's a good idea. There's a difference between questioning a kid and a tough old lady like Miss Smith. Besides, I don't think no old lady is going to be sneaking around shooting anybody."

"That's why Miss Poole will do the questioning, Meenie. She doesn't have your exalted opinion of her own sex."

"I certainly don't," snapped Miss Poole. "And I don't appreciate your remark, Meenie. Women are just as murderous as men. We just haven't had your opportunities until lately."

Charles pinched the bridge of his nose as he listened to them argue. His chest was on fire, his head was pounding, and his belly hurt like he'd swallowed knives. He felt like he'd been rode hard and put away wet—to borrow a Crawford County expression.

"Quiet!" he ordered. "Meenie, you and Raul hit those records. Miss Poole, badger those women, argue with them, gossip, whatever you have to do, but make them talk! And take Finnigan's hat. Surprise them with it and see who breaks. If Mad Dog is telling the truth, then one of them has been worrying about what happened to that hat for fifty years. Find my ace for me, Miss Poole, and whatever you do, be careful. You might not find a poker so close at hand again."

CHAPTER

21

END OF AN ERA
JUDGE POOLE IS DEAD

CARROLL, TEXAS—Judge Daniel Edward Poole died in his sleep at home this past Friday and with him died an era. Born in Fort Worth, Texas, on January 26, 1885, Judge Poole moved to Crawford County where his father established Carroll National Bank in 1903. Young Daniel worked as a teller during the day and read law at night until he was admitted to the bar in 1910 and went into politics. Judge Poole was the first representative from Crawford County to the Texas legislature where he cast the deciding vote in favor of ratifying the Eighteenth Amendment, making Prohibition the law of the land. He lost the next election in a hard-fought campaign in which the *Crawford County Examiner*'s founder, Ben Colchester, endorsed his opponent. Undaunted by his defeat Judge Poole continued his dedicated service to Crawford County. He was instrumental in establishing the first library, supported bond issues for two new schools, Carroll Memorial Hospital, and the present county courthouse. In 1922 he married Elizabeth Green and settled down to domesticity, but the political bug bit him again in 1930. He ran for county judge and was elected, an office he held until his death.

Judge Poole managed the financial and civil affairs of Crawford County in a fair and responsible manner for thirty years. He steered our tiny ship of state through the flood waters of the Depression, World War II, the Korean conflict, and the peaceful days of the last decade. He was the epitome of propriety, integrity, responsibility, honesty, and duty with never a hint of scandal in his administration. Crawford County will never see his like again.

Judge Poole is survived by his daughter, Megan Elizabeth Poole.

Crawford County Examiner
February 24, 1960

From the private journal of Megan Elizabeth Poole:

January 9 [second entry]

Did I ever really know him? Do children ever really know their parents? Would we forgive them if we did?

I underestimated Rachel Smith. I had forgotten her ability to dissimulate and distract.

Miss Poole shifted the strap of her purse farther up her arm. She hadn't realized just how much a Colt forty-five weighed when she borrowed J.T. Brentwood's gun from the sheriff. Actually, borrowed wasn't the right word; liberated was a better choice. That was the word commonly used by GIs for obtaining hard to find, but very necessary goods, during World War II, and this whole case was set during the war, so she might as well use the proper language. In one sense, liberating the forty-five from behind the potted plant on the sheriff's windowsill was a matter of cutting through red tape. There was no point in engaging in an unnecessary argument. Imagine what Meenie would have to say if he knew she was 'packing heat,' but then the chief deputy's ideas of appropriate behavior for a woman were at least forty years out of date. Besides, it wasn't as if she were committing an illegal act. She was a certified peace officer and entitled to carry a gun while on duty. She had just never done it up to now, but then she had never investigated a murder before, never questioned a dangerous suspect before. And of the three suspects, Rachel Smith was the most dangerous.

In Miss Poole's opinion.

Rachel Smith was also the oldest, but that meant nothing. There was no correlation between age and harmlessness.

In Miss Poole's opinion.

She took a firm grip on her purse and rang the doorbell.

Rachel Smith opened the door and smiled when she recognized her caller. "Miss Megan Elizabeth Poole! Come in! How nice you stopped by. I just made a German chocolate cake and was wishing I had someone to share it with. Chocolate in any form just cries out to be shared, don't you think?"

Miss Poole gave the other woman a sharp look as she squeezed past her into an untidy living room. "Don't try to butter me up, Rachel Smith. I don't make a habit of dropping by uninvited, and you didn't just make a German chocolate cake. You're the worst cook in Crawford County, and any cake you baked would be inedible."

Rachel Smith shrugged her shoulders. "All right, it's frozen, but it's the calories that count. I do love sweets and fortunately I've never had to worry about my weight. Some of us are lucky in our metabolism."

"And some of us eat a sensible diet and exercise regularly," said Miss Poole in a tart voice. "I've always found discipline more dependable than luck."

Rachel Smith smiled, the deep dimple in her right cheek lending her a pixie's charm that Miss Poole remembered from one long-ago day—the last day—when she and Albert sat in the library on the second floor of the courthouse. For one awful moment Miss Poole felt herself back in that room, sitting in one of the hard oak chairs that always left her bottom feeling numb and whispering to Albert of her plans for them, always with one eye on the big round clock on the wall behind Rachel's desk, watching the minutes tick away until five o'clock came and she heard her father's footsteps. . . .

* * *

"Megan Elizabeth, it is time to go home," said Judge Poole, pausing in the doorway.

He always said the same thing in that deep, slow voice, and she always gathered her books and followed him downstairs and out the front door of the courthouse to the black Cadillac, one of the last ones made before Detroit converted to building armaments for the war, and her father would drive home to the big, two-story house with the wide veranda on three sides. They would cook dinner and, if it were Friday, she would mix a pitcher of cold lemonade using some of their sugar ration. They talked, but they never visited.

Today she would defy him.

"Papa, I've invited Albert home for supper." She hadn't but Albert wouldn't embarrass her by denying it, and she must act to change her father's mind before it was too late. If he spent more time with Albert, he would see there was no rational basis for disliking him.

Judge Poole turned disapproving eyes on Albert. "I'm certain Sergeant Finnigan would rather enjoy the companionship of those his own age than spend an evening with an old man and a very young girl."

"Good heavens, Judge Poole, you're not an old man." Rachel Smith's dimple flashed as she smiled at him.

Judge Poole removed his Stetson, revealing his thick gray hair. "Good afternoon, Rachel. I trust you've had a pleasant day and that my young minx has behaved herself."

"I'm *not* a minx," interrupted Megan Elizabeth. "And I'm not a very young girl either. I'm sixteen! That's old enough to invite a boy home for dinner."

"But Sergeant Finnigan isn't a boy, Megan Elizabeth, he's a man and much older than you," said Rachel, getting up and walking around her desk to lean against its edge. The pose showed off her long legs to their best advantage in the short skirt she wore. Everyone wore their skirts short to save material for the war effort, but Rachel Smith's were just a fraction shorter than most. There had been complaints about it, Megan Elizabeth knew, but her father, who was also president of the library board, dismissed them as the mutterings of jealous, prudish women. He was not so liberal with his daughter. Her own skirts were hemmed a modest two inches below the knee.

She hated the length, but she hated more her father's double standard. What was appropriate and proper for everybody else in music, in dress, in language, in behavior was somehow inappropriate and improper for her, and no one epitomized that double standard like Rachel Smith. She wore her skirts way above the knee, she danced the boogie-woogie, she used slang, and Megan Elizabeth even heard that she smoked Lucky Strikes in public.

Her father ignored it all.

It wasn't fair.

"My dinner guests are none of your business, Miss Smith," said Megan Elizabeth, beyond caring if she was rude. She refused to stay silent another minute while Rachel Smith preened and showed off her legs and flashed her dimple at Papa and Albert and criticized her.

"Megan Elizabeth, you will apologize to Rachel!" ordered her father.

Rachel Smith tossed her mane of unruly red curls and smiled. "Never mind, Judge Poole. Megan Elizabeth is old enough to show her claws. It's part of growing up."

Rachel Smith defending her? She would rather be forced to apologize.

She felt Albert take her hand and lead her toward the door. "Thanks for inviting me, Meggie, but your dad doesn't sound like he's in the mood to entertain tonight. Besides, I promised Rachel—Miss Smith—I'd help her shift some books, then walk her to choir practice." He squeezed her hand just before he let her go and muttered something under his breath she barely heard. "I'm sorry, Meggie."

The last thing Megan Elizabeth Poole remembered about that day was Rachel Smith smiling at Albert Finnigan—that and her father's angry look.

She didn't eat any dinner that night and neither did her father. . . .

"Megan Elizabeth, is something wrong?"

Miss Poole blinked, then felt her face grow hot with embarrassment, then anger. Daydreaming on duty was as inexcusable as drinking. Whatever had happened to her self-discipline?

"I'm quite all right."

Rachel shook her head. "You don't look all right. Your eyes were glazed, and your face turned red. Do you have high blood pressure like your father did?"

"No!"

"It wouldn't surprise me if you did. The tendency is inherited after all." She pursed her lips thoughtfully. "Although I always thought your father's condition was more due to suppressing his passions all those years after your mother died than to any clinical reason. I told him so, too, more than once, but it always embarrassed him. I often wondered how he managed to raise a daughter when he was so uncomfortable discussing sex. How did he tell you about the birds and the bees?"

Miss Poole was speechless for the first time in her life.

Rachel sighed. "I suppose it's none of my business."

"How did you know my father suffered from hypertension? He never discussed his health," said Miss Poole when she found her voice, then immediately wished she hadn't if all she could think to ask was a question about her father. It only encouraged Rachel Smith.

"We were good friends. His office was next to the library until we moved in the new building, and we often drank coffee together. We weren't at all alike, but we complemented one another. Sometimes that's better than having too much in common. To my mind two people who think and act exactly the same way only double their own worst traits. But at any rate, I knew a great deal about your father, and he, of course, knew a great deal about me. I was grief-stricken when he died. I went to his funeral. Do you remember?"

Miss Poole nodded. "You wore a black suit and a hat with a long veil. Very tasteful, but very dramatic for someone who wasn't a close relative."

"Now you sound like your father. Nicely judgmental. You two prove what I said before. You were so much alike you brought out the worst in one another."

"I'm not here to talk about my father," said Miss Poole, feeling foolish for thinking a revolver was a defense against Rachel Smith. The woman didn't need a weapon to draw blood.

"No, I suppose not, but I've waited more than thirty years to tell you how fond I was of him and how much I've missed him since he died, so don't blame me for taking the opportunity when it presented itself. Now, I imagine you're ready to grill me, but do you mind sitting down while you do it? I'm an old woman, and my feet hurt." She laughed and the dimple looked more like a wound than an attractive feature. "I never thought I'd ever grow old. I always felt so young and beautiful when I was around your father. I was forty-seven when he died and I looked in the mirror and saw an aging woman I didn't recognize because I'd always seen myself through his eyes and he always saw me as I was during the war."

It was such an outrageous statement that Miss Poole challenged it despite suspecting that was Rachel Smith's intent. "And I don't recognize this man you're describing. My father did not have a romantic nature and would never have paid you flowery compliments, and if you were such good friends, I would have known about it. The whole town would have known. If you must make up fantasies, use someone else as your hero besides my father. It's disrespectful of the dead."

Rachel swept a pile of magazines off a worn velvet couch and sat down. "Now you're making me angry. I've done many things in my life that I'm ashamed of, but I would never lie about Judge Poole. You also know that your father was the one man in all of Crawford County that no one ever gossiped about—not since he and Ben Colchester fought to a draw over the *Examiner*'s endorsement of the judge's opponent in 1918. I was just a child, but I remember seeing the fight. Everyone walked easy around your father after that, even Ben Colchester, and he never backed down in front of anyone. You ought to be grateful. Anyone else's daughter who made such a fool of herself as you did over Albert Finnigan would have been the target of every old biddy with a malicious tongue in her head. But not you. Your father wrapped you in his cloak of respectability, and nobody expressed an opinion out loud. I sheltered under that cloak a time or two myself and I was grateful for that protection!"

Miss Poole felt a tiny glow of triumph. Finally Rachel had mentioned Albert's name, and judging by her chagrined expression, she wished she hadn't. Now Miss Poole could go on the offensive and choose the killing ground in this interrogation. She reached in her purse and, withdrawing her first weapon, laid it in Rachel Smith's lap.

"You failed to bury Albert's hat along with his body after you murdered him, Rachel."

Rachel shuddered in revulsion and brushed the hat off her lap, then wiped her hand on her blouse and looked up. "I didn't murder him, you ninny! I couldn't stand to be close to him. I certainly wouldn't have touched him long enough to drag his body to the basement and bury it."

Tilting her head, Miss Poole smiled—and pounced. "Is that so? Then why does the sheriff have several photographs of you not only standing close to Albert, but being embraced by him and enjoying every minute of it?"

And waited.

Rachel sat motionless, her eyes wary. "I participated in the war bond rallies with Albert. It's possible that we posed in some friendly manner for the newspaper photographer. I supported the war effort however I could—even if it meant enduring Albert's pawing."

"You weren't selling war bonds on the picnic down on

the Canadian. Do you remember the picnic, Rachel? Do you remember Mad Dog Treadwell and his camera?"

The old woman closed her eyes for a moment but not before Miss Poole saw a flicker of fear. Rachel drew a deep breath—to steady her nerves, Miss Poole supposed—and opened her eyes. The fear was gone and in its place was defiance. Rachel Smith might be cornered, but she wasn't ready to give up the fight.

"You sound like a jealous woman, Megan Elizabeth. I'm sure you misinterpreted the photographs."

"Did I misinterpret your asking Albert to stay late at the library? Did I misinterpret his walking you to choir practice? How many times did you two stay late at the library, Rachel? How many times did you entice my fiancé?"

"All right! Albert fooled me just like he fooled you! I was his unofficial date to the scrap-metal drives and the bond rallies and that silly carnival we had to honor his heroic service, but that was before I found out what a weasel he was. Your father tried to tell me, but I didn't listen to him anymore than you did. I had to learn the hard way!"

"And what way was that, Rachel? When you arranged to meet in the library after hours in June of 1946, and he told you he'd come home to marry me? Is that why you murdered him?"

Rachel relaxed against the couch, but the wary expression was back in her eyes. "You're repeating yourself, Megan Elizabeth. I already told you I didn't kill Albert. And, my dear, he was not a marrying man as my mother used to say. Whatever reason Albert had for coming back to Crawford County, it wasn't to marry you."

"The library was on the second floor, and his hat was found on the second-floor landing."

"The second floor!" Rachel Smith leaned forward, her hands on her knees, and stared intently at Miss Poole. "Who found it, Megan Elizabeth?"

"Let's just say it's recently been turned over to the sheriff."

"Mad Dog Treadwell! That's where you got the hat and

the photos. Imagine his keeping that hat all these years. No wonder he was nervous when Albert's body was found."

"Why were you nervous, Rachel? In fact, how did you know it was Albert?"

"Oh, for goodness' sake, Megan Elizabeth, don't insult my intelligence. An army sergeant from WWII around twenty-eight years old? Who else could it have been? No native son of Crawford County that age and rank was unaccounted for. Like a bad penny Albert Finnigan turned up, and someone buried him like garbage only not deep enough."

"You only answered one question, Rachel. Why were you so nervous?"

Rachel threw up her hands, then let them fall onto her lap. "Because of having to answer questions—and I knew I would eventually. Somebody would break and give Albert's name to the sheriff. Then the questions would start, and I didn't want to talk about him. I didn't think Mad Dog Treadwell would be the one to break, though. I thought Victoria Dodd would. She was always such a goody two-shoes and weak sister. And her wearing mourning clothes for Albert Finnigan. It makes me sick!"

Rachel stopped abruptly and her eyes narrowed. Miss Poole braced herself for the question she knew was coming. "Why are you talking to me, Megan Elizabeth? Why aren't you questioning Victoria Dodd? She *knew* it was Albert."

"I'll question Victoria, of course," began Miss Poole.

"Why didn't you talk to her first?"

It was a good question, an excellent one, in fact, and she wished she had an answer. Except the real one, of course, that she wasn't ready to hear that Victoria Dodd saw her father murder Albert Finnigan. Then she remembered that she did have an answer, and it was even the truth.

"Because I don't believe she shot the sheriff."

Rachel Smith looked thoughtful. "Of course. I had forgotten about the sheriff. Oh, not really, but I was worrying more about Albert. That was very cold of me and I'm sorry, but one does tend to be self-centered in situations like this.

It happens that I agree with you, though. I can't see Victoria even picking up a gun. Might get her hands dirty. That leaves Mad Dog and me, and I heard at the grocery store this morning that you and Meenie and that nice Raul were at Mad Dog's house yesterday and most of last night. I take it you didn't find anything or Mad Dog would be in jail and you wouldn't be pestering me."

"I cannot comment on the investigation," said Miss Poole.

"No, I suppose not."

"Where were you between midnight and one o'clock on January sixth?"

"You want an alibi? Well, I don't have one. I was asleep, and under our justice system, it's up to you to prove I wasn't."

"Do you own a handgun?"

"I never thought I needed one. Crawford County doesn't exactly have a high crime rate, and I have nothing in this house worth stealing, so why should I have a gun?"

"Will you sign a consent-to-search form?"

Rachel Smith sighed. "I don't look forward to Meenie Higgins pawing through my underwear drawer, but yes, I'll sign your form. Anything to put this behind me."

"Then why don't you tell the truth, Rachel? What are you and Mad Dog hiding? Why is Albert Finnigan so dangerous that one of you was willing to murder Charles Matthews to keep him from asking questions? I won't rest until I know."

Rachel Smith frowned at her. "You certainly rested easily enough up to now. You're the one I expected to be screaming for justice the minute C.J. reported digging up Albert. But you didn't. Why not? And don't tell me you didn't guess who was in that grave because I won't believe you. Why weren't you out for blood from the start?"

"I did indentify him, but I waited too long," began Miss Poole.

"Why wait until someone tried to kill the sheriff?" interrupted Rachel Smith. "What are you hiding, Megan Elizabeth?"

Miss Poole felt perspiration trickle down between her shoulder blades. She knew better than to lie to Rachel Smith. "I believed that whoever murdered Albert was dead, and that there was no point raking over the coals looking for a fire. The fire was out. I didn't realize Albert was still a threat."

Rachel shook her finger at Miss Poole. "Not a good enough answer. If you loved Albert Finnigan so much that you wasted your whole life waiting for him, then you wouldn't have let him be buried without a name, not unless ..." She broke off and her face lost what color it had. "You know who killed him—you and Victoria Dodd both know. That's why you haven't questioned her. You already know what she'll say."

"I don't *know* anything! And I will question Victoria!"

"Don't play semantics with me, Megan Elizabeth. I'm too good at it to be fooled. You *don't* know, but you *suspect*—and it's not Victoria because she's not dead and you wouldn't protect her anyway. On the other hand, I can't see her protecting you. If she saw you kill Albert, the little ninny would have screamed bloody murder—no, I take that back. Victoria would have tattled to Sheriff Treadwell. That would have been more her style. But she didn't, which means either you're innocent or she was too afraid to tell what she saw. Then, too, you're not a terribly good liar, so I believe you when you say the murderer's dead. Besides, if you knew Albert was dead because you killed him, I think you would have married—probably Mad Dog, since he was so crazy over you, and he was a nice boy and enough different from you that it would have been a good match. But you didn't, you waited until it was obvious to even you that Albert wasn't coming back, and then it was too late. Mad Dog married someone else and had a family. So who are you protecting, Megan Elizabeth? You and Victoria? Someone you loved and Victoria was afraid of?"

Then Rachel Smith caught her breath, staring up at Miss

Poole with pitying eyes. "It was your father, wasn't it? And you don't want it to be, that's why you accused me."

Miss Poole considered lying, but as Rachel pointed out, she wasn't good at it. "He had the motive and the opportunity. His office was on the second floor where the hat was found, and he didn't want me to marry Albert—"

Rachel interrupted. "But he didn't shoot the sheriff so he's innocent, you silly girl."

"That's what I thought at first, but the sheriff pointed out that if it was only Albert's identity the three of you feared, then it made more sense to kill me. I knew who he was and eventually I would have admitted it. But someone didn't want Charles Matthews asking questions about the homefront. It's not Albert himself you're all afraid of. He's only the catalyst now as he was then. All of you have guilty secrets you're afraid the sheriff will find. So answer my question, please. Why are you so nervous? What did you learn the hard way about Albert?"

Rachel Smith closed her eyes briefly, then opened them. "All right, Megan Elizabeth, I'll tell you, but it will hurt you almost as much as me. Albert Finnigan was my lover and he rejected me. He stood me up after choir practice that last night before your father sent him back to the army, left me waiting in front of the church like I was some streetwalker. Then he didn't even answer the letters I sent him after he left. Maybe girls today take that sort of thing in stride, but in 1944 it was a sin to sleep with a man you weren't married to. A sin! We knew what that meant in those days, not like today, when preachers in sweatshirts and tennis shoes confuse sin with freedom of choice. They're not the same thing at all!"

Rachel pushed herself off the couch and shuffled over to an old-fashioned china cabinet. She opened a door and took out a bottle of whiskey and poured herself a drink. She knocked it back like an experienced drunkard and coughed. "Sometimes a good belt of Irish whiskey soothes the psyche. Or at least numbs it. So, now you know why I didn't want to talk about Albert. Especially to the sheriff. He's too young to understand how humiliated I was, how devastated. Even after fifty years I still cringe thinking about it. I would have done almost anything not to have to talk about it—except shoot the sheriff. The last thing I would have done is draw attention to myself. I was hoping to lay low until this whole mess blew over."

Miss Poole didn't need whiskey to feel numb. She already was. Like a gunshot victim, she was too stunned to feel the pain. But she would. That was the one certainty in her life—that and her duty. She had nothing else.

"But you already had drawn attention to yourself—when you cut out the pictures in the county history. Why did you do that if you didn't want to be noticed?"

Rachel poured herself another drink and saluted Miss Poole. "Congratulations. You're as tough as your father. You took a knife to the heart and you're still standing, still asking questions."

"And you're still not answering them, Rachel."

"If you recall, I was the last of the sheriff's dogs to bark, and if Victoria and Mad Dog had not acted like such imbeciles, I wouldn't have barked at all. But I knew it was only a matter of time until the sheriff made the connection between their odd behavior and Albert. Then the fat would be in the fire. He would break one or the other—I'm very impressed with your sheriff's persistence—and Victoria in her hand-wringing way would tell everything she knew about you and Albert and your father. I didn't intend for that to happen, so I cut up the county history, the sheriff arrested me, and I kept Victoria and Mad Dog under control. I, of course, would not have said a word—ever."

Shaky with disbelief, Miss Poole sank down in an ancient rocker. "Why would you protect me?"

"Not you, my dear," replied Rachel Smith, sipping her whiskey. "Your father. You're just along for the ride."

"How did you know it was my father?"

"When C.J. Tolliver dug up Albert, I knew immediately who it was and that your father must have murdered him. He hated him badly enough and he had keys to the courthouse just as I did, but you're wrong in believing that he killed him to save his daughter from a life of misery as Mrs. Albert Finnigan. The only other time in his life that Daniel Edward Poole was ever violent was when he fought Ben Colchester because he believed Ben wronged him. Your father would kill to right a wrong, Megan Elizabeth, but he wouldn't kill to prevent a mistake that a good divorce lawyer could correct."

Rachel Smith put her hand over her heart. "Your father killed Albert Finnigan because Albert Finnigan wronged me."

CHAPTER

22

From the private journal of Megan Elizabeth Poole:

January 9 [continued]

There is a difference between being a fool and being foolish. The former is a noun and defined as one who is deficient in judgment, sense, or understanding. Foolish, on the other hand, is an adjective that limits, qualifies, or specifies. It implies poor judgment. One may act in a foolish manner without being a fool. Was I a fool or merely foolish that night after choir practice when Albert stood up Rachel in order to take me out to explain that horrible scene with Victoria Dodd?

I don't know.

But I do know I have lost Albert Finnigan. I have also lost my father. He murdered Albert, not out of a misguided desire to protect me, but to right a wrong done Rachel Smith. I can forgive an overzealous father; I cannot forgive a vengeful man who takes away my choices. I am bereaved.

Miss Poole touched her badge, thankful that she still had her duty. In her experience, work was an excellent panacea for melancholy. It engaged the mind. It restored lost pride. Most importantly, work discouraged tears.

Satisfied that she was in control of herself and no longer in danger of weeping, as she did after leaving Rachel

Smith's house, Miss Poole rang Victoria Dodd's doorbell
and waited impatiently for the older woman to answer. She
rang again, then stepped back off the porch and surveyed
the front of the old antebellum-style house. Drapes were
drawn on all the windows, which even on a blustery January day was odd. The Texas Panhandle enjoyed nearly 330
days of sunshine in the average year, and its residents were
addicted to light. Hardly anyone drew their drapes during
the day unless they were too ill to get out of bed.

Or hiding.

Miss Poole marched back to the door and hammered on
it with her fist. "Victoria Dodd! I know you're in there. Answer the door. It's the sheriff's department." She wanted to
shout "Open up in the name of the law," but thought that
might be a little too melodramatic.

"Who's out there?" cried a muffled voice from the other
side of the door.

"Deputy Poole."

"Who?"

First Mad Dog, now Victoria Dodd. Not being taken seriously as a certified peace officer was wearing a little thin.
"It's Megan Elizabeth Poole, and I *am* a deputy! Now open
the door, Victoria!"

"Just a minute."

In a pig's eye, thought Miss Poole. She wasn't giving another witness time to hide evidence while she waited on the
porch. She hammered on the door again. "Open up now,
Victoria! Or I'll break down the door!"

It was an empty threat, since she had no arrest warrant
and no probable cause to suspect Victoria more than Mad
Dog or Rachel. The elderly widow could sue the dickens
out of Crawford County if Miss Poole so much as leaned
on the door. However, a woman with as guilty a conscience
as Victoria's wouldn't be thinking of the legal niceties;
she'd be too busy thinking up lies.

With a click of the lock and a rattle of a chain, Mrs.
Dodd opened the door and peered around its edge. "Is there
anyone else out there?"

Miss Poole squeezed through the partly opened door. "Meenie and Raul are busy, so I came by myself."

Victoria Dodd slammed the door behind her, locked it, and shoved the safety chain home. "I don't mean deputies! I mean anybody else. Did you see anybody watching the house—or any strange cars?"

Mrs. Dodd's eyes were so magnified by her thick lenses that it was difficult for Miss Poole to judge if their expression was one of madness or fear, or if they merely reminded her of a myopic owl.

"I may have a certain reputation for efficiency and an encyclopedic knowledge of local residents, Victoria, but even I don't know who owns every car in Crawford County. And where might anybody be skulking? It's January and ten degrees outside, if you don't count the wind chill, there's not a leaf on any bush or tree, and I believe I would notice a parked car with its heater on. Why don't you come sit down and tell me why you're so paranoid."

She took the widow's arm and led her over to one of the comfortable white couches that flanked the fireplace. "Don't sit there!" cried Mrs. Dodd, twisting free of Miss Poole's grip and scuttling to the other couch. "Sit on this one by me. It's better."

Miss Poole shrugged and sat down. "Both couches are exactly alike. What difference does it make?"

The elderly woman smoothed her long black skirt. A faint odor of mothballs made Miss Poole's eyes water. "I like this one, and it's not so close to the windows."

"And I suppose that's an optical illusion," said Miss Poole, pointing to a window opposite where they sat.

Mrs. Dodd blinked behind her thick senses. "Oh, there are rosebushes in front of that one, the old-fashioned kind with lots of thorns. No one can get close enough to look in."

"No one can look in anyway. You have the drapes closed."

"But if he gets close enough to listen, then he'll know where we are."

"Who are you talking about, Victoria? Have you had a Peeping Tom? Is that what's frightened you?"

Mrs. Dodd held her fingers to her lips. "Shush, Megan Elizabeth. If he hears you, then he'll know where to shoot."

Miss Poole almost gasped—except in Crawford County she would soon hyperventilate if she gasped at every unexpected or eccentric statement made by one of her neighbors. "Victoria, get a grip on yourself!"

If the other woman heard, she didn't respond, but Miss Poole wasn't surprised. Despite Crawford County's opinion to the contrary, she believed Victoria Dodd had never been blessed with much sense even as a young woman, and age and the discovery of Albert's body hadn't improved her natural condition. Still, duty required her to get to the bottom of this most recent irrational behavior.

"Have you seen someone at your windows? Is that what happened?" asked Miss Poole in a brisk voice.

Mrs. Dodd blinked. "No."

"Someone tried to break in?"

"No."

"Someone threatened you?"

Mrs. Dodd clasped her hands together and swallowed. "I think so."

Miss Poole controlled a sudden urge to shake her. "What do you mean by that, Victoria. Either you were threatened or you weren't. Which is it?"

Mrs. Dodd waved one arm toward the telephone on a lamp table near the other couch. "The phone. I had several calls from him. I finally turned on the answering machine, but he still called."

"Why didn't you call the police?" asked Mrs. Poole.

"I did, but they told me to order one of those call blocking things from the phone company. It was Saturday and the phone company said I had to wait until Monday, but this morning my phone didn't work, and I was afraid to leave the house to go next door and report it. It's my punishment, Megan Elizabeth, he's punishing me for what I did, for what I made him do. I thought he didn't know, but he did. I told him I was wearing widow's weeds so everyone would know how sorry I am and how much I miss him."

Miss Poole felt the hair on the back of her neck stand up. "Victoria, Albert is dead. The dead don't make telephone calls."

"Not Albert! James!"

Disoriented, Miss Poole repeated the name. "James?"

Mrs. Dodd nodded as she began rocking back and forth. "My husband, Judge James Dodd."

As a dispatcher for the sheriff's department, Miss Poole had taken numerous calls from people suffering a variety of paranoid delusions. Her personal favorite was Widow Lowell's fear of Dutch elm disease spreading to humans, a harmless paranoia until the elderly lady took a china saw to her neighbor's elm trees. As delusions went, Victoria's was much more commonplace. Surviving spouses without family ties often spoke to their deceased husbands or wives. Miss Poole always put it down to loneliness, but guilt was a more likely reason in Victoria's case.

"What did James tell you? Perhaps you misunderstood."

Mrs. Dodd sniffed back tears. "He never said anything, but I knew it was him. I could hear him breathing, and you remember how he always breathed so hard because of his weight."

Prank callers often breathed heavily into the phone, but Victoria was too lost in fantasy to listen to reason. "I think you had better tell me why your husband would be calling you after being dead so many years."

"Because of Albert! As long as Albert stayed in his grave, then no one would talk. You know how James hated talk. He always told me that gossip ruined as many politicians as corruption. Now everybody's talking about Albert, and it's roused James from the dead, and he's come back to punish me because it's all my fault."

"What is your fault, Victoria?"

"That James murdered Albert. . . ."

"What!" cried Miss Poole.

"And it's my fault," repeated Mrs. Dodd, looking away and wringing her hands. "Albert and I fell in love, you see, and I broke my wedding vows on several occasions, usually in the mornings after James went to the courthouse—"

"I know," interrupted Miss Poole. "Albert told me that night I saw the two of you in the choir room."

Mrs. Dodd jerked her head around to stare at Miss Poole. "He told you?"

Miss Poole nodded, remembering. . . .

Megan Elizabeth rushed down the narrow hall past darkened Sunday school rooms toward the church's back door. She pulled her choir robe over her head and tossed it away as she ran. Her coat and purse were in the choir room, but she could not bear to go back and get them—not if it meant facing Victoria Dodd again.

And Albert.

She jerked open the back door and ran down the narrow flight of steps. It was chilly without her coat even though it was April, but Megan Elizabeth welcomed the cold breeze blowing against her exposed skin. Perhaps the chilled air would settle her nausea and cleanse her. She felt sick and dirty, as if the shamefulness of Victoria's and Albert's kiss had touched her, too.

"Meggie!"

She heard his voice and the sound of his footsteps and ran. She would have screamed for help, but she didn't want the humiliation of anyone knowing why she ran. And she couldn't lie and accuse Albert of some unspeakable intent. She knew what Crawford County would do to any man accused by Judge Poole's daughter.

"Meggie! Stop and let me explain!"

She glanced over her shoulder to see how close he was and caught her toe in a crack in the concrete sidewalk. She sprawled on her face and, before she could struggle to her feet, she felt his hands lifting her.

"Don't touch me!" she cried and slapped his face.

His head jerked back from the force of the blow, but it

didn't stop him from grabbing her hands and imprisoning them. "Listen to me, then I'll let you go. I'm sorry you had to see that, Meggie. I thought I could leave without you ever finding out."

"Find out you're a two-timer? Then you shouldn't have kissed Mrs. Dodd in front of God and everybody. And in church, too! That just makes it worse. I don't know why God didn't strike you both dead."

"Probably because He's got too much to do overseas."

"That's blasphemy!"

"Or maybe because I'm innocent, Meggie. I won't lie to you and say I never had anything to do with Victoria, because I did. When I first got to Crawford County I was scared and lonely and dreaming every night about blood soaking into the snow and freezing until one day it was my blood, and all my buddies crouched beside me like I'd crouched beside other men when they were shot or blown apart. And I'd wake up every morning sweating and shivering at the same time, and Victoria would be there with her soft voice and soft hands and smelling like lilacs instead of cordite and gasoline and filthy men who had slept and fought in the same clothes for weeks. Do you know how bad a man wants a hot bath and clean socks in a war, Meggie? Do you know how bad he wants a warm woman?"

Megan Elizabeth felt her face turn hot. "No."

The moonlight slanted across his face, and she could see his grim expression. "Bad enough to forget if a woman's married as long as she's willing. And I kept pushing away thoughts about how low-down I was acting—until I met you. You believed I was everything I'm not. You believed I was a damn hero! And I couldn't stand it. I finally had to try to act like a hero, and I started locking my bedroom door and avoiding Victoria. I'm still not a hero, but I'm not sleeping with a married woman anymore either." He released her hands and stepped back. "There, I've said it."

Megan Elizabeth covered her face with her hands. She knew about such things, of course, even knew in a theoretical fashion what went on between men and women, but she'd never talked about it. Certainly not with a man. Her father had never discussed sex with her—ever.

She felt Albert pull her hands away from her face and hold them again, but gently this time. "I don't mean to embarrass you, Meggie, but I wanted you to know the truth. I'm not the hero you want me to be—I'm kind of worthless, really—but I didn't kiss Victoria. She kissed me."

"She's a terrible woman! Only a slut would throw herself at a man when she's married to someone else."

Albert put his arms around her and pressed her face against his shoulder. "No, she's not, Meggie. She's just a woman who's maybe a little lonelier than some, but she's no worse than me. Neither one of us is worth as much as your dad."

Megan Elizabeth leaned back in his arms to look up at him. "My father! My father doesn't like you."

Albert grinned. She could see his teeth flash in the moonlight. "I don't much like him either, Meggie, but I'll say this for him. He's rock solid. It wouldn't matter how lonely or scared he was, or how many nightmares he had, your father wouldn't have messed with another man's wife. He's got standards higher than the Empire State Building, and mine don't reach much farther than the second floor."

"That's not true!"

"Sure it is, Meggie," he said. "But I'm going to fool your old man tonight. I'm going to take you home in the same condition you left in, and that's probably the most heroic thing I've done since the Japs bombed Pearl Harbor. . . ."

"You told James, didn't you?" shouted Victoria, grabbing the dispatcher by the shoulders and shaking her. "Quit staring at me and answer!"

Miss Poole's head snapped back with the force of the widow's assault and her mind snapped forward out of the past. She broke Victoria's hold and scrambled off the couch, backing away from the other woman's reach. "I'll thank you to keep your hands off me!"

Looking like a large avenging black widow spider in her taffeta mourning dress, Victoria Dodd came after her, arms flailing like tentacles. "You always were a nosy brat, Megan Elizabeth Poole!"

Circling behind the opposite couch, Miss Poole debated whether or not to drawn her revolver, and decided she must first warn the maniacal widow. "Stay away from me and control yourself, Victoria, or I shall be forced to use physical means to subdue you!"

Arms outstretched and claws bared, Victoria Dodd stalked around the end of the couch. "It's your fault. If you hadn't told James, he wouldn't have killed Albert!"

"I warned you," said Miss Poole as she dropped her purse on the floor and plucked a pillow off the couch and threw it in the widow's face with the same motion she used as the Crawford County Independent School District employees' baseball team's only woman pitcher. Of course, a cushion didn't attain near the speed of her legendary fastball, but she threw it hard enough to stagger Victoria Dodd. Seizing another cushion she put away the widow with a curve ball that landed on the woman's diaphragm with a satisfactory thud. Victoria went down with a rustle of taffeta skirts.

"Don't try to get up, or I'll be forced to try my breaking ball," said Miss Poole, flexing her arm and hoping she'd be able to move it tomorrow. She hadn't pitched in years and was out of condition.

Mrs. Dodd struggled to a sitting position and pulled her skirt down. "You enjoyed that!"

Miss Poole tilted her head to one side and pursed her lips, considering the accusation. "Yes, I did," she admitted, "and I wish I'd done it years ago. I wish I'd thrown a hymnal at you in the choir room. However, that's neither here nor there. In the first place, I didn't tell Judge Dodd. I left your sins to your own conscience. In the second place, if you don't want me to press charges against you for aggravated assault on a peace officer, I suggest you tell me why you believe your husband murdered Albert. And no lies, please. I'm out of patience."

Victoria Dodd sat up and straightened her glasses. "I saw him do it!"

"You were talking about your husband when you told me that you kept silent all these years because you didn't want a good man to go to prison," said Miss Poole.

"Yes! Who did you think I was talking about?"

Miss Poole decided it was just as well that Victoria Dodd wasn't as bright as Mad Dog Treadwell and Rachel Smith. Otherwise, she would guess the answer to her own question. "Because you thought your own transgressions were responsible?"

"If you didn't tell him, then yes, I was responsible," agreed Victoria, wringing her hands.

Miss Poole leaned against the back of the couch and folded her arms. "Why were you at the courthouse late that night? It was night, wasn't it?"

Mrs. Dodd nodded, pushing her thick glasses back up her nose. "Yes, about ten o'clock. When Albert didn't come back to Crawford County when the war ended, I realized I'd been a fool and went to the courthouse to admit to James that although I'd had a crush on Albert, I had come to my senses and wanted his forgiveness. The elevator wasn't working, so I took the stairs. I had just reached the little landing before you climb the last flight of stairs to the second floor when I heard a grunt and a sound like a watermelon bursting open when you drop it, followed by the sound of something falling. I was frozen for a minute or two because the sounds were so awful and I knew something horrible had happened, but I couldn't imagine what. Then I heard something being dragged down the hall, and I couldn't stand it anymore. I *had* to know what was going on. I crept up the last flight of stairs to the second floor and saw him!" She bent her head and broke into sobs.

"For God's sake, Victoria, stop wailing and tell me what you saw!" ordered Miss Poole, swallowing back nausea. It was one thing to know Albert died of blunt-force trauma; it was quite another to hear a play-by-play description.

The widow hiccupped a few times and then looked up, her magnified eyes looking only faintly red. "I saw James walk down the hall and into the elevator and he was dragging Albert's body behind him!" She covered her eyes as if to block out her visual memories. "It was so awful, Megan Elizabeth. He had hold of Albert's ankles, one in each hand, and was just dragging him along like Albert was a sack of trash. Or one of those Indian sled things—what do you call them, *travois*?—because perched on top of Albert's chest was his duffel bag. I remember thinking that James must have pushed the emergency stop button on the elevator, and that's why it wouldn't come down to the first floor when I wanted it. It's a silly thing to be thinking while you're watching your husband drag a dead body down the hall, but I couldn't seem to take in what I was seeing."

Miss Poole swallowed again. "How do you know it was your husband, Victoria, if all you saw was his back?"

"Do you think I wouldn't know my own husband's back? Who else in the courthouse was his size?"

Miss Poole nodded, feeling so relieved her legs were shaking. Of course, Victoria wouldn't have mistaken the stout Judge Dodd for the much taller and very much thinner Judge Poole. "What did you do then, Victoria?"

"When the elevator doors closed, I watched the needle swing until it stopped at the subbasement level, and I knew James was going to hide Albert's body. I never really thought at that point that James would bury him, although I realized it later when no one discovered the body. I started down the stairs but I had to stop on the landing and sit down. I was shaking so hard that I couldn't walk, and I couldn't think of anything except to wonder how James found out. Finally, I rushed out of the courthouse and came home. I went to bed and pretended to be asleep when James came home. I got up the next morning and pretended nothing had happened. I pretended every morning of my life until James died shoveling snow. It was such a relief not to have to pretend anymore that I didn't grieve for him like I should have. That's why I'm wearing widow's weeds now. I'm trying to make up for not being sorry enough when he died."

Miss Poole heard a clock strike the hour somewhere in the back of the house and wondered if Victoria Dodd might mistake it for the sound of her own doom.

She should—because Victoria Dodd had been lying about everything but Judge Dodd's murdering Albert.

"Did your husband unlock the courthouse door for you, or did you steal his keys, Victoria?"

"The door was open."

"Then your husband was expecting you and he still went ahead and murdered Albert, knowing that you might appear at any minute?"

"No, he wasn't expecting me. I just couldn't stand the guilt anymore."

"You just happened to pick the same night that Albert Finnigan came back to the courthouse?"

"I—I didn't know he was coming back," said Mrs. Dodd, stumbling over her words.

"I don't believe in coincidence. You had an assignation at the courthouse with Albert Finnigan, and Judge Dodd followed you, caught the two of you together, and murdered Albert in anger. Did you try to stop him, Victoria? Did you try to explain that the only reason Albert agreed to meet you was to tell you that he'd come home to marry me, and that he'd appreciate your not making a spectacle of yourself like you did in the choir room? That your relationship had ended when he met me? Is that why you stood back and let your husband murder him? Because he scorned you?"

"No!"

"I think you're lying again, Victoria, and that's why you've deluded yourself into thinking that your husband is calling you on the phone. Because you set him up as a murderer and you feel guilty about it. Your own imagination is punishing you."

"It's not my imagination! I saw James three nights ago—before the phone calls started. I woke up in the middle of the night and saw him standing in the moonlight by my bed. I screamed. I couldn't help it, I was so surprised. And I threw a book at him, the county history I was reading before I went to sleep. I wanted to see why Rachel Smith was cutting out the pictures. Anyway, I threw it and James backed away and disappeared into the dark. The next morning the phone calls started."

Without taking her eyes off the other woman Miss Poole backed up to the lamp table and picked up the phone. Victoria had been honest about one thing at least. There was no dial tone. For which there might be several explanations—none of them having to do with the supernatural. Miss Poole checked the most likely explanation first and found what she suspected: the phone had been unplugged from the wall outlet.

She stood up, the end of the phone cord in her hand. "Did you unplug all the phones, Victoria?"

The widow stared at her. "It must have been James."

"That's enough nonsense, Victoria. Were you trying to fool the sheriff's department into thinking you weren't home? Is that what unplugging your phone and hiding behind drawn drapes is all about? Did you honestly believe that I wouldn't question you? You should have known better. I won't give you anymore peace than your conscience until you tell me the truth."

Miss Poole dropped the phone cord and leaned down to pick up her purse. Opening it, she took out the olive drab hat and tossed it on Victoria Dodd's lap. "The evidence doesn't support your story about Albert being murdered in the hall. Would you like to try again?"

Victoria Dodd's eyes rolled up in her head and she slumped sideways in a faint. On a scale of one to ten, Miss Poole gave the swoon a three. Since she was already sitting on the floor and couldn't sink gracefully from a standing to a prone position, the widow's artistic presentation lacked the necessary drama for a higher score.

Miss Poole retreated to the kitchen for a large glass of cold water. She almost persuaded herself that she didn't enjoy pouring it in Victoria Dodd's face.

The widow came to with a screech, rolled over and pushed herself to her hands and knees, saw Albert Finnigan's hat, screeched again as she grabbed it with one hand, and tried to sit up. Her ears ringing from the high-pitched screams, Miss Poole bent down and seized the widow under both arms and heaved her into a sitting position.

Mrs. Dodd waved the hat at Miss Poole. "You've had it all along! I thought James found it! I waited for years afraid that one day he'd throw it up to me."

Her hands on her hips, Miss Poole stared down at the widow. "Albert was murdered on the second-floor landing, wasn't he, Victoria? That's where the hat was found. That's where Judge Dodd caught up with you and Albert, wasn't it? And in a hurry to dispose of the body, neither one of you thought of the hat."

"No! I dropped the hat when I collapsed on the landing. The murder happened just like I said it did."

"And you kept Albert's hat. What for, Victoria? A keepsake?"

"No! Albert gave it to me before he left."

Miss Poole reached out blindly and clutched the back of the couch. "You're lying. Albert wouldn't give you a momento."

The widow laid the hat across her lap and stroked it. "He looked so smart in his uniform that last morning, his shoes so shiny that I could see the whole bedroom reflected in them. He wasn't smiling though, even looked like he'd forgotten how. I think he was afraid to go to war again. I think he was afraid he'd used up all his luck. It made my heart ache to think about it. I asked for a lock of his hair, and he told me that's what women kept to remember the dead and he didn't want to tempt fate. Then he walked to the window and pushed the curtains aside and looked out like he wanted to store up a memory of Crawford County. When I started crying he turned around and pulled off his hat. He tossed it to me and said, 'I've seen too many women crying overseas, Victoria, and I can't stand to see another one. Take my hat if you want something to remember me by because I've got a feeling I won't be back.' Then he picked up his duffel bag and left. That was the last time I saw Albert Finnigan alive."

"You're still not telling the truth, Victoria. Why did you take Albert's hat to the courthouse if you were planning to confess your misbehavior to your husband? Bringing a momento of your lover to your husband's office hardly seems very diplomatic."

"I was going to burn it as an act of contrition."

"You should have been a romance novelist, Victoria, because I've never heard a less likely story. Your husband was no more given to appreciating romantic gestures than my father was. You brought that hat because you were meeting Albert, and hoped to impress him with your steadfastness. But he spurned you, and you let Judge Dodd murder him. That's why you didn't want the sheriff asking questions. You were afraid the story would come out finally, and everyone in Crawford County would see you for the hypocrite you've always been. That's why you shot the sheriff."

Mrs. Dodd clutched Albert's hat to her breast and stared up at Miss Poole, her face gray as the winter sky outside. "I never shot the sheriff! How dare you accuse of such a thing!"

"Don't waste that holier than thou act on me, Victoria. Save it for Meenie and Raul, or perhaps the jury. You might be able to fool them, but you can't fool me."

"I didn't do it, Megan Elizabeth!"

"Where were you between midnight and one o'clock on January sixth?"

"I was asleep!"

"Will you sign a consent-to-search form, Victoria?" asked Miss Poole. She should have trusted her instincts. Mad Dog and Rachel Smith were far too competent to bungle a simple murder, and Victoria Dodd was too flighty to do anything else.

"A search? What are you looking for?"

"Handguns, Victoria. Do you own one?"

"I won't sign that paper. I won't let you search my house!" cried Mrs. Dodd, her eyes darting toward the couch, then back to Miss Poole.

Miss Poole whirled around and stared down at the couch Victoria had been so anxious she not sit on, the one she hadn't really looked at until now. Leave it to Victoria Dodd not to have any more sense than to hide the forty-five revolver under the pillows she'd thrown at the widow.

CHAPTER

23

Like other western rural communities, Crawford County united to support the war effort. Arguments and rivalries were set aside for the duration and soldiers on furlough while awaiting orders to the European or Pacific theaters were treated like heroes and any unheroic behavior was ignored or overlooked by those on the homefront. In the face of such patriotic fever, no new recruit dared show fear, else he would be called a coward. Not since the opening days of the War between the States in the South had such a premium been set on individual courage nor such public scorn heaped upon those who failed the test.

> *Sociological Traits of a Rural Culture*
> *in Crawford County, Texas*
> An unpublished dissertation by James Crane

2 DOWN—1 TO GO
STAY IN THERE AND PITCH! WE STILL MUST WHIP THE NIP!

Who can blame Americans for going half mad with joy as Hitler's cruel war machine is smashed into dust! For all who have fought and worked and suffered grievous loss, the hour of triumph is deserved.

But our men are still fighting and dying out there in the Pacific. If we let down now, we'll be letting them down!

Let's stick to our labors until Uncle Sam says "Well

done—you may relax!" Let's buy war bonds—they will
be needed now—more than ever.

Crawford County Examiner
May 8, 1945

From the private journal of Megan Elizabeth Poole:

January 9 [continued]

Victoria Dodd's jealous anger stole from me a life that
might have been.

"The museum and the library ain't got the *Examiner* on
microfilm, Sheriff. At least, they don't anymore. Seems like
it sprouted legs and walked off."

"Stolen? *Stolen!*" Charles leaned forward in the hospital
recliner, quivering like a Thoroughbred in the starting gate.
"Damn it to hell! When did it happen, Meenie?"

The deputy scratched his head. "Well, the lady at the
museum can't exactly remember the last time she saw it.
They run that place with one employee and a bunch of volunteers, so the right hand don't always know what the left
hand's doing. It's a nice museum though. The help dresses
up like pioneers—"

"I don't give a damn if it's the Smithsonian and everybody wears pink bunny suits!" yelled Charles. "Stick to the
subject. I want to know when the microfilm was stolen."

Meenie frowned at him. "Well, they don't know, and you
oughtn't to yell about it. That's just how things are."

Charles rubbed his hand over his face. "You're right, I
shouldn't yell. Every damn thing Crawford County does is
calculated to drive a logical man crazy, and I ought to be
used to it by now."

"The librarian keeps a record of who uses the microfilm,
Sheriff," said Raul quickly. "She said it was there last
week."

"So the microfilm was probably stolen after I was shot," finished Charles.

"I reckon that would be a fair guess," said Meenie.

Charles pointed his finger at his chief deputy. "Meenie, the next time I try to make something complicated out of something simple, I want you to kick me. I told Miss Poole that I was shot because I was asking too many questions and rattling too many skeletons. I was wrong! The target was the newspaper all along. God Almighty, a five-year-old kid could figure it out. I got shot because I happened to be at the wrong place at the wrong time." He grinned at his two deputies. "That makes me feel a lot better."

Meenie exchanged a look with Raul. "I don't hardly want to ask this, Sheriff, seeing as how I probably won't get a straight answer, but how come you feel better?"

"Because he—or she—won't be trying for another shot at me. The mummy's identity has been published, the old newspaper records are gone, so there's no point in killing me. But Miss Poole's a different story. She doesn't need to read old newspapers. She's a walking encyclopedia on this town and its people. Where is she, by the way?"

"She called from Miss Smith's," said Raul. "She wanted Meenie and I to search the house, but we thought we'd better tell you about the stolen microfilm first. She said she was going to Mrs. Dodd's next."

"I guess she's safe then. Victoria Dodd is too dotty to be a danger to anyone but herself. Go search Rachel Smith's house, but when Miss Poole calls in, tell her I want to see this morning's statements. And Meenie, why didn't the museum director and the librarian report the break-ins?"

"There weren't no break-ins," said Meenie. "Somebody used a key on both places. And before you get yourself all riled up, me and Raul already asked who had keys, and the answer is damn near everybody in town from the county officials to every volunteer who ever worked at either place. And yeah, our suspects were volunteers both places."

"Even Mad Dog?" asked Charles, trying to imagine Mad

Dog Treadwell dressed up like a pioneer and leading a tour of school children.

"He and Miss Poole were the ones behind building the museum in the first place. He's volunteered one day a week since he retired last year. And while a man don't think of Mad Dog as being the kind who reads much besides the sports page, he's still the president of the library board. He acts ignorant, Sheriff, but that don't mean he is."

"Damn it!" exclaimed Charles. No microfilm and no idea who stole it. Scratch that angle of investigation. But there was more than one way to skin a cat—as Crawford County would say. "Meenie, have you and Raul checked the deed records in the county clerk's office on any real estate transactions our suspects may have made, or have those records been stolen, too?"

Meenie put his hat back on and hitched up his pants. "We ain't checked yet, Sheriff. We been kinda busy in case it slipped your mind. Just little things, like waiting to see if you pulled through being shot and standing guard duty so nobody could finish the job when he found out he missed. Then we spent some time investigating the crime scene and questioning witnesses and searching houses. I guess them deed records got put off in favor of trying to catch the sorry, low-down coyote that put a bullet through your hide."

"I'm sorry, Meenie. I didn't mean to get on your case, but we aren't going to catch that low-down coyote without tracking him through time. We can't do it using the newspaper, so we'll have to check public records." He clenched his fist and pounded on the arm of the recliner. "Damn it, I wish I could get out of here and do some of the investigation myself."

"Well, you can't, so forget about it," ordered Meenie. "And yelling ain't gonna change nothing. You just sit there and read today's paper. Got a real nice article on the mummy."

"I've read the paper!"

"Then take yourself a nap while I go search Miss

Smith's house and Raul looks up the deed records. You gonna be all right till Miss Angie gets back, Sheriff?"

"I'll be fine. If I need anything, I'll call Slim."

"I'll send somebody else over, Sheriff," said Meenie. "Slim's apt to see a killer behind every corner and shoot up the hospital."

"You leave Slim where he is. I'm not in danger anymore, and he's got to learn to be responsible sometime. Better he learn when there's no real emergency," said Charles. "You two go to work and stop worrying."

He watched his two deputies leave, then glanced restlessly around the small hospital room. He felt the walls closing in and perfume from the floral arrangements that crowded every surface choking him. He might as well be in a coffin as suffocating in this room. He coughed just to hear a sound other than the muted voices of nurses and squeak of rubber soles on the tile floor of the hall beyond his door. Damn it, but he was bored!

Sighing in resignation he picked up the *Examiner* and glanced again at the article and accompanying photograph. *Photograph!* Suddenly he sat bolt upright in the recliner. If the newspaper morgue burned and all the microfilm was stolen, where in the hell did Jack Colchester get a picture of Albert Finnigan? Charles felt a cold chill race up his spine as he pieced together details of that last afternoon before he was shot and fitted them into the larger jigsaw puzzle of the investigation since then. He didn't like what he saw.

Charles levered himself out of the recliner and shuffled to the door and opened it. "Slim, steal me a wheelchair."

"Jesus Christ!" exclaimed Jack Colchester when Slim wheeled Charles into the publisher's office. "What are you doing here, Sheriff?"

"I came to ask you some questions."

"Did the doctor release you? No, I guess not since I can see a hospital gown under your coat. What the hell do you think you're doing? Slim, take him back to the hospital before he dies in my office, and J.T. Brentwood comes after me with a gun."

"I can't do that, Mr. Colchester," replied Slim, standing at attention. "Me and the sheriff are manhunters after a vicious killer."

Charles decided Miss Poole was right: Slim was reading too many lurid mysteries. "Slim's following my orders."

"That's what the Nazis claimed, and it wasn't a good excuse then," said Colchester, reaching for his phone.

"I wonder why everybody in Crawford County always tries to change the subject when I say I have some questions. And put down that phone, Jack, or I'll order Slim to arrest you."

"On what charges?" demanded Colchester.

"Attempted murder."

"What the hell!" exclaimed the editor, vaulting out of his chair and leaning over the desk to stare at Charles in disbelief.

"Hands on your head and don't move!" shouted Slim, whipping out his gun in a fast draw and holding it with both hands in a professional stance that Charles knew the deputy owed more to watching Jodie Foster in *Silence of the Lambs* than to any training program Crawford County offered.

"You have the right to remain silent—"

"Put that damn gun up, Slim, and go get a cup of coffee with that young reporter you were staring at so hard you ran my wheelchair over the sports editor's foot," ordered Charles.

The young deputy hesitated. "I don't know, Sheriff. He might try to finish the job and blow you away."

"Slim, you heard me. Put the gun up and get out of here. And Slim, I want you to borrow one of Miss Poole's genteel mysteries, one that doesn't use terms like 'blow you away.'"

Colchester sank back in his chair after Slim left, and Charles noticed his hands were shaking. "You let him have bullets for that revolver, Sheriff?"

"Never mind Slim. He's harmless—most of the time."

"But you're not, are you, Sheriff? Just where do you get off accusing me of attempted murder?"

Charles held the other man's eyes. "You're the only person who knew I stayed late at the *Examiner*. Not even Angie knew because I forgot to call her. I left my car parked at the courthouse, and it was after midnight when I was shot. Who else would expect me to still be here?"

Colchester's face lost color. "You're crazy, Sheriff. It was an arsonist. It must have been."

"That's what I thought, too, after Meenie reported that the microfilm of the *Examiner* was stolen from the museum and the library, but the fire has always puzzled me. Why would an arsonist be so damn inefficient? Even an amateur ought to know to use an accelerant such as gasoline to start a good fire, and Mad Dog Treadwell isn't an amateur. And my other two suspects are elderly women, one of them in her eighties, and looking at them objectively, it stretches credibility to believe either one is guilty."

Jack Colchester's face had gone from white to red with suppressed rage. "Damn it, do you think I'd burn my own building? Destroy my own family's heritage along with Crawford County's?"

Charles felt sweat trickle down his back and shivered. Jack Colchester was telling the truth about one thing: the way he was feeling he just might die in the *Examiner*'s office. But not yet, not until he answered Colchester's questions with his own.

"But you wouldn't burn down your building, would you, Jack? The fire station's just across the street and down the block, so no need to worry about deactivating the smoke alarms. Someone would smell the smoke before the fire got too far out of control. That's why no accelerant was used. A very slow-burning fire, easy to extinguish with little damage. As for your other questions, those are easy to answer, too. It's not your family's heritage. You're adopted. And you didn't destroy Crawford County's history because you have those old newspapers on microfilm. That's where you got that picture of Albert Finnigan you ran in today's paper. That was your only mistake. If you hadn't done that, I might not have remembered the microfilm reader on your desk, and that any newspaper with any money and pride behind it stores back issues on microfilm. You drew attention to yourself, and I realized you had the means, the opportunity, and the motive."

Colchester raked his fingers through his hair. "Damn it, Sheriff, what's my motive? I don't have anything to do with that mummy. I wasn't even born until December of 1945! Do you think I bashed in his head with my teething ring?"

"You said you would have rolled in horse manure and run naked down Main Street to prove you belonged, Jack. You even wanted plastic surgery on your face. It's not impossible to believe you'd carry your fixation on not belonging to the point of killing to protect Crawford County as a sort of bizarre initiation rite."

"You're full of crap, Matthews! It's a big step between horse manure and murder."

Charles nodded. "It happens that I agree with you—now."

He glanced up at the portrait of Benjamin Colchester that hung on the wall behind Jack's desk. Mementos of the *Examiner*'s founder dominated the office—from his old typewriter sitting on a bookcase to framed copies of the newspaper's editorial pages where Ben Colchester had written opinions on issues ranging from Prohibition to Douglas MacArthur's resignation to the Kennedy-Nixon debates. Even Jack's mahogany desk had belonged first to old Ben.

Jack Colchester slumped back in his chair and gripped its arms with still-shaking hands. "You really had me going there for a while. I could almost hear the prison doors clanging shut behind me because I don't have an alibi. My wife was in San Antonio visiting our daughter, and I didn't leave the house after I got home. I got stinking drunk if you want to know. All that talk about being adopted and picking at my psychic scabs got to me, I guess."

He leaned forward and braced his elbows on his desk. "But looking at it from your point of view, I can see where you might suspect me. I'm pissed that you do, but I can understand it. You're sitting there with a hole in your chest and nobody in custody. Hell, I'd be turning over rocks to see what was under them, too."

Charles looked at the man he'd always called his friend and wondered how a single act of violence could destroy lives and friendships nearly fifty years later. "Don't be too quick to forgive me, because nothing has changed but my idea about your motive. You didn't shoot me to protect Crawford County. You did it to protect your right to the Colchester name. Look at this office. It's a shrine to Ben Colchester, and anyone who steps in here is reminded that you're old Ben's great-grandson. You have an identity for as long as no one knows your real name. But what if they did? You wouldn't be a Colchester anymore, you'd be so-and-so's illegitimate son. I think you'd kill to prevent that from happening."

Jack Colchester's eyes took on the expression of a man finally confronting the ghost he'd always known haunted his life, but that he'd never seen until now. "I might," he admitted, "but I didn't, because who I am has nothing to do with your dead sergeant."

"I know about the theft of the birth, death, and marriage records for the decade of the 1940s, Jack. I thought I knew who did it, but I was wrong. That theft worried me because none of my other suspects was born or married during that decade, so I couldn't figure out why any of them would steal the records. But you were born eight months after Albert Finnigan left Crawford County. Your birth would be recorded in that missing volume, and you're the only person who knew I was here in this office. I know that when a child is adopted, the original birth certificate with the mother's name is supposed to be purged and a new one with the adoptive parents' name issued. But this is Crawford County and Murphy's Law is its guiding principal of government. It's not beyond possibility that your original birth certificate was never purged. I think you stole that volume several years ago after you checked those records out of curiosity and found your birth mother's name on your original birth certificate—and your father's name. I think you've concealed that knowledge for years, and when C.J. Tolliver dug up Albert Finnigan and I started asking questions, you knew your own personal skeleton might fall out of the closet."

Jack Colchester released a shuddering breath. "You didn't run this theory by Miss Poole, did you, because if you had she would have told you that there's no way in hell a young girl in Crawford County in 1945 could have been an unwed mother without everybody knowing it. When Edna Manning had a baby out of wedlock people around here talked about it for years. But believe me, Edna was an exception. Girls who got pregnant were sent to relatives who lived as far from Crawford County as possible. That way there might be talk, but no one knew for sure. And there's no way my parents could have adopted a baby born here without the whole damn county knowing who my mother was. And for your information, Sheriff, I was born in Dallas, not Crawford County, and I don't know who my mother is."

Colchester shoved his chair back and stood up in front of Ben Colchester's portrait. "And now I'd like an apology, Sheriff, before I throw your ass, wheelchair and all, out of my office."

Charles hadn't felt this bad when he woke up from surgery; in fact, he hadn't felt like this since the day he realized his best friend and Angie's first husband was a murderer. Except then he had felt betrayed. This time he was the betrayer.

"Meenie warned me that digging up the past was the same as digging up trouble. I didn't take him seriously. I thought I could sit in judgment of whatever secrets I uncovered like I was blessed with some kind of divine wisdom. I was a stranger with no divided loyalties, I could be more objective, more logical than the native born. And where has logic and my own arrogance led me? It's led me into accusing a good friend of attempted murder. I appointed myself God in this case and found out I'm not up to the job."

Charles coughed. "I'm sorry, Jack, for whatever my apology is worth. In your shoes, I wouldn't think it was worth much."

Jack Colchester turned his back to Charles and looked up at the portrait of the *Examiner*'s founder. "Did you know old Ben and Judge Poole had a fistfight in the middle of the street back in 1918?"

"No, I never heard that," said Charles. "And if you're proposing we have one I'll have to take a rain check."

Colchester turned around. "It seems Ben endorsed old man Poole's opponent in a race for the legislature. Poole had voted for the Eighteenth Amendment in his previous term, and being a drinking man Ben took exception to that. Old man Poole took exception to Ben's exception, so they fought it out like that would settle who was right. Each one thought the other had wronged him. The fight ended in a draw because both men fought for their principals and neither one would give in. They were friends before they fought, and enemies afterward. Maybe if I were a Colchester by blood, I'd hold a grudge, too. But I'm not, and I'll be damned if I'll throw away a friendship because I'm too hardheaded to accept a sincere apology. You did what you thought was right and were man enough to admit it when you were wrong."

The editor circled the end of his desk and grasped Charles's hand. "This doesn't mean I'm real happy with you right now, but I'll get over my hurt feelings. And now that we've got our differences settled, I'm telling Slim to haul you back to the hospital. You look like death warmed over."

Charles cleared his throat. "Uh, no, I'm not going back to the hospital. I'm staying here and reading your microfilm."

CHAPTER

24

CRAWFORD COUNTY ON THE SPOT
IN DRIVE FOR SCRAP
WAR HERO VOWS TO HELP

Sergeant Albert Finnigan vows to lead a new scrap drive after national salvage officials advised the local committee that Crawford County only collected twenty percent of its quota. "The steel mills only have a thirty-day supply on hand," says the popular war hero. "All of us fighting men depend on the homefront for our tanks and guns."

We at the *Examiner* echo Sergeant Finnigan's words. When local students led by William Treadwell and Megan Elizabeth Poole stop by your home this Saturday, we encourage you to give generously.

Crawford County Examiner
February 5, 1945

WANTED: 540 MILLION POUNDS
OF GUNPOWDER

American housewives can furnish this much powder if each is willing to save only one tablespoon of *used fats* each day. Mrs. Victoria Dodd shows Sergeant Albert Finnigan the grease can painted with sunflowers that she keeps on the stove to store used fats.

Crawford County Examiner
February 12, 1945

DANCE TO VICTORY

Sergeant Albert Finnigan and Miss Rachel Smith opened
the Crawford County Dance to Victory with a waltz.
Cost of admission was one pound of scrap, and the *Examiner* is proud to announce that over five hundred
pounds were collected.

> *Crawford County Examiner*
> March 7, 1945

Everyone be kind to our own William "Mad Dog"
Treadwell who failed his army physical in Amarillo, and
is feeling bad that he can't fight for his country.

> "All Around the County"
> *Crawford County Examiner*
> June 1, 1945

Miss Megan Elizabeth Poole returned home to Crawford
County after a semester at the exclusive Hockaday
School for Girls in Dallas. Perhaps her father, our own
Judge Poole, will attend to county business now that he
won't be visiting his daughter in Dallas.

> "All Around the County"
> *Crawford County Examiner*
> December 20, 1945

The public is invited to an open house Sunday afternoon
in the remodeled library on the second floor of the courthouse where Miss Rachel Smith, newly promoted Director
of Library Services, will announce expanded hours. Regular library service will be welcomed after the sawdust,
two-by-fours, and the hit-or-miss schedule suffered by patrons during the recent renovation. Judge Poole and the
Crawford County Library Board will present Mrs. James
Dodd with a plaque as Volunteer of the Year at a reception
following the open house.

> "All Around the County"
> *Crawford County Examiner*
> July 1, 1946

* * *

From the private journal of Megan Elizabeth Poole:

January 9 [continued]

All the closets are empty of skeletons, and Charles Matthews is now the keeper of the secrets. There is no man I'd rather trust.

Charles flipped off the microfilm reader and rubbed his burning eyes, then straightened the stack of photocopies he had made of every article in the *Examiner* that mentioned Albert Finnigan or any of the suspects. He knew the weapon that killed Albert Finnigan almost certainly came from the library; he knew the secret that prompted Mad Dog Treadwell's puzzling behavior; he knew the cause of the estrangement between Miss Poole and her father; he knew that Mrs. Dodd and Rachel Smith both had keys to a library full of blunt objects such as tools and lumber, and that both apparently had a closer relationship to the dead sergeant than either admitted to; and he knew Mrs. Dodd had known who was buried in the basement.

He didn't know why the county records were stolen; he didn't know why Rachel Smith cut up the county history books; he didn't know who stole the microfilm from the library and museum; and he didn't know who murdered Albert Finnigan and tried to kill him.

Of what he knew, he could prove nothing except by insinuation. In other words, he could bluff.

Of what he didn't know, only one crime provided a tangible, concrete, hold-it-in-your-hands piece of evidence: the mutilated county history book. He needed to compare it to an undamaged copy and draw conclusions. Add those conclusions to the photocopies, Miss Poole's statements from Victoria Dodd and Rachel Smith, the results—if any—of Meenie's search of the two women's homes and of Raul's search through the deed records, and maybe he'd find his ace—he hoped. Then he'd question his suspects again to see who broke. Someone would. He'd bet on it.

"Looks like you're finished," said Jack Colchester, opening the door and stepping in.

"I'm finished, and with these"—Charles picked up the photocopies—"together with some other information, I should wrap up the case by tomorrow."

Colchester closed the door and leaned against it, his arms folded. "So which one did it, Sheriff? Mad Dog, Miss Smith, or Mrs. Dodd?"

"I don't recall mentioning any names, Jack," said Charles.

"Actually you did. You mentioned Mad Dog's, but even if you hadn't, I could have figured out your suspects. When I scrolled through the microfilm looking for a suitable photo of our sergeant, I could hardly find any that didn't have one of those three in it, too. And Miss Poole. Besides, those names are all over the police scanner in the press room."

"What?" exclaimed Charles, unlocking the brake and trying to maneuver his wheelchair out from behind Colchester's desk.

"Something's going on at the sheriff's department. Started about thirty minutes ago with patrol cars driving past here with their sirens blaring like the devil was on their tail. Miss Poole was on the radio to Meenie, telling him to pick up Miss Smith and Mad Dog on suspicion of kidnapping. It seems she already has Mrs. Dodd in jail."

"Kidnapping! Who in hell has been kidnapped?"

Colchester grinned. "According to what I hear on the scanner, it's you and Slim."

Charles heard the uproar coming from the sheriff's department the minute Slim wheeled him off the elevator, with one voice louder than the others.

"I never should have let Meenie talk me into sending my hands back to the ranch. As long as they guarded that hospital, nobody tried to run off with my boy."

Charles shuddered at J.T. Brentwood's words and wondered when he'd gone from being an unwelcome relation to his father-in-law's 'boy.'

"But that's fixing to change," continued J.T. "I told my hands to get to town as fast as they could and to come loaded for bear. Be damned if I'll let somebody snatch my son-in-law out of his sick bed without answering to me for it."

"I cannot allow your ranch hands to drive around Crawford County like a band of vigilantes, J.T."

Good for you, Miss Poole, thought Charles, motioning Slim to wheel him down the hall to his office.

"A kidnapping requires negotiation, not armed men," continued Miss Poole. "Angie, I insist that you go back home with Raul and wait for a phone call from the kidnappers. I have called the FBI's local office in Amarillo, and they will be sending agents trained to handle these situations."

"I'm not going anywhere with Raul or anyone else, Miss Poole. The kidnapper isn't going to call me. He doesn't want a ransom! He wants to kill Charles! He's already tried once! I should have stayed at the hospital every minute with my forty-five. I would have shot anybody who looked crossway at my husband!"

Charles broke out in a sweat at the thought of Angie with a forty-five. "Slim, help me out of this wheelchair. I've got to stop this and I can't do it if I look helpless. Miss Poole and J.T. would just run over me."

"I don't know, Sheriff," said Slim, helping Charles up. "I think maybe I'd stay in the wheelchair if I was you. Miss Angie sounds like she's ready to take a strip of hide off somebody, and it's liable to be you for running off from the hospital without telling her. Women are funny about things like that. Maybe she won't tear into you if you look helpless."

"When did you get to be such an expert on marital relations?" snapped Charles.

"About five seconds ago—when I figured out that after

Miss Angie finishes skinning you, she's gonna start in on me," replied Slim with as gloomy an expression on his freckled face as Charles had even seen.

"Don't worry, Slim. I'll protect you," said Charles, holding the photocopies and Jack Colchester's copy of the county history against his chest, and striding into the sheriff's department. Actually, he didn't stride as much as he slid one foot ahead of another like an old man, but at least he was walking unaided—if one didn't count his keeping one hand on the wall just in case.

He reached the door by the dispatcher's desk and gratefully leaned against the doorjamb. He saw immediately there was no point in saying anything. He couldn't be heard over the shouting match going on among Angie, Miss Poole, J.T., and Raul. While he was debating whether or not he could walk across the room to stop the argument without falling on his face, a siren sounded. No, not a siren, a scream that slid up the scale to high C, wavered for a moment, then slid down again.

Charles jerked his head up to stare at Victoria Dodd who stood in all her black-clad glory pointing at him. Her chest heaved as she took another breath in the momentary silence, and Charles seized the opportunity to shout. "Stop it!"

"Charles!" screamed Angie, rushing across the room and throwing her arms around him.

"Sheriff! And Slim!" exclaimed Miss Poole.

"By God, is my son-in-law a tough hombre or not. He escaped from that low-down coyote all by himself!" announced J.T. Brentwood, slapping Charles on the shoulder.

"Sheriff, what happened to you?" demanded Raul.

Charles wrapped one arm around Angie and raised his voice. "Not a damn thing happened to me, Raul! I was at the newspaper office reading the *Examiner* on film. I wasn't kidnapped—and Miss Poole, get on that phone and call off the FBI. I've got enough trouble without them. J.T., go intercept your cowboys."

He heard Angie's gasp of outrage and wished he'd taken

Slim's advice about the wheelchair. "You sneaked out of the hospital without calling me or even leaving a damn note!"

"I didn't exactly sneak," began Charles defensively.

Angie twisted out of his arms and glared up at him with her fists clenched. "If you weren't already wounded, I'd take a horsewhip to you. I've spent the last hour thinking about how I was going to tell the baby what a hero you were."

"A baby?" asked Charles, too stunned to move.

"Yes!" Angie shouted. "I was going to tell you sooner, but every time I opened my mouth, somebody else would come barreling into your room. If it wasn't Dad or Dr. Wallace, it was Miss Poole or Meenie or Raul. Once it was one of the pink ladies asking if you wanted grapefruit juice."

"A baby," repeated Charles, then again in a louder voice. "A baby! I'm going to be a father!" He dropped the county history and photocopies on the floor and reached for Angie.

J.T. Brentwood slapped him on the shoulder again. "Don't you worry about a thing, son. I'll teach that boy how to ride a horse just as soon as he can walk."

Angie glared at her father. "Don't talk about horses, Dad. It might bring on a relapse."

"Rachel wore a bright red dress," said Miss Poole, kneeling on the floor and holding one of Charles's photocopies. "Do you remember, Victoria? At open house after the library was remodeled?"

"I remember how she told me what a terrible librarian I was and fired me right in the middle of the open house. And me the volunteer of the year!" said the widow indignantly. "And yes, I do remember that dress. It was not appropriate at all for the occasion, and if it weren't for your father's influence she would never had been hired. Her behavior was a scandal most of the time."

Miss Poole raised her eyebrows. "The pot calling the kettle black, Victoria."

"I didn't shoot the sheriff! That gun hasn't been fired in years."

Charles heard the denial through his euphoria. "What gun?"

"I wasn't referring to your alleged assault on the sheriff, Victoria. I was referring to your misbehavior on the homefront," said Miss Poole, picking up another photocopied article.

"What gun?" demanded Charles, letting go of Angie.

Miss Poole stood up and walked to the dispatcher's desk, followed by a shuffling Charles. "This one," she said, opening a paper sack and letting a revolver slide out onto the desk. "I was very careful, Sheriff. I lifted it with a ballpoint pen through the trigger guard so I wouldn't disturb any fingerprints."

"Charles," warned Angie.

"In a minute, honey," he said, sitting down in a chair and carefully studying the gun. He rolled up a blank incident form into a tiny cylinder and inserted it in the barrel, then withdrew it. "Raul, what do you see?"

The deputy took the cylinder of paper and studied it. "I think rust, Sheriff."

"So do I." Charles swung around in the chair to look at Miss Poole. "She's telling the truth. The barrel's so full of rust, I doubt it's safe to use."

"I told you so, Megan Elizabeth," crowed the widow.

Miss Poole's face was red. "I'm sorry, Sheriff. I was a little overzealous and I'm afraid I didn't look carefully at the gun. I'll have Raul drive Victoria home."

"Do you have her statement? And Rachel Smith's?"

"Yes, they're both in the file on Albert Finnigan, but Rachel's isn't signed yet."

"It doesn't matter," said Charles, cutting her off. "I probably can't prove anything she says anyway. Raul, bring those photocopies and the file into my office. And I want that mutilated county history from the evidence locker. Miss Poole, bring some coffee—and get on the radio and find out what's taking Meenie so long. As soon as I finish reading the statements and comparing the mutilated county history to a complete copy, I want to question everybody again. And I want to do it tonight."

"Damn it, Charles, that mummy has waited fifty years. He can wait another night," said Angie. "I want you back in bed."

"That's right, son," said J.T. "You look plumb bad. Your eyes are sunk so far back in your head, I can only see them every now and then."

Charles took Angie's hands. "Sergeant Finnigan might be able to wait, but I can't. I'm compulsive, I guess, but I have to know the truth, Angie. And there's another reason. This case has been like tossing a rock in a pond, the ripples just keep expanding and touching lives that should be left in peace. I'll compromise with you. Give me two hours, then I'll go back to the hospital whether I'm finished or not. I promise, scout's honor."

Angie hesitated, studying him without expression, then nodded. "All right, Charles, two hours—but I'm staying and timing you."

Charles kissed her. "Thanks, honey—and shouldn't you be sitting down or something?"

"You tend to your knitting and I'll tend to mine," said Angie.

"Uh, right," he said, and shuffled into his office before she changed her mind. He sank into his chair. His head throbbed, his chest and back hurt along with every muscle in his body, his eyes burned—but he felt better than he had in days. He was going to be a father and he was back in charge.

"Sheriff," said Raul, stepping into the office and closing the door. "I found something in the deed records. I didn't tell Miss Poole because I didn't know what it meant, but it looks like her father and Rachel Smith had an arrangement of some kind."

"What kind of arrangement? What did you find?"

Raul laid the file, the photocopies, and the two county histories on Charles's desk, then pulled two pieces of paper from his pocket. "Judge Poole bought Rachel Smith's house on the first of August 1945 for five thousand dollars, and sold it back to her on a contract for deed on June 28, 1946, again for five thousand dollars. She paid off what she owed him, and he signed the deed back to her on September 28, 1950."

Charles looked at the copies of the deeds. "Four years and two months. She must have been paying him a hundred dollars a month. This amounts to an interest-free loan, Raul, and for a generous sum. Five thousand dollars in 1945 was a lot more money than it is today. A family of four could have lived comfortably on it, not to mention a single woman."

"But why would Judge Poole loan Rachel Smith money, Sheriff?" asked Raul. "Unless they were, uh . . ."

"Lovers?" asked Charles, leafing through the photocopied articles until he found the one that reported Megan Elizabeth Poole returning to Crawford County after spending a semester in Dallas. "I don't think so, Raul, not from what I've heard about Judge Poole. I think it was blackmail."

CHAPTER

25

From the private journal of Megan Elizabeth Poole:

January 10

    I could not bear to write this entry last night. I was far too distraught over the revelations during the sheriff's interrogations. To be so betrayed is humiliating.

"Blackmail!" exclaimed Raul.

"There's nothing in these deed records that proves Rachel Smith ever paid back the money. The judge may have signed the house back to her without any money changing hands at all. Remember what Mrs. Dodd said just now, that Judge Poole protected Rachel Smith when the community disapproved of her. Why would a stiff-necked old puritan like him do that?"

"It could be blackmail, I guess," said Raul. "But what did she have on Judge Poole?"

Charles fingered the newspaper article. Rachel Smith didn't have anything on Judge Poole, but she possibly did on his daughter. Jack Colchester said that Crawford County always sent their daughters out of town when one became pregnant out of wedlock. Miss Poole spent the months in Dallas when she would have been most obviously pregnant. She returned home in December, but was not on good terms with her father for the rest of her life. If she was forced by her father to give up her baby for adoption, then she very likely would have held it against him.

It was a very logical explanation. But so was his accusation against Jack Colchester—Jack Colchester who was born in Dallas in December of 1945—and he was wrong then.

"I'd rather not say at the moment. I've already accused an innocent person today, and that's one too many. Go keep Miss Poole company while I read these statements and the county history."

Raul nodded and left, and Charles picked up the mutilated history and Jack Colchester's complete copy and opened them up side by side. His eyes darting between the books, he compared the two. Rachel Smith had cut two photographs and her personal biography from her family's entry. One photograph was of Rachel Smith as an infant in her mother's arms and the other of her alone as a child of four with long curly hair and that deep dimple in her cheek, and Charles saw nothing in either picture that would threaten Rachel. Perplexed, he read her biographical entry.

Rachel Smith was the only child of Edward and Heather Smith and was born January 26, 1913, in Crawford County, Texas. A very precocious child Rachel did well in school and attended the University of Texas at Austin on a full scholarship, graduating in 1935 with a degree in library science. She returned home after the death of her parents in 1936 and became Crawford County's librarian. With the exception of her absence to pursue a graduate degree at the University of Texas in 1946, she served the county faithfully in that capacity until her retirement in 1984.

Leaving the two books open for referral, Charles read Rachel's statement. Frowning, he read it again more slowly, his admiration for Rachel Smith's intelligence growing. The woman had a gift for combining fact and fiction to create believable fantasy. Too bad she let her protective instincts overcome her good judgment. Otherwise, her association with Albert Finnigan might never have come under scrutiny.

Next he read Victoria Dodd's statement, his brows lifting at what the widow revealed. So the other judge in the cast of characters was the murderer. Very interesting. Out of curiosity he flipped through the county history to see what this shadowy figure looked like. Judge Dodd was a rather short, obese man with a face that revealed no trace of laugh lines, and he was at least thirty years older than his wife. No competition for Albert Finnigan in physical attractiveness, and he doubted Victoria Dodd considered anything else when she chose to share the handsome sergeant's bed.

Charles laid the widow's statement aside. He believed almost everything she said—except seeing her dead husband, of course—but he didn't believe she was wearing mourning for the judge. She had managed to keep her conscience at bay since her husband's death more than twenty years ago, and Charles doubted it was hurting her now. Victoria Dodd was mourning Albert Finnigan, and if any ghost haunted her, it was the dead sergeant whom she had allowed to lie in an unblessed grave for nearly fifty years, and all her good deeds since hadn't atoned for that sin.

Charles flipped on the intercom. "Miss Poole, send in Meenie and Raul with Mad Dog. And bring in the coffee."

He leaned back in his chair and folded his hands as his two deputies filed in with Mad Dog, followed by Miss Poole carrying a tray with mugs and a thermos. "Put it down, Miss Poole, and thank you."

Mad Dog dropped into one of the chairs in front of Charles's desk. "Ain't she gonna stay, Sheriff? She's been in on every grilling so far."

"I don't think you want her to, Mad Dog. You see, I know your secret, but I don't think you want Miss Poole to hear it," said Charles, pushing the article across the desk to Mad Dog.

Mad Dog picked up the photocopy and read it, his face slowly turning pale and old as color and vitality seeped away. Finally he looked up. "I guess your sins always catch up with you, don't they? How did you figure it out?"

Charles glanced at Miss Poole, but Mad Dog interrupted before he could say anything. "Let her stay, Sheriff. The punishment ought to fit the crime, and I can't think of no worse punishment than having Megan Elizabeth learn the truth about me. So let her rip, Sheriff. How did you figure it out?"

Charles cleared his throat. "Certain things you did, and other things that you said. You were so emphatic about not being perceived as a coward. You even gave up photography, which you obviously loved and were good at, in favor of one of the most dangerous professions imaginable. When the body was discovered you immediately took up a very risky hobby. And you were terrified that anyone would believe you shot me in the back. A back-shooter is a coward, and you've gone to extremes in your life to convince everyone that you're no coward. But you protested too much, Mad Dog."

"And that's what tipped you off?"

Charles shook his head. "When you told Miss Poole that Albert Finnigan had some useful advice and then I saw this clipping I knew—or strongly suspected. I think the final piece of evidence was when I noticed that in the first article that mentioned you and Finnigan, you were referred to as William. In the last article, the one you have, you're called Mad Dog. I assume the infamous incident with the algebra test occurred in between, and that it was a trial run?"

"Yeah, but I had too much soap in my mouth."

"You two gonna let the rest of us in on what you're talking about, or are you just gonna talk around in circles?" asked Meenie, shifting his tobacco and taking aim at the spittoon.

"Mad Dog was a draft dodger," said Charles. "And unlike the Vietnam War, avoiding military service during WWII was the most shameful thing a man could do. Mad Dog would not only have gone to jail, but he would have been ostracized in Crawford County." He heard Miss Poole gasp but continued. Better to get this over with than to drag it out. "I believe Mad Dog simulated epilepsy. At that time the disorder was diagnosed by symptoms only, and the induction centers were running men through their physicals like cattle through a chute. I doubt any of the doctors took a very close look. Mild convulsions, drumming heels on the floor, a tiny sliver of soap to provide the necessary frothy saliva, and Mad Dog was rejected for military service. Did I miss anything, Mad Dog?"

Mad Dog drew a breath and squared his shoulders. "You got it all. My sister had epilepsy so I knew what an attack looked like. Albert Finnigan coached me, and I'll say this for the son of a bitch. He was sincere about it. He said the war was nearly over, that the Nazis and the Japs were on the ropes, and he didn't see any sense in one more kid getting his head blown off. I hadn't hardly made it back to Crawford County from the induction center than I started feeling guilty. What the hell made my neck any more valuable than any of the rest of those boys that were drafted? That war had to be fought, and it had to be fought by boys no braver or less scared as I was. The only difference was that they did their duty and I didn't."

He rubbed his hands together and glanced at Miss Poole's still face before looking back at the sheriff. "I was afraid everybody would figure out what I'd done, so I did everything I could to prove I was the most fearless bastard around. Hell, I've been running away from myself for years, Sheriff. It's almost a relief not to have to run anymore."

"Go home, Mad Dog," said Charles. "Your secret stays in this room with us, and by the way, it takes a brave man to confess in front of a woman he cares about. Frankly, I think I'd rather be shot at."

Mad Dog stood up, glanced at Miss Poole again, then walked out of the office.

"Are you all right, Miss Poole?" asked Charles.

Miss Poole moistened her lips. "He has moral courage, don't you think, Sheriff? It couldn't have been easy for Mad Dog Treadwell to admit being a coward. And I can't judge him now by what he did then. He's a different person—I think."

"I think so, too, Miss Poole."

"Wait a minute, Sheriff," said Meenie. "What about his shooting you? Seems to me he had the best motive a man could have. Lord Almighty, but Crawford County would ride him out of town on a rail if anybody ever found out."

"I don't know if he shot me or not, Meenie," said Charles. "Let's talk to Mrs. Dodd, shall we? I don't want to jump to any conclusions."

Meenie gave him a sour look and spat in the spittoon again, but thankfully didn't have time to say anything more before Victoria Dodd rustled into the room in her black taffeta and scent of mothballs. Charles gritted his teeth at the sound. Of all his suspects, he found her motives the most despicable.

"Sit down, Mrs. Dodd," he said in a firm voice. "I've read the statement you gave Miss Poole. You weren't entirely forthcoming, were you? For instance, didn't you have keys to both the courthouse and the library because you were a volunteer?"

"Well, yes, I did, but I didn't think to mention it because the courthouse door was already unlocked. And I was a library volunteer."

"Who was fired."

"Yes! And Rachel Smith had no right. If it hadn't been for me, the library would have closed during the remodeling, but did Rachel think of that? No!"

"Are you certain your husband murdered Albert Finnigan?" This time it was Meenie and Raul that gasped.

"Yes, Sheriff," replied the widow meekly.

"Because he found out you were sleeping with Albert Finnigan?"

She put her hands up to shield her face. "Please, Sheriff, do you have to say such things in front of these men?"

"Yes, I do, Mrs. Dodd. Answer my question."

"Yes, that's why poor James killed him. I feel so guilty about it."

"Good. You go home and continue feeling guilty. And no more calling the police to report ghosts, Mrs. Dodd. I'll keep your gun, by the way. It's unsafe."

"But I need it for protection!" cried the widow.

Charles shook his head. "If your husband didn't wring your neck when he was alive, I doubt if he'll bother now. Escort her out, Miss Poole, and bring in the formidable Rachel Smith."

The elderly woman strolled in Charles's office with all the nonchalance of a saint on a Sunday walk. Unlike the day he arrested her in the library, she didn't look like anyone's grandmother. She wore a scarlet tunic and black stirrup pants, eye shadow and lipstick. He had a feeling that this was the real Rachel Smith.

She pinched Raul's cheek, leaving him blushing, and sat down. "Yes, Sheriff, you wished to see me?"

Charles studied her for a few minutes, but she merely raised her eyebrows at his delay and lit a cigarette. He grinned at her audacity and leaned forward. "You cut up the county history so I would arrest you and you could persuade Mad Dog and Mrs. Dodd to keep quiet about Albert Finnigan."

"Yes," replied Rachel. "I owed it to Judge Poole."

"You also owed him five thousand dollars, Miss Smith. Did you pay him back, or did he just sign over the deed to your house?"

Other than a few second's delay in answering, Rachel showed no other reaction. "My, but you are efficient. The deed records I suppose?"

"Yes," said Charles, pushing the copies of the records across the desk to her.

"I don't need to look at them. Age has not impaired my memory."

Miss Poole snatched the papers, glanced through them, then looked at Rachel. "Why did my father give you five thousand dollars?"

"Your father didn't *give* me five thousand dollars. He

loaned it to me, and I paid back every penny. It was the only way I'd allow him to do it."

"You're being evasive, Rachel. Why did he loan you the money?" demanded Miss Poole.

"It was a business arrangement."

"And this so-called business arrangement was one of the reasons you felt you owed it to Judge Poole to protect his reputation?" asked Charles.

"Certainly, Sheriff, and because I knew he murdered Albert for my sake," replied Rachel. "I was willing to take a chance as a suspect."

"It wasn't much of a risk, was it, Miss Smith, since you had an alibi for the time of Albert Finnigan's death and were in no danger from a criminal investigation. You were in graduate school at the University of Texas from August 1, 1945, when Judge Poole bought your house, until June 28, 1946, when you arranged to buy it back from him. Judge Poole in effect loaned you money to leave town, more than enough money in those days to pay for a year of graduate school. But you needed a little extra cash, didn't you? For doctor bills and hospital bills. Judge Poole must have been very fond of you to not only provide funds for your confinement, but to save your job. I'm certain he bullied the library board into remodeling the library while you were on leave, and arranged for Mrs. Dodd to work as a volunteer."

"My God, it was Albert!" cried Mrs. Poole

Rachel Smith knew when she was beaten. "Of course, it was Albert, Megan Elizabeth. Why else would I be so upset and angry when he left? I meant to tell him that last night after choir practice, but he stood me up, and the next day he was gone. I wrote, but never received a letter, and I was getting desperate. I didn't want to end up like Edna Manning, swelled up like a watermelon and no one in sight to blame it on, but at least she had family to take her in. I had nobody but your father. I think he loved me, but my affair with Albert was one scandal too many. He wouldn't have married me after that if he had died of sexual frustration.

Too much pride to take Albert's leftovers, and I was too fond of him to force the issue by seducing him even if I could have. So we remained friends. Not the sort of thing that would happen today I suppose, but it was different then."

Rachel Smith paused to dab her eyes with a handkerchief she took from her purse, then continued. "At any rate, I told your father what happened and he helped me. He even put you in that horrible boarding school you hated so much so he would have a reason for being out of town. He came to Austin to check on me, and when the time came, he took me to Dallas for the birth and arranged for the adoption. That way no one would connect an illegitimate birth in Dallas with Rachel Smith who was attending school in Austin."

"But he never worried that someone may have suspected me," said Miss Poole. "I was in Dallas."

"Oh, for goodness' sake, Megan Elizabeth. No one would suspect Judge Poole's daughter, but everyone in Crawford County would suspect Rachel Smith of anything except murder."

"That's quite a story, Miss Smith," said Charles. "And I believe it. But there's another chapter, isn't there? One that explains why you mutilated the history book."

"I told you why, Sheriff. So you would arrest me, and I could intimidate Mad Dog and Victoria into keeping their mouths shut."

"There was no way for you to know that I'd connect their behavior to Albert Finnigan. I hadn't questioned or arrested either one. No, Miss Smith, you had another reason. You were afraid. You saw suspicion where there was none, and you tried damage control. There was nothing to be done about the copies of the county history in every home in Crawford County, but how many people actually looked at them. But the library copy was different. Anyone reading it might be paying attention, and might notice how much your baby picture resembled that of another person. You weren't protecting the judge, you were protecting your child that had been adopted. That's why you never mentioned your alibi. You would rather go to jail for murdering Albert Finnigan than call attention to those dates that seemed such red flags to you."

"Please stop, Sheriff," said Rachel Smith, a note of pleading in her voice that Charles would bet had been absent since the day she asked Judge Poole for help. "I'll admit everything you've said is true, but please don't identify my child."

"I'm sorry, Miss Smith, but I have to. Angie and I are having a child of our own, and I have no intention of risking being shot again because of secrets you and Mad Dog and Victoria Dodd still hold. Your son is Jack Colchester. It was the dimple in the cheek."

"Please don't tell him, Sheriff. It's enough to know he's my son. He doesn't need to know I'm his mother—because I'm not. I only gave birth to him, but I was never his mother. It would be too embarrassing and uncomfortable for him."

"Nothing will be repeated outside this office, Miss Smith. Just as long as none of you tries again to kill me, and I don't think you will. The incentive is gone. Your secrets are known. By the way, Judge Poole didn't murder Albert Finnigan."

"Then who did, Sheriff?" asked Rachel.

"If I keep your secrets, can I do any less for Mad Dog and Mrs. Dodd?"

Rachel Smith sighed and got up. "I suppose not, Sheriff." She opened her purse and tucked her handkerchief inside. She had cried for the last time. "Well, this has been an interesting little talk—soap opera in Crawford County—but if you've finished, I'd like to go home. I think I'll watch a Walt Disney movie. I need a vicarious happy ending."

When the door closed behind her, Meenie spat, then shifted his tobacco to the other cheek and looked at the sheriff. "So which one of them shot you, Sheriff?"

Charles shrugged. "I don't know, and what difference does it make? The case is closed. We'll bury Albert Finnigan and the past along with him."

CHAPTER

26

SOLDIER FINALLY BURIED
IN HALLOWED GROUND

Sergeant Albert Finnigan was laid to rest today at the
Crawford County Cemetery. A graveside service was
held with Reverend Lundy of the First Baptist Church of-
ficiating. Volunteers from the local post of Veterans of
Foreign Wars served as pallbearers, and soldiers of the
United States Army fired a twenty-one-gun salute.

Rest in peace, Sergeant Finnigan.

Crawford County Examiner
January 20

From the private journal of Megan Elizabeth Poole:

January 20

"The wicked flee when no man pursueth: but the righ-
teous are bold as a lion."—Proverbs 28:1

"A nice turnout, Sheriff."

With his cheeks pink from the cold wind and his eyes
sparkling with vitality, Jeremy Worchester looked in better
shape than Charles felt. Of course, he was one day out of
the hospital and Jeremy was one day back from his honeymoon, so maybe that accounted for the difference.

Charles looked around at the crowd. It was a nice

number of people, nearly all of them older and now claim-
ing they remembered Albert Finnigan and couldn't imagine
why they hadn't thought of him before. Miss Poole, Rachel
Smith, and Mad Dog came, but Charles doubted it was to
pay their respects. More likely, it was to be sure that the
sergeant was well and truly buried this time. He noticed
that Mrs. Dodd hadn't attended, and wondered if Miss
Poole or Rachel Smith had discouraged her. Given the widow's penchant for melodrama, perhaps the other women
were afraid she would indulge in a graveside confession
and let the cat, or secrets in this case, out of the bag.

"I guess no one could resist going to the most talked
about funeral in Crawford County history," said Charles.

"I barely remember the boy myself," said Jeremy. "I was
too busy trying to drill wells on a shoestring budget and
damn near no help. Any man healthy enough to work more
than an hour or two was overseas, and I was hiring the
army rejects and hoping they'd live long enough to bring in
a well. Even my partner up and enlisted and left me holding the bag. That was back in early '41 before we'd even
gotten in the war, but he suffered from terminal patriotism.
Even when he came home on furlough in late '43 he didn't
have his mind on business. Anyway, between one thing and
another, I didn't get to any of the bond rallies or dances or
such in town, so I just saw our sergeant a couple of times."

"Why did you come to the funeral then?" asked Charles.
"Did you want to see the excitement, too?"

Jeremy shook his head. "I've got all the excitement I can
handle these day what with being a newlywed and all. In
fact, it was Marcie who wanted to come as much as me."
He nodded at the young girl who stood a few feet away.
"She thinks this whole business about Albert Finnigan is
romantic, but she's young and young girls are gullible. Now
me, I came because the way I see it, this funeral is a social
ritual. We're closing the books on the homefront and all
that went on. At least I am. But I guess you can't, what
with being shot and all. You got any idea who did it?"

"The case is closed."

Jeremy nodded his head, a knowing look in his shrewd eyes. "In other words, you got your suspicions but you've decided not to push it for some reason or the other. Sure sounds like you're fitting in with Crawford County, Sheriff. We overlook a hell of a lot when we figure it's the best thing all the way around."

"I don't really have any comment, Jeremy."

"It's best you don't. The only safe secret is known to just one man." He buttoned up his coat and shivered. "I believe I'll grab Marcie and go home. It's a tad brisk out here for an old man."

The old man tipped his hat to the sheriff and walked off, hugging his new wife to his side, looking rejuvenated and satisfied with the world. Charles wished Miss Poole would use the funeral to close the books on Albert Finnigan. The dispatcher had been looking very fragile lately, as if the ground had crumbled beneath her feet and she was looking for a soft landing place.

Shivering, Charles turned toward the patrol car, and saw Jack Colchester standing alone by the grave holding the flag that had draped the coffin, and veered that way instead.

"Jack."

"Sheriff. Good to see you up and around."

Charles nodded. "I feel good enough to go to work for a few hours this morning." He cleared his throat. "I called the Parker brothers to arrange for the funeral, and they told me you'd already paid for it."

Jack Colchester shrugged and looked down at the flag in his hands. "I could afford it."

"It was a generous thing to do."

Colchester raised his head and met Charles's eyes. "I figure it's a little more than that. I looked in the county history after Meenie returned it to me. I never noticed before what interesting old photographs were in it. Of course, I didn't know exactly where to look until now."

"You can't be sure, Jack."

"Oh, I think I can."

"Don't bother her, Jack. She says she's not your mother."

"She's not, Sheriff, and I'm not her son. I did what old Ben told me to do. I became a Colchester. Still, I'm glad to know who I was when I started out, and I'm glad to know that I'm a native son of Crawford County after all even if I wasn't born here." He looked over Charles's shoulder. "I think Meenie's looking for you. He's got that mother hen expression on his face."

Charles turned to go. "You need a ride, Jack?"

"I'm going to stick around until everybody leaves so I can visit with the dead a minute. I'll bring him up to speed on the kin he left behind. It's something I feel like I have to do, then we'll be done with each other."

All the way back to town Charles carried the image of Jack Colchester standing by that grave with a flag in his hand and farewell in his heart.

Charles walked up the courthouse steps with Meenie and Raul each clutching an arm and Miss Poole hovering behind him. He felt restless, uneasy, as if he'd left something important undone. When he entered the elevator and Meenie pushed the button for three, he realized what it was. He needed the same kind of closure that Jack Colchester did. He needed to go down to the basement and bring Albert Finnigan up to date, tell him all that had happened. Because Albert wasn't at the cemetery; he was still waiting by his makeshift resting place for Charles to tell him farewell—one interloper to another, one soldier to another.

Goodbyes were important. Goodbyes tied up loose ends.

"I need to check the basement, Meenie," said Charles when the third-floor doors opened.

"Well, you ain't going down there by yourself, and you ain't going down there at all till you have a cup of coffee and warm up some," said Meenie, taking a firmer grip on Charles's arm and steering him off the elevator and down the hall toward the sheriff's department.

Charles decided not to argue with Meenie when he was in his mother hen mode. He'd drink the coffee, excuse himself to go to the men's room, then duck down to the basement. It wasn't a foolproof plan since he had his own private bathroom attached to his office, but it might work.

Slim looked up from the radio. "The man sitting by Meenie's desk is waiting to see you, Sheriff. And Howard Worchester stopped by and left you a note." The deputy looked around, checked the floor around his chair, and searched his pockets. "I had it just a minute ago."

"Slim, I'm concerned that one morning you may get up to find that you've misplaced your head," said Miss Poole.

"I'll find it, Miss Poole, I promise," said Slim.

"My God, I don't believe it!" exclaimed a tall elderly man rising from his chair. "Meggie? Meggie, is that you?"

Miss Poole turned utterly white. "No. *No!*"

"What is it, Miss Poole?" asked Charles.

The dispatcher slowly turned around to face the stranger hurrying across the room. "Albert? My God, Albert!" Then quietly and with the dignity Crawford County expected of her, Miss Poole's eyes rolled up in her head and she fainted.

"Madre de Dios!" shouted Raul as he caught her before she hit the floor.

"Meggie, are you all right?" asked the stranger, sinking to his knees beside Miss Poole.

Charles leaned down and grabbed the stranger's arm. "Who the hell are you?"

"I'm Albert Finnigan, and I read about my death in *The Dallas Morning News.*"

Charles raised his head to stare at Meenie. "Then who did we bury this morning?"

"Are you all right, Miss Poole?"

"Yes, thank you, Sheriff, and I apologize for my unseemly behavior. I've never fainted before in my life."

"You've never confronted the deceased immediately after attending his funeral either, Miss Poole. Do you want time off to visit with Mr. Finnigan while he's in town?"

"I don't know Mr. Finnigan, Sheriff, and he doesn't

know Miss Poole. We can't go back and start over, so what do we have to say to one another?"

"Perhaps a proper goodbye, Miss Poole," said the sheriff.

For a young man Charles Matthews was wise beyond his years. Farewells must be said, the last chapter finally written, but later, when Miss Poole came to terms with Meggie, and Albert made peace with Rachel—if that were possible. For now, she had a job to do.

"He has other farewells to make, and we have a case." She folded her hands and crossed her ankles. "Who did Victoria Dodd see her husband murder, Sheriff? It had to be someone who looked like Albert for her to make such a mistake."

"Obviously Mrs. Dodd didn't tell us everything. His Honor, her husband, had a grudge against somebody besides Albert Finnigan."

"I had a difficult enough time believing Judge Dodd would murder Albert when I knew he had a very good reason, Sheriff. I can't imagine such a placid man killing anyone else for a lesser motive," said Miss Poole. "It's not logical."

"Logic has been in short supply in this case, Miss Poole," said the sheriff, rising and reaching for his hat.

Miss Poole was still turning the puzzle over in her mind as she followed the sheriff up the sidewalk to the Dodd house. Of all the revelations the morning had brought the most surprising was that Judge Dodd would murder anyone *but* Albert. What didn't surprise her was that Victoria's drapes were still drawn or that there was no answer when the sheriff rang the doorbell. The widow was so lost in her delusions that there was no telling who she imagined was at the door. Ghosts perhaps.

While the sheriff huddled with Meenie and Raul discussing probable cause to break down the door, Miss Poole slipped quietly off the porch and hurried around the house. As she recalled, the back door had a very flimsy lock rather than a chain or dead bolt, and she saw no need in kicking in a perfectly good front door if there was another way. Besides, this was her case as much as the sheriff's, and she had no intension of being relegated to a minor role.

Selecting a credit card from her billfold, she slid it between the doorjamb and the door and jiggled it up and down until she felt the lock give. She opened the door and slipped inside.

"Victoria, it's Megan Elizabeth. I need to talk to you."

She listened, but the house was still. Deathly still. Miss Poole heard no sound of breathing, no creak of floors upstairs. She sighed. She hadn't liked hide and seek when she was a child, and liked it no less now, but supposed she would have to peek inside closets and look under beds until she found Victoria. The woman was tiresome.

Miss Poole passed through the kitchen and into the living room, but saw no sign of the widow and no place to hide. She heard the sheriff and the other men on the porch and started toward the front door, but caught sight of something out of the corner of her eye as she walked past the stairs. She retraced her steps and looked up toward the second-floor landing.

Her last thought before she started screaming was that Victoria Dodd needn't be afraid of ghosts anymore.

CHAPTER

27

ALBERT FINNIGAN ALIVE AND WELL
IN CRAWFORD COUNTY

Sergeant Albert Finnigan walked into the sheriff's department shortly after his own funeral. Although three different informed sources swore it was his mummy in the courthouse basement, Sergeant Finnigan persists in living. Sheriff Charles Matthews says the case of the unknown soldier will be reopened and appeals to Crawford County for help.

Crawford County Examiner
January 21

From the private journal of Megan Elizabeth Poole:

January 21

Victoria Dodd was murdered, hanged to be precise, from the railing of the second-floor landing of her own staircase. According to the sheriff, and I will defer to him in these matters, someone strangled Victoria before tying a rope around her neck and dropping her off the landing. He expects the pathologist to concur with his theory. I'm quite ashamed of my deplorable lack of self-control upon discovering the body. I've never been the type to scream like a banshee at the sight of something unpleasant, but I suppose there are exceptions. Victoria's purple face and protruding tongue were quite horrible.

The sheriff, of course, blames himself for her murder, but I pointed out that no one would have taken seriously Victoria's claim of seeing her husband's ghost. I certainly didn't.

Charles paced his office. "I don't blame myself for not taking Mrs. Dodd's ghost stories seriously, Miss Poole. I blame myself for jumping to conclusions. If I hadn't been so quick to accept Albert Finnigan as our Sergeant Doe, I might have looked further than I did. And I for damn sure wouldn't have left loose ends like those missing county records. I took everything Mrs. Dodd said at face value and never asked the most rudimentary question."

"What question is that, Sheriff?"

"Were you wearing your glasses, Mrs. Dodd, when you thought you saw your husband kill Albert Finnigan?" said Charles, pausing to lean against his desk.

"Oh, my goodness!" exclaimed Miss Poole. "I never thought of that."

"Neither did I, Miss Poole. Victoria Dodd was blind as a bat even as a young woman, and never wore her glasses in public, so no one knew how poor her vision was. It was another of her secrets like the affair with Albert Finnigan, but it was fatal. If she couldn't see the soldier well enough to identify him correctly, then she couldn't see the murderer either. Whoever she saw wasn't her husband, but a man who looked enough like him that she couldn't tell the difference without her glasses. The question is why did the murderer wait so long to kill Victoria Dodd?"

"Because he didn't know she was a witness," said Raul.

"Exactly," said Charles. "He didn't find that out until yours truly, the brilliant Charles Matthews, pulled her in for questioning. I couldn't have set her up any better to be murdered if I'd tried."

"You're getting complicated again, Sheriff," said Meenie. "How was he going to know it was Mrs. Dodd? How come her instead of Miss Smith or Mad Dog?"

"Rachel Smith wasn't in Crawford County at the time of the murder and everyone knew it. And the murderer probably believed, based on Mad Dog's reputation as a brave man, that he would have never stayed silent all these years out of fear. That leaves Victoria Dodd."

"But there's a fallacy in that theory, Sheriff," said Miss Poole. "It isn't logical for anyone to believe Victoria Dodd saw a murder committed and stayed silent for nearly fifty years, so why would the murderer assume that she was a witness at all?"

"But he did, Miss Poole, unless we believe that on the same night he burned the newspaper morgue and shot me, somebody else appeared in Victoria Dodd's bedroom. Unless we believe someone else made threatening phone calls to her for the next two days, then stopped once Sergeant Doe was identified as Albert Finnigan. And finally, unless we believe someone else murdered Victoria Dodd on the day the real Albert Finnigan showed up. I don't believe in coincidence."

Meenie spat a stream of tobacco juice in the spittoon and shifted his wad to the other cheek. "Word never got around town that Albert Finnigan was alive till this morning when the paper come out, Sheriff, so how did the murderer find out so fast?"

Charles rubbed his temples. "Damn it, I don't know! All we know—pardon me—suspect is that Mrs. Dodd's murderer is the same man who killed Sergeant Doe. We don't know who that man is and we don't know the mummy's identity. We're right back where we started from when C.J. Tolliver dug up that body."

He slapped his knees and leaned over to look at his cadre. "So we ask our questions over again. Who of our senior citizens acted out of the ordinary after the body was discovered? Who are my barking dogs, damn it?"

"Jeremy Worchester," said Miss Poole in a pensive tone. "He married little Marcie Gray, and there's never been a word of gossip about his interest in young girls. Although she's not that young. Twenty-five, I think. And he was a county commissioner during the Forties."

Meenie straightened his hat and sat up. "He left town to marry her about the time you were shot, and came back for the funeral yesterday."

"And he asked me about the case," said Charles. "But why would he steal the county records?"

"I don't have any idea, Sheriff," said Miss Poole. "His wife died about twenty years ago and he never remarried, and Howard was born before the war. I can't think of anything related to him that would be in those records."

"I certainly wouldn't know," said Charles. "But I'll find out. I'll take copies of all the birth and marriage announcements as well as the obituaries from the *Examiner* and I'll consult with the resident expert. Since Reverend Lundy has probably married, buried, and baptized three-fourths of Crawford County in the last fifty years, he ought to catch any oddities. While I'm at the church, you look up the deed records again, Raul. Miss Poole, go by the library and museum and get their lists of volunteers who have keys. Meenie, you'll have to drive me. Angie still won't let me have my car keys."

Brother Lundy stacked the copies on his desk and folded his hands. "I'm afraid I'm not going to be much help, Sheriff. If my memory serves, and it usually does, I didn't see any vital statistics missing from the *Examiner*. Except one, and it's to be expected."

"What was it?" demanded Charles.

"There was no announcement of the birth of Edna Manning's baby, but it was illegitimate, so it wouldn't be published. Ben Colchester had a firm rule about that. He believed no child should be embarrassed by published notice of its illegitimacy. I found Edna's obituary, but no notice of her giving birth." He passed it over to Charles.

Died from a fall, Edna Manning, 20. Services will be at the First Baptist Church, May 30, 1946. She is survived

by her parents, Mr. and Mrs. Peter Manning, and one
daughter, Carla Manning.

"What kind of a fall?" asked Charles.

"That was Ben Colchester's way of glossing over Edna's
suicide. She jumped from one of the library windows and
broke her neck. I think of poor Edna every Memorial Day."

"Who was the father of Edna Manning's child?" asked
Charles.

"Carla? I believe it was a man named Carl Armstrong, a
brilliant young geologist. At least, they were keeping company during the time she must have conceived, and Edna
never denied it. She never confirmed it either, but girls
didn't go in for broadcasting that information in those days.
She always referred to him as 'Carla's daddy,' when she
spoke of him at all, and was sure he was coming home to
marry her. She never wavered in that belief until the day
she went headfirst through that window. It turns out he was
in Dallas all the time."

"Excuse me, Sheriff, I've got those deed records," said
Raul, stepping into the minister's study.

"Thanks, Raul. I hope you've found something because
I haven't, or rather, Brother Lundy hasn't. I'm beginning to
think those missing records have nothing to do with this
case." Charles skimmed the copies of the deed records and
whistled, then looked at the minister. "What was Carl Armstrong to Jeremy Worchester?"

Brother Lundy hesitated a minute. "They were partners
for a short while, but Jeremy bought him out after the war.
Jeremy was bitter about it for a long time because he had
carried the business while Carl was in the army. Then, after
the war when Jeremy was drilling well after well and finding oil everywhere and just about to pull himself out of
debt, Carl demanded that he buy him out at market price.
Jeremy was up to his ears in debt again, but the worst
thing, the most despicable thing was the fact that Carl only
contributed the most niggardly sum to his daughter's support, and he only did that after Jeremy threatened to help

the Mannings pay for a lawyer and sue for support. And he never came to see his own child, and when Carla married her invitation to her father came back marked address unknown. I was never so disappointed in a man in my life as I was in Carl Armstrong. For one of the few times in my ministry, I was totally fooled. I never thought he would be such a scoundrel."

"These deeds don't mention the money amount, Sheriff," said Raul, "but there was a lot of property that Carl Armstrong sold to Jeremy Worchester."

Meenie leaned over Charles's shoulder. "Looks like Jeremy bought him out in July of 1946. Leastways, that's the date on the deed."

Charles crushed the copies in his fist and threw them across the room. "Damn it! There's nothing. Nothing! I guess he married Marcie Gray because he's a dirty old man, and there's no connection to Sergeant Doe at all."

"Oh, my, I don't agree with that at all, Sheriff," said Brother Lundy with a faint look of disapproval at Charles's outburst. "Not that I favor old men marrying women young enough to be their granddaughters even when they have known each other for years, but in Jeremy's case I consider it an act of generosity rather than lust of the flesh. He's sharing some of the financial largess denied her grandmother and mother. Much of Jeremy's wealth began with those few pieces of ground surveyed by Carl Armstrong."

"Marcie Gray is Edna Manning's granddaughter?" asked Charles in disbelief.

Brother Lundy looked surprised. "I thought you knew that."

"Oh, absolutely," said Charles. "Just like I know where the billiard parlor used to be."

The minister chuckled when he caught Charles's meaning. "I guess we do have our little quirks, don't we, Sheriff."

There was nothing he could say to that, so he nodded.

"Sheriff," said Miss Poole, entering the study and hurrying over to him. "I have the lists, but our suspect isn't on either one."

"Why am I not surprised? None of my other ideas has panned out. Why should this one?"

"You're jumping to conclusions again, Sheriff," she said, handing him the lists and pointing to a name. "I wonder if you've considered an alternative?"

A jumbled series of images of the day he was shot flashed through Charles's mind: smug faces, defiant faces, his own tight with anger as he taunted Victoria Dodd. How did the murderer learn that she was a witness? From Sheriff Charles Timothy Matthews, of course.

"Sheriff!" exclaimed Jeremy Worchester, opening his door. "And deputies. This must be serious to bring out the best part of the Crawford County Sheriff's Department."

"May we come in, Jeremy?"

"It's too damn cold for me to stand outside, and I don't guess I'd have much luck telling you to go peddle your papers, would I?"

"None at all, Jeremy."

The old man led the way into the living room with its big picture window that Charles remembered. Marcie Gray, now Worchester, leaped nervously off the couch. "Good afternoon, Miss Poole. Would you like to sit down?"

"Good afternoon, Marcie. You look lovely today. Marriage must agree with you," replied Miss Poole.

Marcie smiled and looked at her husband. "Oh, it does, Miss Poole. Jeremy is wonderful!"

Charles felt an instant's regret for what he was about to do. Marcie Gray obviously worshiped Jeremy Worchester and saw a knight in shining armor instead of an ancient husband whose reasons for marrying her had little to do with love or lust.

"Could we trouble you for coffee, Jeremy. None of us has had lunch, and maybe the caffeine will take the edge off," said Charles. "Maybe we can get our business out of the way while Mrs. Worchester is making it."

Jeremy seemed to relax. "Marcie, honey, would you

make some coffee and maybe some sandwiches. We can't have folks going hungry."

Marcie nodded. "I'll make a tray, Jeremy." She squeezed his arm as she left the room, and Charles saw the old man's eyes soften and take on a bemused expression.

There was nothing soft in his eyes when he turned to Charles. He was the tough, hard man who had built an oil and gas empire and held it for fifty years. "So what's this all about, Sheriff?"

"I believe I know the whereabouts of your former partner. He's residing in the Crawford County cemetery under the wrong man's name."

"Can you prove that?"

"I'm not certain, but there's a possibility. A DNA test using his dried tissue and comparing it to a DNA sample from his granddaughter would, I think, prove his identity."

"I hadn't considered that," admitted the old man. "But I took action anyhow. As old as I am and as close to seeing the Lord up close, I thought I best undo some of the meanness and make things right, so I married Carl's granddaughter and I've already fixed up my will to leave her half of everything I've got."

"That's not a bad try, Jeremy. It's not an admission of guilt, but by inference you're trying to mislead me. But I never have believed in deathbed conversions—or, in your case, near-deathbed conversion. I don't believe leopards change their spots. If you wanted to make things right, you would have done it years ago. Why wait until now? Because Carl's body was found. And you didn't have to marry Marcie. You can will your money to whomever you please. But you wanted to give her the protection of your name because you didn't want your son cheating her out of what was due her after your death as he cheated her mother and her grandmother when he murdered Carl Armstrong."

The old man didn't flinch, but then Jeremy Worchester had had enough time to prepare himself. "That's some accusation, Sheriff. Can you prove it?"

"Not unless some of the bankers and lawyers he used in

Dallas are still alive and can remember his hiring them under the name of Carl Armstrong to arrange the sale of certain property to you. I saw the deed records. Everything was handled by mail from Dallas, even the pittance he paid in Armstrong's name to Edna Manning's daughter. He was young, but he had all of Carl Armstrong's identification, his discharge papers, so I don't imagine the lawyers or bankers thought too much about why the army inducted such an overweight man. He had a real gift for fraud, didn't he, Jeremy?"

"You're right, you got a weak case. I don't think banks or law firms keep records for fifty years. There wouldn't be room for all that paper."

"I do have Mrs. Dodd's statement in which she swears to witnessing the murder by a rather short, stout man she mistakes for her husband because she's nearsighted. Howard does look a lot like Judge Dodd. I don't know what if anything I can prove about Edna Manning other than she wasn't in a suicidal frame of mind according to Brother Lundy. She believed that Carl was coming home to finally marry her. And he was. But that would mean half the business—half the money—would be his, and I don't think that pleased Howard."

Charles saw the slight flicker in Jeremy's eyes that told him he was on target. "Howard killed Carl Armstrong for money and killed Edna Manning for the same reason. He didn't want to risk your making any kind of settlement on Edna in Carl's name. I think he stole the county records of births because Edna gave Carl's name as the father. Maybe he hoped that he could persuade you the baby wasn't Carl's. I'm sure he must have been enraged when he had to pay support for Carla."

Charles thought he saw a faint expression of amusement in Jeremy's eyes. Even all these years later the old man appreciated the humor of forcing Howard to pay Carla support. "I don't know how Howard learned when Carl would be coming, but I imagine he intercepted a letter to you. Carl would certainly want to talk to you about the business, so it's a logical assumption that he wrote you. But we'll never know unless Howard chooses to tell, and he won't. He loves secrecy almost as much as he loves money. I'm sure he got a real kick out of knowing that there was a body buried in the courthouse when no one else did.

"But I won't be arresting him for Carl Armstrong's murder or Edna Manning's either. He's going down for murdering Victoria Dodd. That's a fresh crime scene, and I'd be very surprised if we can't tie him to it with trace evidence, not to mention other evidence we have. Howard heard me say that Mrs. Dodd knew the mummy was in the basement when he came to my office to threaten me with a recall petition. And he was in my office again yesterday morning when Albert Finnigan walked in. That's when he knew that the mistaken identity wouldn't hold up."

Jeremy walked slowly to the couch and sat down. He lit a cigarette and inhaled, his eyes unfocused. Miss Poole, Meenie, and Raul stood or sat without moving, almost not breathing, as they waited along with Charles for Jeremy Worchester's reaction.

"I didn't think of it being Carl down there at first. Oh, I knew that the height and age were right and that it had to be somebody with ties to Crawford County, but I shied away from admitting it. Because if I did, then I'd have to ask who would want to kill him and I knew the answer to that question. Howard. He hated Carl because of the money just like you said. And he hated Edna Manning because I'd been slipping her a little cash now and then when I had it. Still, when Edna went through that window I didn't think of Howard even though I couldn't figure out how she got in the library. It was locked up for remodeling, and when it was open, Mrs. Dodd was there. But I had a key and it wouldn't take anything for Howard to borrow it. Hell, he probably had copies made of all my keys because that was the kind of kid he was. Sneaky."

Jeremy took another drag on his cigarette, then looked up at Charles. "But a man doesn't think of his son being a murderer until he can't help himself any longer. I got out all those papers that Carl supposedly signed and I took a good long look at the signatures and compared them to some geology reports he had written. The handwriting was close, real close, but not quite close enough if you looked hard. Then I started thinking of what kind of a man he was, and I couldn't reconcile his refusing to see his baby girl with the man I had known. And that piddling support he paid was more like what Howard would do than Carl. Then there was the fact Howard was in Dallas that summer. It all fit and I got sick at my stomach. That's when I decided he wasn't going to reap the benefits of what he'd done. I married Marcie Gray so my old partner's granddaughter could inherit the money that should of been Carl's. It was the best I could do to set things right without accusing Howard. I couldn't bring myself to do that. He's my son, and in Crawford County we protect our families come hell or high water."

Jeremy leaned over and stubbed out his cigarette. "You're wrong about one thing, Sheriff. I didn't marry Marcie just so I could leave her my money and maybe protect her from Howard. That was the idea at first, but it didn't last long. It turns out that she always thought I was such a gentleman because I was always kind to her when she was growing up—gave her Christmas presents and remembered her birthday, stood up for her whenever I heard somebody remark that her family was white trash for no better reason than because her grandma had a baby out of wedlock. After fifty years you'd think folks would forget, but not Crawford County. I wasn't risking my good name by taking up for Marcie's family, but she thought I was. She believed I was a damn hero like is in some of them books she reads instead of just an old man so rich that everybody thinks twice about crossing him. How can a man resist a young girl who looks at his wrinkled old carcass and sees a hero. I couldn't, didn't even try. So when I said I'd love, honor, and cherish, I meant it."

Charles decided that maybe Marcie married a knight on a white horse after all.

EPILOGUE

From the private journal of Megan Elizabeth Poole:

January 22

I invited Albert to my home. It was the first time he'd ever been there, since my father never allowed him to set foot inside the door, but I wanted our meeting in private.

He bore the marks of his farewell to Rachel and Mad Dog. I believe Rachel was responsible for the knot on his forehead. A terrible waste of good whiskey in my opinion, and Rachel is on a fixed income. I'm sure another bottle is not in her budget. Mad Dog didn't bother with weapons, and Albert's black eye and split chin are testimony to Mad Dog's skill at fisticuffs.

I didn't resort to physical violence. The young girl who was Meggie would never hurt Albert, and the woman who is Miss Poole understands that one's life is not the sole property of a single individual. Those few weeks Meggie spent with Albert belong to her, not to me. Had Albert returned after the war, he would not have found Meggie. She already dwelled in the past. Megan Elizabeth Poole as a very young woman would not, I think, have loved Albert. Certainly Miss Poole does not. I believe Albert felt the same although he didn't say so. He is not the same man who visited Crawford County all those years ago. He is different as I am different. We spoke of the Meggie he remembered, and I believe he was truely fond of her. I spoke of the Albert I remembered, and realized, at last, that I had created him from my own dreams. But every young girl needs dreams. My mistake was trying to keep Meggie's dreams. All because Albert and Meggie never said a proper goodbye.

We have now.

Charles stepped out of the elevator and into the subbasement. "Sergeant Armstrong, I've come to tell you that Howard Worchester is under arrest. Justice is served, or as close as men can come."

Charles didn't feel as foolish speaking to the blackness as he thought he would. He knew he had a listener, not because he saw a ghost or even believed in them, but because he believed in life. When a life is unjustly cut short, a part of it lingers, not as a diaphanous figure that materializes in the dark, but as a sense of grief and loneliness that can be felt by those with sufficient imagination or empathy. Only when that remaining part is reassured will it vanish.

"You have a granddaughter, Carl. She married your old partner, Jeremy. They love each other so don't worry about the age difference, but maybe you wouldn't anyway. The dead have a different perspective."

Charles described the investigation and all his mistakes, the funeral under the wrong name, and the return of Albert Finnigan. Then he told of his own war and his own wounds and all the changes time had brought to Crawford County.

Finally, he was done except for a few last words. "Farewell, Carl. Rest in peace."

He closed his eyes and heard only the empty silence of a dank basement.

He stepped back in the elevator and pushed the button for the first floor. The case was closed with a proper goodbye.

Look for these marvelous
mystery novels by

D. R. MEREDITH

in your local bookstore.